Tripp Unleashed

Darren Simon

Tripp Unleashed
Tripp Unleashed ©2021, Darren Simon

Tell-Tale Publishing Group, LLC
Swartz Creek, MI 48473

Chapter 1

The Reluctant Hero

Just after 11 p.m. I slid my skateboard to a stop in front of the 7-Eleven on 86th Street, ten blocks from my house. Light from the store spilled onto the parking lot, barren save for two lone cars. Shadows danced across the edges of the building. No one followed me.

A small sign, posted next to the glass doorway, stopped me. It read, *Smile, You Are Being Watched By A Surveillance System.*

A camera attached to the roof had me square in its sights, but video footage of my presence wouldn't matter. Why should it? *I'm just another late-night customer like anyone else with the munchies.*

With my wiry frame, I barely cracked the door to gain entrance. The clerk behind the counter didn't look much older than a teen with short red hair, freckled cheeks and a long neck. He was most likely a new hire since I didn't recognize him. I made it a point to hit different twenty-four-hour spots around my Jackson Heights neighborhood and all over Queens, so no one would become too familiar with my face.

The clerk, David according to the nametag on his shirt, stared at me from the register. Probably thought I was up to no good. He wasn't completely wrong.

I glided past the counter, my skateboard tucked under one arm. From then on, I pretended not to notice his suspicious glare. I wasn't the only one in the store. A rather large brutish man, who looked groggy and kept trying to clear his throat, had a bottle of Benadryl. A young woman dressed like a nurse, her hair pinned up in a ball, filled a mug with coffee. When I determined they had no interest in me, I drew in a long whiff of the treasures filling the shelves.

A bucket and mop leaned against the far edge of the counter. Others might focus on the ammonia emitted by the liquid inside, but my nose separated that pungent scent from the sweet aroma of chocolate bars and red licorice. I lifted a chocolate bar to my nose and absorbed the aroma of coco and sugar. Pure heaven!

On another aisle, I lifted the plastic lid to a container filled with doughnuts and cinnamon buns. I reached in to pick up a chocolate doughnut, but quickly closed the lid.

Why did I put myself through this? I didn't have a good answer. Still, the saliva building at the sides of my mouth compelled me to continue searching through the store.

I reached the frozen burritos—my favorites—and the Slurpee stand nearby. With the five-dollar bill in my pocket I could purchase any of these untouchables then sneak off like a rat to enjoy the moment—regardless of the effects. With no one around me, nothing bad would happen. I was sure it would be all right, as long as I controlled the portions.

Time to choose. If I stayed too long, my dad might notice my absence. Not that he would care. I was not exactly his favorite person. His odd son—me—was a real disappointment, I guess. Still, the old dude could be severe with his punishments. No reason to risk it any more than I already was.

I decided on a frozen burrito. Couldn't eat the whole thing, but a few bites would tide me over. With my burrito in hand, I turned toward the register. The mucous guy now leaned over the clerk's counter to make his purchase. Along with the Benadryl, he had a bottle of Tylenol. The nurse stood behind him, her mug filled with coffee.

Sicky made his purchase and then swung open the glass door only to bump into a creepy looking millennial type, short and thin like me, dressed in a long dark coat. Gesturing with his middle finger, the sick fellow rushed from the store, got into his vehicle and drove away.

Meanwhile the woman waited for her change after paying for her coffee.

A few steps past the burrito rack, I fumbled through my pocket for the cash but dropped my five spot to the floor. *Duh.* I bent down to pick it up.

"Hey, let's hurry it up. I don't have all night," the creep in the long coat blurted. He stood in line behind her. Nothing in his hands. Was he going to buy some cigarettes from behind the counter?

Something about him made my forehead break out in a cold sweat. A hood covered much of his face. Who would dress like that on a warm Spring evening?

His fingers twitched.

Something bad was going to happen. I had to get out of there. I stood, placing the burrito on a shelf. Skateboard in hand, I started toward the door. *I just want out of—*

Whipping out a handgun from his pocket, the man grabbed the nurse by the shoulder with his free hand and shoved her to the side. She tumbled to the floor, her coffee splashing over the tile.

The man aimed the barrel of his weapon at David. "Hand over the cash now!"

The nurse screamed.

Oh my God! My heart raced. Blood rushed from my head; my knees buckled. I dropped my skateboard. *He's got a gun! He's going to kill us. What do I do?*

"Shut-up!" The scum raised a hand as if to strike the nurse. "Don't move. Don't cry. Don't breathe. Or you're dead!"

He swung toward me. His bulging eyes were streaked with red. He pointed the gun at my chest. "I see you there. I've no problem shooting a kid, understand me?" The seriousness of his threat laced a thick high-pitched New York accent.

I never had a gun pointed at me. I stumbled backward into the Slurpee machine, knocking over a tray of cups. They crashed to the floor.

My body froze. Fear stole my breath. My chest ached. If only I hadn't ventured out tonight. I didn't want to die. Not now. My head swooned. What was I supposed to do? *Be brave, dude.* How was I supposed to be brave? *Think. You know what you have to do.*

The robber waved the gun at me. "Kid, I said do you understand me?"

I nodded.

He returned his attention to the clerk. "Where's that money?"

With his focus away from me, I grasped the handle of the wild cherry Slurpee nozzle. I forced myself to breathe, swallowing a lungful of air. My face flushed. How could I do the thing I feared most? The thing I swore I would never do in public. I had to. It was the only choice. He was going to kill us all. His hand shook like crazy.

Dollar bills slipped through David's trembling fingers as he handed the money from the register.

"Fifty dollars... that's it?" The bastard slammed his hand against the counter. "There better be more or everyone in this store... I'll put a bullet in each of you."

"That's it." His cheeks reddened, David backed away from the register.

"Don't lie." The robber leaned over the counter and grabbed him by his shirt, then jammed the barrel against the young worker's forehead. "Do you want to die right here? Where's the rest?"

"Leave him alone," the woman shouted.

Sneering, the attacker turned the weapon on her. "Shut up, lady. "

"Just stop," I begged. My heart beat rapidly. Sweat dampened my curly brown hair. Why did I say that?

Ignoring me, he spun back to David. Gripping the young clerk's collar, he shoved him against a glass case filled with cigarettes. The glass shattered, shards crashing to the floor. David dropped to one knee.

"Is this store really worth dying over?" The robber knocked over a candy wrack next to the register. "There's got to be a safe in the back."

"Just give him what he wants," the nurse urged.

She was right. Maybe if he got what he wanted, he'd leave without killing us. No, look at him. His red-tinged eyes. He was bound to pull the trigger. Even if by accident. I had to do it now. Take a drink of wild cherry. See what would happen. Before it was too late.

David slowly stood. Blood dripped from the side of his neck. He'd probably been cut by a sliver of glass. "There is a safe." His voice trembled. "It's in the back."

"Let... let's go." The barrel of the jerk's handgun danced around. "Lock the door. The four of us are going to walk to the backroom. Get that safe open—maybe I won't kill you all. If you don't...." He pointed the gun at each of us.

I ducked as the barrel targeted me. He was going to kill us if I didn't do this.

The gun pressed against his back, David changed the *Open* sign to *Closed* and locked the door.

"G... good." The robber pushed him toward the storeroom, gesturing for us to follow. "You better pray he knows the combination."

David gulped. He wrung his ghostly white hands together.

The oaf didn't know the combination. That was clear. The time had come. I had to release a part of me I worked so hard to keep hidden. I dipped my head under the wild cherry Slurpee dispenser and twisted. Icy cold red liquid cascaded into my mouth. I swallowed as much as I could.

"What was that?" The gunman raised an eyebrow. "Did you just steal a drink during a robbery? Boy, you got guts."

I held my hands high as the last bit of the frozen drink carved a glacial path from my throat to my stomach.

The robber grabbed the woman and placed the gun to her head. "Boy, you best get your ass over here, or I'll kill her. Is that what you want—her to die because you can't listen?"

She cried. Her eyes begged me to listen.

I wanted to listen, but...

A gurgle rose from deep in my stomach. A belch escaped my lips. Everyone could hear. Searing heat spread like lava flowing through my veins into my heart, pumping the molten liquid through my arteries out to my limbs, setting them afire. I hunched over and screamed.

The robber took a step toward me. "What the—?"

I screamed again. My knees buckled. I clutched my stomach. Something grew inside of me, pushing its way out. My body twisted.

The woman shrieked. Her eyes bulged in horror at whatever was happening to me. She turned her head away, covering her face with her hands.

"Holy crap." The clerk bent over as if to vomit. His chest heaved. Lips parted to let out the spew.

A muffled cry escaped my throat. *God, make it stop!* My bones cracked louder. What had I done? What beast had I unleashed?

My pain subsided. Gasping for air, I glanced up.

The woman fell to her knees. The clerk gripped the counter with both hands. His arms trembled.

The gun-wielding punk slumped against a display of potato chips. His mouth agape in a silent scream. He staggered to his feet, gun aimed at my head. "What are you?"

"I... I don't know." My voice sounded gurgled, like I was speaking underwater.

Instead of arms, I had four long green tentacles covered in suction cups. A security mirror on the ceiling revealed the rest of my transformation. Bile rose halfway up my throat. I was going to be sick. My hair fell away. Lizard green scales covered my bald head. I no longer had a nose—just two tiny slits. My brown eyes, larger and spread farther apart, glowed yellow.

I'd become a walking squid, a new horror even for me.

A round exploded from the robber's gun. The bullet pierced one tentacle, plunging deep into my flesh. Blood spewed. The tentacle recoiled from the pain, ten times worse than any wasp sting. I drew shallow, quick breaths through clenched teeth. "Uhhhh!'

An animalistic desire for survival took over. I became the prey facing a predator in the ocean deep. I should flee. I didn't owe the others trapped in the store anything, especially my life. *Squids are loners. We save ourselves.* No, I couldn't abandon them. I had to become the predator. I launched my tentacle arms at the gunman. Two wrapped around each of his hands. I squeezed until he yelped, dropping the gun. The weapon clattered to the floor. With my other two tentacles, I grabbed his shoulders, then dragged him closer.

"Don't... don't hurt me." He closed his eyes.

I didn't answer. Instead, a foul cloudy substance spilled from my mouth, encasing his body in a murky blackness that hardened into a slimy shell. Only his face was free of the nasty gook.

Oh my God, that was disgusting. I'd gotten strange *abilities* before but nothing like this. I couldn't stop myself. I didn't want to stop myself. The robber had hurt me. He needed to pay for that.

The woman screamed again. She fled to the front door, banging her fists against the glass. The clerk fumbled for his keys.

"You're a freak!" The man struggled to free himself.

With a tentacle, I wiped some of the black residue from my chin. Boiling hot blood rushed to my head. My body shook with each beat of my heart. How easy it would be to kill him. Woe, wait a second. I had to maintain control. Couldn't let the squid's instincts takeover. Raising a tentacle, I slapped him hard enough to knock him unconscious.

Spying his gun on the ground, I sucked up the weapon and placed it on the counter.

I finally took a deep breath to calm myself.

The woman stopped banging long enough to stare at me with wild eyes. David, the clerk, eyed the gun. They saw me as the robber did. A freak! I slithered toward them. They retreated a few steps.

"Please, stay away," the woman pleaded.

"Stay back," David ordered. He lifted the gun and aimed it at me.

"I'm not going to hurt you." Could they understand my gurgled words? Anger built inside of me. I just saved these two and now they treated me like a monster. I guess I couldn't blame them, but still. *Harsh.* "You don't have to be scared of me."

Tears formed in the nurse's eyes. She backed into a newspaper stand and nearly toppled over it.

David stepped in front of her. The gun unsteady in his hand. "I… I'm… warning you. I'll shoot."

I lowered my head and sighed. Dad was right when he told me to hide my powers. No one would accept me. Just look at these two. I saved them, but it didn't matter. They saw nothing but a beast. Hate seethed inside of me. Blood rushed to my head. My cheeks boiled. I needed them to know I was not a monster.

I slid closer to the clerk. "Listen to me—"

David slunk away. Tripping over his own feet, he lost his balance. His gun hand flew backward. The nurse was in the line of fire.

Oh no! I sprang at him, wrapping a tentacle around his wrist, lifting his hand away from the nurse.

The gun cracked to life. A round struck the wall inches from her head. She cried out and scurried on her hands and knees to the front doors.

I tore the gun from the clerk's hand and straightened him on his feet. "I'm sorry." I didn't know what else to say. The nurse could have been killed, and it would have been my fault. I placed the gun on the counter and hurried to the doors. I needed to get out of there. Away from them. Away from everyone until I returned to normal.

Slamming my shoulder against the double doors, I split the lock and threw them open.

A hand grabbed my shoulder before I could run off into the night.

"Thank you." It was the nurse.

Tears overcame her.

I turned to face her, but she retreated again. Fear still etched into her face.

The clerk raked his trembling fingers through his hair, damp with sweat. He kept his distance. His eyes darted back and forth between me and the gun. Damn. He still contemplated using it on me. He spoke with a shaky voice. "Wh... who... or... what... are you, man?"

I could feel my green skin flush. "I'm no one."

Chapter 2

I Probably Shouldn't Have Done that

As it turns out, riding a skateboard as a squid boy takes great effort. My tentacle arms waved clumsily, throwing me off balance. I slipped off the board ten times, racing through alleys and across darkened streets.

I had to reach the park a block from my house. Under the cover of night, I could hide there until I became human again.

Two streets away I burst from an alley and skidded to a halt when a man walking his Chihuahua crossed into my path.

"Watch where…." His words trailed off as he shined a flashlight into my face. Mouth wide open, he grabbed his dog and ran away.

I started toward the park again but fell in the middle of an intersection when one of my stupid tentacles slapped me in the face. Fumbling to lift my board, a bright yellow light engulfed me. A car screeched a few feet in front of me. I squinted into the beams. *Oh no!* I'd been spotted again. I scanned the street for others who might catch a glimpse of me under the spotlight. My heart thudded louder than a drum. Fear stole my breath.

The squid in me reacted. A spray of black gook spew from my mouth, just like before. The oily substance coated the windshield.

A woman inside the car screamed. The driver gunned the engine, throwing the car into reverse. The vehicle sped back the way it had come until disappearing around a corner.

Reaching with a tentacle, I sucked up my board and bolted across the street, but the damage was done.

I was dead. I wouldn't be able to hide this from my dad. I'm sure my change was caught on the store's surveillance camera. Come morning, everyone would know. He always warned me against transforming. Yep, Dad would kill me.

Once across the street, I ducked through some bushes. I peered through the greenery. No one else walked on the street. I climbed on my board but before I could push off, my tentacles froze. A tingling sensation spread through my squid limbs. They convulsed; my body shuddered. Inside, bones cracked. Muscles twitched. Flesh popped and sizzled. I scanned the street one more time. A chill rose up my back. Was someone out there shrouded in the dark?

Flesh from my tentacles melted away in a gooey mess of slime. In their place, arms returned.

"Ride, dude!" I leaped on the board and charged toward the park, the wheel bearings screaming as if just as frantic as I was. My foot pounded the pavement as I raced faster. I barely breathed. I didn't dare look back. Didn't want to see who might be following me.

My tattered shirt, covered in black goo, flapped around me like a cape.

Nearing the park, my hair follicles tickled as they spread and grew across my head. By the time I reached the park, I had changed back into myself. I ran my fingers through my curly hair and touched my nose and cheeks. I never really liked my looks, but right now I appreciated my human face right down to every tiny little zit on my forehead and chin.

I rode through the park, eyes shifting in every direction. The raggedy remains of my shirt slid off one shoulder. Dad would know. He'd find the shirt, and he'd know. No, maybe not. Most times, he ignored me.

I breathed in the cool night air. The night's events played over and over in my head like a movie. I'd saved those people. I really did. I didn't have a choice, right? I had to do something. I just could never do it again.

The looks on their faces even after I stopped the robber was a reminder this power I have is a curse.

Twisting my torso with each kick of my foot, the two-quarter–shaped valves in my right lower abdomen stuck out. Another reminder I'm… different.

A pitch black settled across the night sky. Glowing stars spotted the late-night canvas. Digging my cell from my pocket, I breathed a sigh of relief. It survived the transformation. I checked the time. "Damn, almost midnight!"

Silence filled the park. Hazy orange light from poles around the stone walkway barely cut thin lines through the darkness.

I should have headed home right then, but my right arm ached as if the bullet pierced flesh. Lifting my board with one hand, I lumbered over to a bench, then slumped against the wooden seat, cradling my arm. I checked for any wound, but there wasn't even a tiny scratch. Still, my scrawny bicep throbbed.

My head spun with thoughts. Did someone get a video of my transformation? Would I have to run away? Would everyone call me a freak?

"Out kind of late, aren't you?"

The raspy voice startled me. I jumped from the bench, scanning the darkness for the speaker. No one appeared. Then something slithered from the trees. The shadow took the form of a rather tall man holding a cigarette that burned bright orange. Smoke surrounded his face. He seemed more ghost than man.

Like a frightened rabbit, my first instinct was to flee. But I froze. My legs unable to budge.

"It's impolite not to answer your elders, kid." The man took a puff from his cigarette and wiped ash from the trench coat.

"Uh." Forcing my legs to move, I scrambled behind the bench.

"I'm just kidding." His smile revealed yellow teeth. Bones stuck out through gaunt cheeks. "But really, shouldn't you be getting home? This is a safe neighborhood, but you never know what unsavory types might be out at this hour."

His words, spoken with a hint of an English accent, sounded threatening. He took another puff. The tip burned brighter. Though he smiled, his deep-set eyes did not.

"You... you know, you're right I should get home. My dad will be worried."

"Of course he will." He ran bone-thin fingers through his unkempt hair. "He should be worried, especially with all the crazy things happening in the city tonight."

I reached for my skateboard, but he scooped it with a long hand.

"Hey," I blurted. "Th... that's mine. I just got it for my birthday. Give it back."

"A birthday, you say." He lifted the board to his face. "Very nice. And how old are you, mate?"

"Thirteen." I reached for my board. "Please, it was a gift from my dad."

He handed it back. "Thirteen. That sounds about right."

What did he mean by that?

The man leaned closer to me. "Do not fear me, lad. I mean you no harm. I just... I understand there was some excitement at the 7-Eleven on Main Street. Little over an hour ago now." His smile widened.

I stopped. My heart beat heavy in my chest. A cold sweat formed along my forehead. "What happened?"

The man dropped the cigarette to the ground and snuffed it out with his foot. "There was a robbery, but the punk was stopped by someone very special."

I gulped. "What do you mean?"

He placed a hand on my shoulder. "Someone with powers."

"How do you know? Were you there?" I shrunk away.

"Maybe." The man sneered. "You know us homeless types. We get around. We know New York City and its boroughs like no one else. Even if I wasn't there, you'd be surprised how fast word spreads on the street."

"Well, like I said, my dad's going to be worried." I dropped my board to the ground, placing one foot on top. I tried to ride off, but he grabbed my shoulders. My heart nearly stopped beating. He leaned even closer until his face was just inches from mine. I glanced toward the ground. Anything to avoid his stare.

"You wouldn't know anything about that person with powers?" His breath stunk like an old ash tray.

"What? No! Why would I?" I struggled to break his grip, but his fingers dug into my flesh. He knew something. He knew it was me. He was going to report me. "Let me go."

The stranger released me. "Sorry, mate. Like I said, you don't have to be afraid of me. You don't have to be afraid of anyone." He stood tall, towering over me. "You know, I sure wish I had that certain someone with powers in front of me, so I could tell him to stop hiding in the dark. This city… this world… needs a hero, you know—someone who will stand up to the evil and give us all hope."

He pulled out another cigarette. "Oh well, what am I telling you for? You're just some kid who should be getting home to Daddy." He winked at me then sauntered into the night. He disappeared behind a grassy knoll in the park.

I blew out a lungful of air. He knew what I did. But how? I didn't see him there. A chill rose up my back. I focused on his words. *You don't have to be afraid of anyone.* Was he right?

The little hairs dancing on the back of my neck told me otherwise.

Chapter 3

A New Day

My alarm clock blared to life at 5 a.m. A soft emerald glow spilled through the curtains. Daylight would soon cast away the night. I lay in bed, groggily staring at the ceiling. My lips cracked in a wide yawn.

"Jeez, didn't I just crawl under the covers?" I rubbed my tired eyes. Had any of last night really happened or was it all a dream? Could I have been that much of a freaking idiot to play a hero? To risk being killed? Worse, to risk the wrath of my dad?

"Dream or not, I have to get up and begin my dumb routine." One thought echoed through the sleepy haze. *Please let today be no different than any other day. I just want to take a shower, get dressed and go downstairs for my liquefied breakfast.*

Then I could go off to school and pretend like I wasn't different.

Unfortunately, I was pretty sure last night happened. And that it was all caught on camera.

"Dude, today could bring the kind of trouble that could really mess with my life." I slid from my bed.

If people already knew what happened... if I had been identified... if the news already had my picture... then nothing could ever be the same.

"Plus, Dad would ground me forever." I shuffled to the bathroom, shivering at the idea of facing my dad downstairs. My stomach ached, maybe because I was scared; maybe leftover from the transformation.

"Maybe they won't tell," I said, remembering the woman and the cashier. But what about the robber. "If he says anything, it won't really matter. No one is going to listen to him anyhow. And if there is a video, maybe police will think it's fake. No, nothing has changed—nothing."

What about that homeless man in the park? He seemed to know something.

"It doesn't matter," I mumbled. "He's nobody. Just do your thing and don't worry."

Shaking off the last bit of sleep, I switched on the light in the bathroom, undressed and prepared to step into the shower. When I caught my image in the mirror, I jerked to a stop. The two circular holes in the right side of my abdomen seemed bigger than ever. They made me... different. A freak!

Most people don't even know I have valves in my side, even if they saw me shirtless. They barely protruded above the skin, and fake flesh made of a synthetic substance sealed the holes. Doc Torren liked to think of my feeding tubes as a marvel of modern medicine. Some marvel. He didn't have to live with them.

Once showered, I threw on a white T-shirt, purposely a size too big. The shirt draped loosely over my thin frame, all the better to keep the valves hidden. Next, I grabbed a pair of jeans, slipped into my Vans, then lumbered downstairs to the kitchen.

Dad lifted a mug of coffee to his lips. He didn't bother to look up from his newspaper.

"Good morning, Dad." I shuffled past him.

"Is it?" he uttered.

I didn't answer. Why bother?

Slumping into a chair at the far end of the table, I attached myself to N.E.R.D. Otherwise known as Nutrient Enrichment Rationing Device—a Doc Torren invention that feeds some colorless ooze into my body for nourishment.

N.E.R.D looked like a Star Wars droid. The contraption stood waist high with a rounded metal shell for a body, like R2D2. Plastic bags of liquid food filled one side of the machine, and tubes from the opposite side attached to the valves in my abdomen. Lights blinked, like the twinkling lights on a Christmas tree, and every minute or so N.E.R.D. bleeped, indicating a fully charged battery. I swear N.E.R.D. had a single purple eye that watched me, but Doc Torren assured me it was a scanner to keep the machine locked on its feeding target—me.

Activating the device, I connected its feeding tubes to my valves. The familiar whish of suction, followed by a click-clack, signaled the tubes locked into place.

N.E.R.D hummed to life as if to welcome me for breakfast.

"So is it eggs-and-bacon-flavored slop today?" I joked.

Dad rolled his eyes. Wow! I got a reaction out of him.

I was just kidding about the flavor. The elixir had no taste. Just this magic juice that flowed into my abdomen, where it somehow slid around my stomach and fed my body. Not only that, but the brew also made it so that I never felt thirsty. I have little syringes of the stuff if I get thirsty. Prick myself in the arm and that's how I drink. Fun, huh?

N.E.R.D. hummed louder.

I waited for the gentle swish of the N.E.R.D. juice flowing through the feeding tubes into my valves. Although Doc Torren told me I would never feel the wet stuff move in my body, I did every time. My veins ached as the juice reached my limbs. A cold sweat formed over my brow. Doctor called it a phantom sensation, but, as usual, I trembled as the cocktail snaked from my gut to my arms and down to my legs.

I ignored it and concentrated on my dad.

He peeked up from the newspaper. His gray eyes locked on me. Deep lines, like trenches, furrowed into his brow. He shook his head, then buried his face back in the newspaper.

My face felt hot, but I tried to control my breathing. I didn't like that stare. Was that the sign of trouble?

No way the *Times* got wind of last night, right? But what about TV? What about the Internet? Sooner or later Dad's going to know what I did. Should I just tell him. No, that would be crazy.

Dad would be pissed. He and Doc Torren had one rule. Never use my powers. I never did. Until last night.

"Anything interesting this morning?" I asked.

"Not really." He shrugged.

He took one more drink of coffee, cleared his throat and rose from the table. Grabbing his wooden cane from the table's edge, he limped stiffly from the kitchen. Though only fifty-six, he might as well have been eighty with his thin gray hair, paunchy stomach and leathery pale skin. His torn beige sweater hung loosely over his shoulders and drooping jeans didn't help.

He stopped at the doorway, then peered over his shoulder. "Clean up when you're done and get yourself to school. I'll expect you home by 3:30. You have chores to do."

"Whatever." My hands balled into fists.

"What was that?" He leaned heavily on his cane.

"Nothing, sir." My cheeks grew hot.

"Remember, get home early." He continued into the living room. His ridged right leg creaked with each step. Slumping into his rocking chair, he sat in silence, staring out the front window.

"I hate you," I whispered.

He probably hated me, too.

Because of my *condition*. How much had he sacrificed? A single father. No one else to depend on. No other family. No friends. No life except to care for his freak son. He couldn't even eat around me—not really.

If he knew anything from last night, he kept quiet. From that point on, I tried not to worry. I was in the clear so far.

"What if someone lurked in the shadows and filmed me on their phone?" I whispered. "What if they made it viral? What if it had a thousand views already?"

When my feeding cycle ended, I detached from N.E.R.D., ran upstairs, and grabbed my cell phone. The little hairs on my arms bristled. Fear prickled against my scalp. I quickly searched the Internet for any videos from last night. My breath stalled.

Nothing displayed. No YouTube, Facebook... nothing. My secret remained a secret. A wave of relief washed over me.

Still, I couldn't help wonder what challenges school might bring today. I slid my phone into my pants and glanced out my window at the neighborhood. A slight breeze rustled the trees and bushes. For no good reason, I felt someone watched me from the brush.

I chill spread between my shoulder blades.

***

When I walked through the front gate of Melody T. Poopter Junior High, also known as JHS 104, I scanned the crowd of wandering students for the one I needed to talk to first. Lucas. My best and only friend.

He knew my secret, though I kept that little factoid a secret, too. I never told my dad about sharing my problem with Lucas. He would not approve. I trusted Lucas and besides, even before I told him, he had vague memories of a time at pre-school when my powers first appeared. I finally told him the full story during our first year of middle school. He demanded I show him. I did by eating an apple in front of him. The effects came fast. Lasers shot from my eyes. I singed one of his eyebrows, but he didn't care. He called it the coolest thing he'd ever seen.

"Tripp... Tripp, wait up."

I stopped at the voice calling me from behind. A cold sweat formed across my brow before I turned. My pits dampened. The voice belonged to Maria Hernandez, a math and science whiz and all-around genius.

"Uh, hi." I turned toward her, my head bowed. I glanced up at her once, then focused on a rock on the ground.

She smiled wide, a soft blush across her brown skin. Her pixy hair danced around her green eyes. "Hi, Tripp. Um, will I see you in mathletes club today. You weren't at the last meeting, and, well, I need... I mean, we need your Algebra skills for the upcoming match against PS 105."

I gazed at her again. My cheeks felt hot. I had to keep myself from staring into her eyes. "Yeah, I'll be there." I wasn't sure that was the truth, but I wanted to be there. It's just that mathletes met after school, and Dad expected me home. But I didn't want to disappoint Maria. She was just about the only girl in school who seemed to like talking to me even if I was a little strange.

"Good." She smiled even wider, revealing her braces. "Well, I'm going off to first class. Would you like to walk with me?"

Yes, I would. That's what I should have said. Instead. "Oh, I need to find Lucas before the morning bell."

Her smile vanished.

Stupid.

She retreated a couple of steps. "I'll see you later, Tripp. Remember, mathletes." She turned and walked away.

"She likes you, dude, and you're a goof." Lucas punched my arm from behind.

I swung toward him. "She's just being nice."

"Open your eyes." Dressed in a wrinkled plaid shirt and torn jeans, a backpack hanging off one shoulder, Lucas shook his head and raked his fingers through his curly blond hair.

"Whatever." I studied his body language for any signs he knew something. He yawned and swept his disheveled hair from his red-streaked eyes.

"What's going on? You don't look so good." Lucas raised a thick eyebrow and tugged at the collar of the Polo button-down shirt his parents made him wear. In protest, he wore it un-buttoned, and a Metallica T-shirt was visible underneath.

"I'm cool... spent last night studying for Philips' history test." I lied of course. I never did study for that test.

"Really? You studied? What are you trying to do, make me look bad?" Lucas laughed, revealing one dimple in his left cheek.

"Listen, after school let's hit the mall and play some air hockey or something."

"Can't."

"Your old man?" Lucas frowned.

"Yeah." I lowered my head.

Lucas placed a hand on my shoulder. "Are you sure you're—"

The morning bell cut him off.

"See you in Philips' for third period." I scurried away before he finished his thought.

The rest of the morning passed by as usual. No stares. No odd looks. Kept my head down, walking from class to class. Never once raised my hand during the first two classes. Mr. Smith, my second period science teacher, shushed me for tapping my fingers on the desk while he showed a film on amoebas and how they have the ability to alter their shape.

During third period, I did my best on the history test, which would get me a "D". I didn't care. One bad history test wouldn't destroy my life.

When the bell for lunch rang, I quickly turned in my test, avoiding eye contact with Mr. Philips. I glanced over my shoulder at Lucas. He sat at his desk still filling in a few answers.

Lucas had brains and did well on most tests. He typically turned in his tests last. He took his time with everything—never rushed.

I, on the other hand, dashed out of the classroom and made my way to the abandoned trailer on the far edge of the school yard.

"How are you, Tripp?" Mrs. Ramirez held the trailer door open for me. She smiled, revealing crows feet on the sides of her brown eyes and gentle laugh lines around her mouth. Her long auburn hair flowed over her shoulders.

"Uh, fine, I guess." My muscles, usually tense, relaxed as if a weight had been removed from my shoulders.

Her perfume, a mix of apple and cinnamon, surrounded me. I breathed it in deeply.

Mrs. Ramirez ushered me in and closed the door, sealing us in—more important, keeping others out. Beams of sunlight spilled in through cracks in the curtains, the only light since the trailer had no electricity. As always, she had her iPad on the counter by a window tuned to the local news.

"What's for lunch today?" Her voice was kind—even comforting—as always. "I personally have a peanut butter sandwich and an apple."

"I have the usual." I tried not to stare at her. I forced myself not to smile or show any emotion. I didn't want her to know how I felt. Like she was, well, the only real woman in my life. Besides Lucas, she was the only one I could trust with my secret.

I unpacked a protein patty that might have resembled hamburger meat except for its green color. Another of Doc Torren's tasteless creations. I also had a nutrient shake concoction. Like the N.E.R.D. juice, it didn't have any color or smell. Just a vegetable flavor from an additive he developed safe for me. That's how I learned how veggies, like carrots and celery, taste.

For some reason, I could swallow the patty and drink the special veggie shake without going into my change.

I stared at my lunch, cringing. "You know, I've never understood why Doc Torren and my dad think it's a good idea to let me eat this crap at school. I should stick with the feeding through my tubes."

Mrs. Flores tied her long hair into a ponytail, then crossed her slightly plump hands on the table. "They just want your day to be as normal as possible. They know how tough your unique circumstances can be. And that's why they shared the truth with me, so I could watch over you. Make it a bit easier. Honestly, Tripp, I feel honored that they trusted me enough to clue me in rather than the lie they told Principal Jones about you needing to be out of the sunlight as much as possible because of a skin condition. This way, no one bothers us, and if you lose control, no one will know."

"Yeah, what if I turned into a monster and busted out of here?" I folded my arms.

"That hasn't happened yet, and I don't believe it will." She took a sip of bottled water.

"Yeah, right. I forgot. You grownups got it all figured out, huh." I grabbed my cardboard burger. I didn't mean to be rough on her. *Stupid, she's all I have. Don't push her away.*

Mrs. Ramirez folded her arms. "Sorry, Tripp."

"No, I'm sorry. I didn't—"

"You have nothing to be sorry for." She tilted her head, like a concerned... *mother.* "Would you mind grabbing my iPad? You know how I like to hear the news."

I did as she asked. I placed the device on the table so that we could both see it. She nodded and grinned. I liked her smile and not because I had a crush on her or anything. It's just that Dad never smiled at me. Ever. And Doc Torren just looked at me like I was lab rat. Mrs. Ramirez looked at me like I think a mother might.

I focused on my patty, but I couldn't bring myself to lift it to my mouth.

Mrs. Ramirez must have noticed. "Tripp, we've eaten lunch practically every day since you started school here this year."

"I know."

"Then why are you so uneasy eating around me."

"It's just hard."

"Relax." She took a bite of her sandwich. "We've had a lot of talks in our time together about being real, about being who we are. Someday, and I hope sooner than later, you will learn to be comfortable with who you are."

"Maybe someday." I took bite of my green food and swallowed it slowly. I felt it slide down my throat into my stomach.

Rumbling started deep inside my gut. *Oh no, please don't change.* This wasn't supposed to happen.

Mrs. Ramirez's eyes became concerned. She reached for my hand. "Don't fight it, Tripp. It's not a bad thing. Whatever change comes, let it come. It will be all right."

My body tensed. I tried to break away from her grip, but she held my hand tighter.

An explosion ripped through my body, throwing me out of my chair back against the far wall of the trailer.

"Tripp!" she shouted.

"I'm all right." I lifted myself from the floor and gasped. My arm stretched like a rubber band, and she still held my hand across the trailer.

"Oh my goodness, Tripp." She blinked and shook her head. "Truly amazing."

I jerked my hand free from her. It snapped back toward me like a slingshot, slapping me in the face. I fell to the floor.

"Are you all right?" She rushed over to me.

"I think so." I rose to my feet.

"Can you do that again?" she asked.

"I don't think I want to."

"Tripp, try. See if you can control it. See if you can pick up my sandwich from the table. Don't be afraid."

I scowled at her. "Fine."

Stretching, my arm extended to the table. I listened for the snap of a bone or the pop of a ligament, but my arm reached farther as though all my bones had turned to rubber. The only sensation was a slight tug in my shoulder.

My fingers wrapped around the sandwich. Sometimes the beasts I became, like the other night, were nightmarish. Not this time. This change was cool. Exhilarating. I felt the blood rushing through my head.

"Now see if you can pick it up." Mrs. Ramirez placed her hand atop mine, squeezed gently, then released.

I did as she asked with no problem. My hand functioned normally. I wiggled each finger, tightened my grip—anything I wanted.

"Can you do the same with your other arm?"

"I think so."

"Tripp—"

Blaring sirens from the iPad captured Mrs. Ramirez's attention. She walked over, leaning against the table. I pulled my arms back to my body then joined her.

The Channel 12 News showed video of firefighters, police and many others gathered in what appeared to be an open field next to a row of houses.

A reporter's voice explained the crazy scene. "You are watching live footage as rescue crews struggle with how best to reach a three-year-old boy who has fallen forty feet down a drainage pipeline adjacent to his family's home. We are told the child is wedged inside a narrow shaft, making extraction dangerous."

"I know where that is," Mrs. Ramirez snapped. "It's an old neighborhood of Corona. It's not far from here."

I started to back away.

"Tripp, your powers." Her eyes bulged.

"No."

"Tripp."

"I can't."

"That child needs help and right now you have the power to help him."

"I don't even know how long these powers will last."

"You have to try, Tripp." Mrs. Ramirez approached me. "I know you're scared, but I believe… I have always believed… you have these powers for a reason. I realize how hard your father has worked to protect you, but maybe it's time for you to unlock the real you. Tripp, you can do this. You need to do this for that boy and for yourself."

"Why should I care about some boy." I turned from her.

"Tripp, I know you better than that." She placed a hand on my shoulder.

"Maybe you don't." I knocked her hand away. "Besides, if I did anything I'd be seen. Everyone will know. My dad will kill me. I know he doesn't give a squat about me, but this whole power thing is a big deal to him."

"Tripp, please."

I retreated farther. My stomach ached. Breathing became difficult, like someone placed a heavy weight on my chest. A cold sweat dripped from my forehead, down my cheeks. I twisted back to the images on the iPad.

The camera angle quickly moved to a woman crying.

Mrs. Ramirez picked up the iPad. "Tripp, I know that woman. Oh my God. It can't be."

"What is it?"

"Tripp, that's Mrs. Hernandez, the mother of that girl I see you talking to sometimes. Maria. And if I'm not mistaken, she has a little brother. Oh, Tripp. That could be Maria's brother trapped in that pipe."

I stumbled against a wall. *No... no... no.* It couldn't be, but what if it was? I had to help Maria's brother. I just had to. But if my dad knew, he'd kill me. *Screw it.* Right now, Dad didn't matter. Maria did.

"Okay, I'll try, but I can't be seen."

Mrs. Ramirez grinned. "I have something in my car that might help with that."

$\mathbf{C}$hapter 4

A Hero's Time

Mrs. Ramirez's compact car raced down the street. Each jerk of the steering wheel sent me crashing against the car door. I flinched when she narrowly swerved around a black Mercedes. Was she trying to get us killed?

"Mrs. Ramirez, what are you going to tell the school about me ditching classes?" I gripped the dashboard, digging my fingers into the plastic to stop from sliding.

"I'll take care of it." Her knuckles whitened over the steering wheel.

"But my dad. The school will call my house."

"I'll handle it. Tripp, see that paper bag in the back seat?" Her foot never eased off the gas pedal. Eyes never shifted from the road.

"Yeah."

"It's for you. Open it up." She switched lanes to slip past another car

I grabbed the bag. Something about this made my stomach churn.

"What is it?" I asked.

"Just open it."

Taking a deep breath, I reached inside. At first inspection, it appeared to be a pink dish towel. On closer examination, this pink embarrassment, with little white flowers sewn on either side, had eyes and nose slits and an opening for the mouth.

"I'm not wearing a girl's ski mask." I threw it into the back seat.

"It's the only thing I have to protect your identity." Mrs. Ramirez veered around another car. Her tires screeched in protest.

I grasped the sides of my seat. "What are you doing? Why are you driving like an insane person?"

"We have to get you there. We don't know how long your powers will last."

"If we're dead, it won't matter anyway."

She didn't respond, but the car noticeably slowed. We still dodged car after car but at safer distances.

"Wear the ski mask," she ordered. "There's no other choice."

Mrs. Ramirez, I don't want to do this."

"You need to."

"Why?"

"To break out of the shell you've built around yourself... the shell others have forced upon you."

"Why are you pushing me?"

"Because it kills me you see yourself as a freak. That's not what I see. I don't think it's what others will see, either." Her foot pressed harder on the gas pedal. The car shook as if ready to come apart. "Don't you want to see what you can do with this ability?"

"Not really. And Dad's made it clear I'm never to power up."

She glanced at me. "Maybe your dad's wrong. Do you do everything he says?"

My body tensed. Was she pushing me to defy my dad? Why? What was it to her? Then again, why should I listen to him? It's not like he gave a rat's ass about me. He looked at me like I ruined his life, or something. My head ached. "I... I don't know."

"Listen, Tripp, you can be so much more than you are." Mrs. Ramirez's eyes shifted back to the road.

I gnawed on the inside of my mouth, then blew out a lungful of air. "If I do this, it's a one-time thing for Maria's brother. Got it?"

"Sure, Tripp," she uttered.

I stretched my arm into the backseat, tapping into my elastic power, and retrieved the ski mask. Slipping it over my head, I gazed into the rearview mirror. My face grew hot. I could see the headlines in the *Times*: *Pink masked avenger saves boy*. Sweat plastered the mask to my brow.

"No way!" I ripped off the mask.

"It's not that bad." She eyed me for a second before returning her attention to the road. "We're almost there."

"So what am I supposed to do? They're not just going to let me walk up there. There's going to be a lot of police and firefighters. They'll be keeping people away."

"I'm not sure how you get past them, Tripp." Mrs. Ramirez slowed and eased into a right turn. Police and fire trucks lined the street ahead. "You're the hero. You'll have to find a way. Isn't that what heroes do?"

"Funny."

She maneuvered cautiously, like a cat stalking its prey along the street. Aging wooden and brick houses lined one side of the cracked roadway. A section of fencing around the lot had been torn down so crews could get to the trapped kid.

More police cars and fire trucks screamed past us.

Curious onlookers huddled together behind police tape. Rescue crews shouted orders. A helicopter flew overhead.

Mrs. Ramirez reached for my shoulder but recoiled. "Are you ready?"

I breathed deeply. "No."

"Yes, you are."

"Mrs. Ramirez—"

"You can do this. I'll be waiting here for you."

My face went numb. "You're not coming? I can't go out there alone. Mrs. Ramirez, please."

She grasped my hand. "You have to do this alone, Tripp. I'll just slow you down. I believe in you. It's time you believed in yourself. Besides, I have to keep the engine going. I'm the hero's personal chauffer."

I took another deep breath, stepped out of the car, and slid the ski mask into my pocket.

First, a test of my powers to make sure they still worked. I stretched my arms beyond their normal length. Both responded, but the stretch felt tighter than before. The powers were fading. It was now or never.

I crept from her car to the crowd. Fifty onlookers gathered across the street from the vacant lot. I pushed through them until I reached yellow police tape.

Maria's mother wept at the edge of the lot. Police surrounded her. Another woman embraced her.

A police officer stood guard just beyond the yellow tape. Not sure how I would get around him. Across the street, inside the lot, rescue workers gathered in a tight circle. Not far from them a machine pumped like a human heart. The attached tube disappeared into the shaft. They must be feeding the little boy oxygen to keep him alive.

What was I supposed to do? How was I going to reach that drainage pipe? They'd stop me. I scanned the street for an answer. A white construction helmet lay in the gravel where the pavement gave way to the lot. I could grab it and pretend to be a rescue worker. It was a dumb idea. How would I reach the helmet? Police would be on me fast. I shook my head. *Just try.* If I got to the drainage pipe before anyone stopped me and used my powers, then they'd have to see I was there to help, right?

The police officer stood like a statue, keeping watch over the crowd. If only he could be distracted. Even a second would be enough. *Wait! My powers!* I slid my hand into the waistband of my jeans then concentrated on my right index finger. Hidden in my pants, it stretched along my leg until it reached the ground. Snaking out from the pant leg, the finger slid along the street toward the officer. It was the weirdest sensation—like my finger bone was being tugged from my hand by some unseen force. Sweat dripped from my forehead. I stopped breathing. So far no one noticed, but that could easily change. Then I'd be screwed.

From behind him, my finger climbed toward the officer's shoulder. *Here we go.* I tapped him three times, and then I snapped back a heartbeat before he swung around.

This was my chance. I slipped under the police tape, head lowered. My footsteps quickened. Muscles tensed.

Once at the lot, I bent down and picked up the construction helmet. Placing it on my head, I blended among the rescue teams. It worked. No one paid attention to me. I trekked on toward the pipe. An arm's length from the circle, I removed the pink ski mask from my pocket, removed the helmet, tugged the mask over my head and threw on the helmet again.

What was I doing? This wasn't going to work. *Turn back.* No, I couldn't stop now. That kid needed me. *Oh my God, I'm really going to do this.*

Someone grabbed my arm from behind. "Who are you?" a gruff male voice asked. "You don't belong here."

I never bothered to look back.

I ripped away from him and broke through the circle, pushing a couple of firefighters and police officers out of the way.

"Hey, what are you doing?" one officer grumbled.

"Who is this?" a firefighter asked.

"Get this nut out of here," another officer ordered.

I didn't answer. I ignored the hands reaching to drag me away. Having only seconds to help, I studied the narrow shaft, no wider than your average bucket. A kid's faint cry echoed up from the darkness.

A hand clamped onto my shoulder. A second grabbed my other shoulder.

"No. Stop! I can help!" I struggled to escape their grasp.

"Arrest this fool! Get him out of here!" someone from behind commanded.

"No!" I ripped away from their grip and stretched my neck until my head towered over them. I must have looked like a giraffe wearing a pink ski mask decorated with flowers.

"I can help. Please, let me!"

The rescue workers backed away, their jaws dropped in shock. Police aimed at least a dozen weapons at my chest, but no one said a thing. The crowd beyond the police tape hushed. Cell phones held high captured pictures of me, the freak in the pink ski mask.

Like an annoying gnat buzzing around my ear, the whoop-whoop of whirling blades drew my gaze skyward. The Channel 12 News helicopter. The squeal of tires on the street announced the arrival of news vans with video cameras attached to their roofs. The whole world would know now! I pushed away that frightening thought, and my neck retracted to its normal length, but the officers still targeted me with their weapons.

"Let me help," I repeated. "There isn't much time."

"Let him try." A woman's tearful voice rose from behind the police. They parted, revealing Maria's mother. She stared at me with grim determination. She had the same green eyes as Maria. The same warm skin and plump cheeks. The same pixy hair. "Help my child."

I nodded. "I'll try, if they'll let me."

One officer with three golden stripes on his sleeve stepped toward me. His weapon aimed at my head, he glowered at me with gray eyes and bushy white eyebrows. His eyes then shifted to Maria's mother. "Ma'am, this is a job for authorities, not *stretch* here. For all we know, he's the reason your child is trapped in the drain. As far as I'm concerned, he's a suspect, and I'm taking him downtown to the precinct."

"What?" I extended my head to the officer. "That's not true. I saw this on the news and came to help. That's all."

Maria's mother stepped in front of the officer. "Please, give him a chance. I beg of you. Please."

"Ma'am, you need to let us do our job." The officer kept his gun on me. "You need to step away. Someone, get her out of here. Take her—"

"Please!" She grabbed his arm.

The officer shook his head but slowly lowered the weapon. His eyes shifted back to me. "First, take off your mask. Let me see your face."

"No!" I raised my voice a little too loud. "I can't do that, sir, but I can save the kid."

The officer rubbed his wrinkled forehead with the back of his hand, and then leaned closer to me. "I don't like this. Not at all." He took a long breath. "I can't believe I'm saying this but go ahead and do what you can. But if I suspect, even for a second, you're doing more harm than good, I'll make sure you're locked away in some stinking prison. You have one chance. Hear me?"

"Yes, sir." I barely whispered the words. The weight of this moment, of the eyes all locked on me, made my body shiver.

Maria's mother gripped my hands. New tears slid from her swollen green eyes. "Save him. Please."

What if I fail? What if her child dies because I blow it? How would I deal with that? What was I doing? What had I gotten myself into? This was a mistake, but at this point, I had to try.

She removed her hands.

Licking my dry lips, I stared into the abyss and hollered down to the kid. "Don't be afraid. I'm coming for you. Just hold on."

I motioned two firefighters. "Hold my feet."

They gazed at each other, then got down on their knees and wrapped their hands around my ankles.

I scrunched into the drainage ditch, stretching like a rubber band. My eyes watered from the stench of the gunk clinging to the sides. Air pumped into the shaft hissed like a snake, but I only managed shallow breaths. The dank, suffocating darkness pushed against my chest.

Descending into the darkness, I extended my arms deeper and deeper. Shoulders tightened. My rubbery abilities started to give way. Tendons snapped like tiny explosions. Much farther and my bones would split. *Can't give up! Can't fail!* Grunting, I reached deeper into the pit. Sweat soaked the ski mask and stung my eyes.

"Stretch!" I mouthed. Instead, my right shoulder popped. My limbs could not stretch farther.

"Kid, where are you?" I realized he hadn't cried for a while. "Let me hear you."

He whimpered—faint at first, then louder. Just a few more feet, and I'd be on top of him.

"I can hear you!" I shouted. "I'm coming. If you see my hands, reach for them. Reach as high as you can."

I willed my limbs to stretch farther. My muscles burned in protest.

The boy listened. Tiny fingers made contact with my own outstretched hands. *Yes, thank God!*

I strained just a little more until my lower back cracked. If I kept this up, my body would break in two. Muscles tore and skin ripped. I fought the urge to scream. I had to keep it together and finish this. "Hold on, kid."

Our hands latched together. I hauled him closer, but the slime coating both of us broke my grip. *Oh no!* He slid farther into the abyss. His cries of terror rattled my eardrums. I had to catch him before he slipped beyond my reach. I stretched the only part of my body with any elasticity left. My fingers! I lassoed him, fingers wrapping around his body, tying into a knot.

"I have him! Pull me up," I yelled.

We ascended the tunnel. Searing heat spread through each muscle fiber in my limbs. My body demanded I shrink back to normal size, but I couldn't. I had to stay stretched; otherwise, we'd be trapped. *Come on, Tripp. Hang in there.*

Pinpricks of light cut through the darkness. Fresh, breathable air filled my lungs. "We're going to make it, kid. We're going to make it."

"He's got him! He's got him!" somebody shouted.

In the next instant, the rescue workers lifted me from the hole with the boy still wrapped in my arms. The cheers and applause grew deafening. The kid, his face dirty and scratched, cried.

I handed him to a firefighter then dropped to my knees. My chest heaved as I sucked in air. Arms sprawled out like strands of spaghetti. I just wanted to close my eyes and sleep, but I dare not let that happen.

"Stay with us," someone urged.

Hands tilted my body, and a stretcher slid underneath me. No! I couldn't let them take me away. They'd know who I was. I had to escape. Rescue workers carried the stretcher toward an ambulance.

Thank goodness, they didn't remove the ski mask.

"You're going to be okay." A young woman with blond hair in a ponytail smiled as she used a stethoscope to listen to my heart. She wore a blue jacket with the initials NYFD sewn into the chest. Eyes wide, she leaned closer. "How did you do that? Who are you?"

I didn't answer. I had to get up. I flexed the muscles in my legs and arms. They responded. I wiggled my fingers and toes. They moved as directed. My strength returned. I had to get up and run. I couldn't let them take me to a hospital.

With shaky hands, I lifted myself from the stretcher.

"Get back down on that stretcher," the police officer with the three gold stripes lifted his revolver and aimed the barrel at me. Other officers brandished their guns, all pointed at my chest. "You're under arrest, punk."

"Huh?" My hands clenched. Body twitched. Numbness spread out like spiderwebs from my chest to my limbs.

The woman with the NYFD jacket stood in front of me, her arms crossed. "What are you doing? Whoever this is just saved that little boy."

The officer nudged her out of the way with his free hand. "For all we know, he threw the kid down there in the first place. Until proven otherwise, he's a suspect."

"He's a hero," the woman snapped, stepping behind me.

"I said back down on the stretcher." The officer inched his revolver closer to me. The wrinkles in his forehead deepened. "Let these medical folks make sure you're healthy. If you do not comply, I'll haul your ass off to the precinct now."

What the hell? This is the thanks I get? I'm a damn suspect? It was just like at the 7-Eleven. All they saw me as was a monster. Rage quickened my pulse. I scanned for a way to escape. No way was I going to the hospital or to a police precinct.

The officer pulled back the hammer of his revolver. "I'm just going to tell you one more—"

"Leave him be." Mrs. Hernandez, Maria's mother, walked up to me, escorted by two women. She held her son in her arms.

"Thank you!" Tears welled in her eyes. "Thank you for saving my child."

I nodded but didn't speak.

She turned to the officer with the gold stripes. "I said leave this one alone. I tell you he is an angel from God sent to save my child. That's what he is. How dare you wave your guns at him. You should be ashamed."

A commotion behind the police yellow tape caught everyone's attention. Camera crews jostled for position.

I had to get away! Now!

With a bit of stretchiness left in my legs, I bounded away, crossing to a fence on the far end of the dirt field in just a couple of strides.

I expected a hail of gunfire to slam into my back, but the police never fired. I stopped at a chain link fence to gaze back once. Some officers sprinted after me. Others were running to their cars.

I sprang over the fence, crossed a narrow street and ducked into an alley filled with tall brush and old tires.

The screech of tires signaled a car approached. The police? A news van? *Keep running, stupid!* For some reason, I didn't listen to myself. I slid to a stop and peaked beyond the alley's concrete wall to the street.

A familiar car screamed around the corner. *Mrs. Ramirez!* My heart nearly leaped from my chest. I swallowed a lungful of air and jumped from my hiding place as her car skidded to a halt. She threw open the passenger door. "Hurry. Get in."

I climbed inside and threw off the sweaty mask. She patted my shoulder and drove away—calmly as though taking a leisurely drive through the neighborhood.

Sirens sounded in the distance, but no one stopped us. Still, someone would know it was me. Somehow, I'd be discovered. Life as I knew it was over. Such an idiot. Why'd I listen to Mrs. Ramirez? What if Dad found out? I'd be dead. So, screw him.

"You did it, Tripp! Mrs. Ramirez smiled wide. "You did it! I'm so proud of you!"

"Never... again."

Chapter 5

What Comes Next?

On the examination table in Doc Torren's office, a clock ticked loudly on the wall behind me. The only noise in this sterile room other than the crinkle of white tissue paper under my butt.

The stench of medicine tickled my nose.

Dad paced back and forth with the *Times* in one hand, cane in the other. Seated in a chair, Doc Torren quietly reviewed papers on a clipboard.

Finally, my dad cleared his throat. He threw the newspaper on a metal counter. "Look at that headline, Tripp. *Elastic Hero Saves Child, Then Disappears.*"

I threw up my arms. I preferred the silence. "I know, Dad."

He limped closer to me. "I don't think you do. Let me read the story to you."

"You don't—"

Dad grabbed the paper and started reading. "*A masked rescuer with what appeared to be superhuman elastic abilities reminiscent of fabled comic book superheroes saved a three-year-old boy who fell down a forty-foot drainage pipe Thursday in Queens. According to witness reports, the mysterious hero who wore a pink ski mask disappeared before authorities could discover his identity. The rescued child is listed in good condition at an area hospital. Investigators say there are reports that the boy may have been kidnapped and thrown down the shaft, but no one has been arrested. Investigators are not ruling out the masked hero as a suspect.*"

He stopped reading, then threw the paper to the linoleum floor.

"What do you want me to say?" Anger laced my voice.

"I want you to think, Tripp." Dad leaned against his cane, his graying eyes reddened. Frown lines deepened.

"What does that mean?" My fingers tore through the tissue paper.

He banged his cane against the floor. "Do you know what happens if anyone finds out that was you? Already, Channel 12 had a story. And there've been Facebook posts. How long until it links back to you?"

I slid off the table. "Did they get my face. No, I don't think so."

"Don't give me lip—"

"Henry, please." Doc Torren stood from his chair and placed a hand on my dad's shoulder. He stared at Dad through coke-bottle lenses. Veins spread across his bald head like spider webs. "Both of you need to calm down."

Dad retreated across the room, but still glowered at me.

Doc Torren turned to me. "Well, Tripp... or should I call you Mr. Hero... how do you feel?" He grinned, his pudgy cheeks widening his face. His coffee breath nearly made my eyes water.

"I'm fine, doc, really." I wanted to escape, but my dad wouldn't allow that. He dragged me here after learning what I'd done.

Placing a blood pressure monitor over my wrist, the old doctor crossed his arms. The machine buzzed then slowly tightened over my vein.

"Your blood pressure is fine." Doc Torren finished by inspecting the valves in my abdomen. "I don't see anything wrong with you, my boy. You are a healthy teenager in every way, with obvious differences, and you apparently decided to explore those differences, didn't you, Tripp?"

My heart beat wildly. Hands formed into fists. "Jeez, why are you both on my case about this? I had to. I mean what was I supposed to do, let the kid stay trapped down there?"

Dad placed a hand on my shoulder. "Son, I get why you did it." His voice was noticeably calmer. "You made a choice, a courageous choice, and that deserves praise. Sorry, if I haven't given any."

"We're both proud," Doc Torren added. "You saved a life."

I almost didn't hear the doctor's words. I was blown away by the kindness from my dad. Really, I was blown away by even a hint of pride from him. So why bug me about this? "So what's the problem?"

My dad's face tightened. "But what if things went wrong? What if that kid died in your hands? What if someone ripped that ridiculous mask off your face? So many things could have gone wrong. Then, where would we be? Where would you be? I know you saved that boy, but maybe you shouldn't have."

"What?" Blood rushed from my head.

Doc Torren stroked his graying goatee. "You have to understand, your dad is concerned for your safety. It's his mission to watch you… care for you. That's why he brought you here today—for your health and safety."

Mission? What the hell did that mean? I let that thought slip away. "But I'm fine. You said it yourself."

"Tripp, how long have we known each other? How long have I been your doctor?"

"Since I was in preschool; since my powers started."

"Right." Doc Torren's smile faded. "And in all that time your dad and I have spent a considerable amount of time exploring ways to keep your abilities in check. Why do you think that is?"

"I don't know. So people don't think I'm a freak?"

"Is that really what you think?" Dad held his cane with both hands.

"Yeah, well, I don't know." I stared down at my checkered Vans.

"Tripp," Doc Torren continued, "that's not it at all, and you're bright enough to know that. The surgeries, the feeding tubes, all the effort to conceal your unique situation… it's all been done to ensure your safety."

I didn't buy that. "Safety from who? From what?"

Silence filled the room until Dad snatched up the newspaper. "Safety from headlines like this. Son, if your identity became known, people might try to hurt you. This kind of press is a… problem. You see it, right? Now they think the masked one is a suspect. We don't want this getting back to you… to us. It's too dangerous."

"Why is it dangerous? I didn't do anything wrong."

Doc Torren cleared his throat. "We are just concerned there are people out there who might seek to exploit someone with your abilities. Can you understand that? Already, police are investigating whether that child was thrown into the pipe, and whether that hero is responsible. You see how people react?"

The whole suspect thing weighed heavy on my shoulders as if unseen hands pressed against me. "That's not my fault. I don't know why they're saying that."

"Tripp—"

"Come on, doc, I've done everything you guys have told me to do. I eat when you tell me I can eat. I eat what you tell me to eat. And half the time I live with that liquid diet you feed me through tubes. But enough is enough. Stop telling me what to do. Maybe it's time I decide for myself what's best. Maybe my condition is a gift and not a disease."

"Whoever called your abilities a disease?" Dad asked.

"You treat me as if I'm sick." My body trembled. Voice cracked. "Doc, you're supposed to be some super genius scientist, but all these years you've never been able to tell me why I'm like this."

"There's just no simple answer, Tripp. This case, as you know, is so unusual."

"I get it, but maybe this happened to me… I don't know… because of God, or something." I couldn't believe the words coming from my mouth. "Maybe, I'm a freak for a reason, and I've just been wasting it."

Doc Torren sighed with a glance at my dad. "First, you are no freak. Second, you can't control your powers, Tripp. I wish I knew how to help you learn control, but I haven't discovered that answer yet. Until I do, you could be a danger to yourself and others."

"I don't think so." I retreated to the office door and leaned against it. "Look how my powers helped that kid."

My dad gripped his cane. "This is ridiculous, Tripp. You're a thirteen-year-old boy. You don't make the decisions here, I do. And I say—"

"You were lucky this time," Doc Torren interrupted. "You said you changed after eating that protein patty. That shouldn't have happened. We have worked long and hard through trial and error to create food you can eat. I'm still mystified at that. We will have to go back to the drawing board and rethink the formula. As for the change, you could have transformed into anything. That you gained elastic powers at a time when those powers were needed was a fortunate coincidence, nothing more. Tripp, you must be careful. You don't know what you might do."

Dad slowly approached me. "You have to listen to us, Tripp. You're just a kid. You're not ready to decide what's best for you. That's my job, and you will listen."

"That's your job, huh. That's all I am to you." I rolled my eyes. "Whatever, Dad. Can we just go."

Dad sighed. "I didn't mean it like that."

Doc Torren motioned for me to sit back down on the examination table. "I promise you, Tripp, I will find the code to control the way your system reacts to food. You have put your trust in me all these years. Don't lose faith now."

"Son, just listen to us," Dad urged. "For your own good, let's not see any more of these headlines."

I lowered my head. "Fine."

"For curiosity sake, Tripp, have there been any other incidents lately involving your abilities?" Doc Torren asked.

I stood there in silence.

"Tripp," Dad demanded.

"Maybe one other time," I mumbled.

"Damn it, Tripp." Dad stomped his foot.

Doc Torren cocked an eyebrow. "Care to tell us about it?"

I stared at my feet. "It was nothing. It happened at a 7-Eleven. I stopped someone very bad from hurting other people."

"What were you doing at a 7-Eleven?" Dad exchanged a worried glance with the doctor.

I shrugged my shoulders. "Sometimes I go just to get some real food. I just eat a few bites. I've never hurt anyone. It's just there was this guy with a gun—"

"Oh my God!" Dad blurted. "Tripp, you're taking too many chances."

"I'll be more careful."

Dad's eyes widened. "I know you will because I'm not letting you out of my—"

"Henry," Doc Torren interrupted. "That won't help."

"Then you tell me what to do." Dad swung toward the doctor. "You started this."

Doc Torren hesitated. "Tripp is fine. He wasn't seen. No harm done. But, Tripp, no more going off on your own to eat. That's very dangerous. Agreed?"

"Sure." I was lying.

"Good." The doctor's wide grin returned. "Henry, Tripp, I'm going to double my efforts. For now, go home and live life. And be thankful you have each other."

Dad grumbled but didn't say another word. As we left Doc Torren's office, one thought filled my mind. What life? Dad was a recluse who hated me most of the time. I was a freak doomed to hide from the world. And Doc Torren was wasting his time.

Maybe I should explore my powers… but on my terms. Screw everyone else.

Chapter 6

A Hero's Utility Belt

For the past two hours, I contemplated the pink mask. It silently nudged me from its perch atop my computer monitor. I reached for it. A rap on my window jolted me. I recoiled and sprang from my desk chair.

"I bet it's Lucas." I grabbed my chest to quiet my racing heart. "Not the right time, man. What the hell could he want?"

A louder second clink rattled the window. "Dude, let me in. You know your dad can't stand me. This is the only way to avoid him."

Yep, Lucas. I checked my clock—9 p.m.—and threw open the drapes. Lucas' face was mashed against the glass. His blond hair nearly covered his eyes. "Dude, come on."

I laughed and unlatched the window, sliding it open. "What are you doing here?"

"You skipped school today. Why?" He jumped into my bedroom and landed with a thud.

I winced. "Quiet, man. You want the old man to know?"

"Oops, sorry. Answer the question. Why'd you skip?"

"Sick."

"You're not sick, dude." Lucas ripped his phone from his pocket. "Your absence wouldn't have anything to do with this?"

He hit a button and a grainy YouTube video appeared on the screen. Shaky images of a guy in a pink ski mask with an elongated neck played for a few seconds.

"You're all the rage." Lucas slapped my shoulder.

"That's not me."

"Right, and that pink mask on your computer is just a decoration." Lucas grabbed the ski mask and hurled it at me. "Dude, did you know that was Maria's brother you saved? Of course, you did, huh. She talked about it all day. She also asked about you—you know, why you were absent."

I tried not to smile. Heat rose from my cheeks. "She asked about me? Really?"

"Yeah, serious, man."

"What did you tell her?"

Lucas winked. "That a hero needs a day off."

"Shut up." I threw the mask on the bed.

He chuckled. "I told her you were sick. That's all. So admit it. You're *el stretcho,* right?

I folded my arms. "All right, it's me. Just shut up about it."

"Maria's going to think you're a stud." He flexed his arms as if he had some muscles to display.

I shook my head. "She can't know. No one can."

"Does your dad know?"

"Of course he does, and he's pissed. Took me to see Doc Torren today. That's why I missed school. They both chewed me out. Told me never to do it again. Said I'm a danger to myself and others."

"That's rough." Lucas dropped onto my bed. "What are you going to do—listen to them?"

"I really don't know." I slumped into my desk chair. "I'm not looking to be anyone's hero. But not because of my dad. It doesn't matter what he thinks. I'm old enough. I don't have to live by his rules anymore. Whatever I do, it's my choice."

"Chill, dude." Lucas slid onto the floor. "You want my advice?"

"No."

"Hero up."

"What?"

He wiped strands of hair from his eyes. "No, I mean it. Stop all this hiding and get out there."

"That's easy for you to say." I glared at him. "Remember, when I singed off one of your eyebrows in preschool after eating a pizza?"

He nodded. "You know it. That's when we became friends. I thought anyone who can shoot lasers from his eyes must be cool."

I lowered my head into my hands. "I could have killed you."

"But you didn't." He punched me in the shoulder.

"Yeah, but that's when all this crap started." My hands balled into fists. "That's when Dad took me to Doc Torren, and they figured out I was different. That I'd never eat or drink like others. That I could be a danger to everyone. That I needed to hide this… power."

Lucas shrugged. "I know all this, man."

"You don't get it. I'm a freaking monster. I may get lucky once in a while and do something good, like saving that snot-nosed kid, but who knows what I might become. I could kill, just like I nearly did with you. I can't control it. No matter what I eat, I change into something. I mean, what if I became Godzilla or King Kong and smashed the whole damn city?"

"Right, look at you—a skinny little dude. You're going to become Godzilla. Don't think so. More likely you'll become a Powerpuff Girl." Lucas laughed.

"Shut up." I threw a pillow at him. "You know, I just really wish my mom was alive. I wish she'd been here from the start. She'd know what to do. And my dad wouldn't be such a dick. He wouldn't have a reason to hate me for being born."

Lucas frowned. "It's not your fault, Tripp. You were a baby. If you're old man can't see that, the hell with him. You're a cool guy even if you dad's a turd."

I felt my eyes watering. "Thanks. You know, I don't want any of this. I just really want to be normal. Eat a Big Mac and large fries. I've never had one."

"Ain't missing much." Lucas headed for the window. "Look, I know I kid around a lot, but seriously, I think there's a lot of good you can do, and I'm ready to help any way I can, bro. But if you decide not to, that's cool, too. Chicken. But cool." He started to climb through the window. "See you in school, tomorrow?"

"Yeah, I'll be there."

"So what are you going to do about the hero thing?"

I shrugged. "Still don't know."

"Well, when you do know, clue me in. I really do want to help."

"Yeah… why?"

"The girls, man! Girls love a hero. Batman, Superman… even Spiderman. They get the chicks." He climbed through the window onto the roof, then stopped. "There's one weird thing about all of this. Don't you think it's strange that the kid who falls down a pipe is the brother of someone you know."

I hadn't thought about it, but Lucas was right. "You're right."

"Probably just one of those things that happens. See ya." From the roof, he scurried down a gutter line, dashed across the yard then disappeared up the street.

"Damn, Lucas has a good point." His question nagged at me, but I tried to ignore it. I stared into the night. Stars filled the nearly cloudless sky. A slight breeze whistled through the neighborhood.

That's when I caught a glimpse of *him*! The stranger from the park. A lighted cigarette cast his face in a red glow. I ducked beneath the window. Terror held me in a vice grip. I couldn't move. I couldn't breathe. My stomach turned to ice. He knew where I lived. He followed me home.

"Come on, Tripp. Maybe, it's just your imagination. Look again." Taking a few short breaths, I slowly peaked back over the windowsill.

No one was there. Had he even been there? Could it have just been my imagination? Maybe, but a lone puff of white smoke rose into the trees. A cold streak rose between my shoulder blades.

I quickly closed my window and the curtains and shut off the light. I crawled to the wall farthest from my window. Heart pounding, I huddled there I guess until sleep came.

***

"Tripp, you lied to me." Maria marched up to me when I entered the school yard. Her foot tapped the ground. Her hair covered one eye.

I nearly choked on my own saliva. What was she talking about? "Wh… what do you mean?"

"You said you were going to mathletes, but you didn't show up." She brushed the hair away from her eye. Her nostrils flared.

"Oh, I'm sorry." I shrugged. "My dad needed me home."

A smile crossed her lips. "I'm just kidding. I'm not mad. I'm glad you're feeling better."

"Huh?"

"Lucas said you were sick yesterday. That's why you missed." Maria took a step closer. "You don't look sick."

My pits started to sweat just like they always did when I spoke to her. "Oh yeah, just a twenty-four hour bug or something. "Hey, I heard your brother had an accident. Is he all right?"

"Oh my God, Tripp, you heard what happened, right? He could have died." She scratched her arm, her nails leaving slight marks in her soft skin. "Crazy thing, he fell down a drainage pipe. Not even sure how it happened. He said the boogie man threw him down, but he's little. He believes monsters hide in his closet. Still, police are asking us a bunch of questions. But thank God, he's okay. The most amazing part was the hero in the mask who came out of nowhere to save him. It's unbelievable. I mean I didn't think people with superpowers really existed. I wasn't there, but my mom said the man in the mask could stretch or something. Tripp, he saved my brother. He was a hero."

My heart danced. She called me a hero. "I'm glad to hear he's okay."

She took a long breath. Her body trembled. "Tripp, if there's heroes, do you think my brother is right? The boogie man is also real?"

A shiver climbed my back. The image of the stranger in a trench coat flashed through my mind. I forced a grin. "Uh, no. Let's just be glad there's someone out there willing to help."

"You're right." Maria nodded. She turned as if to walk away, and then stopped. "Hey, Tripp, there's still time for you to join mathletes. Will you?"

"I really want to." I rocked back and forth on my heels. "Um, I better get going."

"Okay, see you." She strolled away, peering over her shoulder once before turning down a hallway.

The first bell sounded.

I rushed off to class and struggled to pay attention. Maria had called the stranger a hero. *Me*, a hero. During each of my classes, her words played over and over. Visions of the drainage line filled my mind. Of her little brother grasping my hand. Of the people cheering. Then, I thought about what my dad and Doctor Torren had said.

Maybe they were right. I couldn't do that again. I couldn't risk being seen. What chance would have I have for a normal life if people found out it was me? None. And what of this boogie man Maria's brother had mentioned? Could someone have really shoved him into the pipe? If so, why? I tried to push those questions away, but they lingered.

At lunch, I joined Mrs. Ramirez in the trailer.

"Missed you yesterday, Tripp." She chewed a bite of her sandwich. We sat at the table in the darkened trailer. From outside came a chorus of sounds as the rest of Melody T.

Poopter's Junior High students laughed, ate, played basketball or whatever else they did during the lunch hour. "Did you get into a lot of trouble?"

"No." I contemplated the two plastic bottles on the table filled with colorless, odorless shakes then pushed them away. Doc Torren had me back on a strictly liquid diet until he figured out why the protein patty caused the transformation. "What about you—any trouble?"

She smiled. "Thanks to you, no one knew I was involved. Thank you for not telling your dad, though I suspect it makes me a hypocrite for you to be who you are while I hide in my car."

"I understand." I yawned.

"You know if I did come forward, I'd probably lose my job, and I just can't—"

"I said I understood." Silence filled the trailer. Why had I barked at her? I softened. "If you lost your job, I'd have to eat alone every day, so don't feel bad. I need you around."

"Thank you, Tripp." She opened the day's *Times*. "The hero in the pink mask is quite famous."

She pointed to the article on the top of the second page but didn't need to show it to me. I'd seen it earlier. The paper had done a follow-up on the story. The article said police no longer considered the rescuer—*me*—a suspect but did have evidence the boy had been thrown down the shaft. Police still wanted to find me to offer thanks.

The 12 News also reported the story. One broadcaster referred to me as *The Elastic Hero.*

"At least they don't know my identity." I dragged a shake closer and stirred it with a straw. "Do you think they'll keep trying to find me—I mean the person in the mask?"

"Some will. Yes."

"That's what my dad is afraid of."

"And he wants you to stop, right?"

"Well, yeah."

Mrs. Ramirez sighed. "What do you want to do?"

I paced the trailer. "Be left alone. Like I said, there won't be any repeat performances of the other day."

"But why, Tripp?" She sat back in her chair and folded her arms. "Didn't it feel good to help that little boy? To help your friend's brother?"

Does everyone know Maria talks to me?

"That's another thing." I tapped my fingers on the table. "It's just weird something like that happened to someone I know… and just when my powers showed up?"

Mrs. Ramirez tilted her head and raised an eyebrow. "What are you thinking?"

I tapped harder. "Nothing. I don't know. I guess anything is possible."

She took a swig from a bottle of water before speaking. "I don't have an answer, but it's an interesting question. Maybe one you should explore."

"Maybe."

She leaned closer. "You didn't answer my question. Did it feel good saving that boy?"

"I guess." Truth be told, it did feel good. I didn't even mind being called *The Elastic Hero* by the press. But I could never be like Superman or Batman or any of those comic book heroes. I'd always be an out-of-control freak. "Why do you even care?"

"I care about you, Tripp." She clasped her fingers under her chin. "Ever since your father and doctor entrusted me to watch out for you at school, I've been concerned they're holding you back from doing great things."

I stood and pushed away from the table. "Stop pushing me. I'm not supposed to be some hero."

"That's your father talking."

I turned my back to her. "Maybe, but like I said, I'm done."

Mrs. Ramirez crossed in front of me. "I don't mean to push, Tripp. I only want what's best for you. You know, I kind of see you like my son. I probably shouldn't say that, but I really do care about you."

I stared at her. I wanted to throw my arms around her. I couldn't remember the last time anyone had hugged me. But that was stupid. *Settle down, Tripp.* "Uh, thanks, Mrs. Ramirez."

"Don't thank me. Look, Tripp, I just ask that you think about it. And, I wanted you to have this." She handed me a large paper bag. Her lips parted in a gentle smile.

"What is this?" I asked.

"A little present."

"Whatever it is, it's heavy." I dug out a new ski mask, black with two yellow lightning bolts sewn into the sides near where my ears would be. I glanced at her then back at the mask.

"The pink mask just isn't right for you." Mrs. Ramirez's brown eyes widened.

My head spun. Did she want me to become some kind of vigilante wandering the streets in search of trouble? She had the wrong teen. How could I make her understand? The paper back crinkled in my hand. It was still heavy. What else had she gotten me? I wasn't sure I wanted to see.

"There's more. Keep looking," Mrs. Ramirez said.

I lifted out a belt, like something a police officer or a soldier might wear. Camouflaged with a number of pouches. "What am I supposed to do with this? I don't have any weapons."

"True, but what brings about your powers?"

"Food."

"Right." She placed her hand on top of mine. "Consider this your utility belt."

"Kind of heavy isn't it." I held the belt closer to my face to examine it. "How am I supposed to fight bad guys when this weighs me down? Do you see any muscle on this body?"

"Tripp, that's just silly."

I placed the mask and the belt back in the bag. "Mrs. Ramirez—"

"Tripp, don't say anything. Just think about it. You can toss them if you want, but just give it some thought before you do."

Chapter 7

Bad Night for a Stroll

The clock on my desk read 10 p.m. Dressed in jeans and a black sweatshirt, I sat staring at the black ski mask and utility belt. My fingers tapped the table. My legs shook. By now, Dad was passed out downstairs in his armchair in front of the TV, an empty can of Budweiser in his lap.

It would be easy to sneak out.

I grabbed Mrs. Ramirez's gifts and tossed them in the trash can under my desk. "I told her I wasn't interested. What happened at the 7-Eleven, I did to save my life. Helping Maria's brother—I'm glad I did it, but that was the last time."

Still, I needed some air.

Grasping my skateboard from the floor by my window, I stopped for just a moment. What if the stranger was out there waiting for me? Who cares? He's just some homeless jerk. If he bothers me, I'll ride away. Better yet, slam him with my board. How's that for a hero? Maybe I should be a villain, instead. I chuckled, then headed out.

As I guessed, Dad was asleep in his armchair, his head slumped to his chest. But I was wrong about having a Budweiser in his lap. It was a half-finished bottle of Corona. Oh, something different. A stained robe loosely tied around the waist covered his body. MSNBC was airing some international news on the TV. His cane lay on the ground beside him. I shook my head. It was the same scene every night, except for the brand of beer.

"Night, Dad," I whispered. I wondered if he dreamed about mom when he slept. Maybe he was happier unconscious.

I slithered like a snake out the front door onto our brick porch. Sliding my fingers through my curly hair, I scanned the neighborhood. No signs of anyone lurking. Just rows of quiet houses bathed in soft orange of street lights overhead. A soft cool breeze rustled yellowing leaves. A dog barked down the street.

Off in the distance, a siren interrupted the calm. Then another, and a third. I shrugged. Not my problem. Not tonight. Not ever. I just wanted to ride my board. Clear my head.

I rode from one neighborhood to the next. All the while more sirens screamed.

Hard to say how far I skated. Maybe a couple of miles, but when I neared Roosevelt and 111th, a helicopter roared overhead. Then a police car, followed by a second and then a third, raced past me.

"Turn back, Tripp," I urged myself. "You don't want nothing to do with whatever's going on."

I didn't listen. Curiosity tugged at me. More squad cars flew by. Must have been a big emergency. Their red lights served as a beacon guiding me toward them. "Turn back, dude." I still ignored myself, even as the little hairs on the back of my neck stood at attention. Even as my heart fluttered.

There! Up ahead! The red and yellow beams from the lights splashed like waves against the walls of buildings. Police tape held back a crowd of onlookers, but from what?

A couple of blocks up the city sprawl gave way to the greens of the Queens Zoo.

I skidded to a halt, kicked up my board and ran through the crowd. Just beyond the yellow line, an army of police officers in helmets with shields and shotguns huddled together. Fire crews joined them.

"What's going on?" I asked.

"I heard the police talking about the zoo animals breaking out of their enclosures," a man near me answered.

"The animals are rampaging," said a third person.

"They're going to break through the zoo fence and get into the city," another warned.

Their words weighed on me like heavy backpacks filled with thick textbooks slung over my shoulders. *Just get back on your board and get out of here.*

"Who cares, this isn't the Central Park Zoo. They don't have the big animals here," a teen blurted.

"Didn't you read the local paper?" an elderly man added. "This week the lions and tigers are here on loan from Central Park. I think there's more, too… the rhinos and elephants."

"How'd this happen?" I asked.

"I don't know," the man next to me answered, "but I hear police may have to start shooting the animals."

I slunk to the back of the crowd. What the hell was going on? I use my powers one time, then all of a sudden crap like this just happens. A kid down a pipe. Zoo animals busting out into the city. I rubbed my head. My teeth clenched. Damn it. What was I supposed to do? I didn't want the animals to be killed. I paced the street away from the onlookers. Finally, I reached a decision. Let the police and firefighters do what they do. I was a teenager. I should do what teens do. My own thing. I don't know what strange twist of fate was going on to drag me into using my powers, but I wasn't going to play along.

"Screw you, fate. I'm going home." I jumped on my board, then a hand grasped my shoulder from behind.

I fell, landing on my butt. Peering up, I gasped. "Mrs. Ramirez!"

Chapter 8

What Would I Become?

Mrs. Ramirez stood over me, her brown hair disheveled. Her purple blouse half tucked in, one side hanging loosely over her jeans. Her eyes were red and swollen. A helicopter buzzed overhead, spotlight zeroed in on the zoo.

"Tripp, you have to help," she uttered.

I climbed to my feet. What the hell was she doing here?

"Mrs. Ramirez, what—"

"There are people in there who need your help." She pointed past the crowd to the zoo. Her hands shook.

I retreated a few steps. "Why are you here?"

She lifted a Three Musketeers from her pant pocket. "Look, you can eat this. Become something that can help them."

A group of police in battle gear, shotguns in hand, ran past us.

More squad cars roared along the block. A second helicopter hovered in the night sky. A news chopper.

I shook my head. She was out of her mind if she thought I was going to help. "We talked about this. I don't even know why I came here. I should be home doing homework. And I really don't know what you're doing here. It kind of freaks me out."

She thrust the candy bar at me. "You don't understand."

"No, I don't care." I grabbed my board and swung around to leave. "I'm out of here."

"Tripp, my daughter Elizabeth is in there." Mrs. Ramirez started to cry. "I came here because she's doing an internship at the zoo and was working tonight. I tried calling her cell, but she didn't answer. Please, Tripp. She's in danger. I just know it. Save her. You're the only one who can."

I bit my lip and cursed under my breath. She'd told me about her daughter before. Twenty-four. A student at NYU. Studying to be a veterinarian. Damn. What was I supposed to do now?

Head lowered, I turned back to her. "I… just… can't. The police are there. They'll help her. That's their job."

Mrs. Ramirez approached me. Tears slid down her face. "What if they can't. Tripp, I'm asking as a friend. She's my only child. Tripp, I've tried to be there for you. Be there for me now. Please."

I took a deep breath and slowly released it. Why didn't I just stay home? Why didn't I ever listen to Dad? I reached for the chocolate. "Okay."

She gently placed it in my hand. "Thank you, Tripp. Thank you. Please hurry. Before it's too late."

My hand closed around the chocolate. Short breaths slid from my lips. Every muscle tensed. "Whatever I become, it's on you," I told her.

"Whatever it is, you'll still be you, Tripp." She wiped away her tears.

"Do me a favor, when my father kills me, don't bother coming to the funeral." I rode my board away from her and the crowd to a quiet intersection. Circling in the middle of the street, I searched for the right spot to transform. Shadows covered a large, metal trash bin against the wall of a closed deli. I ducked behind the bin.

"This is stupid. You don't know what you're doing." I shook my head. "Yeah, but I have to try. For Elizabeth."

Closing my eyes, I unwrapped the candy and bit down on the chocolate. I quickly devoured half of it, forcing the sweetness down my throat.

My stomach grumbled. I held my breath, but nothing more happened. My stomach quieted and besides a slight bout of nausea, nothing changed.

"What the heck? What's going—?"

A stronger rumbling rose from my gut. Tiny explosions tore through my stomach like hundreds of landmines detonating deep inside my belly. I collapsed to the dirty concrete and folded my knees into my chest. My insides blazed. Groaning, I writhed across the ground. *Please, end! Hurts! Bad! Burning up!* Sweat dripped from my forehead. "Change… now! Can't! Take! More!"

I tried lifting myself, but my limbs wobbled like wet noodles. Only my eyes worked, which I wish didn't. I didn't want to see what came next.

A slimy warm substance oozed from my nose and ran down my chin. *What's happening—?* My stomach heaved. Something gurgled up my throat. It poured from the sides of my mouth, pooling around my head. I coughed and spewed some more. *Can't breathe! Drowning!* With a shaky hand, I wiped goo from my lips. Green glowing gelatinous ooze slid between my fingers. My body went limp. Bones became jelly, quivering under a mass of loose flesh. Skin melted away from my arms, revealing bloody muscles and veins. I screamed in silence. *Air! Need air!* More slime bubbled up from my exposed insides, coating my shirt, pants, socks and shoes.

"Help….

The word came out as a barely audible murmur. Before I could finish, my lips, nose, ears—my entire head—dissolved into a slippery mass. I sloshed along the ground, a formless disgusting puddle on the street. My clothes floated on top of me.

The transformation ended. I had become—snot. Something people sneezed from their noses.

Able to breathe again, I slurped in air. I had no idea how I could breathe, see or even think, but I could. Somewhere in this gooey mess I even had a heartbeat, and right now it thumped wildly. I couldn't move. Scream. Cry for help. I panted. My gaze darted back and forth from the trash bin to my skateboard to the crowd near the zoo. What now? This was useless. No, it couldn't be. I had to make this work. Had to think. What could goo do?

I stopped gulping air like an overheated dog. I had to get to the zoo, but how? I no longer had arms or legs—nothing to propel me forward. *Wait a second! In science, we saw amoebas through telescopes. How do they move? Think, Tripp. Come on. Oh yeah, they stretch, re-form then stretch again.* I willed myself to slide.

With a silent grunt, I snaked along the pavement, leaving my clotes behind.

As I got the hang of it, I picked up speed, gliding along the street. I slithered under the crowd unnoticed and then flowed around a line of police cars, fire trucks and ambulances. I reached officers dressed in full riot gear and seeped past them through the zoo's entrance.

A chorus of animals bellowed—some guttural barks and growls, others, high-pitched squeals—from deep inside the zoo grounds. How many of them were loose? How many were a threat? How would I stop any of them?

The answer came immediately.

"Please, help me!" A woman clung to the upper branches of a tree just beyond the entryway. Dressed in brown khakis, she had to be a zoo worker. A police helicopter shined a spotlight on her.

Beneath her, captured in the spotlight, two lions clawed at the tree. Their roars filled the night.

From the looks of it, the lions had already injured her. Blood dripped from a shredded pant leg. Crimson stains along the tree trunk marked her desperate climb to escape the massive predators. Her pleas excited the beasts. They circled then leaped at her over and over, their claws digging into the bark a few feet from her legs. Any moment they could leap high enough to strike her. Worse, they could climb the tree and drag her to the ground… and to her death.

Behind me, police piled into the zoo. Their boots stomped against the pavement. Red laser beams sliced through the night as police rifles targeted the lions. Little glowing scarlet dots spotted the lion's orange fur and brown manes.

"On my mark, open fire," one officer ordered.

"No," the woman shouted. "Don't kill them. It's not their fault."

I had to act now to save the woman and the lions. My mind raced. *Wait! Maybe ooze can reshape itself.*

I twisted and stretched into a snot-colored worm, rolling forward like a slinky on its side until I came within an arm's reach of the lions. With a sharp exhalation of breath, I hauled up one end of my gelatinous body from the ground, towering over the beasts.

Twirling wildly to pick up speed, I slung myself toward the woman like a cowboy throwing a lasso. I snagged the branch next to her and wrapped myself around it in a knot. Then I reshaped into a thin slide to carry her over the top of the lions to the police.

"Oh my God." She hugged the tree, squeezed her eyelids shut and turned away from me.

"Come on, lady! Move it!" I urged but without a mouth she couldn't hear me.

The lions leaped at her with snapping jaws. She whimpered and tucked her legs tight against her chest. One lion started to climb. Police rifles clicked. Drops of me slid down the tree, covering the bark in slippery goo. The lion struggled, wildly thrashing about to maintain its hold, but couldn't. The beast dropped to the ground. Immediate problem averted, but I still had to get the woman to trust me.

Come on, head! Think!

What happened next came straight out of some gory horror movie. My head rose from the green goo. I had no body—just a head.

"Lady, it's all right. Trust me." Slime dripped from my mouth; my voice sounded phlegmy.

She screamed louder.

Police aimed their targeting lasers at me. Tiny red dots marked my face.

"What is that?" someone blurted.

"Do we take the shot?" another asked.

"Not yet," a third commanded.

"Please, lady, move... before they shoot," I begged.

Tears streamed down her cheeks. Her body trembled. "What are you?" She stuttered her words.

"A friend."

She glanced at the lions, then back at me and nodded. Slowly lowering her body onto the slide, she glided to the police who carried her to safety.

"Now take out those animals," one officer commanded.

"No!"

I reshaped into a dome around the lions.

A thunder of gunfire erupted. Rounds plunged into my flesh, one plop after another after another. The bullets lodged inside me but never reached the lions. I froze. Who knows how much hot lead my body absorbed. Was I going to die? How could I survive this..., but somehow my heart still beat and my lungs moved air.

For a second time, my head rose from the goo, and I spoke to police. "Knock it off. Help me find a safe place for these animals." From underneath my dome, the lions roared and scratched at me, their claws like razors. "Hurry! Can't hold... them... much longer."

One of the officers stepped away from the rest. He approached me, a handgun aimed at my head. A helmet hid his face. Four gold stripes lined his sleeve. "Whatever the hell you are, stand down. We've got a job to do here."

The woman I rescued pushed past the wall of police. "Here. There's an empty enclosure." She pointed to a building surrounded by a wall of boulders.

"Get her out of here." The officer with the four stripes commanded his men. "Get her to an ambulance."

"No, wait," she protested with a shaky voice. "I'm the head zookeeper. Listen to me. There's a steel door attached to the wall. I have the keys. Get the animals inside, and I'll lock them in. They'll be safe."

"No." The officer grabbed her arm.

I swatted the officers hand away from the woman with a long jellylike arm.

More lasers targeted me, but the police held their fire. Of course, they did. The woman was too close.

She ran to the steel door, unlocked it and swung it open.

With the lions still protected inside the dome, I skidded them into the enclosure then dissolved into a glowing slick and drained away.

The woman slammed the door, locking the lions inside.

I sighed in relief, but more had to be done. The cries of animals running loose echoed from every direction.

I don't know how I did it, but I reshaped into a vaguely human form with gummy arms and legs. The glowing green goo dripped from my face. Under the ooze, no one would recognize me. At least, I hoped no one would.

The officer with the stripes removed his helmet, revealing cropped jet-black hair. He still aimed his revolver at me but studied me with deep-set coal eyes. "Are you that elastic hero everyone's talking about?"

I shook my head. "No."

"Then who?" He took a step closer. His title and name showed in yellow letters on his police jacket. Captain Weaver.

"Just someone here to help." I crossed to the zookeeper. She was arming a rifle with darts. "Do you know where Elizabeth Ramirez is? Is she all right?"

The zookeeper cocked her weapon. "Elizabeth? The intern vet student? She's not working today? I haven't see her. I sealed off the zoo. There's no way she could have gotten in. I hope she's not here."

"I have to go see." I turned on oozing legs toward the zoo's stone pathways.

"You're not going anywhere, except downtown for questioning." The captain blocked my path.

A man's scream rose from within the zoo. Weaver turned toward the sound.

I splashed to the ground and left him behind. My heart pulsated like energy waves rippling through my slime. I glowed brighter with each beat. What could make a man cry out like that? Would it be worse than the lions?

I rounded one corner into the path of a rhinoceros. The great beat slowly stalked a man who backed away from the animal, his hands held out before him as if to calm the creature.

I skidded to a halt in between them. "For real? A rhino?"

The great beast bowed its head and stomped its front hooves. Its massive horn seemed deadly; its armor impenetrable. A rifle lay crushed on the ground next to the beast. Darts clung to the animal's side, but the rhino still huffed and stomped its hooves vigorously.

How do I stop a rhino? What could slime do? A dome wouldn't contain it. I had to think of something else.

Before I could develop a plan, the rhino bellowed a guttural cry then charged.

"No!" The man ran but there would be no escape. No way to outrun a freaked-out animal. The beast would flatten him, crushing his bones like it did the rifle.

Now, Tripp! Like a volcano, I erupted into the air then landed on the rhino's head. In the next heartbeat, I willed myself into a green, gelatin mass large enough to cover the beast's head. The creature slid to a stop and tried to shake me off. I held on as tightly as I could, mainly because I didn't know what else to do.

Shots whizzed through the night and struck the animal. There must have been at least ten thuds into its body. The rhino wobbled, fell onto its hind legs, and dropped to the ground. I dripped off the beast. Behind me, Weaver stood with his officers. Those with tranquilizer guns held them aimed at the animal.

Heavy breaths poured from the rhino. Good.

"There're still others in danger." The captain nodded at me.

I reshaped into my dripping human form. "I'm on it." I turned to search the rest of the zoo but stopped at a steel gate to one enclosure. A round hole had been burned into the entryway.

Charred remnants hung loosely from hinges.

"Holy crap! This was no accident." I rubbed my gooey forehead.

"That's why I'll be taking you for questioning when everyone's safe." Captain Weaver approached from behind.

"I didn't do this, Captain." I swung toward him.

Another cry for help came from somewhere in the zoo.

"We'll see." Weaver lifted his gun and ran in the direction of the shriek.

For the next couple of hours, I helped save zoo workers and rounded up the rest of the animals. But no Elizabeth. I guess I could see how Mrs. Ramirez would have been scared since she couldn't reach her daughter. Couldn't blame her for that.

I let that thought fade away as my mind wrestled with the real mystery. Someone made it possible for the animals to escape. Who could have done this? Why? How could no one have noticed?

So many questions, but I figured the police could handle it. I'd done my part.

Before the captain could arrest me, I turned back into a puddle and disappeared from the zoo. I didn't want to think about how much news coverage this would get or what my dad would say when he found out about this.

I was a bit surprised when I didn't see Mrs. Ramirez waiting for me on the street. After all, I did this for her. Had she gotten a hold of her daughter? Still, why wouldn't she wait to see if I was safe?

I oozed back to the trash bin where I'd left my skateboard, reaching it just in time. The change started. My body reformed and the slime vanished. I became a human boy again, only naked. My body ached. My knees buckled and I slumped onto the concrete. I could have fallen asleep right there, but I couldn't allow that to happen. I had to get dressed. And get home.

Reaching for my clothes, a searing pain rippled up my right side just above the waist. I winced and panted through gritted teeth. *Ouch.* It freaking stung. I gingerly touched my side, expecting to find skin shredded by the lions' claws. Nothing! No scratch. No blood. No sign of injury at all. Just a phantom shockwave of pain that left me sprawled on the concrete. But I had to get up and move.

I painfully dressed, grabbed my board and lumbered away. One new thought filled my mind on the way home. There would be no hiding this.

Dad would know, and he'd kill me.

Chapter 9

Consequences

News of *Slimer,* as 12 News called me, spread quickly. Poorly recorded images from someone's phone ended up on all the major news stations. With the appearance of *Slimer* and the earlier arrival of *Rubberband Man*, again named by the same newscaster, the media speculated whether a team of heroes had arrived in Queens. None of it linked back to me, but Dad reacted worse than I expected.

At our dining table, as I hooked up N.E.R.D. to my feeding tubes, he shook his head.   "Trip, you deliberately defied me!" His crusty morning voice drowned out the hum of the N.E.R.D.

"Dad, it wasn't me." My feet fidgeted under the kitchen table. What a stupid lie. Did I really think that would work?

Dad slammed his hand on the table. I jumped. "Really, Tripp? You would try a lie… now?"

I stared into N.E.R.D.'s one eye as my breakfast flowed into my feeding tubes. "All right, it was me, but I helped those people. You saw."

"You shouldn't have been out there in the first place." He leaned forward, hands twisting the newspaper. "We talked about this. We agreed."

"I didn't agree to anything," I snapped. "By the way, I'm fine. You didn't even ask. You know, I got clawed by lions, but my powers protected me. Not one scratch on me. Not that you care."

"Don't care?" Dad rose from the table, kicking his chair away. His robe untied, revealing a white undershirt and gray boxers. "You ungrateful little…. Do you know what I gave up for you?"

I jumped from the table, ripping away from N.E.R.D. The thick clear substance spilled onto my striped shirt and jeans. "No, Dad, tell me what you gave up. Go on say it. You blame me for mom's death. That she died giving birth to me. Just say it. I ruined your life."

He limped toward me, grabbing me by the collar. His eyes bulged. Lips quivered. Was he going to hit me? Let him. I didn't care. Somehow, he stopped himself. Blinking fast, he released his hold on me and retreated.

I wasn't finished. "That's it, huh, Dad? I'm right."

He frowned at me. There might have been a tear in his eye. "I care, Tripp. I've always cared from the first moment you were given to me."

"Huh?"

"Tripp, you don't know what's at stake. People could find you. Worse, he could take you away." He tightened the string around his robe.

"What are you talking about?" My cheeks burned as if a fire ignited beneath my skin. "What people?"

Dad crossed to the refrigerator, threw it open and grabbed a beer. He twisted the cap and took a long swig. He swallowed a mouthful, then spoke. "I just mean people will eventually find out it's you performing these deeds, and they won't understand. Who knows what the government might do if they found out. They might try to take you away. Experiment on you. Do you want that to happen, Tripp? Do you?"

"No!" I wasn't at all sure that's what he meant.

Dad took another sip from his bottle. "I've made a decision, Tripp. I decided you are not to leave this house for the time being unless supervised by me."

"Wait! What? How is that even possible? I have school."

"You'll be homeschooled for now," Dad explained.

"So I'm a prisoner now—a prisoner in my own house!" Hot tears formed. How could he do this to me?

"It's not like that, Tripp," Dad shook his head.

"Yes, it is." I turned my back to him.

"You've left me no choice. I have to protect you." He placed the beer bottle on the counter. He stared at the floor.

"This isn't fair!" I shouted. "Not fair at all!"

Dad stepped toward me. "That may be, but that's the way it is for now. I'm sorry, son. Like I said, I have no choice."

"Yeah, well maybe I do." Before he could stop me, I bolted into the living room, snatched up by skateboard and flew out of the house.

He shouted for me to stop, but I didn't listen. I had to get away from him. I had to figure things out for myself.

I skated frantically down the street. The engine of a familiar truck revved behind me. I turned to see Dad's F-150 following me. I rode harder, but he quickly caught up to me.

"Tripp," he ordered through the open passenger window, "come home so we can talk. Don't do this."

"Leave me alone," I cried.

"Tripp, please!"

I didn't answer. Instead, I made a ninety-degree turn onto 85th then veered into an alley between homes. Dad couldn't stop in time, and his pickup flew by the alley's entrance. If I could reach the other end before he doubled back, I could hide somewhere. One foot on the board, my other pushing off the ground, I rode as fast as I could. Sweat poured from my forehead. The other end of the alley neared. Then a thought splashed through my mind. I was running away from my dad. None of this made any sense. He was my dad, not the—

I struck a tire, hurtling off my board. I crashed against pavement, rolling several times. I ended up on my back. Stinging pain radiated from scrapes along my arms and legs. A moan slid from my lips.

"Tripp!" Dad called from his pickup, which screeched to a stop at the alley's exit. He slid from the pickup and limped to me.

He still wore his robe. Slippers covered his feet. Leaning on his cane, he slowly dropped to both knees. "My God, Tripp! Are you all right? Son, are you hurt?"

"Well, duh," I answered. My body ached all over. Blood dripped from my right elbow.

Dad wrapped his arms around me. "Son, I'm so sorry. Please come home and talk. I don't blame you for what happened to your mom. It has nothing to do with you. It's me, son. Not you. I know I've been a lousy dad. I know I've lost my way. I won't keep you out of school. I promise. Just don't run away again."

I hugged him. "Dad, I don't mean to mess up. I don't know what's going on with me. I'm… confused."

"I know that." He helped me to my feet and, with a hand around my shoulder, walked me to the pickup. After I climbed into the passenger seat, he grabbed my board, then gently placed it in the bed of the pickup.

"Dad, can I please just go to school today?"

He sighed. "If that's what you want. But… we need to talk. I guess… we can do that… after. You'll have to change first. Can't go to school bleeding and with that N.E.R.D. crap all over your clothes."

We drove home in an uncomfortable silence. I guess we were both shaken up, and I'm not sure we completely trusted each other. I had the feeling nothing would be the same between me and my dad… or in my life.

Chapter 10

Have to Save Him

I made it to school a little late. My dad accompanied me into the front office to manufacture some excuse about a flat tire. The office staff didn't question it. They handed me a note and sent me to my morning class. I remember the look on my dad's face as I left the office. He watched me for the longest time. His brow furrowed. His face fixed in a gloomy stare. I don't know if he felt guilt or concern… or both. He probably felt the same way I did— our troubles had just begun.

I headed to my first class along a quiet hallway. I got to within a stone's throw of my classroom, and a hand grabbed my shoulder.

"What the…?"

"Dude, quiet." Lucas spun me around, dragged me to a bathroom and pushed me inside.

"What are you doing?" I protested.

"You did it." He patted my shoulder. "I really didn't think you had it in you, but I was wrong. You're a hero, dude."

"What do you mean?" I played dumb as I scanned the bathroom stalls for anyone else listening. We were alone.

"You know." Lucas frowned. "Don't play stupid. The zoo. It's all over the news. *Slimer* is all the rage."

"Hey, you don't know that was me." I uselessly kept up the charade.

"Dude." He raised an eyebrow.

"All right, it was me, but shut up about it." I didn't want to talk about it… not here at school. Too dangerous. Someone would hear. School grounds were not the best place for keeping secrets.

"Look, man, I understand." Lucas leaned against a sink. "I just wanted to let you know I think you made the right choice—I mean to be a hero and all."

I shook my head. "My dad doesn't think so. He wanted to keep me at home and make me a prisoner."

"What? Why? No one knows it's you."

"You know."

"Yeah, but—"

"Look, I've got to get to class, and so do you." I headed toward the bathroom door. "Just forget about this. I don't want to get in anymore trouble. I shouldn't have done what I did last night."

"Hey, Tripp, you and I both know you're not done being a hero, so whatever dude." Lucas moved closer to me. "I just want you to know I'm your bud. If you need me for anything, I've got your back—unless you become that slimy thing again. I want nothing to do with that scary dude."

I nodded. "Thanks—I think."

The rest of the morning went smoothly. I went to my classes and buried my head in my books. A few students whispered about *Slimer* but no one gave me a second thought. How could the weird kid who eats lunch in a dark trailer be a hero?

In English, Mrs. Thayer called out a girl for using her phone in class. When Thayer snatched the phone, the girl said she just wanted to see a YouTube video of the slimy hero at the zoo. My heart stopped until Thayer threw the phone into her pocket.

"You can get this back after school," she told the girl.

At lunch, I headed to the trailer to eat with Mrs. Rodriguez and tell her off. When I threw open the door to the trailer, she greeted me with a wide grin.

"You really did it, Tripp." She led me inside and closed the door. "You saved everyone. You were the hero I knew you could be."

I folded my arms over my chest. "You told me your daughter was trapped in the zoo, but she wasn't."

The smile on her face vanished. "Tripp, I didn't know. I couldn't get ahold of her. I was so scared. That's why I was there last night. It was so fortunate that I ran into you. You saved everyone."

I stepped back from her. "Where were you when it was over? You didn't even wait to see if I was all right. The only reason I went there was because of you, and you just left. Do you know how much trouble I got in? My dad was beyond pissed."

Mrs. Ramirez sat down at the table where we usually ate. "I'm so sorry. I finally got ahold of Elizabeth. I was so happy she was safe, I just had to hold her. I knew you'd be fine, Tripp. You're a hero."

I kicked a chair beside me. "Stop saying that. You should have waited. This little lunch thing we… it's over."

I stormed out of the trailer. And never looked back.

I avoided everyone, even Lucas and Maria, the rest of the day. I really just wanted the day to end, so I could get home and have it out with my dad. Maybe, we could finally work things out.

Then came the second to the last period of the day—science class.

Mrs. Rodriguez rushed into the classroom and said she needed to take me to the office. I trembled all over. What now? She didn't say another word, but rather led me down the hallway toward the office.

"What is it?" I asked. "I told you to leave me alone."

"Tripp, follow me!" She turned away from the office and steered me to the trailer. She jerked me inside and then slammed the door shut. "Tripp, there's real trouble. At a bank. And I think I saw your father."

"What?" I backed away from her. What day was it? Thursday? My dad went to Queens National Bank every Thursday to make a deposit. My heart pounded. A weight pressed against my shoulders as if invisible hands pushed against me.

"Look." She pointed to her cell phone. "It's happening right now."

In shaky images beamed from a helicopter, police surrounded a bank with their guns drawn. It was Queens National Bank. A man in black military fatigues held another man at gunpoint just outside the front door. The camera zoomed in. My heart sank. *Dad!* The bastard held my dad, gun pointed to his head. My body froze. No… no… no. This couldn't be real. I grabbed the cell from her hands and held it up to my face. My dad peered up toward the camera as if he could see me watching him and shook his head. Was that a message to me? Was he telling me to stay away? Was he crazy?

The gunman dragged him inside.

Then a newscaster's voice blazed to life. "We have reports of an unknown number of armed assailants holed up inside the bank. There are hostages, like the one we just saw, though we don't know how many or whether there are any injured so far. Sources have reported that the gunmen have said they will start to kill hostages if they're demands are not met."

Shots rang out from the television. The reporter's voice quivered. "Shots have been fired, but we're not sure from where—whether police fired on the gunmen or whether the shots came from inside the bank. What is clear is that the situation is growing increasingly violent and dangerous."

Mrs. Ramirez had her lunch on the table. Without hesitation, I lifted a red apple and bit through it until there was nothing left. "Dad, hang on. I'm coming."

More shots rose from the television. I glared at the images of armed police around the bank.

From the table, I picked up a can of soda and slurped it down. "Dad—"

The change came fast.

Like always, my stomach thundered. Limb by limb my body started to shake. I dropped the apple core and grabbed my belly. My insides boiled. The searing heat radiated from my gut to my heart into my limbs. Brown fur grew from my forearms and claws tore through my fingertips. My jaw cracked. My face pulsated. My nose stretched into a snout. *My God, what beast am I becoming now?*

I screamed, but it came out as a howl.

Fangs sliced through my gums. The bones in my feet snapped and my legs, covered in fur, rippled with new muscles that burst through my pants. My heart raced. Lungs expanded like massive balloons pushing against my chest. The pain eased. My limbs flexed. Strong! I felt so strong! More than that... I felt wild... like I just wanted to run.

The change stopped. Mrs. Rodriguez backed away to the other side of the trailer. I panted for air, wheezing and gasping for each breath. Sprawled on the floor, I studied my hands. Long, thin and bony with dagger-like nails. I'd become a werewolf! Was I still in control? I couldn't tell. I hungered for flesh. Raw flesh!

It would be easy to give in to the animal. It felt so good. Each sense had come alive. I drank in the musty odor of fear from Mrs. Rodriguez's sweat. My ears detected the soft whimper she tried to suppress.

My muscles rippled under the fur. I picked myself up from the floor. With the strength in my legs, I could have bounded through the roof. I howled a second time, but not from any pain. I just had the urge, like a wolf in the moonlight.

"Tripp, is... is that you?" Mrs. Rodriguez asked gently. "Can you understand me?"

My tongue slid over fangs extending from my snout. "Yes, I'm still me—only better." My voice sounded rough, threatening. As I stared at Mrs. Rodriguez, a hunger rose from inside me. I smelled the warm blood pumping under her skin. It would be so easy to feed. Just one slice of her neck. My mouth watered. *Wait a second! Stop that!* I wasn't a wolf. Not really. I needed to maintain control. I stepped toward Mrs. Rodriguez, but quickly stopped and backed away.

"Tripp..."

"Mrs. Rodriguez, get out of here. Now!"

She scooted past me and threw open the door.

Crouching like a tight spring, I leaped through the open trailer door. With a wolf's speed, I raced through the school yard, bounded over a fence and charged through the neighborhood toward the bank.

I didn't bother to hide my presence as I raced on all fours, sometimes on the sidewalk, sometimes on the street, dodging traffic and people. I had to get to my dad. That's all that mattered. Adults gasped and kids screamed. Cars screeched and skidded. I didn't care. I liked the hunt. I imagined myself a wolf flying through the forest where no obstacle could stop me.

Rounding a corner, I jumped onto a building's fire escape and climbed the five stories to the roof. From there, I sprang to another rooftop and then another.

I crossed ten city blocks in just a few heartbeats, stopping atop one tenement that overlooked Queens National. An officer, perched on the same roof, hadn't noticed my arrival. He held a rifle aimed at the bank. I slid behind an air conditioning unit to stay hidden and forced myself not to howl. The wolf inside of me didn't like that. He wanted to attack now, to tear apart the gunmen for threatening my dad, but if I barreled in like a wild beast, hostages could die. He could die.

I devised another plan.

If I could make it onto the bank's roof, I could find a way in and surprise the gunmen before they had a chance to hurt anyone. Maybe I could stop them without killing them.

Peering over the air conditioning unit, careful to remain hidden from the officer, I scanned for a route to the bank's roof. I could never make the jump to the Queen's National across the street. Nevertheless, a path presented itself. Two billboard signs with narrow platforms—one to the left of the bank and the other just to the right of the tenement—would do the job. With my wolf strength, I could leapfrog one billboard to the next to reach the bank. If I did it fast enough, no one would be sure what flew through the sky. I had to try—had to test my wolf abilities.

Stepping from behind the air conditioner, I lowered down on all fours. My blood flowed fast; my heart raced. *Go!* I bolted toward the edge of the roof. The officer must have heard me because he whirled toward me. Before he could pull the trigger, I leaped over him, soaring toward the first billboard platform. I reached it gracefully then vaulted again for the second billboard. After I landed on it, I flew one more time toward the bank's roof.

Stretch! Stretch! Make it!

I stealthily touched down on the roof and skid to a stop. I looked back just once to see the officer pointing toward me. He had to be calling to the other officers, but I had no time to worry about them.

A faint breath rose from the far ledge to my right. The scent of gunpowder made my nostrils tickle. A gunman dressed in black armor, his face covered by a mask, resembling something out of a ninja movie, hid in the shadows. His calm breathing indicated he hadn't seen me yet. His attention focused on police, but he could spot me any moment. My plans would be ruined. He'd signal those inside the bank. They'd hurt the hostages… or do worse.

The hunt began.

Like a wolf in the wild stalking its prey, I crouched low. A harsh growl rose from deep within my throat. I couldn't help it.

With powerful legs, I pounced on the gunman before he could react. He couldn't even scream. Though the wolf wanted to slaughter him, I maintained control. One claw strike to his face knocked him unconscious. He dropped his rifle then slumped against the roof like a bag of trash.

I turned my attention back to the air conditioning unit. That would be my way in. With super strength, I ripped the metal shaft from the unit, exposing an air duct just large enough for one person—or a wolf. The air duct dropped into darkness. Stale air wafted up from the depths.

With my claws extended, I slid into the metal pit. I landed with a clunk where the duct shifted from a vertical drop to a horizontal crawlway split in four directions. I could feel the base sag under my weight. I sniffed the dusty air. The stink of sweaty human flesh came from the farthest right shaft.

Following the stench, I crawled from one vent to another. The thin metal rumbled underneath me. I winced with each movement. They would hear me approaching. All would be lost.

I stopped and listened. Hushed cries, whispers, the click of a gun, and a mother's words of comfort to a child from up ahead.

My wolf ears detected more voices.

"This is stupid, man. What are we doing here?" one man complained, his voice shaky.

"What we're hired to do. Don't worry. Our ride's on the way."

"For now, it's about time we kill a hostage. That's what our benefactor paid for," a second man declared.

I sensed no hesitation in him. I had to move quickly.

I crept down the shaft, which led me around a bend to the vent above the bank's main floor. I studied the scene. Four gunmen, armed with rifles, stood over hostages, who sat cross-legged on the floor. There could have been maybe twenty, a mix of men, women and children. Where was my dad? I couldn't see him. But he was there. The earthy scent of his oak cane was unmistakable.

The gunmen wore the same black armor and masks as the man on the roof. Two of the gunmen faced each other. Probably the two I heard talking. The other two stood by a doorway leading into the bank.

Blood pooled around two uniformed security guards, sprawled on the floor a few feet apart. Neither moved. I prayed they might still be alive, but I feared not. I shook my head. Rage burned my insides. The wolf wanted to avenge them, and so did I. If I let the wolf take control, the gunmen would pay, but the attack would be sloppy and bloody. I would place too many lives at risk. My attack had to be fast, quiet and calculated.

The two gunmen who faced each other argued over who to kill.

"Let's ice a kid," a short stalky thug said.

"No way. The old fool with the cane," the other responded. He was tall with a long neck. "I don't like the way he looks at me. Like he's superior, or something."

"Then just do it and get it over with," the first one blurted.

The tall gunman walked through the hostages. He reached down by a kiosk and lifted… Dad.

Dad, no! I had to move. No time to think. No time to plan.

The wolf crashed through the vent to the floor. My vision turned crimson. Screams echoed around me. I slashed wildly, pouncing on the short gunman. I then swung toward the taller one who held my dad. Only, he was already on the ground. Dad bent down, smashing the gunman's face with a fist. He then peered up at me, shaking his head, pointing to the exit.

How could my gimp dad have taken the dude out so quickly? A gunshot rang out. Something ripped into my chest. Searing heat radiated through my body. I slowed and touched the fur just above my heart. Thick scarlet liquid dripped from my claws. Was it mine or the gunmen's? I couldn't be sure.

More gunfire rang out. I leaped at the two remaining gunmen, cutting through their armor, ripping through skin, muscle and bones. Their flesh hung from my nails. Blood splattered across the bank floor and splashed screaming hostages.

The gunmen cried out in agony.

I howled. The human in me lost control. My world went dark.

Chapter 11

Not Him Again

"Hey, wake up, kid."

The voice spoke as if far away and yet I recognized the English accent. *Him!*

A foot nudged my side. "You don't want to be found like this, kid. Come on, get up now."

My head felt woozy. My eyes slowly blinked open. A blurred image hovered over me. I blinked again, and the blur became a shadowy figure. I didn't want it to be him, but the accent didn't lie. "Where am I?"

"In a park not far from your home," he answered.

The man who had spoken to me in the park the night of the convenience store robbery found me again. That night he knew about me, knew what really happened. He creeped me out then, and here he was again. The little hairs on the back of my neck stood at attention. The uneasy feeling in my gut warned me he was dangerous.

I blinked again and rubbed my eyes. The same trench coat covered his body. He had a cigarette in his mouth just as before. He seemed older under the fiery glow of a sunset. Wrinkles lined his forehead and eyes. A scraggly, thin, black and gray beard covered his cheeks and neck. Messy hair spilled around his face and nearly covered his dark eyes.

He removed the cigarette from his mouth and blew out a ring of smoke. "I hope you realize you were lying here naked and covered in blood. Thank goodness you had enough sense to hide in bushes at the far end of the park where no one could see you."

I looked at myself. I wore a trench coat, just like his. How did I get here? Did he give me this coat? The last thing I remembered was—the wolf.

I rose up on my elbows. "What happened? Did you bring me here?"

He knelt on one knee. "It was you, wasn't it? It's all over the news, my boy. You saved everyone in the bank, well, except for those two unfortunate security officers. But you had no way of saving them." The man grinned broadly and puffed on his cigarette. "You're a real hero."

"What... what are you talking about?" I lifted myself to my knees. "Where's my dad. Is he okay?"

"I should say, my boy." The man frowned. "Don't play coy with me, boy. You know what you did. What you became. You not only saved everyone in the bank, but you did it without killing the men who sought to rob the bank. Of course, they were critically hurt by whatever attacked them. One even lost an arm. But he probably deserved that. They say a man dressed as a wolf or a wolf man saved everyone then fled. They also say the wolf was shot. Look at your chest, boy. If I am not mistaken, there is an outline of a bullet hole not far from your heart."

Still on my knees, I peeked under the trench coat. The outlines of a wound barely showed through the skin, like a scar healed over time. My mind swirled. I needed to find my dad. Needed to get home.

I stared into the man's dark eyes. He knew too much.

"You didn't answer my question. Did you bring me here? How did you know I was here?"

He took a drag on his cigarette and flicked it away. "You got yourself here, kid. As for me, it's like I told you the other night. We homeless see things others don't. We get around in ways that common folk don't. We pay attention to what happens on the streets because they're our home."

"You're lying. You're following me, aren't you? I saw you outside my window watching me. Why?"

He leaned in closer. "In time."

What did that mean?

He started to walk away. I grabbed his arm. "Hey."

He shoved me away with more force than I expected.

"Don't ever grab me."

I backed away, aware of the clear threat in his words. He shook his head and rolled his eyes as he struck a match and lit another cigarette.

"Sorry, mate. Look, I think what you are… what you can become… is something special. I'm glad to see you start to use your abilities instead of wasting them like some commoner. You are not bloody common—at all. Don't let anyone tell you otherwise. Good luck, kid. Tough times lay ahead, I'm sure."

He strolled away, a trail of smoke left in his wake. "By the way, keep the coat. Consider it a gift."

I thought to follow but let him go. I had to make sure my dad was all right, even if he flipped out at me. He had to understand I just wanted to save him. He just had to.

***

"Dad, I know we have to talk," I announced as I ran through the front door. I expected he would be in the front room on the couch ready to yell at me, but no. Darkness shrouded the house as day bled to dusk. "Dad?" No response. *Weird.*

I stepped into the kitchen. Empty, lights off. A cold sweat dripped from my brow. *Run!* The sensation was overpowering, but first I had to find him. What if he had been hurt. What if something worse than that had happened.

"Dad, are you here?" I ran up the stairs to his room, then his office, then my room. All deserted. The strange man in the trench coat—did he have something to do with this?

The sound of a window sliding open came from downstairs. I snuck to the stairs with light, cautious steps. I took quiet shallow breaths and listened. No more noise. Crouched low, I slid down the banister to the living room. Movement came from the kitchen. Was it my dad? Had to be.

"Dad, is that you?"

Silence greeted me until I reached the kitchen. Two rather large men in black suits sat at the table. I didn't recognize either man.

One of them, a blond-haired man with a scar on his chin, spoke. "Good evening, Tripp. You've had a busy day."

His unfeeling voice made me shiver. He didn't smile or frown or show emotion of any kind but continued to speak.

Where had they come from? A moment ago the house had been deserted. *How--?*

"I think you've done enough for one day. You need to come with us." The blond with the scarred chin stood. The second man, an Asian with jet black hair, followed his lead.

"Who are you? Where's my dad? How do you know my name?"

"Just come with us, young man." The blond one stepped around the table toward me. "We're not here to hurt you."

"What have you done with him?" I ran to the front door. Two more men, dressed in similar dark suits, blocked the way.

"Leave me alone!"

Two others appeared at the top of the stairs.

"What's going on here?" I backed away from the two at the front door. "Who are you? Why are you in my house?"

"Tripp, there's nowhere to run." The blond man took a few careful steps toward me. He used my name again. How did he know me? Using it freaked me out. "We are not the enemy. We just need you to come with us."

"No way!" I whirled in each direction in search of an escape route. I found none. I could try to smash through the front window. If only I had some food. Whatever creature I changed into would help me escape.

My gaze shifted between the six men. They each slid cautiously toward me, their hands outstretched.

"Come on, Tripp," blondie urged. "Make this easy on everyone."

"Where's my dad? Tell me." Desperate, I reached into the pockets of the trench coat for any kind of weapon. The right pocket hid something in a wrapper. I quickly lifted it from the coat. Chocolate! Had the man in the park left it for me? Did he know I'd walk into a trap? I lifted the candy to my mouth.

Before I bit down, something whished through the air and struck my left arm with a thud. A bolt of energy zapped my body. My limbs twitched. The candy slipped from my fingers. I couldn't breathe. My legs shook violently. I fell, my body convulsing as I writhed wildly on the floor.

"Sorry." Blondie picked up the chocolate bar and took a bite. "It wasn't supposed to go down like this."

"Where... Dad?" My teeth chattered.

"He is with us," he whispered. He knelt down, removed a syringe from his pocket and injected something into my arm.

"What are... you doing? What did you say... about... my dad?" A gray void engulfed my vision.

"He's the reason we're here."

"Huh?" My eyes blinked and became heavy.

"He sent us for you."

No! That was a lie.

Chapter 12

Where Am I?

I hid in the air duct of Queens National Bank. On the floor below, a wolf pounced on four gunmen. The beast slashed its claws through one man's chest, ripping through his armor. Blood spewed from the wound as he dropped to the floor. Hostages covered their eyes. Their screams bounced off the walls.

Gunfire erupted. The beast spun around as a round struck it in the chest. Crying out, the wolf threw itself at the two remaining gunmen. Both dropped their weapons and tried to run, but the creature's attack came too swiftly. The wolf sliced their backs. They fell quickly and squirmed on the ground, begging for mercy, but the wolf had a taste for blood and wanted more.

Saliva dripped from its fangs. The creature bent down toward one of the men. A little boy, one of the hostages, shouted, "Please stop!"

The monster glanced at the boy who couldn't have been much older than five or six years old.

Unleashing a howl, the wolf crashed through a window in the bank, charged past the police and the crowds and raced away. Only one clear thought filled its mind. What have I become?

My eyes shot open, but my thoughts swirled with visions of the beast. Then came thoughts of the men in black suits.

The bastards stuck me with something. What did they do to me? Where did they take me? My breaths froze in my throat. My head pounded. I blinked away the last bits of haze and realized I lay on my side in a small bed without sheets.

"This isn't my bed!" I leaped to my feet, but my wobbly legs failed me. I dropped to the cold, hard floor. "Hey, where am I?"

No one answered.

"This isn't right?" I forced myself to take a breath. Tried to quiet my racing thoughts. "Anyone… help me!"

I tried standing again. Though my legs were shaky, this time they supported me. I lumbered around my surroundings.

I was in a room that resembled my own bedroom, but it wasn't. I had the same dresser, desk and chair. The walls were even decorated with posters of my favorite rock bands, but this place couldn't be my room. My room always felt warm and stunk of dirty clothes. This place had a cold draft and smelled like cherry cough medicine. Pale white lighting overhead cast a faint glow instead of the Darth Vader lamp in my room. My computer was gone, too. White walls surrounded me instead of the ocean blue paint in my real room. I didn't even see my cell phone. One more difference—the door to this room had no knob, and there were no windows.

I'm trapped! I ran to a wall and pounded a fist against it over and over. "Let me out of here!"

Still no response.

Who did this to me?

My eyes bulged. Throat tightened. "Is anyone out there? Please! Let me out of here! Why have you brought me here? Tell me where my dad is? Come on! Talk to me!"

"Tripp, you are in no danger," a voice finally explained. The words penetrated the walls, surrounding me. Even though I couldn't see him, I recognized the speaker right away.

"Doc Torren!" I circled the room. "What's going on? Those men attacked me in my house. I think they have Dad. Help me!"

"Tripp, I need you to listen to me." Doc Torren spoke calmly, just like he always did.

The overhead lights in my prison dimmed. A section of wall to my right slowly slid away, revealing a window. Doc Torren appeared behind the glass. A couple of men in dark suits—like the men who kidnapped me—stood behind him.

"Tripp, like I said, you are safe."

"Doc?" I dropped to my knees. "Did you do this to me?"

He lowered his eyes. "You left us no choice, Tripp. We urged you, for your own safety, not to continue down this path of exploring your abilities. We were trying to keep you safe, and now we have to take drastic measures to protect you. I'm sorry."

"I don't understand." I rushed toward the window. "I just want to see my dad."

"I'm here, son." My dad spoke, but I couldn't see him.

"Dad, where are you?"

He stepped into view. Standing next to Doc Torren, he sighed and shook his head. "Tripp, this is the only way to keep you safe. Something's going on. You're in danger."

I placed my hands against the window. I remembered what the dark-suited man had said back home. *He's the reason we're here.* He hadn't lied. Whatever was happening to me was because of Dad and Doc Torren. My stomach cramped. More tears fell.

"I don't understand. Please let me out of here. I promise I won't change. I promise to do everything you tell me!"

"Tripp, this has gone too far," Doc Torren explained. "We may be close to a breakthrough on your condition. If we can focus right now on a cure I have been developing, we can bring some normalcy to your life. But I need you to be in a safe place where I can monitor you and prevent further changes."

I backed away from the window. "Where am I? What is this place?"

Rather than respond he eyed my dad.

"Tell him," Dad commanded. "If we're going to keep him here, he deserves to know where he is."

Doc Torren nodded. "Since I started treating you as a child, I knew one day we might reach this point where you would become a danger to yourself and others. I prepared this facility especially for you. It is located on land I own outside New York

City. Tripp, I had hoped it wouldn't come to this, but after so many years of research, I am so close to having the answers we need to cure you. I can't… I won't… let anything or anyone get in the way of that. This is for your own safety and well-being."

I slumped onto the bed. My head ached. Doc Torren's words spun in my mind. I wanted to believe him but couldn't. "You're lying!"

"No—" Doc Torren started to say.

"Stop it! Just stop it!" I hit the bed with both hands. "You're lying. I know you are. You never told me you're close to a cure. You're just saying that now, so I won't try to break out of here. You don't know how to cure me. You don't know anything, and now you're just going to lock me away and why… because I saved some lives?"

I glared at my dad. "Dad, I went to the bank for you. I'm your son. How can you let him do this to me? Please."

My dad placed his hands against the glass. "Doc Torren's not lying. He's closer to a cure than he's ever been. We have to give him a chance and protect you while we give him time. This isn't forever. I am grateful you tried to save me. Really I am. But you shouldn't have. You should just have been a teen. That's all you need to be. And we're going to make that possible."

I turned my back to the window. "I'll never forgive you for this, Dad! Not ever!"

"I know." His voice cracked.

Footsteps drew my attention back to the window just as Dad walked out of view, leaving Doc Torren and one of his dark-suited goons.

My body shook. I wanted to eat something so bad just to change and break through the window to reach Doc Torren.

"Tripp, we are going to give you all the comforts of home." Doc Torren lifted a clipboard and scribbled something on it. "I'll have a television brought in and your iPod—"

"What about my computer—my cell phone?" Maybe I could reach out to Lucas. He'd know what to do.

"No, I'm sorry. You cannot have any communication device for now." He smiled faintly. "I stress *for now*. We will see what we can do in the future, but right now, for your own protection, we must limit communications with anyone outside this facility."

"Then this is a prison."

"Think of it as a safe house."

"Prison."

"Tripp, I know you must hate me, but I am still a friend and your physician. I am going to stick this out with you until the day we can give you a normal life, and I think that day will be soon."

"What if I don't want a normal life?" I pointed at him. "What gives you the right to make me change what I am?"

"This is what we've been working on for so long, Tripp. You've only become confused as you've experienced the changes that food brings."

"So what if I have. It's my life."

"There's more at stake than you know." He sighed deeply.

"Tell me."

He examined his clipboard before responding. "Tripp, for the time being you will receive the proper nutrients through N.E.R.D at designated hours of the day. I personally will supervise your feedings. I will also be including a new medication with each feeding that I think will be the catalyst for the cure."

Feedings! He was treating me like I was some caged animal in the zoo. Well, that's exactly what I was—a caged animal. More tears dribbled down my cheeks. "Please, just let me out of here. I will do anything you say."

"Not today, Tripp. Not today." The glow that illuminated the window went dark. The overhead lighting rekindled. The window vanished, leaving a solid white wall.

Everything I knew had been taken away from me.

Chapter 13

An Unexpected Visitor

Hate and a thousand questions zigzagging through my mind made my head spin. My temples throbbed, and not even sleep—what little I got—helped. My eyes burned from a mix of dried tears and restless hours of staring at the walls. How could they do this to me? How could my dad allow this?

Damn him! Damn Doc Torren!

I don't know how long they kept me locked up, but it felt like an eternity. It was hard to breathe as if these walls closed in on me. Was it day? Night? Would I ever see the sky again?

I tugged at the collar of the stiff, blue denim shirt left for me. A stack of them lay inside the dresser along with pairs of blue jean pants, white socks, underwear and scratchy pajamas.

Sitting cross-legged on the floor at the base of the bed, I tried to keep calm. My jaw ached from clenching my teeth. The inside of my mouth stung from gnawing at the flesh. I rubbed the cracked skin over my knuckles. Spots of blood marked the wall I'd punched over and over.

Numbness had set in. My arms hung at my side. Head drooped against my chest. I no longer wanted to think but flashes of rage exploded through my thoughts. I'd make them pay for this.

The door to my room swished open. Doc Torren strolled inside, clipboard in hand and a N.E.R.D feeding machine in tow.

I ignored him.

For four feeding cycles he had entered my room. This visit made it five times. The first couple of times I begged him to release me. He refused. I asked to see my dad, too, but he had only said… *in time*. Crying didn't work either. The next two times I didn't bother to say anything. I just sat as he hooked me up to N.E.R.D.

This time would be different.

Doc Torren knelt down beside me and placed a hand on my shoulder. "Tripp, I know you hate me, but in the end, you'll see this is for the best. We're going to give you a normal life. A life you deserve."

He reached for the feeding tubes to connect them to the valves in my stomach.

My heart raced. *Now!*

I lunged at him, slugging him with both my fists, The crack of my knuckles against his cheek bones reverberated through the chamber. Blood spewed from his mouth. He fell onto his back. He moaned. His eyes blinked rapidly.

My body tingled. Breaths rushed from my lungs. *Don't stop now, Tripp!*

Before Doc Torren could react, I grabbed the keycard to the door he kept in his lab coat pocket, and then I ran to the door.

"Tripp, please." Doc Torren slowly lifted himself.

I shook my head, then thrust the card into its slot. The door swished open. *Freedom! Finally!*

I burst through the door into the arms of two men in black suits like the men who brought me here. *No, damn it.* Doc Torren had my cell guarded. I should have known. My pulse slowed. Ice flowed through my veins. My body trembled.

Their eyes covered by dark glasses, the guards showed no emotion. They gruffly grabbed my arms and hoisted me from the floor without uttering a word.

"Let me go!" I thrashed my arms and legs to wrestle free, but it did no good.

Their fingers squeezed my scrawny arms tighter. They hauled me to Doc Torren, then forced me to my knees.

My chest heaved with each breath. A pain spread through my stomach as if I'd been punched in the gut. Whether it was hunger or despair, a feeling of emptiness coursed through me with each pump of my heart. I never had a chance to escape. I was a fool to ever think I did. So stupid.

I glared at Doc Torren. "Get these bastards off me."

Standing over me, he wiped blood from his mouth. "Gentlemen, that will no longer be necessary."

The men released their grip on my arms and slowly backed away.

"We'll be right outside if you need us." The taller of the two men adjusted his tie.

The two guards passed through the doorway, and the door slid closed behind them. I was once again locked in. My head drooped to my chest. If only I could find a scrap of food… even a crumb. Then I could use my powers to escape this prison. Maybe even use my powers to make Doc Torren and those guards pay for what they've done.

Doc Torren lowered to me and went to work attaching the feeding tubes to my valves. I let him. "I know how you feel, Tripp. I know you feel betrayed, but I am going to make you better. Please have faith."

I lifted my head. "No, you're not. You're going to keep me locked up here like I'm some kind of freak. Like I'm a danger to society or something."

Rubbing his jaw, he stood again.

I'd hurt him. My lips parted in a grin.

Crossing his arms, he paced in front of me. "Tripp, I need to ask you something. Is anyone influencing this new attitude of yours? Is anyone asking you or telling you to use your abilities?"

A chill climbed my back. Did he know about the stranger? Did he know Mrs. Ramirez had asked me to save her daughter in the zoo? For a heartbeat, I thought about telling him everything. No!

Why should I tell him anything? How many lies had he told me? What truth was he keeping from me now?

"No one." I pounded my fists against the floor. "You think I need someone to tell me to help others? Maybe I just want to use my powers to make a difference. What's wrong with that?"

He interlocked his fingers under his chin. "Nothing's wrong with that. My boy—"

"I'm not your boy." I tried to stand, but I remained tethered to N.E.R.D.

Doc Torren shook his head. "Tripp, I just want you to be safe."

N.E.R.D. beeped to indicate the end of the feeding cycle. He detached the tubes. "Tripp, listen—"

"Just get out of here." I crawled into bed, my back to him.

"Don't give up on me, Tripp." He sighed and walked away, his checkered Vans squeaking along the floor. The door swished open then closed behind him.

Doc Torren was right about one thing. I hated him. Dad, too. If only I could see my dad one more time… and spit in his face.

Another face flashed before my eyes. *His!* The strange man in the long trench coat who smoked cigarettes! He knew so much about me but how? He always showed up as if he followed me but why?

I shrugged my shoulders. None of that mattered. I would never see him again, either. I'd never see anyone again.

My head sunk heavy into the pillow. Sleep overcame me.

***

The swish of my door opening awakened me. My head popped up. How long had I been out? I blinked away the sleepy haze.

Time to feed the zoo animal, I guess. I expected to see Doc Torren enter the room with N.E.R.D.

102

Darkness seeped in from the open passageway, but no Doc. Torren. I climbed from my bed and inched toward the door. "Hey, anyone there?"

I stopped and held my breath, listening for an answer. Nothing. A cold sweat formed across my brow. The door remained open. This was my chance to escape, but my legs refused to cross to the murky passageway. Whatever lay beyond was hidden from view.

The lights overhead doused, surrounding me in pitch black. I flinched. Something wasn't right. I shrunk back to my bed. My pulse spiked. I breathed in quick bursts. "Who's out there? Say something."

Still no response. Like a child scared of the boogey man, I slid underneath the bed.

Lights beyond the door flickered. Shadows spread across the floor like snakes slithering toward me.

Something squeaked on the other side of the doorway. Doc Torren's shoes?

Two stubby legs lumbered into the room. I glimpsed Doc Torren's checkered Vans through the dim, sputtering light. He gurgled words I couldn't understand followed by thick, raspy breaths.

I frowned and inched my way from underneath the bed. "Doc, what's going on?"

He didn't answer. His clipboard dropped to the floor.

"Hey..."

Doc Torren slumped to his knees. Blood dripped from his mouth. His lips parted as if he wanted to speak, but a phlegmy cough bathed his chin in more blood. He clutched at his neck, and then reached for me with a crimson-soaked hand.

I backed away. I wanted to cry for help, but fear gagged me. I could only utter, "Doc Torren?"

"Tripp... get..." His face contorted. With one last long breath, he collapsed, no longer moving. Blood oozed from his body.

I crawled away, pressing my back against a far wall. A bone-chilling panic shackled me there. My mind screamed, *run*, but my limbs refused. Where would I run? Each flash of light revealed the agony etched in Doc Torren's face. His dead eyes stared at me. *No! This can't be happening.*

I looked away, concentrating on the doorway, but the flickering, murky lighting showed little of what lay beyond my room. My stomach churned. Heart pounded in my ears. I needed my powers. Anything to face whoever killed Doc Torren—whatever might be coming for me. I whispered, "Who... who's out there?"

"Come with me," a voice commanded.

"Who said that?" I tucked my knees into my chest. "Show yourself."

"You know who I am." A familiar English accent stabbed through the room's darkness.

From the shadows, *he* appeared. The homeless man in the long trench coat. A long knife in his hand. The glints of light revealed droplets of blood trickling from the blade.

"If you want to live, come with me." He tucked the knife inside his coat. "No time to explain. Trust me, I'm a friend. Doc Torren was not your doctor; he worked for your government and had orders to keep you here. I'm trying to free you, and time is not an ally."

I buried my head in my arms. "I... I just want to go home."

"Mate, you haven't been home for quite some time."

"What?" I gazed up at him.

"Nothing." He reached toward me. "There's no going home for you now. You have a different destiny, and I'm the only one who can help you realize it."

My focus shifted from the stranger to the blood pooling around Doc Torren. A chill froze the back of my neck. *Dad, where are you? Help me.* "I want my dad. Where is he?"

The man glared at me through distant eyes as though he looked past me.

"Forget him. If you want to live, come with me now. If you want to discover your true self, I have those answers… not that imposter you call dad. If you want to remain a prisoner, by all means, wait for him to come for you."

He headed toward the door. "I have no more time. Best of luck. Don't say I didn't try to help, but you're on your own now." Stopping, he removed a handgun from his trench coat and aimed it into the bleakness beyond the door. A quick nod back to me, and he disappeared through the doorway.

What was I supposed to do? The stranger's words reverberated through my mind. Dad an imposter? I had no idea what that meant. I couldn't think. The flickering lights made me dizzy. I gazed once more into Doc Torren's lifeless eyes. He'd been kind to me through the years, but it had all been lies. He thought me a monster. Nothing to do now but flee.

With an icy deep breath, I stood and followed the man. I had no idea what lie beyond the door. The darkness only made it worse.

I burst through the door and nearly slid on a wet substance coating the floor. I glanced down and gasped. On either side of the door lay the two guards. Their bodies slumped against a wall. Blood poured from gashes across their necks.

Dry heaves overtook me. I hunched over, struggling for a breath. I'd never seen death before. I wanted to close my eyes. Maybe these images would be gone when I opened them, but this was real. God help me. This was real.

"Come, lad." The stranger grabbed me by the collar and dragged me away from the bodies.

"What have you done?" My feet dragged across the floor as he pulled me.

"Only what was necessary." He released my shirt. "Now move."

A narrow hallway stretched before us. Shattered ceiling lights sparked, casting shadows along the walls. I crept along a tiled floor, crunching shards of glass. His hand grabbed my shoulder.

"Walk quietly!" The man pressed a finger to his lips.

He grabbed my arm and walked beside me along the hallway. In this bleak light his cheeks seemed thinner than before, more bone than flesh. His dark eyes sunk deeper into his skull than before.

He grimaced at me. "Stay focused."

We hastened down the hallway until I stumbled over something. Falling to my knees, a pair of unblinking eyes stared at me. Blood seeped from a hole between the eyes. I jumped to my feet. A woman—someone I had never seen—lay on the floor, her head twisted upward, her legs folded to her stomach, arms across her chest. She wore a white coat, now soaked in blood. I couldn't take my eyes off her.

How many people had this man killed for me? That thought rattled me. Their blood was on my hands. I placed my hands against my mouth to suppress a scream. My eyes were hot with tears.

The man clunked my head with the back of his hand. "Keep moving!"

"What have you done?" I shoved him away. "What are you doing this for?"

"I killed to save you. Now move." He stepped around the woman's body with a long stride and continued along the hallway.

"I didn't ask for this." I retreated from him.

"Didn't you?" He aimed the barrel of his gun at me. "Each time you transformed you beckoned to be free of the bonds that constrained you, and I'm the only one who can show you a way. So you bloody well did ask for this."

He clutched my arm again and dragged me toward him.

"Please, I'm begging you." I shook myself free and tripped over something else—legs. A man in a uniform with a badge on his chest sat against the wall, his head bowed. A handgun lay at his side. He didn't move. Blood snaked from his left side.

My head spun. I dropped to my knees. This time, vomit spilled from my mouth in spasms. When it ended, I collapsed.

From the corner of my eye, I spotted something glowing green through the hazy lighting. It slid along the floor... kind of like me as that slimy creature at the zoo. The oozing *whatever* disappeared around a corner or maybe into the wall or a vent.

Had I really seen something, or was I losing my mind? Why would there be glowing slime here? No, I hadn't seen anything. I couldn't have.

The man's grating voice startled me. "Come on, boy, we don't have time for this. Get up and move."

"No." I spit out a last bit of vomit. I shook my head to try to clear it, but it didn't help.

"Then you leave me no choice."

Thwack. Something hard clubbed the back of my head.

A blinding light flashed, and then my sight tunneled into a gray void. A blistering wave of pain rippled from the base of my skull to my forehead. My legs crumbled; my body slipped to the floor.

Gray gave way to black.

Chapter 14

The Labyrinth

"Oh, my little Ilan, you are destined for such greatness."

The Englishman's words ripped me from unconsciousness. My eyes snapped open. I sucked in a lungful of stale air. The back of my head ached. My stomach gurgled. I was going to be sick. Hot bile rose from my stomach, burning my throat. I closed my mouth and held my breath until the sensation eased.

Where was I? What happened to me? Who was Ilan?

I lay on a cot. The pillow stunk of sweat. A musty odor hung heavy around me. I blinked my eyes, but a blurry haze limited my vision.

Footsteps struck the ground nearby. It had to be him. The British dude in the trench coat. What was he going to do to me? He'd killed Doc Torren and those others. Struck me with something. Why? To free me? It didn't make any sense. Nothing made sense anymore.

I tried to lift my hands to rub my eyes, but my wrists were tethered to the sides of the cot with thin straps. My ankles, too. My pulse raced. Pricks of cold sweat danced across my forehead like sharp needles. I wrestled against my restraints, but it did no good. The straps dug into my skin. The slightest movement rattled my brain and made me nauseous. I cringed and stopped.

I was his prisoner.

"Why is this happening to me?"

I trembled. More sweat dripped down the sides of my face. *Where am I?*

The Englishman's shoes squeaked. I heard his raspy, smoker's breath. I felt tears coming. What was I going to do?

I struggled for a deep breath. Either my lungs were too frozen with fear or the air was too thick and musty. *I can't breathe! I need air!*

The Englishman started to whistle cheerfully.

I wanted to cover my ears. I closed my eyes. If only this were a nightmare. *Wake up!* I painfully shook my head. This was no dream.

I opened my eyes again and willed myself to slowly breathe in and out. Losing it was not going to get me out of this. "Get a grip, man. Use your head. First, figure out where you're at."

Lowering my head into the pillow, I stared at my surroundings. It was a cavernous chamber. A ceiling of concrete and metal pipes jutted from the shadows. A long table, covered with computers—some buzzing with life, others silent—stood near my cot. A cracked lamp gave off an eerie yellow glow, casting shadows off dingy concrete walls.

Dust floated in the glow. Damp air pressed against my chest.

What was this place? An abandoned warehouse? A cellar buried deep below ground? Would anyone ever find me? Was anyone even looking?

A new wave of panic radiated through my body. I shook uncontrollably. *God, help me!*

I had to get out. Get away from him. I jerked against my restraints. The straps tore into my skin like tiny blades piercing my flesh. I couldn't break free. I blinked away hot tears. *Think, Tripp.* There had to be a way out of this.

"Oh, my Ilan, we have so much work to do." The Englishman's voice echoed around me, but he remained out of sight.

I froze; didn't dare breathe. I pretended to sleep. My head throbbed worse with my eyes closed. My thoughts spun out of control. Why had I gone into that 7-Eleven? Why did I save Maria's brother? Or those people in the zoo? I just wanted to go back to my old life. What had I done?

"Dad, how could you and Doc Torren lock me away?" Maybe they were right. Maybe I was a danger to myself and everyone else.

What did it matter now? The doctor was dead, and I was imprisoned by some crazy man in a trench coat.

Anger and fear raged inside me. My head pounded harder. My dad abandoned me to this nut job. I knew my old man hated me, but—

"Ilan, you can't imagine how long I have waited for this moment." Joy resonated in the man's voice. He almost chanted his words.

Again, he spoke the name Ilan. Who in the hell is that? I closed my eyes.

"All the sacrifice and loss will now be worth it." His footsteps clomped on the floor. His voice grew faint. "You will be the realization of my dreams. Everyone will know I was right to do what I did—that I saved the world by giving them you."

Cold air wafted through this concrete vault.

Somewhere a train whistle echoed and a crescendo of thunder rumbled until the cot shook.

Oh my God, we were under the subway? Yes, we had to be, but where? The complex labyrinth of tunnels beneath New York City meant no one would find me. I was alone. More tears formed. I couldn't help it. *Stop it, Tripp. Don't be a scared baby.*

After the train passed, quiet returned. I studied my surroundings some more.

Two microscopes sat atop another table. Next to them rested test tubes filled with rainbow-colored liquids.

Wires from the equipment snaked through his freaky lab to the ceiling where they disappeared among the concrete and exposed rods. That must be where the power came from.

"I see you are awake. Good. I was concerned I hit you too hard." He spoke above and to the left, the opposite direction from where my attention was focused. "I hope I did not injure you too badly, but you left me little choice."

Stupid! I should have been more careful. I turned my head toward him. The movement rocked my skull. I wanted to close my eyes and slip back into unconsciousness to escape the pain. Instead, I bit down on my tongue until the blinding shockwaves eased and my brain no longer rattled against bone.

The Englishman tilted his head. His raven-black eyes and furrowed brow conveyed concern. He offered a slight grin, kind of like a parent trying to soothe a child.

A stained, white lab coat replaced his dirty trench coat. His scruffy, graying beard snaked along his cheeks. His hair, thinning around the forehead, hung long in the back and covered his ears.

"What's going on?" Even speaking caused my head to ache more.

"Ahh, that's a good sign." He nodded his approval. "You're asking questions, so your brain is working."

I fought against the straps binding my wrists and ankles. "Let me go. Please."

He knelt, and his bony fingers gently lifted a bandage wrapped around my head. I hadn't even realized it was there.

"Wha-what are… y-you doing?" I trembled.

"Just checking a slight laceration on the back of your head. Good, it's healing nicely. Sorry about conking you there, mate. Wasn't very civilized of me, but you didn't leave me much choice, did you?"

"I said let me go."

"Oh, where are my manners, of course." From a satchel at his side, he removed a black-handled knife like the kind hunters use on survival shows. He slid the long blade over the straps and freed both my hands and feet. "Again, my apologies, but I couldn't have you trying to escape before we have a little chat."

I rubbed my wrists but stayed on the cot. I tried to hide my fear. To be brave. "Who are you? What are you doing with me?"

He chuckled. "So many questions at once. Let's start with the first one. Who am I? That is such an interesting question and not one that comes with an easy answer. What I want you to know is that I am a friend. A *true* friend. Not like those you have looked to as your friends and family."

"I don't understand any of this." I blinked to try to focus.

He retreated to a table and then returned with a damp cloth, which he placed over my forehead. "I know it must all be so confusing for you. That is because of the lies you have been told your whole life."

One more time, he walked to the table. This time he returned with one of those medical devices doctors use to check your eyes.

"Can't you just let me go home, so I can see my dad?" I lifted myself onto my elbows, but my stomach churned. Spew rose in my throat, but I forced it down, slumping into the cot.

"I'm afraid that cannot happen." He lowered his face within inches of mine and studied my eyes with the device. He smelled of sweat and medicine. "Your eyes look clear. I actually have given you a thorough exam, and you are a healthy young man— except for those valves in your side. What an injustice of medicine to take someone as perfect as yourself and try to change you. Such Neanderthals! I should have been there to protect you. I assure you I will be from now on."

"Where am I? Why'd you kidnap me?"

"Kidnap you? I saved you." He shook his head. "You must know I mean you no harm."

"Then give me answers." My bellowing voice echoed off the walls.

After grabbing a wooden chair, he scooted beside me. He intertwined his fingers as if in prayer and placed his hands just under his chin. "We will have to explore all your questions over time as none of what I have to tell you will be easy."

"Please, tell me something." With a deep breath, I rose to a sitting position. The room spun. The blood rushed from my head. I wrapped my arms around my torso to steady myself. "Your name... what's your name?"

"Yes, I suppose you should know my name. I am Cardan."

What kind of name was that? "Is that your first or last name?"

"It does not matter." He glared at me. "You can simply call me Cardan."

I tried to match the chill of his voice, but inside I trembled. "Fine... Cardan... then tell me why I'm here."

"The place I liberated you from was actually a military installation far from the city. It is where your Doctor Torren and this bloody government imprisoned you because they deemed you a threat. I should have realized they would take you the moment you started to use your abilities. If I had, I would have acted sooner. I should have taken you right after you stopped that bank robbery, but I figured you and I needed more time to develop a relationship."

Relationship? What was he talking about?

"I brought you here to give you a new life," he explained, as if every word he said made sense.

"If it's true about that place belonging to the military, how'd you break in and free me? Why are you following me?" The room still spun. I closed my eyes and concentrated on breathing. When the spinning slowed, I opened my eyes and focused on the wrinkles in his shallow cheeks.

"I have my ways," he answered. "It should be enough for you to know that I cared enough about your future to intervene."

"That's not enough." I tried to stand, but my shaky legs buckled. "Why'd you kill Doc Torren and the others?"

"They left me little choice." His voice revealed no remorse. Who else had he killed?

"Why'd you hit me?"

"You were most disagreeable, my lad. If we delayed, we'd be caught."

"What about my dad?"

He rolled his eyes. "What about that imposter?"

I tightened my hands into fists. "Is he all right?"

"I have not harmed him."

"Where is he?"

"I do not know the answer to that."

His words stung. Lies! They had to be lies. He held back answers. Why?

I gazed up at Cardan. "What do you want with me?"

He leaned in closer. "I know who you are and what you can do. I know the fear you have of consuming food because of the transformations it brings, but I can help you to control it. You ask what I want with you. I want nothing for myself. I wish to help you become the hero the world needs."

"How do you know so much about me?" I searched his eyes for any signs of the truth.

With shaky hands, he produced a cigarette from his lab coat. Placing it in his mouth, he lit it. He seemed to savor the moment as he breathed in the smoke. The tip glowed red hot. Blowing out the smoke, Cardan studied the cigarette for a moment, his hands much more steady.

"You, my boy, were engineered to destroy evil wherever it exists in the world… to defeat terrorism, aid the hungry, make streets safe for the good people who are crying out for a savior. What you are is no accident. And I think you are beginning to realize that."

"Did you say I was engineered? What does that even mean? On wobbly legs, I backed away from him.

He stepped toward me. "It means that you're special."

His words made no sense. *What was I… a test tube baby? Was I created in a lab?* I raked my fingers through my damp hair.

My head hurt worse than ever, like someone twisted a screwdriver into my brain.

"You're crazy, dude."

"Maybe." He puffed again on his cigarette. "But I can help unlock your true potential."

"Just let me go," I pleaded.

"I cannot do that. We belong together."

I stumbled, nearly falling to the floor, but caught myself on the edge of a table. What was that supposed to mean? This was a nightmare. It had to be. "What? Why?"

"All your answers will come in time."

"Look, man, thanks for freeing me and all, but I just want out of here, okay? I don't know what any of this is about, and I want to go home." I turned from him and lumbered on heavy legs toward a far wall in search of a door in murky lighting. I felt around the slimy concrete wall but found no exit. There seemed no way out of this tomb.

A click sounded behind me. I swung back toward Cardan. He held a revolver, the barrel pointed at the ground.

"My boy, all you need is the proper training, and you will be able to harness untold power." He placed the gun on the table beside him. "I can provide that training. In return you will go into the world and bring hope to the hopeless and peace in an age where people have grown weary from the violence around them. Isn't that worth staying for and exploring with me?"

I shook my head. "I'm just a teenager. I'm not a hero."

He blew out a ring of smoke. "That is what you have been brainwashed to believe. It is time to open your eyes, free from the tyranny of those who asked you to hide your gift. All I ask is that you allow me to be your guide."

Cardan extended his hand to me. "Together, we can unlock the secrets of your power. The key is not to suppress your ability, but to tap into its full potential. Here, in this abandoned tunnel, we can prepare you for the challenges ahead. Are you ready to begin a new phase in your life—one that has always been your destiny? What do…?"

Overhead another train raced through the subway. The ceiling shook and chunks of concrete fell from above. I had to find a way to escape—to reach the higher levels where the trains passed. I studied his outstretched hand. Agreeing to work with him might be my only way out of here. What else could I do?

"I'm ready." I lied.

His lips parted in a wide grin. "This truly is a miraculous day."

I glanced around Cardan's underground lair. "I have one more question. Who's Ilan. I heard you speaking to him?"

He dropped his cigarette to the ground and stomped on it. White smoke rose from the ashes. "As I have said, all will be revealed in time."

Chapter 15

Eat up

Sweat dripped from my brow. My toes tapped the floor. I clawed at the glass walls that confined me.

"Let me out of here!"

How could I have been so stupid to fall asleep? How long had I been out? Long enough for that snake to lock me inside a glass box no bigger than my dad's walk-in closet. At full height, my head nearly struck the ceiling, just a few inches above.

I was caged like an animal! With probes attached to my forehead!

Inside with me was a table with three plates spaced evenly apart. One held a banana, the second a sizzling steak and the third a loaf of bread slathered in peanut butter. A glass of milk was behind the plates. The smell of burnt meat surrounded me. Saliva dripped from the sides of my mouth.

I pounded my fist against a glass panel. Nothing happened. I threw my shoulder against it once, twice, three times. The glass withstood my assault.

"That will do you no good." Cardan's voice twanged through a speaker somewhere above me. "I assure you this glass is impenetrable."

"Let me out of here." I slammed my hand against the table. The glass of milk tipped over. "What are you doing to me?"

Cardan strolled up to my glass prison in his white lab coat with a clipboard in hand, just like Doc Torren. "After our little talk, you fell asleep. I took that opportunity to prepare you for our first round of testing as you and I explore your powers together."

I dropped to my knees. "Please, let me out. I'll do anything you want. Any test. Just not like this."

Cardan pressed his face to the glass. "Do not fear. This is not permanent. It is simply for your safety. We have to be careful with these initial tests because we do not know how you will react. That's why I assembled this chamber. As soon as you have better control of your abilities, we will no longer need to use it."

"You're lying."

"I will never lie to you, my boy."

"Cardan, please."

He backed away. "If you want out, the instruments to do so lay in front of you. Choose from any of the plates. Eat and transform. Perhaps you will gain the strength to break out without my help."

My stomach rumbled. I wiped my mouth. Yes, I should eat. That was the only way out. No, that's what he wanted.

I flung the plate with the banana against the glass. The plate shattered into pieces on contact. "I'm not doing it! I'm not some lab experiment."

I ripped two of the probes from my forehead.

"Stop!" Cardan pointed at me before I ripped away the last two. "This just won't do. Those probes are attached to my computers, so I can analyze your brainwaves as you transform. We need a better understanding of how much control you maintain through the change. You must remain calm. Trust me. I can teach you to control your transformation."

I slunk to the back of my glass cage and dropped into a sitting position, my head buried into my hands. "Trust you? You say you saved me from Doc Torren. All you've done is taken me from one prison and locked me in another. I can't trust you or anyone."

Cardan shook his head and lit a cigarette. "That's not true. In time you will see that I want nothing but the best for you."

"Just words." I glared at him. "You even sound like Doc Torren."

"Enough." He slammed his clipboard onto the floor. "I will not be compared to those who have led you down false paths. Now listen to me. I know you more than you know yourself."

I wished he would shut up. His words were driving me crazy. "Leave me alone!"

"I cannot."

I jumped to my feet. "Who are you... really? A doctor? A stalker? A mad scientist?"

He picked up his clipboard. "A bioengineer." He lifted the cigarette to his mouth. The burning tip caused his coal-like eyes to glow red.

"A what?"

He took a long drag on the cigarette then lowered it. "Let's just say I study the body and all living organisms to understand them better."

"Then tell me why I'm like this." I stepped toward the table, my eyes locked on the steak. A stabbing pain exploded in my stomach. I clutched the table with both hands. My arms trembled. More saliva dripped from my mouth. I could transform into something and break out of this. The English dude would never see me again.

He ran his fingers through clumped strands of hair by his ear. "Do you believe in God?"

I ignored him.

"I asked—do you believe in God?"

"I guess."

"Then perhaps that is answer enough."

"What does that mean?"

"Every day children are born throughout the world. At a molecular level, they are pretty much the same, but every now and then someone is born with a mutation that makes them different. You are one of those fortunate few. As I told you, it is a gift to be cherished and developed for the good of mankind."

I pushed away from the table. "That's a lie. You said I was engineered. Those were your words, man."

"I did not mean that in a literal sense." He paused. "Enough of this discussion. I know you're hungry, and you're scared." He took a long drag on his cigarette. He must crave it as much as I wanted the food. "I can assure you everything will be fine. You are in no danger, so feel free to eat the food you see before you."

"I'll change."

Cardan beamed. "I know."

"I don't know what I'll turn into."

"Together, we'll make it so that you can control your metamorphosis."

"I don't want to control it. I want to be rid of it."

"That's the others talking. Not you. It is time you learn to accept who you are and that you have a greater purpose. Food is the ignition for your power. You must understand that if you are to master this ability, you have to utilize food in a way no other human being can. You are a very special young man. I think that is where our lesson must begin. I need to help you realize how important you are to the world. Your transformation is a remarkable advancement in our species."

"Whatever." He was lying, but despite my fear, I edged back to the table. I wanted the steak like a dog begging for scraps. The hot buttery scent penetrated my nose. My stomach gurgled louder. I had never eaten a steak before. A hamburger, yes, one of those dollar burgers under a heating lamp at convenience stores. Never steak.

I reached for it with shaky hands. Cardan followed my every move, jotting down notes on his clipboard, waiting for me to take that first bite to see what monster I might become.

Grabbing the steak, I lifted it to my mouth. I shouldn't. I was playing his game. Becoming his lab rat. But I had to. I couldn't fight it. Like somewhere deep inside, a ravenous dog was taking over my conscious.

I took a small bite and chewed the tender flesh. A mix of salt and grease mixed together in a savory blend of flavors. I couldn't hold back. I tore at the steak. The juices spilled down my chin. I couldn't stop myself. I devoured the meat until nothing but bone remained.

Panting, I stepped away from the table. I placed my hand against my chest to steady my breathing. My heart raced—thump, thump… thump, thump… thump, thump—like it would explode into a million pieces. My eyes darted back and forth from the table to Cardan.

My body trembled. I stumbled back against the wall behind me.

"Don't fear whatever is to come next," Cardan urged. "If you fear it, you'll fight it, which I am sure takes away from your ability to control the change. Just breathe steady. Listen to the rhythm of your heartbeat."

I wanted to listen, but if I had no reason to be scared, why had he locked me up?

"Please, just let me out of here!"

"Soon."

"Please!"

"Stay calm." Cardan turned toward a computer screen to his right. He threw his cigarette to the ground. "You have to calm down. Your brain activity is rising to dangerous levels like someone about to have a seizure. You're letting your fear and anger take control. It doesn't have to happen like this."

"I don't care about any of that," I cried. "Let me—"

Searing heat tore through my insides as if flames might burst from my gut and spew from my mouth. I screamed and grabbed my stomach. "Help me!"

"You're doing this to yourself," Cardan explained. "You're harming yourself because you're letting your emotions control you."

I slammed my hands against the floor. His words no longer made sense. I screamed again. My head throbbed. When would the transformation come? When would the agony stop? None of the times I had changed before felt like this.

Crackling echoed from my stomach. Fire charred my insides. The skin on my arms sizzled and glowed bright red. Smoke rose from my hands.

"I'm boiling!" I tore away my shirt and kicked off my pants. "I'm burning alive! I can't take—"

Flames burst from my fingertips and crashed against the glass panel in front of me. The blaze ricocheted from one panel to the next until a circle of fire engulfed me.

"No!" I covered my eyes and twisted wildly, thrashing my body to try to extinguish the flames.

Cardan banged on the glass. I glared at him through my fingers—and red flames. He shouted something but the dancing flames deafened me.

"He-help… me." My own words sounded muffled.

I dropped to my knees. My head lowered against my chest. Smoke penetrated my lungs. I coughed and wheezed, clutching at my throat.

From outside, Cardan still banged on the glass. His words rose above the fire. "Control your fear. Listen to me. Listen to my words. You are in control, not the transformation."

I slowly breathed in and out. I coughed some more. Then air! Through the blaze, I inhaled air. *How?*

I climbed to my feet, concentrating on each breath.

"Stop fighting it and look at what you have become." Cardan, drenched in sweat, took a step from the glass. "It is remarkable. I have never seen the like but for comic books or superhero movies that common man views as impossible. But look at you."

Despite the flames that engulfed me, I no longer felt pain. My burning skin tingled. Underneath the fire, my skinny arms sprouted muscles. Energy coursed through my body, giving me strength.

The fire crackled and danced as it leaped from each limb. I waved my arms, and the flames grew brighter. I pointed my fingers at the panel in front of me and a blast of fire flew from my hand, crashing against the glass.

Cardan smiled ear to ear.

"You are beautiful." He dashed to another section of his lab, rifled through some items and returned with a mirror. "Just look at yourself. See what you can become."

Orange flames covered my body. A mask of fire concealed my face. I no longer had distinguishable eyes, a nose or a mouth, but I could still see, breathe and talk.

"Great, so I've become a fire demon." I couldn't look away from my image "Are you going to let me out now?"

Cardan's grin revealed yellow-stained teeth. "I think not. We don't know how controlled your powers are right now. We don't know the risk."

"I said let me out!" I held my hands in front of me like trying to push open a door. Streams of fire shot from my palms. The blaze slammed against the glass. My cage held. I threw more fire but the glass didn't crack or melt. Not a scratch.

Cardan chuckled. "I like that fight in you. You'll need it for the challenges that lie ahead, but as I told you for now, as we continue our tests, you must remain inside this chamber."

I lowered my arms. "Because you're afraid of me, isn't it? Because you know what I'll do to you if I break out of here."

"Perhaps a little." Cardan leaned against a table. "You're right, mate. I have no desire to be baked to a crisp, and I do understand how angry and afraid you are. I hope to help you alleviate that fear and anger. More to the point, we need to understand this power, and I'd like to try to understand why your transformation took this form. I do not think it was because the meat had a specific effect on you. You might eat a steak under different conditions, and your transformation would take another form. Right now. we don't have control over your powers. Soon we will. Soon you will be free."

"So what made this change hurt so much, Mr. Genius?" I glowed brighter.

"Emotions." He glanced back at his computer.

"What?"

"Your emotions were out of control as you changed. You were frightened, terrified and angry… angry I wouldn't let you out. I could see your emotional state on this monitor. Your mind's neurons were spiking off the charts. I was afraid you might have a seizure, but instead the transformation took over. Your emotional state has some effect on the change, but to what degree I cannot yet say."

"I don't understand anything you're saying."

"Let me explain it another way." His expression grew serious. "I'm sure you have heard of the Incredible Hulk, right?"

"Yeah."

"Well, what happens when Bruce Banner gets really angry?"

"He Hulks out."

"Correct, my lad." Cardan lit a cigarette and puffed once. "To put it mildly, you just Hulked out."

"Now what?" I shot a flame from my fingers at the glass walls just because I could.

Cardan puffed once more on his cigarette. "Now we test our theory."

"Do I have to eat more?"

"Most certainly."

"Does this mean you'll let me out of this box?"

"No, I am sorry, not until this transformation ends."

"I see." My flaming body glowed red hot. I was his prisoner, for now. But if he slipped up just once, I'd escape. Had to find my dad. Do whatever I could to get my life back—not that I knew what that meant anymore.

Chapter 16

The Next Test

I lay in my little glass box, legs tucked into my chest. My stomach bubbled like boiling water. Groaning, I rubbed my belly to calm the inferno, but it didn't help. My chest ached like someone stomped on me. I struggled to take deep breaths, gasping and wheezing with each breath.

No more. It hurts. I couldn't take it. Too much food. All morphed out. Needed… sleep.

Cardan studied his charts, the lines on his forehead furrowed deep.

For what had to be hours he fed me all kinds of food, slipping the morsels through a slit at the base of a side panel. He studied me as I transformed over and over again—sometimes into horrific monsters and beasts. At other times, I had more heroic powers, like superior vision and hearing. I even gained super-strength, though not enough to break through this box and win my freedom.

The constant morphing sapped my energy. I had never eaten so much food or transformed so often.

I wanted to pass out. Sleep might bring relief, but each time my eyes closed, Cardan's voice shook me back to consciousness.

I suffered for nothing. He didn't know what made me change or how to control it. He pretended like he had learned so much, but he lied.

No more. I was done with this.

"This has to stop," I pleaded. "It hurts."

"I know, my boy, and for that I am truly sorry." Cardan glanced up from his clipboard. "But we have learned so much in such a short time."

More lies.

I tried to lift myself from the glass floor. "Yeah, you're full of it. All you've done is torture me."

He pressed his face to the glass. "The lessons of science come with some pain, but I promise you will not suffer for long. It is time to let you out of this box so that we might try one more test."

I stood on wobbly legs. "No, I'm sick and need sleep."

"We cannot stop. Not yet. Not when we are so close to breaking the riddle of your transformation. Will you please trust me for just a little longer? I ask for so little but can provide you so much."

Did he think I was stupid? Some dumb kid? I gazed into his dimly lit lair. Somewhere there had to be a doorway out. If agreeing to one more test freed me from this box so I could escape, I would do as he said. For now.

If he took his eyes off me just once, maybe left me alone even for a minute, I'd find that door. I had to make him think I trusted him. If he believed that, he might slip up and give me a chance to break out of this underground prison.

A train racing by overhead rattled the cavern. More dust and chunks of concrete fell from the ceiling.

"Fine, one more test, that's it." I wiped damp hair from my eyes. Wet rags, once a white T-shirt and gray sweatpants, clung to me. After my change into that fire creature, Cardan gave me the clothes but after so many transformations, they were torn to pieces. Sweat glued the shreds to my body like sticky strips of fly paper.

I stumbled to the glass door and held my breath as he punched in a code on a side panel. The deadbolt unlatched with a loud click. The door swished open, and I collapsed into Cardan's arms.

"Easy, young one, you've been through a lot." Placing an arm around my waist, he helped me walk. I wanted to push away but lacked the strength. My feet slid along the floor. Arms dangled loosely. My stomach churned. Head swirled. "Don't worry. Your strength will soon return."

He guided me toward the cot.

"My boy, after so many transformations, your odor is a bit ripe." Cardan relaxed his grip around my waist. "If I might be so bold as to suggest a shower, if you think you can stand for a time on your own."

"Uh, you have a shower down here?" I took a few clumsy steps away from him.

He grinned. "I rigged one up with an old water line. No heat, but perhaps you'll find the cold water refreshing."

"So you're a plumber, too, huh?"

"I have my talents." He gestured to a circular curtain at the far side of his lair. "You'll find soap and shampoo inside. I'll leave a towel and some clothes for you."

I lumbered toward the shower, Cardan beside me, his hands outstretched as if to catch me should I fall. He walked alongside without speaking. Once we reached the shower, he lifted a cigarette from his lab coat, lit it and took a few puffs.

"Are you sure you can stand on your own?" White smoke billowed around his face.

"I think so."

"Right then, I'll leave you to it." With a wink, Cardan retreated toward his computers.

He no longer watched me. What was he doing? He knew I wanted to escape. What was his game? Was he testing me? Jeez, he probably had security cameras everywhere.

I turned my attention to the shower. Slimy mold coated the curtain in brown muck. Inside, a rust-covered pipe dangled from the ceiling. Black goo hung from one side of the shower head. The same substance blocked up the drain.

It was gross, but right now I didn't care. Disgusting water was better than nothing. I tore off the rags and threw them outside the shower curtain. Twisting a rusted knob, the pipe above growled and shook in protest. It took several moments, but chilled water, more greenish than clear, spurted from the showerhead. It stank like dirt muddied by rain. The first icy spurts stung my skin. My teeth chattered, but that didn't matter. For the first time in a while I felt human again… I felt like Tripp, not some monster. Dizziness faded away. My gurgling stomach quieted.

I lingered there a while, expecting Cardan to order me out at any moment to start a new round of experiments. He never did.

Revived enough, I turned the knob and peeked through the curtain. A white towel and clean clothes—another white T-shirt, a pair of boxers and a new pair of gray sweat pants—sat on a portable table just outside the shower. White socks and a pair of Nikes also waited for me.

I stepped from the shower and quickly dressed, scanning for Cardan. I spotted no one. Not Cardan. Not some other stranger named Ilan, who still remained a mystery. I listened for movement, but still nothing. Only the computers hummed. Had he left me alone? No, that didn't make sense. Maybe he had gone for more food for the next test? Could this be my chance to try to escape? I tiptoed through the lab. There had to be a way out of here. I surveyed the walls. Nothing resembled an exit.

From above a subway train's whistle broke the quiet. The ground under me shook. I ducked as the train seemed to pass right overhead. When I looked up, Cardan stood over me.

"I see you found the clothing I left for you." He folded his hands behind his back.

"Uh, yeah… thanks." I lowered my eyes, my hopes of an escape ruined.

"I trust you are refreshed and ready for the next test." He placed a hand on my shoulder, his touch colder than the water. The hairs on the back of my neck stood.

"I gu-guess I'm re-ready."

"Good, then come with me." Cardan traded the white lab coat for his old trench coat. The wardrobe change shifted his appearance from mad scientist to homeless man. He smiled as if to reassure me everything would be fine... head titled to the side, right eyebrow lifted, one side of his mouth curled up just a bit higher than the other.

He motioned for me to follow. "I have something to show you."

Cardan's footsteps echoed as he walked to the wall farthest from his lab equipment. The dim lighting barely touched this corner of his lair. At one time the wall might have been made of smooth marble, but over time bits and pieces eroded away, leaving a rough concrete surface. Wording had been chiseled into the wall overhead. *Ninet--th Str-et St---ion, Tr-ck N--e.*

"Nineteenth Street Station, Track Nine?" I mumbled. Nineteenth Street. Where did that put us? I could really use Lucas right now. He knew the city better than any kid, thanks to his dad, who worked for the Transit Authority.

Another train passed. Dust cascaded from the ceiling all around me.

Cardan reached into a coat pocket and removed something resembling a credit card. He lowered his gaze to me. "Mate, this is a key card. I'm about to open a door to this chamber. But first, I must share I have not been completely honest with you."

My heart nearly leaped out of my chest. The way out! I could make a run for it. Now was my chance. "What do you mean?" At this point I didn't really care what lies he told, as long as he showed me the way to freedom.

"I told you I didn't know where the man you call your father is." He took a long breath. "That's not exactly true."

My elation faded. Muscles tensed. "What... where is he? What have you done?"

"Let's just say, he is safe for the moment, but he is at an undisclosed location where his very life depends on me. If something happens to me, he will never be found, and he will die—maybe of starvation—maybe from lack of air."

"What?" I grabbed his trench coat. My body numbed. "What have you done? Take me to him, you bastard."

He wrapped his long fingers around my neck and effortlessly slammed me against the wall. My head struck concrete. Blinding pain radiated from the base of my skull. Spittle flew from my mouth. A gray fuzz boxed in my vision. I blinked over and over to remain alert.

Lifting a knife from his pants, Cardan held the warm blade to my neck. "If you try to escape. If you disobey me in any way, his fate will be the same. Whether he lives or dies is in your hands, mate. Do we understand each other?"

I tried to struggle free, but he tightened his grip. "You're... lying. I don't... believe you."

He leaned in closer. His smoky breath brushed against my face. "I was wrong to lie to you before, boy. I am not lying now."

"At least let me see him." The haze over my eyes lifted.

"In time. If you prove your loyalty to me." He slowly released his grip and slid the knife away.

I slumped to the ground, covering my head with my hands. What was I supposed to do? I couldn't escape. Not now. Or ever. I couldn't risk my dad's life. But what if the Englishmen was lying? Damn it. *Dad, where are you?* My hands balled into fists. I screamed inside my mind. Then, I climbed back to my feet.

"Do we understand each other, mate?" he repeated.

"Perfectly," I uttered.

He placed a hand gently on my shoulder. "I'm sorry it has to be this way. Soon, you will come to know me as a friend. There is so much I have to reveal to you when the time is right."

"Just open the door." I brushed his hand away.

Retrieving the key card from his pocket, he slipped it into a crevice in the wall. As if by magic, a slab of concrete shaped like a door swung open from the rest of the wall with a loud crunch.

Cardan led me from his lair into an abandoned subway tunnel. Darkness hid its true length. Another train passed overhead. Concrete crashed to the ground around us. I dodged one large chunk that almost struck my head.

How far below the surface were we? How many stacked tunnels were there? The thick, dank air pressed against my chest. I missed fresh air.

"Welcome to the underbelly of your city." He spread his arms like some crazed ruler overlooking his kingdom. "Citizens of the world above have forgotten this world, but the evil here claws its way to higher ground. It hungers to infest the world you know."

"What are you talking about?" I backed away.

"This is the perfect place to test your abilities. And your resolve."

"Resolve to do what?"

"All that must be done." He peered ahead.

He led me along the tunnel until we reached a bend where he nudged me up against the wall. He placed a finger to his mouth.

"What?" I asked.

"Speak quietly."

"Answer my question."

"Look around this corner and tell me what you see."

I strained through the gloom until I spotted a round man from the side seated in a chair a stone's throw away from us. Ten short people formed a semi-circle around him. They looked like kids because they were shorter than me. Of course, their height could have been an optical illusion caused by the dim lighting and the distance between us. Some handed the man bags, and he patted one on the head before handing each of them duffle bags. With a snap of his fingers, the group disappeared down the tunnel while he chuckled like a hyena.

"What do you think you're seeing?" The whites of Cardan's eyes seemed to glow.

"How should I know?" I threw up my arms and kicked at the ground.

Cardan shook his head. "You have no idea."

"About what?" I inched farther away from him.

"About the level of crime… the level of evil… in your own city." He grabbed my arm. "Look again at that man."

I did as he ordered.

"That man is known as *The Moose*. He runs a crime ring that preys on children who have nowhere else to go. They come from broken homes or the streets. He uses them to steal what his clients ask for. In return, he gives them a few measly dollars so they can buy a meal or two. Rather than find better shelter, they remain down here with him. They see him as their protector, but he is destroying any chance they have at a future. This kind of filth must be stopped for good."

"Why tell me? Tell the police. They can stop him and save these children."

"Don't be a fool." His hands tightened until his knuckles turned white. "The police can do nothing. Don't you think they've arrested him before? Don't you think social services has been in these tunnels before and taken children away? It means nothing. The Moose gets out of jail, returns to his tunnels, and always finds new children."

I glared at Cardan. He must have been down here weeks, months, maybe more to be so familiar with The Moose. Had he been watching me all that time? "How do you know all of this?"

"I have eyes. They see the truth." He spit on the ground. "No, my boy, he must be stopped permanently."

"What are you saying?" A chill rose up my back. *Permanently?* I spun away from Cardan but he grasped my arm.

"The Moose is your next test."

I ripped my arm from his grip. "What do you mean?"

From his trench coat Cardan handed me a carrot stick and half of an apple. "Stop him."

I pushed away the food. "No. What do you want from me? Look, I know you think I can be some hero, but you've got the wrong guy. I'm nobody. A loser. Just let me go. Let my dad go. I won't tell anyone about you. I promise."

"You are so much more than you can even imagine." He forced the food into my hands. "I've seen you stop criminals, even those armed with guns. You have the ability to stop evil."

"But I can't control my power. You haven't cracked the code yet."

Cardan reached out as if to touch my shoulder, but I slid away.

"This test, and how you respond to it, will get me that much closer to understanding what foods cause what changes. I only want you to achieve your real potential."

"I can't do this."

"Do as I say. Remember the consequences if you disobey me." He grasped my wrists.

I peered down the tunnel at The Moose, who must have been counting a wad of money. He kept licking his fingers and shuffling something in his hands. He coughed and labored for each breath.

My legs trembled, my stomach already ached, and I hadn't taken a bite yet. What did Cardan want? What did he expect me to do? It didn't matter. I had no choice but to do as he said.

I took a bite of the carrot and then the apple.

From deep within my gut an icy chill coursed through my arms and legs, as if someone injected freezing water into my veins. With each pump of my heart, frost extended to my fingers and toes. White mist poured from my nose and mouth.

"S… so cold." My teeth chattered. My body spasmed. "F… fr… freezing. Lungs burning. Can't breathe."

My sweat turned to icy droplets that shattered against the ground. My limbs stiffened. I tried to bend my arms and legs, but they cracked at the joints like an iceberg splitting in half.

I fell on all fours, heaving as I struggled to breathe. I tried to lift my hands, but they had frozen to the concrete. A pulsating blue glow rose from each hand up my arms until it coated my skin. The icy sheet tore away my clothes and shoes, encasing me. *S… su… suffocating! N… need air! He… help!* I trembled violently. Tiny jagged pieces of ice ripped at my insides.

When I lifted my head and twisted my neck to try to free myself, the ice swept over my face. My cheeks and eyes stung.

A last gasp escaped my mouth before I became an ice sculpture. I couldn't blink. Wiggle my nose. Move my mouth.

Cardan knelt down, his face inches from mine. "You need to free yourself from this frozen cocoon to become the butterfly."

He… help me. He couldn't hear me. He didn't know my suffering. To him this was a test. To me, this was a frozen prison with no escape.

"Break free, my boy," he urged.

I can't! My voiceless cry caused my body to shake beneath the shell. A crack echoed around me. I willed myself to vibrate harder. Fractures in the ice formed. I managed to break my hands free and then my arms and legs. Slowly I stood, ice chips falling from my limbs.

My chest glowed blue.

"You're a work of art," Cardan whispered. "I have never beheld a creature such as you."

My hands reminded me of blue gemstones. I slid ice-coated fingers over my crystal-like arms. I breathed normally and welcomed the chill flowing through my veins.

I had become an ice man.

"What can I do with this power?" I aimed my hands at the ground. Nothing happened.

I concentrated harder. My hands shook. The blue glow brightened. A white laser shot from my fingers and caked the concrete around my feet in an icy crust.

"Truly amazing," Cardan folded his arms over his chest.

I glanced at him. "Now what?"

"Now, my boy, you permanently chill The Moose."

Permanently chill? A white laser accidentally shot from my fingers. The ray struck a rat a few feet away. It squealed and then fell on its side. Stiff. Silent.

"I won't kill him." I shook my head.

"He may leave you little choice." Cardan lifted a cigarette to his mouth but didn't light it.

A new thought wound through my mind. Freeze Cardan and make my escape, figure out a way to find my dad. End all of this. But, what if I didn't find him? What if he died because of me? I couldn't let that happen.

Pointing my fingers toward the ground, I focused a white beam at my feet. Ice formed around them, which I sculpted into a pair of skates. I slid closer to Cardan. "I'll go deal with this Moose dude, but I want to see my dad after that."

"I guarantee you and your father will be reunited soon." He nodded, the cigarette still nestled between his lips.

Like an Olympic skater, I launched myself toward The Moose.

His head swiveled toward me; whatever he held dropped to the ground. He screamed and fell from the chair. He tried to rise, but his massive size caused him to trip and fall back to the ground.

I slid to a halt in front of him and crossed my arms, trying to appear more sure of myself than I was.

"Don't hurt me!" he begged, wheezing and gasping. His eyes, blood shot and rimmed by black shadows, bulged.

"You're done here, Moose." I lowered my voice. Thought that might scare him more, though the sight of an ice man in these tunnels probably frightened him enough. He whimpered through gasps for air.

"Y… you got the wrong guy. Y… you're I… looking for some other guy." His cough gave his voice a throaty sound. His shorts revealed stumpy legs, while a T-shirt, nearly the size of a tent, barely covered his stomach.

"Don't lie to me."

"Y… Yes, I'm The Moose." He started to crawl away.

I shot a white laser at his right foot, freezing it to the ground. He screamed again and then pleaded for mercy.

"Your time in these tunnels is over. Leave here and stop using children to carry out your crimes." I shot another laser inches from his head. The ground next to him exploded in ice.

"I'm sorry… so sorry. Take my money. Take it all."

He picked up the money and tossed it at my feet. Thousand dollar bills lay on the ground. How could a crook hiding beneath the city collect so much? What did he have the kids doing?

I stared at it the bills too long. When I looked up, the barrel of a revolver pointed at my head. *Stupid Tripp.*

"No one tells The Moose what to do. No one." With a shaky hand, he fired the weapon.

A round bounced off my chest. Ice chips flew around me. I cringed, but I was bullet proof.

Another round echoed through the tunnel, deflecting off my icy armor. I shook off the memories. "Enough!"

He fired off a third, but I swatted the bullet away. "That was a mistake, jerk."

Before he could fire again, I encased his gun hand in ice. The weight caused his arm to droop. He could no longer lift the weapon. Puckering my lips, I blew a cool mist from my mouth, wrapping his body in a giant snowball.

Only his chubby face remained visible. His teeth chattered and his cheeks turned blue. If I left him in there, he would freeze to death, but I didn't want a frozen Moose popsicle on my conscious. I reached inside the snowball and yanked him free. His color immediately returned, but he shivered uncontrollably while rolling on the ground. I ripped the gun from his hand and then threw it down the tunnel.

"What do you want from me?" Still on the ground, he rubbed his arms.

"I told you—leave this place and leave the kids alone. If you don't, I'll know and make you suffer."

"Anything. Please, just let me go." He tried to rise to his feet but fell again. "I'll do whatever you say."

"No, he won't." Cardan stood beside me with the man's gun in his hand. "You know he's lying. This filth is incapable of anything but evil. He must be stopped—forever. Use your power. Freeze him."

"What? I told you… I'm not going to kill." I slid away from The Moose and Cardan. "You're right. He's scum, but he doesn't have to die." My eyes shifted from the gun to Cardan. What was I supposed to do now?

"You heard me. He must die. There is no choice. His crimes warrant death. This is your test. Use your power to do what must be done."

"No. There're other ways."

"Do not fail this test." He pointed the gun at the shivering man.

"I'm not going to kill, and I'm not going to let you to kill either." I raised my arms and pointed my fingers at him.

Cardan smiled. "You dare threaten me… your father?"

I lowered my arms. "What did you say?"

"Your entire life has been a lie, my son." He tilted his head. "That man I have hidden away is an imposter, a government plant. I am your true father."

"I don't believe you." Blood rushed from my head. I lost balance, dropping to one knee. It couldn't be true. He was lying. Everything he said was a lie.

"You will come to know the truth and you must learn to accept it. Your future, just like your past, is tied to me."

He fired the gun once into The Moose's head.

Chapter 17

A Hero Trapped

The gun. I stared at it on the lab table next to Cardan. Images of The Moose's head snapping back as the bullet pierced his forehead raced through my mind. His blood stained the tunnel wall. My stomach cramped as vomit rose up my throat. Covering my mouth, I swallowed the bile. I wouldn't let myself be sick in front of Cardan.

My transformation faded and my human flesh returned. My whole body felt heavy. Numb. Cardan placed his lab coat over my shoulders back inside his lair. I wrapped it tighter around my body. The stench of his cigarettes clung to the course fabric.

For some reason, tears formed. Why would I cry over The Moose?

The massive man had knelt an arm's length away, his eyes first focused on me, then vacant. His body slumped to the ground, blood spilling from the wound, pooling around his head. In the last few days I'd seen bodies but hadn't witnessed their deaths. I'd never seen a cold-blooded killing.

Why had Cardan killed him? The Moose might be scum, but he didn't deserve to be gunned down. That's not what a hero would do, and isn't that what Cardan—my father—wanted me to become—a hero?

My mind circled back to his revelation. *I am your true father.* My knees buckled. Dizziness swept over me. My head drooped.

"You look weary, my son." Cardan once again spoke kindly. He held a cigarette with one hand; the other rested inches from the handgun. "You can grab a chair and sit if you like. I suppose we have much to discuss."

I dropped into the nearest chair. "Why did you kill him?"

"Because you didn't, but that is not what I wish to discuss right now." He picked up the gun and held it with both hands. "Such an ugly destructive device—just an example of the kind of evil mankind has brought into the world. I detest such weapons."

"Really?" This guy was a killer. How long before he pointed that thing at me?

He turned the gun over and over as if studying it from one angle, then another. With sure hands, he released the magazine from the handle and then placed the weapon and ammunition in a drawer. Removing a key from his trench coat, he locked the cabinet.

"I do not wish to discuss the justification for my use of the gun." Cardan swung back to me. He lit the cigarette, then took a long puff. He blinked red eyes several times. "We have more important topics to address."

"Just let me go already." I started to rise.

"Please, Ilan, sit and listen."

I crumbled back into my seat. He used the name again, only this time he referred to me as Ilan.

"That's not my name."

A train roared overhead.

Cardan rubbed his eyes from the falling dust and sighed. "Yes, your real name is Ilan, and you are my son. I know this can't be easy for you to hear, but it is the truth. You cannot imagine what it means to reunite with the child who was taken from me so many years ago."

He leaned against the table. His arms shook.

"What are you saying?" I rocked back and forth in my chair. "You're insane. I'm not your son. I have a dad. You took him from me. You just threatened to kill him if I don't do what you say."

Cardan shook his head. "The man I hold is not your father. I know that cannot be easy to hear, but it is true. He is a secret service agent, assigned to keep you in line from a government that fears your power." He banged his hand on the table. "Oh, how they've twisted your mind. Thank God your poor mother is not alive to have to experience the kind of pain I have had to face, but that is in the past now. I have you again."

I lunged at him, grabbing the collar of his trench coat. "Don't you dare talk about my mom. She died giving birth to me. You have no right to speak of her."

Cardan pushed me away, his hands grasping my shoulders. "I am not referring to whatever woman you were brainwashed into believing was your mother. I refer to your real mother... the woman I loved, the woman who brought you into the world."

"What?" I broke away from his grip and paced in front of him. "I don't believe any of this."

My teeth clenched. Body trembled.

"Yes, son, you were taken from me and your mother—kidnapped by those who feared me and feared what you could become."

"You're lying." I held my hands to my head. I wanted to block out his words, but they pierced my brain.

"I am not. You see, I was a scientist of some standing back home in our native England, and it is because of me that you were gifted with your powers. In a sense, I engineered you while you were still in your mother's womb."

I slid back into my chair. My head spun. *Engineered. Womb. Gifted.* I covered my eyes, trying to quiet my thoughts, but it didn't help.

"Dude... wh... what... did... y... you do to me? How could you? Why?"

Cardan ignored my questions. He stared off toward some distant point. "Oh, you were this little perfect creature that your mother and I loved. I can still picture her face when she held you for the first time. It is a moment etched in my memory for all time."

"I don't want to hear any more."

His eyes shifted back to me. "You must hear it all. You were our perfect child for a month until that day… that one horrible day. I thought I had hidden us away from those who would seek to take you from us, but I was terribly wrong."

"Who wanted to take me away?"

"The British scientific community, the Crown's Guard and the government—they all knew of your birth. My so-called scientist friends proved disloyal, stealing information about my experiments and sharing it with the military." Cardan paced in front of me. His hands formed into fists. He squeezed them until his knuckles turned white. "They all feared my breakthroughs in genetic science. My ability to create a more perfect life. To manipulate genes, so there would be no more disease. No more suffering."

He knelt beside me, grabbing my hands. His eyes widened. "Can you imagine what I could have accomplished, and you were the beginning of it all. My first creation."

Cardan tightened his grip. I tried to shake free but couldn't. "My friends betrayed me, and when I learned of their traitorous action, I hid us. I found a cottage in the back country and changed our identity."

He took a long breath and released my hands. "But they still found me a month after your birth."

Pain etched into his face. His chin quivered. Lips curled into a frown. The lines in his long, drawn cheeks deepened. He blinked away tears.

Cardan slumped into a sitting position and started to rock back and forth. "I fought as best I could, as did your mother. All I had was an old rifle. I fired on them, and when they broke through our door, I swung wildly at them. All I could hear were your terrified cries. I begged them to leave us be, but they wouldn't listen. Those monsters feared me. Feared you…my creation. Your mother held you. Wouldn't let you go until they struck her.

Then, they tore you from her arms. I rushed at them, but they smashed me over the head. I blacked out."

His nostrils flared. Face reddened. "When your mother and I awoke in a prison, she was in one cell, I in another. And you... I had no idea what they had done to you. Can you imagine what that felt like? I pleaded with them to let me see you. To let me be with my wife. But they turned a deaf ear to my pleas."

I rose and retreated from him. Could it all be true? Could my life be a lie? I contemplated his features. Curly hair. Thin build. Just like me. I looked more like him than my dad.

My head pounded. "You said my mo... your wife... died. How?"

He lit a new cigarette with shaky hands. His chest heaved as he inhaled the smoke. "I can't say how long they held us in that prison. Time no longer had meaning. The only relief from my agony came from hearing my wife's voice from her cell. We spoke every day. Then one day, she didn't speak to me. I called to her but nothing." He took another long puff. New tears slid down his cheeks. "I screamed for our jailers to check on her. When they did, I heard a commotion from her cell. My God, Ilan, the next thing I saw was them removing her with a sheet covering her face. She was gone. My love was dead." He stomped his foot on the ground. "I was told she took her own life, but that's a lie. She wouldn't leave me. She wouldn't abandon you. Ilan, your mother died of a broken heart. There was no other explanation."

I stopped pacing. "What became of me?"

He threw the cigarette. "For far too long I had no idea. I remained locked away in that prison with nothing but my feelings of anguish and hatred for what they had done to me, your mother—to our family. I wanted to die. I can't tell you how many times I contemplated taking my life. But then I thought of you, my son. I had to stay alive for you. I had to find you again. Somehow! I just had to."

I kicked the chair in front of me. I wanted to curl up in my comfortable bed in my own home, but that all seemed impossible now. If Cardan's words were true, I didn't belong in that bed. "How did you get out? How did you find me?"

"A friend saved me. Patrick was his name." Cardan reached for another cigarette. "He was a fellow scientist, one of those who betrayed me to the government. One day he showed up at my cell and told me how sorry he was for what had befallen me and his role in it. He was filled with regret. I still remember the click-clack of the cell door unlatching as he freed me. I don't know how he orchestrated it, but he'd drugged the guards, and then led me deeper into the prison until we reached a sewer hole. From there, we crawled through a narrow pipe just large enough to slide on our bellies. We crept for what could have been a mile through the worst filth you could imagine. I couldn't breathe. Thought I'd die. But I couldn't. I had to survive for you. We reached a stream in the dead of night. By then, we heard the dogs. They were hunting us. But we still managed to slip away. He led me to an abandoned warehouse and told me to hide there. He said he would come for me in a day and provide me all the information about what had happened to you."

"And did he?"

Cardan lit the new cigarette. "He never returned. I later learned his body had been found in a lake. He gave his life to save mine, but I was left alone to find the answers that would lead me to you."

"How did you find me?" The little hairs on the back of my neck stood at attention. A warning not to believe him? Why was I even listening to this?

"It took years, but I pieced it together, Ilan. The government smuggled you from the country and sent you to the U.S. You were a creature to be managed while this country's best scientists and doctors tried to *cure* you from the gift I bestowed upon you. They deemed you a danger. At first, they locked you away to study you, but then your Doctor Torren took over your case. It was his idea to place you with a man who would pretend to be your father, but it was a ruse, my son. Your bloody doctor told you he wanted to treat you. That was partially true, but he was really trying to duplicate your genetic code to create another being like you, only one whose power was manageable. They lied to you my son. They manipulated you. They tried to keep me away from you."

I retreated farther from him. "They knew you escaped. Didn't they think you'd try to come for me?"

Cardan crossed to me. "I knew they'd come for me, so I had to keep moving. I had some money hidden away in an account they couldn't trace. I escaped England and hid in Scotland. When I thought they were close, I fled to South Africa. I kept running. Always one step ahead. Always praying for the day when I could reach you. Always hacking their files for any information about you. When I learned the truth, I began to plan for the day we'd be reunited. For this day."

Cardan grabbed me with both hands and pulled me in close. "I found you, Ilan. A father cannot be kept from his son. I found you and I have freed you."

He hugged me tighter.

I broke away. My cheeks burned. I pointed a finger at him. "You did this to me. You made me this way. You gave me this curse. I'm a freak because of you. I can't eat like normal people because of you."

"What I gave you is a gift, one to be shared with the world." He reached for me, but I held my arms up to block him. "Those who took you from me made you believe you were ill. If I had had more time, if I had been able to raise you, I could have taught you to control your power, to harness it for good. Your life would be so different. You are no freak, and I will spend the rest of my life proving it to you."

This time he succeeded in wrapping an arm around my shoulders. "I know this is more than you can possibly understand right now, but in time you will see all I have told you is the truth. I am your father, and I want what is best for you. I want you to cherish your gift and learn to harness it. More than that, my son, I hope one day you can learn to love me as I love you."

Yeah, sure. I stared at the cabinet where he placed the gun.

Chapter 18

A Father's Demand

I lay on my cot unable to sleep. I can't say how many hours passed. If I closed my eyes, images of death flashed before me. Thoughts of my dad—the crabby old dude who raised me—filled my mind. Was he really held captive somewhere? Was anything Cardan said true? Could he be my father? Could my whole life be a lie?

Staring at the pipes embedded in the vaulted ceiling, I tried to measure the time between the trains passing in the tunnels high above. Hard to do with no phone, no clock. Nothing. No idea whether it was day or night. Still, I guessed roughly an hour passed between the rumbles and whistles.

Always present was Cardan. His footsteps plodded against the concrete floor. The stench of his cigarettes was constant. He occasionally hummed. Other times he grumbled. Did he ever sleep?

"Ilan, time to rise, my boy." His words startled me. My pulse quickened and stomach clenched. What now?

He stepped into view and sat down on my cot. He wore his dark trench coat and held a cell phone. "Ilan, I hope you have rested because it is time for your next test. And I think you'll be pleased. We'll be venturing out of the tunnels."

I peered at him. A wide smile crossed this gaunt face. Was he serious, or just playing with me? Was he actually going to take me up to the streets? That could be my chance to figure out where I was. "Great," was all I said, trying not to appear too excited.

He held up the cell phone so that I could see the screen. "Before we begin, however, I must show you something. I hope you appreciate it. It's what you've been asking for."

I shuddered. "What is it?"

He pressed a button on his phone and a video began to stream. I gasped. It was Dad. The image was grainy, shadowy, but it was him. Inside a room no bigger than a closet. Slumped against the floor. Stripped down to his underwear. His bad leg extended. The other knee bent to his chest. His head bowed, but he was alive. His chest moved up and down. One hand formed a fist. *Oh God, Dad. I'm sorry.*

I lunged for the phone. Cardan snapped it away from me.

"Dad! Dad!" I shouted. "Can you hear me?" Blood rushed to my head. My face became hot. I leaped from the bed. "Dad!"

"That man cannot hear you." Cardan climbed to his feet. "Ilan, what you are seeing is live. I wanted you to trust me when I say his very life depends on your actions."

"You son-of-a-bitch. Where is he?" I grabbed the cot and flipped it over. I breathed so fast I started to hyperventilate. "Let him go. I'll do whatever you want."

"Oh, I know you will, my son." He held the phone toward me again.

My dad looked up. I dropped to my knees. One of his eyes was swollen. Sealed. A gash crossed his forehead. He'd been beaten. He slowly lowered his head again.

"Why'd you hurt him?" Tears came. I couldn't hold them back.

"He has gotten nothing less than he deserves for what he has done to you." Cardan slid the phone into his pocket. "For keeping you from me. For making you feel ashamed of the power I gave to you. He is lucky to be alive. Now, Ilan, know this, with one push of a button on my phone, deadly gas will be released into his chamber. His death will be slow and painful. Do you understand?"

I crawled to Cardan and grabbed his leg. "Please, just let him go. I'll stay with you no matter what. He doesn't even like me. He never did. Just take me to him one last time so I can say goodbye. I promise that's all I want."

Cardan grabbed me by the shoulders and lifted me to my feet. "My son, that's impossible. He is too far away, and we have much to do. I do understand your feeling for the man, and I am touched. Though he be an imposter, he is the only father you know. I pray someday you will have those feelings for me, your real father. I know I cannot rush it, but in time you will come to love me and know that I offer you a real future... one that embraces all that is special about you. I offer you a future in which you will change the world as you were meant to do."

He wrapped his arms around me, forcing my head against his chest. I was too numb to push away. "I'll give you a moment to compose yourself; then, we must be off. Ilan, I am not an evil man. I am just a father who would do anything for his son. Even kill. All of this is for you. To make you better. Stronger. I love you, son."

***

Cardan led me through the gloomy lower shafts. We trudged from one tunnel to the next, rounding one bend, then another. Shadows made it impossible to tell the different passages apart. It felt like we walked in circles.

Maybe we did. His way of keeping me confused.

We marched in silence, but my thoughts rang loudly in my head. I was his prisoner and there was no escape—even out on the streets—not as long as he had my dad. What if the man who raised me wasn't my dad, like Cardan claimed? Why would anyone do that to a kid? Lie all this time. Just to keep me from using my powers because the government feared me? Was I actually starting to believe Cardan? My head spun. I didn't want to think anymore, but I had to stay focused.

At a steel door, Cardan stopped. "The way to the surface is through this door."

He swung it open and then we ascended through a narrow shaft with a steep grade as if traversing a mountainside path. The icy chill of the lower tunnels gave way to an embracing warmth the higher we climbed.

I counted the steps. When I reached one hundred, we arrived at another steel door. Cardan pushed it open and ushered me through the doorway. We stepped onto a platform with a railing on the edge of what had to be an active subway tunnel. Lights lined the ceiling above. A few feet below, tracks stretched along the passageway. Just beyond the walkway, voices—maybe hundreds of them—bounced off the walls.

I held myself to keep from trembling. People... actual people... were close by. I don't know how long he'd kept me below, but I'd almost given up on ever seeing other human beings again. Now, they were close.

"Let's keep moving." Cardan spoke just above a whisper. "A new beginning awaits you, my son."

We continued along the walkway, which was just wide enough for one person to pass over at a time. I walked in front with Cardan just behind. His hot, smoky breath brushed against my neck.

He grabbed my shoulder and stopped me. Leaning close, he lifted the phone from his coat, a finger placed against a side button. "Remember, Ilan. Don't do anything foolish." Cardan slid the phone away and nudged me forward.

My body trembled. Nausea bubbled inside my stomach, but I kept walking.

The voices grew louder with each step. Light from whatever lay ahead spread toward us. The brightness stung so much I had to shield my eyes. I didn't realize how accustomed to the dark I'd become.

Finally, we emerged from the tunnel into a subway terminal. Light washed over me from every direction. Eyes burned like glaring into the sun. I slowly scanned my surroundings. People crowded together waiting for the next train. Some sat on benches. Others leaned against concrete columns. Their voices rattled my brain. Too much noise at one time. Deafening.

I covered my ears.

Cardan placed a hand on my shoulder. "It's okay, Ilan. You'll soon be reacquainted with the surface."

I froze under his touch. He did this to me. Turned me into some kind of subsurface dweller. Scared of light… people.

Releasing his grip, he strolled on alone toward stairs that led to the surface. He didn't glance back at me. He just expected me to follow.

What choice did I have? I stumbled after him to the steps. A sign next to the staircase read, Liberty Avenue Station. We were in Brooklyn. Not all that far from Queens. From my home.

Nighttime had fallen when we slithered like rats from the subway onto the streets above. The fresh air, though tinged with exhaust and city grime, was still a welcome relief from the stale dampness of the manmade caverns below. The stars above had never seemed so bright, like I hadn't seen the night sky for years.

Closing my eyes, I concentrated on my breathing and listened to the city's music. Honking car. Stomping feet. Blaring sirens. Screeching brakes.

The Liberty Avenue terminal spilled onto an older part of Brooklyn. Brick and stone buildings lined the streets. Graffiti marked gang territory on the sides of apartments, storefronts, and bars. Trash cluttered chain link fences; steam rose from manholes. The Brooklyn Bridge, brightly lit against the night sky, peeked through some of the high-rises. Manhattan's skyscrapers rose in the distance.

A cigarette dangling from his lips and white smoke billowing around his face, Cardan ushered me along.

"I have a question, *Dad*." I used the word more out of spite than affection. Cardan noticed.

"Ilan, I ask you to refrain from calling me *Dad* until you can do so and mean it. To use it in any other way belittles both of us. Some day you will say it and mean it, and I will rejoice when that day comes." Cardan raised an eyebrow. I avoided his stare, kicking a rock on the sidewalk with the slip-on Vans he gave me.

"Ask me your question," he continued.

"You said Doc Torren held me in some kind of government stronghold. That's where you found me and freed me. You could have taken me anywhere you wanted. We could have disappeared, but instead you brought me back to the city—back home. I mean sure I was living in the suburbs, not downtown, but it's still NYC. Why? Why bring me back here?"

He puffed on his cigarette, which lit his face as the end of the cigarette burned bright. "As you should be able to tell by now, I went to great lengths to establish myself in, or rather, under this city. This is where I built an underground laboratory. When the time was right, I could help you unlock your true potential. More than that, if ever a city needed your help, this is it. I decided this is where you will train and grow in strength. From here, we can use your gift to heal the world."

"You do know I'm just a kid, right?"

"You are my child. You are extraordinary."

He strolled faster, and I jogged beside him to keep pace. Off to the right, two police officers patrolled on foot in the opposite direction. It would have been so easy to call out to them that a crazy man had kidnapped me.

One of the officers gazed my way, but I let the officers pass without uttering a word. I couldn't risk my dad's life. I had to figure this out on my own. Until then, I had to do what Cardan said.

"Okay," I blurted, breaking the silence between us. "What is it I'm supposed to do?"

"Bring change."

"Stop speaking in riddles? Answer me straight."

"I will show you."

He rounded a corner and led me along a street with buildings lit by neon signs splashing a rainbow of colors. A row of bars and shops, selling everything from cheap clothing to rugs, filled the block. Posters advertising Broadway plays covered buildings. More graffiti, some artistic, some hastily sprayed, spread from one building to the next.

We stopped outside a bar where the musty odor of liquor and urine hung heavy.

Cardan peered through the window and pointed inside. "There, look."

I put my face close to the glass but couldn't see much through the brown muck. "What am I supposed to see?"

He tapped on the glass. "Do you see the rather large fellow dressed in black sitting at a table with his back to us? He is joined by two others, one short and thin the other rounded with a red beard."

"I see them."

"The one with his back to us is a high-ranking member of the Police Department. His name is Ryan Billes, and he is a lieutenant in the organized crime unit. Those two he is speaking with serve a mob boss known only as *Ghost.*"

"What... how do you know all of this?" I backed away from the window.

"I read, I study, and I have my sources." He dropped the cigarette to the ground and stomped on it. "Tonight, Lieutenant Billes is being paid off to allow a shipment of guns to be trucked into Brooklyn and placed into the hands of Ghost's henchmen."

I leaned against the glass just in time to see a case pushed across the table by the bearded man. Lieutenant Billes took the briefcase and walked toward the rear of the bar where he disappeared through a door.

Cardan grabbed my shoulder and ushered me to the edge of a narrow passageway, a bit more than shoulder length wide, separating the bar from another brick building.

"Stand casually against the wall and watch, but don't look like you're watching." Cardan lit another cigarette and eased back against the building, like some loafer with nothing better to do on a cool Brooklyn night.

Soon Lieutenant Billes slid from the back alley, the black briefcase in one hand. He walked right by without paying us a second thought. I studied him out of the corner of my eyes. A large muscular man with chiseled features, he walked slightly hunched over—maybe on purpose. He wore a black coat with the collar up like someone trying to hide their identity.

Billes stopped once to scan the city street then slunk into the night.

"Let's move." Cardan glided with long strides through a crowd of night walkers to keep pace with Billes.

I didn't want any part of this. I already had a sense of what my role would be and didn't like it. I hadn't eaten anything yet, and my stomach growled in anticipation of what would come next.

"Come on, keep up," Cardan directed. "We don't want to bloody lose him."

"Why are we even following him?"

"Because Billes is not only a crooked cop, he's a stupid one. He wants to see the shipment of weapons when he should be as far away from it as possible. Yes, he's going to lead us right to the truck."

We followed him for two blocks before he stopped at an intersection where a black sedan pulled to the curb. He climbed into the back and then the vehicle, its windows darkened, whisked him away.

Cursing under his breath, Cardan signaled for a taxi. One immediately stopped.

"Where to?" the taxi driver asked.

Cardan nudged me into the yellow cab then sat before slamming the door. "Just drive, mate. I'll give you further instructions in time."

"It's your buck." The taxi driver, a heavy-set man with pudgy cheeks and a billowing mustache, chuckled. His puffy eyes darted back and forth between staring at us through the rearview mirror and watching the traffic.

"I see them just ahead," Cardan whispered. He leaned forward in his seat. "They're turning… turning right. Sir, I need you to make a right at the next intersection."

The taxi driver nodded.

The black sedan, just a few car lengths ahead, continued straight, passing through four or five intersections. Buildings on either side of the roadway became larger as we drove toward the waterfront. The Brooklyn Bridge loomed in front of us.

One more right turn at an intersection and the sedan came to a stop in front of a warehouse a block from the harbor.

"Driver, please stop there." Cardan pointed at a six-story high rise across the street.

The taxi driver swung the car into a U-turn against traffic and stopped next to the curb.

"That will be ten dollars, friend." He swiveled to face us.

Cardan pulled a twenty from his trench coat. He never looked at the cab driver. His eyes remained on Billes. "Keep the change, good man."

We watched Billes from behind one parked car along a quiet stretch near Brooklyn's waterfront.

Billes, briefcase still in hand, tapped the roof of the black sedan as he exited and the car sped away. He dashed across the street to the sidewalk close to us and stopped maybe ten feet away. His foot tapped the ground, and he checked the watch on his wrist. Never once did he look in our direction.

"So this is where it will happen." Cardan grinned.

"Where what will happen?" I looked from Billes to Cardan.

"Ghost, the crime lord I mentioned, owns the warehouse across the street. He runs it as a legitimate import storage facility for goods shipped from around the world, but in reality, it's a stash house for the underground. Drugs, weapons, money—they all cross through here first. Well, here and other warehouses like it. This particular weapons shipment is important to Ghost. We're talking thousands of assault rifles with armor-piercing ammunition—enough to declare war on those police Ghost hasn't already corrupted."

Cardan placed his hands on my shoulders. "Are you hungry, Ilan?"

"What… no." I pushed away his hands. I should have run but didn't. "What am I supposed to do against something like this?"

"You, my powerful son, are going to stop that shipment and send a message to this city that a change is coming. That a hero is here to bring new hope."

"You're crazy."

His hands shook. He formed them into fists and then released a long breath before he spoke again. "Believe in yourself, Ilan, as I believe in you. Whatever you transform into, you can use your ability to stop this shipment. I am not asking you to kill. I merely want you to stop that truck, dump it somewhere it cannot be found and let those criminals and Billes know they cannot get away with such crime any longer."

"What if I don't want to?"

"Then you will have failed me a second time." He held up the phone.

"Wait… wait." My limbs shook. He asked too much. I couldn't do something this big. "I thought this was supposed to be about helping me learn to use this power."

He lowered his head to mine. "Indeed it is."

"Then let's start slower." I whispered. "Maybe rescue a kitten from a tree or something."

"Ilan, you've already done so much more than that. The convenience store robbery. The boy you saved from the drainpipe. The zoo. The bank. I wouldn't ask you to do this is if I didn't think you capable. It is only through extreme moments of stress that we can truly understand your transformation."

He knew everything I'd done. Had he been there each time? Watching me? "I'm scared."

"It's okay."

"I don't want to die."

"That won't happen. I won't allow it." He pulled me from our hiding place to a deserted narrow alley. Once we stood in the shadows, he reached into his trench coat.

"I brought something I think you will enjoy." His hand emerged holding a burrito, one that would have come from a convenience store. "I am sorry if it is a little cold, but at least it is no longer frozen."

My mouth watered. I snatched it from him with a trembling hand and held it up to my face. My stomached growled with anticipation.

"Go ahead, my son, and meet your destiny," Cardan urged.

I lowered the burrito. "I don't think—"

"Don't be afraid." He gently gripped my hand.

A big rig lumbered up the street. Was that the truck carrying the weapons?

Cardan turned toward the street. "You see, the police do nothing, thanks to Billes. Ghost pays Billes and he pays his officers to look the other way. It is up to you, Ilan, but you must act now. Keep these weapons off the streets."

Wiping saliva from my lips, I bit into the burrito. A chilled, spicy mix of beans and meat slid down my throat. The second bite came with less hesitation. A third bite and a fourth followed.

Before I knew it, I'd eating half the burrito. Bits of tortilla and cheese clung to my fingers.

The transformation started as I swallowed my last mouthful.

A familiar pain rose from my gut as if someone had just punched me in the stomach. I keeled over and wrapped my arms around my body. "It hurts."

Cardan bent down so his face was even with mine. "Don't fight it. Don't be scared. Your emotions affect your change, make it more painful, more volatile. Just accept the change like welcoming an old friend. Will yourself to want the transformation. Use your mind to control the change."

I shoved him away. His words meant nothing. Bones cracked. The skin along my back ripped open. I covered my mouth to muffle a scream. Something grew from my shoulder blades.

"Ilan, it's beautiful," Cardan declared.

Panting, struggling for each breath, I gazed over my shoulder. Four wings, each as dark as a raven's, extended from my back. "Oh my—"

An ache stabbed my sides. A second set of arms burst through my flesh. These new limbs had sharp talons, like an eagle's, in place of hands.

The transformation continued to twist my body. I touched my face. Cheekbones projected through the skin. My jaw popped and cracked, stretching into a long hard beak. Feathers covered long, pointy ears. All of me throbbed, worse than the time I had five baby teeth pulled at once.

I slid my hands over the beak. Was I becoming some kind of crazed bird?

When the change ended, I shuddered and released a lungful of air. The four wings attached to my back towered over my head. My blood pulsed through each black feather.

I wanted to soar into the sky.

"Ilan, you are truly a heroic creature." Cardan retreated a few steps. "Now go and use your power."

I fought the urge to squawk. "What am I supposed to do? I'm a bird."

"Let your powers guide you."

"Yeah, right, that's easy for you to say." I flapped my wings softly at first, then with greater strength, rustling unseen garbage in the darkened alley.

With a last look at Cardan, who nodded back, I thrust my wings with such force that I shot skyward like a bullet. I soared over the alley to land on the roof of the building across from the warehouse.

Standing on the ledge six stories up, I studied the big rig, a gray truck without any distinguishing marks, stopped in front of Ghost's warehouse. Like ants emerging from the earth, men spilled onto the deserted sidewalk and gathered at the truck's rear. Billes remained across the street leering at the crime he had been paid to ignore.

What should I do? Those men had to be armed. What good would wings be against guns? I stared at the stars above and off toward the horizon beyond New York City. With this power, I could easily fly away. How would Cardan find me? How would anyone find me? Why should I care about the city after all the crap I've been through? Why should I care about that man who raised me if he wasn't even my father? Because he was my dad no matter what Cardan said. I had to stay. Had to do this to keep him alive. And if I flew away I'd never know the truth, and I needed answers.

The men below opened and unloaded a crate. One in a black leather coat, his curly hair greased, held up a rifle, pointing the barrel toward the sky. The others, at least fifteen, cheered.

Cardan hadn't lied. The truck held a shipment of guns.

"With these assault rifles, we'll bring war to the other crime bosses," the man who held the gun shouted. His high-pitched, hyena-like voice carried up to me. "We'll spread blood through the city until only Ghost remains."

I shook my head. How many innocent people would be killed? I paced back and forth as the men carried more crates from the truck. "Okay, Tripp, or Ilan, or whatever the hell my name is, let's do this."

Under the cover of night, I leaped from the ledge and glided to the truck. I touched down gently on the trailer then tucked low and crawled to the edge. Maybe my freakish appearance would be enough to scare them away.

Standing with all four of my arms crossed, wings spread to their full height, I shouted, "Stop what you're doing!"

My words came out as nothing more than a screech. Oh no, what happened to my voice?

I tried again. "I'm not going to let you have these weapons." Once again, a squawk replaced the words.

The men stared at each other in confusion, shrugging their shoulders and backing away. Some chuckled.

"What are you supposed to be?" The man holding the rifle with one hand stroked his goatee with the other. "Fly away birdy before I clip your wings."

I didn't budge even though every instinct screamed at me to fly away to safety.

"Does anyone know what this thing is?" The armed man strutted along the street. "I know, you're one of those vigilantes I've heard about. What? You think you can stop us, little birdy man? You're mistaken, pal."

He aimed the rifle at me. "Time to die, you feathered freak."

Before he fired a round, I dove at him, slashing with my talons. The rifle fell to the ground. Blood spewed from gashes in his palms.

Don't just stand there, shoot that thing," he ordered.

Ghost's men drew handguns on me.

"You're going to die, you freak!" declared one large man in a Levi's jacket with a scar across his cheek.

I shot into the sky as he opened fire. Rounds whizzed by me, some close. I spun and shifted direction. One bullet tore through a wing. My body tensed. The wing retracted. Searing heat radiated from the wound. A second round clipped another wing. A yelp escaped my mouth. Feathers and blood sprayed from the injury.

I lost altitude as if my wings could no longer keep me aloft. No! I couldn't give up. I spread my wings wide and climbed high, evading more rounds until their guns silenced. Now it was my turn. Panting to ease my pain, I dove toward the city street, charging like a hawk after its prey.

"It's coming," one of them shouted, frantically reloading his weapon. Some of the bullets dropped to the ground.

More gunfire erupted, but too late.

I smashed into them like a bowling ball striking down pins. Seven dropped fast, knocked off their feet. I, too, crashed against the pavement, rolling several times. I quickly rose to my feet, swinging my wings wildly at those who remained standing.

Two more, struck in the head, slumped to the concrete. Then, I don't know how I did it, but I unleashed a screech from deep in my throat. The sound acted like a shockwave, hurtling everyone backward.

None of them moved again.

I dropped to my knees. Blood spilled from wounds in my side. I'd been shot there, too, and hadn't even realized it. I peered across the street. Billes had disappeared. I searched for Cardan, but no sign of him either.

Cold swept over me. My head felt heavy. I just wanted to lay down in the street, but I still had to get rid of the weapons. Coughing and spitting out blood, I struggled to my feet, limped over to the crates of guns already removed from the truck.

"Look at that thing," someone gasped.

"What is it?" someone else asked.

I swung around. People, perhaps stupidly drawn to this block by the crack of gunfire, crouched behind parked cars, pointing at me. Some had their phones out filming. I had to get away before my powers faded.

Though pain radiated though my body, I gripped the gun crates one at a time and hefted them into the truck as easy as lifting empty cardboard boxes.

When finished, I flexed all four arms. Muscles bulged from my forearms to biceps. They tingled as if energized with superhuman strength. Could I do the impossible? Lift a truck? I had to try.

Sliding my hands and talons underneath the bed of the truck, I lifted with whatever unnatural strength flowed through me. My limbs screamed in protest, but the tires rose from the pavement. I was doing it! I screamed out, hoisting the cargo section away from the cabin. My body shook, shoulders popped, but I pushed the trailer over my head.

Spreading my wings, I took to the air.

More gasps came from hidden onlookers.

"I don't believe it," someone uttered.

My muscles quickly weakened against the truck's weight. Tendons snapped. Arms burned. Wings flapped wildly, straining to stay airborne. I grunted uncontrollably with each labored breath.

I had to get the guns away from Ghost's men, but I couldn't hold the trailer much longer.

There! Several blocks away stood a five-story building marked NYPD 68th Precinct. Yes! The police could figure out what to do with the guns. Let them question Billes about how these weapons got into Brooklyn.

"That will do. I just—"

My wings shrank, slithering under my skin. I lost altitude. "Oh my God! I'm not going to make it." Desperately flapping what was left of my feathered appendages, I flew as fast as I could, but my strength also failed me. "Come on, just a little farther! Hang on!"

My arms trembled from the strain. Grunting, I lifted with every last bit of strength, but I couldn't keep the massive truck airborne for long. Something in my right shoulder snapped. Like bone crunching into fragments. A shockwave of pain tore through me. Gasping, I peered at the streets. Homes underneath. "Can't let go yet! God… help… me!"

I slowly dropped from the sky, thrashing my wings to gain altitude. Sweat nearly blinded me. My lungs burned from exhaustion. Chest heaved. Each heartbeat brought stinging waves of agony.

"Hold on!" Below, houses slid from view. I reached the precinct. My muscles failed. The truck slipped from my grip.

With a thunderous crash, the rig crushed squad cars in the parking lot. Twisted metal, guns and ammunition spewed right up to the building's front door.

As police ran outside, weapons drawn, I struggled to stay aloft long enough to get away.

I aimed for a schoolyard up ahead. No one would be there at night. My head spun. The sky seemed to flip upside down.

My body plummeted. The ground rushed at me. I'd splatter into a bloody mess. I was going to die. *No! Fight! Survive! I have to—*

Darkness overtook me.

Chapter 19

What have I done?

A fog blocked my view of anything beyond a few feet in any direction. Four raven-black wings rose from my back. Feathers covered my four arms. My wounds bled. Dark pools of crimson liquid surrounded the ground beneath me.

Voices pierced the gray vacuum.

"Hide your eyes from the beast!"

"Kill the freak!"

The crack of gunfire sounded in the distance.

"I'm not a freak," I shouted. "Don't call me that."

I slashed blindly with each talon, ripping and tearing at whatever stood beyond this barrier of gloom. I didn't stop until a breeze lifted away the murky haze. I stood on the street where I had faced the thugs unloading the guns shipment. Only now, those same men lay at my feet, their faces and necks slashed apart. Blood oozed from my talons.

"No! I couldn't have," I screamed. "I couldn't—"

"Ilan, wake up, son. Ilan."

The bodies vanished. The fog returned, closing around me.

The voice spoke again. "Ilan, you're safe. Come on, my boy, open your eyes. You are no longer in danger."

The haze began to fade. I blinked. Coughed. Sniffed stale air. A train whistled overhead. The ground shook. Just like in Cardan's lair. What?

My eyes shot open. I lay on the cot in his lab underneath the city. It had been a dream. A terrible dream. I didn't kill anyone. I couldn't. I'm not a killer.

Memories flashed through my mind. The transformation, facing those men who shot at me, swooping down and knocking them off their feet, lifting the truck and flying it to the police precinct, then falling. I remembered it all up until the moment I blacked out. How did I survive the fall?

Why the nightmare about killing? I didn't kill anyone. I couldn't have.

Cardan leaned over me with a syringe in his hand. "Easy, Ilan, you're all right now."

"What happened to me?" I tried to rise, but he placed a hand on my chest.

"We're back in my laboratory." He placed the syringe into a tube attached to a needle in my wrist. "I wish I had a more comfortable bed, but this cot will have to do."

"What are you doing to me?" My eyes followed the tube up to a bag like something sick people have hanging over them in a hospital. A clear liquid flowed from the device.

"This is just an IV line with some nutrients to help you regain your strength." He checked the tube. "You were shot, my son, several times, but your body has already healed itself. As soon as you transformed back to your human form, the wounds sealed themselves almost as if they had never been there at all."

He gripped my hand. "Son, what you did was nothing short of miraculous. You have made me so proud."

His attempt to comfort me just made me edgy.

"I want to get up." I tried moving again, but he forced me down with both hands.

"You need to rest. You have sent a message to this city, just as I hoped you would. Now you deserve to rest. There will be more to do soon. This city needs to see its hero again, and we shall not disappoint... but when you're ready."

"No more of—" I stared at him closely and what I saw shut me up. A square bandage covered his right cheek and three blood stains leaked through. "What is that? What happened to you?"

Cardan touched the bandage. "You did this, but do not let it trouble you."

"What do you mean? How could I have hurt you? The last thing I remember was falling from the sky." I searched my memories. Nothing. Not one single hint of a moment when I cut him. I didn't do it, did I? Could I have lost control like I did as the wolf?

He lit a cigarette. "I saw you land. Thankfully, your wings slowed your fall. When you hit the ground, I ran to your side. You were unconscious, but then you awoke and went wild, maybe with rage from being shot. It was like the animal in you took over. I tried to calm you down, but you slashed at me and did this." He pointed to his bloodied cheek. "Then you flew off."

"What are you saying? I don't remember any of this." He was lying again. But how could it be a lie? Look at his face. What else happened? What else couldn't I remember? Oh no, the nightmare! The bloodshed!

"Ilan, you must listen carefully now. What you did to those men who worked for Ghost was not a bad thing."

I shook my head. "What are you talking about?"

"In your anger, you flew back to Ghost's building, found those men who hurt you and you killed them."

"No! It's not true. It was a dream—a nightmare. I didn't kill anyone." I turned away from him.

Cardan tried to touch my face, but I pushed his hand away.

"The city is a better place for what you did." He grasped my shoulder.

"I don't believe you." I couldn't hold back tears. They streamed down my cheeks onto my pillow.

"It is the truth." He placed a laptop on the cot near my face. "This was on the local news tonight. The video is all over the Internet. The world has seen you now."

He pressed play and a newscast filled the screen.

"This was the scene by a waterfront warehouse, according to images provided to us by witnesses at the scene," a newscaster reported. "We must warn you the images may be disturbing to some. Based on unconfirmed reports from police sources and eyewitnesses an illegal shipment of guns was delivered downtown this evening but the guns were confiscated by what amounts to the latest reports of individuals with extraordinary powers making themselves known throughout the city. This one, dressed like a bird with the ability to fly, stopped the shipment. That individual then, with apparent super strength, lifted the truck carrying the weapons and dropped it at a police facility. The story, however, took a much more violent turn. That flying vigilante, as some are calling him, returned to the scene and then apparently killed the men allegedly connected to the gun shipment. We remind you the images you are about to see may be disturbing. We will not show all of the footage provided by witnesses."

As the newscaster stopped speaking, a grainy shaky image appeared on the screen. A grotesque bird creature flew in from the right edge of the picture, dodging gunfire. The screeching beast attacked the gunmen. The newscast cut away from the picture.

The newscaster spoke. "The police are officially refusing to comment on this—"

Cardan stopped the video and closed the laptop.

"Oh my God, what have I done?" My stomach tightened. "I'm going to be sick."

I bent over the cot and spewed. Nothing came out but yellow slime, some of which clung to my mouth. I wiped it away and lay down again, gasping for air.

"You did what you had to do," he offered.

"No." I'd become a killer. An out-of-control monster. How did I let that happen? This is what my dad and Doc Torren warned me about. I didn't listen. Why didn't I listen?

"Do not despair, son." He sat in a chair beside the cot. "Rejoice in this step you've taken. You know what you can do. What you're capable of. Unleash your power, as you did against those thugs, and you can save the world from the evil that corrupts it."

I slammed my fists against the cot. "But I didn't want to kill anyone. How could I do that? How could I not remember? How could you let me? This has to stop. You have to let me stop before I hurt anyone else."

Cardan hugged me tightly. "This cannot stop. You have only just begun your journey. Their deaths are on Ghost's hands—on Lieutenant Billes' hands—on the hands of everyone who would do evil. For some reason, when you transform, the longer you are in that other form, the less control you have of yourself. I promise you we can learn to control this."

"I'm tired of the promises." I shoved him, ripped the needle from my arm and sprung from the cot. I had to get away from this labyrinth. Away from him. This city. I would never use my powers again.

Cardan grabbed me from behind. "I will keep my promises to you, Ilan. Together, and only together, can we fully understand your amazing ability and tap into your full potential."

"Don't you understand, I don't want this power." I wrestled to break free, but his grip tightened. I thrashed about like a wild animal, kicking my legs, trying to stomp on his feet. I still couldn't break free. Winded, my head and limbs slumped. Cardan lowered me to the cot. "I'm a monster because of you. Everyone out there now thinks I'm a killer because of you. I am a killer. I just want to be a normal kid."

He sat beside me. "You were never meant to be normal. The sooner you accept that and embrace all you can be, the sooner your new life can begin."

I rolled onto my side and peered over the edge. On the floor lay tattered clothing stained in dried blood.

Was that the shirt I had worn during the transformation?

I closed my eyes. "What if I don't want a new life, Cardan? What if I just want the life I had with my dad? At school? With my friends?" For the first time in a while, my thoughts turned to Lucas. My best friend. I missed him. And Maria, too. Would I ever see them again?

"The life you knew was an illusion, Ilan. It was never real."

"Yeah, well it felt real."

Cardan sighed and slid a sheet over my shoulders. "Rest now. Later you will come to see the reality I offer you is so much better than anything you have known. When you awake, it will be time for the city to see its hero once again."

"No… I… can't." Still groggy, my eyes dimmed.

"You can and you will." Anger laced his voice. "If not for yourself, if not for me, then for the safety of anyone you care about."

"What… do… you mean…by that?"

"Do you think that imposter father is the only one I know about?" His eyes grew wide. "I am very well aware of a boy you call a friend. His name is Lucas. And a counselor who knows of your gift. Ramirez is her name. There's a girl. I believe her name is Maria. She's such a sweet little thing. I could make them suffer, too. It would be so easy."

"No… please."

Through hazy eyes, I watched him light a cigarette. "Then sleep now, and when you awake, you will do everything I tell you to do. I only hope you can open your mind to the truth, so we can be family and all of this can be so much easier."

"Yes… father." Those were my last words before sleep came.

Chapter 20

A Hero's Hunger

I awoke from a fitful sleep without any way of telling how long I'd been unconscious. Sweat dampened my pillow; strands of hair plastered my face. I wore only white underwear, and my skin seemed glued to the cot. The IV, which I tore from my wrist, was gone.

Images of the dead haunted me, but I forced myself up. My limbs ached.

With my feet resting on the floor, I searched for Cardan. No sign of him. Could he have left me alone? Most likely not. He had to be close… watching me.

I shivered.

I scanned the dimly lit lab one more time. Still no sign of Cardan. My heart raced. Maybe he had left me alone. An idea formed. Use his computers. Try to get a message out to Lucas. Warn him of the danger.

Rising from the cot, I stumbled to the table where Cardan had his row of computers. Once at a keyboard, I glanced over my shoulders. My body trembled. Heart beat like a sledgehammer. I held my breath. Still alone? Yes! I clicked the mouse next to the keyboard. The screen glowed bright, revealing the Explorer icon. He had the Internet!

If I could access an email account, I could send a quick message to Lucas.

"Ilan!" Cardan appeared from nowhere, swinging a baseball bat at the computer. I fell to the ground as he smashed the desktop over and over, shattering the monitor. With one more swing, he knocked the computer and monitor off the table. They crashed against the concrete, wires hanging uselessly from the dented hard drive.

He breathed heavily, bat still held high over his head. His eyes bulged.

I didn't dare move or speak.

He sighed then lowered the bat, letting it fall to the ground. Without speaking a word, he removed a cigarette from his lab coat and, with shaky hands, lit it. After one puff, he focused on me. His lips parted in an eerie grin, and he winked at me.

"All right then, happy to see you up and about." He spoke calmly and lowered a hand to me.

I swallowed a bit of saliva then grasped it and climbed to my feet. I still didn't speak; just watched as he stepped over the wrecked computer and walked to a far corner of his lab.

"I suggest you take a shower to refresh yourself. We still have much to accomplish together."

Dad or not, he was freaking insane. How long until he lost it completely and killed me? I had to find a way to message Lucas, no matter the risk.

For now, I did as he said—made my way to the shower. A towel had been placed on a table nearby along with clean clothes. Stepping into the shower, I turned the faucet. The pipes rumbled. Cool water trickled over my head. The constant drip and occasional spurt that burped from the pipes comforted me, almost like washing unseen blood from my skin.

I lingered in the shower a little longer, then turned off the faucet, grabbed the towel and wrapped it around my body. Once dry, I dressed in the clean clothes Cardan left.

"Good shower I trust." Cardan stood at my side. All signs of his earlier rage had vanished. "I figured a shower would be in order after you slept so long, but you needed it. I did not want to disturb you."

"How long was I out?" I studied him for traces of his madness. A stubbly uneven beard spread over his thin cheeks. His hair stood almost straight up as if it hadn't been washed for days. He might have stunk but the only odor I could detect was smoke.

"You slept nearly twenty-four hours." He wrapped an arm around my shoulder and ushered me over to a makeshift kitchen. He had me sit at the table. "You look well. While you slept, I examined you and saw your body had completely healed itself, at least on the surface. That is an amazing effect of the transformation—your body's ability to recover."

I glanced toward the smashed computer, but the shattered pieces were gone, the concrete floor swept clean.

"Ilan, are you all right?" he asked.

"I'm not sure." I didn't know what he wanted me to say, so I answered honestly. "I feel numb inside."

"Those men you killed wanted to kill you. They shot you. They hurt you. They would have killed you if you didn't react." He sat beside me. "You must understand that. You may not have been yourself, but the creature you became knew enough to protect itself, and it knew only to harm those who would do evil. You did not hurt any bystanders. You are a good boy, and you carry that with you through the transformation."

"I guess."

Reaching into a pocket of his lab coat, he retrieved another syringe filled with blue liquid.

I leaped up from the table. "What's that?"

He smiled. "Don't be afraid. From my studies, I have prepared an enzyme that I think will act as a counteragent during your transformation. It will not stop the transformation food causes, but it will help prevent at least some of the pain you experience. I administered one dose while you slept, but I need to give you a second dose."

"I don't think so." I retreated a few steps.

He stood. "Ilan, there's something else. Unfortunately, I cannot be certain until you go through the change, but after studying your cell structure, I think this enzyme might enable you to maintain greater control through the transformation. In essence, you will remain you with all your thoughts, senses and beliefs. Will you allow me to administer it, and then test my theory?"

I wanted to say no and run away, but I nodded. If he was going to make me morph again, better that I maintain some kind of control.

"Don't worry, you won't feel a thing. The dosage is low—just a test." He placed the syringe to my right upper arm, just beneath the shoulder. "We will need to wait about a half hour to see what effects this enzyme has, enough time for us to make our way to the next test of your abilities."

He inserted the needle into my arm and the blue liquid slowly disappeared. He didn't speak until the syringe emptied into my vein. As the enzyme flowed through me, my limbs tingled like the time I suffered a quick jolt from an exposed Christmas light wire. The sensation quickly vanished.

"Another test?" I lowered my head and rubbed my neck so hard I could have ripped through the skin.

"Why, yes, my boy, the city still needs its hero."

"Dammit! Not again!" I ran across the labyrinth until I slammed into the wall where the door had appeared. I pounded against the concrete surface, but nothing budged.

"Ilan, the world needs you." Cardan sprinted toward me.

"No it doe—"

Warmth washed over me from my chest to my arms and legs. The sensation felt almost soothing.

I stopped pounding the wall and took deep easy breaths, my chest rising and falling rhythmically. My head felt light and clear, like a weight had been lifted from my forehead. My fears faded. What was there to be scared of? Nothing. With my powers, no one could hurt me.

I wanted to transform.

"I don't understand it, but I feel really good, you know, like hanging at the carnival on Coney Island good. What did you do to me? What was in that blue juice?"

Cardan folded his arms. "The enzyme is having an effect sooner than I anticipated."

My stomach grumbled and my mouth watered. "I'm so hungry all of a sudden, like I haven't eaten anything for days. Come on, what do you have for me? I want to scarf something down. Maybe a donut or a hot fudge sundae—I don't even care."

"You know it will bring about a transformation." Cardan tilted his head and raised an eyebrow.

I grabbed him by the lab coat. "Sure. Bring it on. I want to transform. Let's go after some bad guys."

Drool dribbled from my mouth.

***

Thirty minutes later, Cardan and I climbed from the abandoned lower tunnels to the Liberty Avenue subway terminal. We entered a train and zipped along toward some unknown destination. I didn't care where we headed. He sat quietly while I paced up and down the car, dodging the feet of people who sat on either side. My face felt flushed and my limbs tingled.

Cardan, now in his trench coat, had stuffed his pockets with junk food. A bag of Doritos filled one pocket, a Hershey's bar another, a Hostess cupcake a third pocket. The mix of sweet and salty scents tickled my nostrils. Like some ravenous beast, I wanted to devour all of it. Why was I like this? That enzyme he had injected into me—what was it doing to me?

I tripped over one passenger and almost fell into the lap of another.

"Ilan, sit down," Cardan scolded me.

Like a dog swatted on the butt, I sat at his side, but my eyes dodged back and forth to his pockets and the train exit. "How much longer? I'm so hungry. You don't understand. I can't wait. Really. I can't."

"Just a little longer, son." He placed his forefinger to his lips to quiet me.

I sat against the plastic chair and repeatedly bumped my head against the window. My feet tapped on the floor, legs danced. Eyes closed, I listened to the rhythmic clicking of the subway train racing over its tracks. The car swayed back and forth as its engine roared through the tunnel.

The subway train slowed. I peered out the window as the tunnel's walls gave way to a terminal. When we stopped, Cardan left his seat and I followed. The sign on the wall read 149th Street. The Bronx.

"Come with me," Cardan ordered.

"Can I eat something now, please?" I tugged at his coat. "Come on, just a little something."

"Soon." He led me up the stairs to the city street. Sunset had fallen, and a purple haze settled over the storefronts lining the block. Of all the New York burrows, I spent the least amount of time in the Bronx. The neighborhoods had a grittier feel than my own Jackson Heights, and I guess, in the past, that made me scared of the area—you know, fear of the unknown.

Right now, though, I feared nothing. As long as I had some food and could transform, bring on the crime.

Traffic roared by on this busy storefront street. A helicopter flew overhead. A siren wailed in the distance.

"Okay, so what are we doing here?" I trailed after Cardan. "I know you want me to transform, but to stop what?"

"I appreciate your enthusiasm. You are going to need it for tonight's challenge."

"I'm ready for anything. Just feed me."

"Soon."

We walked several blocks, crossing streets and rounding corners. The city grew darker as the soft colors of dusk gave way to the shadows of night. We passed from rows of neon-lighted businesses to the quieter residential neighborhoods where street lamps cast a soft orange glow across sidewalks in front of homes and apartments.

Cardan stopped in one particularly quiet neighborhood with rows of brick, two-story houses bathed in darkness. Shutters and curtains over windows hid any sign of light inside the homes. Only a few had porch lights. A thick murkiness, the kind which rests heavy on the shoulders, spread through this area.

"What do you see?" Cardan asked.

"Not much," I answered, a little frustrated.

"And why do you think that is?"

"How should I know?"

"The answer is simple." He strolled around me, an unlit cigarette between his fingers. "The people who call this part of the city home live in fear."

"From what?"

"Not from what—from whom. Two streets gangs are at war for control of this neighborhood, the 140th Rhinos and the Midtown Warriors. Their actions have led to far too many deaths, not only of those who claim to be associated with the gangs, but also the innocent people who just want to live in peace."

"Man, for an English dude not even from here, you sure seem to know a lot about this city. How long did you say you've been in NYC?"

He rubbed his head. "Much too long for my taste, but that is far from the point. I do not bury my head in the sand and pretend violence doesn't ravage the world around us. It does, Ilan, and that's why you're here. You can't hide from it anymore. You must confront it."

"Okay… okay, but what am I supposed to do about two flipping gangs? Even with powers I can't stop a gang war."

"Can't you?" He grabbed my T-shirt. "I believe you can. Not all at once, but in steps, and the first comes tonight."

The enzyme must have still been working because I nodded. "Fine, I'm ready. Just food me, man."

He released my shirt and evened out the wrinkles. "Wait, there is more you must know. Tonight, members of the two gangs will clash over the recent killing of one gang member."

"How do you know?"

He flashed me a look of annoyance and let the question slip away. He just knew, just like he seemed to know every corner of NYC—every neighborhood, every alley—and the city's ugly underworld of crime.

"There's something else, Ilan, These gangs are armed with weapons that came from Ghost. The crime boss is arming these gangs and using them as foot soldiers for moving drugs."

"I get it. Tell me where this *clash* will happen."

"Not far from here is a park surrounded on every side by homes." He pointed down the block where the homes gave way to a line of apartments. "If you follow the streets around those apartments, you'll come to the park. It's controlled by the Rhinos. They're there every night. Tonight, the Warriors will attempt a drive-by in the park against the Rhinos. Both gangs are heavily armed."

"But, how—"

"I've been monitoring police scanners. Police have an idea what's supposed to go down tonight. They've tried to keep gang members off the streets all day, and undercover units are nearby, but blood will be shed tonight, unless—"

"Unless I stop it."

"Yes."

"Look, man, I've heard enough. Like I said before, I'm ready and starving." I stepped closer to Cardan, my body swaying from side to side. "I need to eat. I can't wait any longer."

Smiling, he retrieved the bag of Doritos from one of his pockets. Before he could hand it to me, I snatched it from him.

Ripping the bag to pieces, I poured the cheesy tortilla chips down my throat, barely tasting them.

Dropping the empty bag to the pavement, I reached out to Cardan with both hands. "More."

He handed me the cupcake next, which I devoured just as quickly.

When finished, I stood quietly, my chest heaving like a sprinter who had just finished a race. I waited for the pain. I wanted the change, needed it. I listened for the rumbling that would rise from my belly, the first sign of a transformation. Silence greeted me. I placed my hands against my stomach. Not one bubble danced in my gut.

I peered at Cardan. "I don't under—"

A wave of warming energy coursed from my insides and enveloped me in a white glow. The change felt… comforting. No stabbing pain in my gut, no cracking bones or tearing skin. Had Cardan's magical enzyme caused this painless morph? Had he truly found a way to help me?

A blinding flash exploded around me. I dropped to one knee and shielded my eyes.

Blinking away a sea of colors, I stood and glanced at myself—only I couldn't see me. *What the heck?* I'd vanished. I could still feel my limbs, my body, but I had become invisible, except for my clothes. They hadn't disappeared, just my flesh.

"Ilan?" Cardan reached out toward me.

I didn't answer at first. *I'm the invisible teen.*

"My son, are you all right?"

"Yeah, better than all right." Though I couldn't see my legs, they felt stronger, like superhuman strong, as if I could leap high into the night sky, maybe even jump over a high-rise.

Cardan frowned at me. Was he worried? Good. Let him worry. I wanted to make him worry some more. I tore off my clothes—everything, even the shoes, socks and underwear.

I stood before him naked, cloaked in invisibility.

"This is great, man." I danced around him, poking at his back and stomach. "Where am I, *Dad*? Can't see me, can you?"

"Ilan, stop." Annoyance filled his voice.

"Why, *Pop*, isn't this what you want?"

"Ilan, there is work that must be done." His annoyance turned to anger.

I stopped circling him. "This is the best I've felt in a while."

"You feel this way because of the enzyme. Its effect is stronger than I expected. It worked faster than my research indicated. Son, this is a step toward our ultimate goal—the ability to control your change. Look at how this change happened. You did not suffer, did you? In fact, you were excited about the change, weren't you?"

"Yes."

"And that was just a small dosage. Imagine what would be possible if we increased it." He reached out and found my shoulder. "Don't you see? This is a breakthrough."

"I do want to help, but—"

"But what?"

"I don't want to kill."

He sighed. "Just do what must be done."

I scanned the dark neighborhood. These people shouldn't have to live in fear. No one should, and if I could help, I should.

"All right, I'll play the hero one more time." I slipped away from Cardan.

He followed. "Will you return to me, son?"

"I don't have much choice, do I?"

I bolted toward the park.

Chapter 21

Under the Cloak of Invisibility

I stood on the southwest corner of the park, a block-long grassy area with a playground and kiosk in the center. A sign at one entrance read, *Welcome to 140th Street Park. Please Keep This Park Clean and Safe For All. Paid For By The City Parks Commission.*

Old homes boxed in the park on all four sides. Streetlamps bathed it in an orange glow. Some blinked on and off.

This would have been a perfectly nice place for kids and families in any community if not for the graffiti marking the playground and signs. Tennis shoes dangled from telephone lines at the four corners. Even I knew gangs marked their territory that way. A bullet casing lay on the pavement next to my foot.

Sadness draped this park like a shroud.

I scanned for signs of trouble, but the grounds seemed abandoned. Maybe Cardan goofed and sent me to the wrong place. I stepped from the sidewalk onto the grass but stopped.

Three gray cars, headlights off, snaked into the neighborhood and lined up along the curb at the north corner.

Tinting covered the windows, which made it impossible to see how many people filled the vehicles. Almost in unison, the doors of all three cars opened and, like clowns at a circus, a crazy number of rough-looking young men, eight from one car alone, climbed out to gather on the sidewalk.

They laughed loudly, pushing each other. Some held bottles. Others waved handguns. They marched into the park like they hadn't a care in the world.

Despite my invisibility, I crawled to a clump of bushes.

Still more of these gangsters piled from the cars. This new wave carried rifles, kind of like the ones in the crates at Ghost's warehouse.

My mouth dried and my face numbed. Maybe the enzyme started wearing off because my confidence slipped away. What was I doing here? Sure I was invisible, but what good was that going to do if a barrage of bullets flew at me?

I counted twenty-four in the group. They made their way, laughing and taking swigs from the bottles they held, to the kiosk where they assembled around benches. Most continued to drink and wrestle. A few armed with the rifles took positions around the kiosk. The guards, I guess.

From my hiding place, I searched the neighborhood for signs of anyone else. A child's tricycle in front of one house caught my attention. So did a soccer ball on the porch of a second home. A bike leaned against another house. Kids had to be inside these homes. This park should belong to them, not these drunken Rhinos, or were they Warriors. Did it matter? They all had to be stopped, but by me?

"Jerks," I whispered as my focus returned to the group at the kiosk. If they meant to have a gang war tonight, rounds could hit these homes, putting everyone in danger. How could I stop that from happening?

Where were the police? Were they carefully hidden, ready to strike at the right time? I hoped so.

"I have to get these puke faces out of the park before the other gang gets here," I told myself. "Stop this before it even starts. But that's not what Cardan wants me to do. He wants me to take them all out. That'll scare all the gangs in NYC. Send a message that someone is around who'll kick their butts."

Digging my fingers into the dirt, I ripped out blades of grass. What would a real hero do? Save lives, right? Even these punks deserve a chance to change. Forget Cardan. There had to be another way.

I stepped from the bushes. *Screw it. I should sneak up on them, knock their guns away and smash their faces.* No, that was stupid. The enzyme in me messed with my head. It would be like taking on one heavily armed small army.

"Besides, I'm nothing more than a ghost right now. What can a ghost do?"

I pondered that for a moment. "I can scare them. Make them think this park is haunted so they never come back. That won't work. If these are hardened gang members, they're going to be scared of some ghost? I don't think so."

As I tried to form a plan, another group of cars with headlights off, four in all, inched toward the park.

"Oh no, it's happening already." I ran toward the gang members at the kiosk but stumbled over a sprinkler.

Before I could pick myself up, the new cars gunned their engines and charged into the park, headlights suddenly switched on to blinding high beams. The cars skidded to a halt on the grass, doors flew open, and the rival gang members threw themselves on the ground, weapons targeting their enemy.

Wild bursts of gunfire shattered the quiet neighborhood. One fell. A second one cried out as a bullet caught him. Rounds struck the invading cars. The rat-a-tat-tat of bullets ripping through steel echoed through the park.

I had to stop this battlefield before the war spread to the nearby homes.

I dashed toward the kiosk. My heart beat triple time. Head swirled. Rounds zipped through the air. Windshields shattered. I ducked but charged forward like a soldier rushing an enemy. Only I didn't have a gun. This invisibility power had to be good for something. What? Create a force field between the gangs? Shoot a ray to make others invisible? I skidded to a halt a stone's throw away from the waring gangs.

Let's see what I can do. Raising my hands, I tensed my body as if to will something—anything—to happen.

A tremor raked through my limbs. Crippling pain exploded inside my torso. I crumbled onto the grass. Had a bullet struck me? Struggling from my back onto my hands and knees, I crawled like an inchworm away from the battle. Searing heat spread through me. I coughed through labored breaths. *Oh… my…. God!* What was happening? *Feel strange. Not like… I was shot.*

A yellow glow, faint at first, flowed from my chest. The soft light intensified and expanded. My transparent body pulsated with a burning radiance.

I'm… changing… again! How? I slowly stood. My skin—like glass—revealed simmering energy inside of me like a ball of light.

The gunfire silenced.

"What the…?"

"Do you see that?"

"Is that a freaking ghost?"

The two gangs glared at me. Some pointed their fingers. Others aimed their weapons in my direction.

I had become a vaguely human glow stick. And I was visible! They were going to kill me!

A pulse of even brighter light blazed from my chest, spread to my arms and down to my trembling hands. A fiery red bloom circled inside my palms like a spiraling hurricane. I don't know why, but a primal urge compelled me to thrust my hands toward the combat zone. Scarlet rays fired from both palms.

The red energy smashed into their vehicles, flipping them over and over, glass and metal breaking apart. Two cars landed on their sides. Two others flipped upside down, tires in the air. Gang members shielding themselves behind the cars leaped out of the way. Three didn't.

I stared wide eyed at the damage I caused, my hands still aglow. What had I done? How did I do it?

No time to figure it out.

Guns cracked to life, shredding the dirt around me. *No… no… no! Run!* I spun away from the exploding rounds but stumbled to the ground. Dirt and grass sprayed around me. Rolling onto my side, another crimson beam launched from my palm. The glimmering laser struck a table, knocking it into gang members who crumbled onto the grass.

A helicopter thundered overhead, flashing a spotlight over the park. Squad cars, sirens blaring, poured into the neighborhood. Officers surrounded the park with guns drawn.

"Down on the ground, everyone!" one policeman ordered from a bullhorn.

I started to crawl away but stopped when the gangs turned their weapons on police. The war worsened.

Police officers huddled behind their squad cars, rifles and handguns exploding as they pressed their assault. The two gangs refused to give up the fight, though outnumbered. They would fight to the death and try to kill as many police officers as possible.

I pressed my feet hard into the grass to steady myself. I breathed deeply; listened to my rhythmic heartbeat. I squeezed my hands into fists, then opened them wide, palms aimed at the gangs. One more time, crimson beams crashed into them. They flew backward like ragged dolls, slamming back onto the grass. Some didn't move. Others tried to stand. I fired a third time, striking down the rest. Their moans and cries spilled into the night.

Had I killed anyone? I prayed not.

From above a chopper's spotlight ensnared me. The police stopped firing. Their attention quickly squared on the glowing mutant captured under the beam. Four officers with rifles slid from behind the squad cars, their weapons aimed at me.

"Down on your knees, hands up," one of them demanded.

I stepped back, but the spotlight followed my every move. I couldn't be caught. There'd be too many questions that I couldn't answer. They would lock me away like some kind of freak. Maybe turn me over to those black suits who invaded my home and locked me away in that military prison or whatever it was for Doc Torren to study me, like some lab experiment. I couldn't let that happen.

My mind spun and my head ached. How could I escape? I couldn't use my powers against the police. What kind of a hero would that make me? What was I supposed to do?

The officers marched toward me.

"I ordered you down on the ground," the same officer barked.

"I'm the good guy." I retreated a few steps, then turned and bolted for a group of trees sitting atop a grassy knoll.

Diving into the trees, I landed hard on the ground and rolled. Smashing myself up against one tree, I held my breath as the chopper swung its light toward me. Of course, they had no problem following me. I cast a yellow trail in the darkness. I had to conceal myself. I surveyed my surroundings. There! Something black lay in the grass just beyond the trees.

Darting from my hiding spot, I pounced on the object—a blanket caked in mud and home to dozens of crawly bugs. The cloth wreaked but that didn't matter. I swatted away the bugs and draped myself in it, dousing the light from my glowing body. Once cloaked, I dashed away from the park.

I had to find a place to hide until my powers vanished.

A shot rang out from somewhere and a round slammed into my glowing right shoulder. I dropped to my knees. Cried out. Blood oozed from the gaping hole. Stinging pain radiated from the wound. I panted, grasping my shoulder.

Why did I keep getting shot? This hero thing really sucked.

My eyelids grew heavy, my head drooped, but I lifted it just enough to spy one of the gang members in the street just outside the park with a handgun aimed at me.

I fell onto my back. Muffled voices sounded off the distance. What were they saying—something about calling for an ambulance.

An icy chill replaced the burning sting. I shivered, blinked and coughed.

Sleep—I just wanted to sleep. I blinked again and again. Had to stay awake. Couldn't be caught.

My sight dimmed. I forced my eyes open one more time. *Must get…*

A shadowy figure stepped over me. Cardan? No, this specter couldn't be much taller than me. Wrapped in a dark cloak, like mine, the eerie newcomer glanced at me before firing a beam into the park. The stranger then marched toward the gangsters.

My eyelids closed. Blackness surrounded me. I slid into unconsciousness, but not before one last thought filled my mind. The face beneath the cloak was my own.

Chapter 22

The Vigilante

The stench of thick smoker's breath hovered just above me. A familiar chill and the roar of a train passing overhead told me I was alive. And back in Cardan's lair. I fluttered my eyes, shaking off unconsciousness.

His voice cut through the haze. "Ilan, you've returned to me. You're all right." Dry fingertips stroked my hair. A shiver pulsed down my neck and spread to my limbs. My hands clenched into fists. I wanted to scream, *don't touch me!*

How did I return here? Memories flashed. A gang war. A neighborhood under siege. A change into a glowing star kid. A bullet wound in my shoulder. The stranger shrouded in a dark cloak. With my face.

No, I must have been hallucinating.

That enzyme he gave me. The change didn't hurt so much, but I became different. His lapdog. Ready to do his bidding. Even if it eased my transformations, I couldn't take it again. I wouldn't.

"Ilan, can you hear me?" Cardan asked.

"Yeah, I hear you." My eyes fully opened.

"Thank God." He wrapped his arms around me and squeezed.

"Enough! Let go of me." I pushed him away. He'd drugged me. I sat up in the cot, my feet rocking on the ground. I dropped my head into my hands. I had a pounding headache. My stomach gurgled as if I'd be sick. The last thing I wanted was a hug. My cheeks heated with rage. How could he do this to me?

Running his fingers through his uncombed hair, Cardan stepped away from me. His face was more gaunt than normal. Eyes droopy… marked by red lines.

Another train passed above, rattling this labyrinth. Dust fell around me.

I titled my head toward the small bandage that covered the area where the round entered. "So how bad am I hurt?" Just like the other times I'd been shot, there were no traces of pain.

"Look." He lifted the bandage.

If a bullet had ripped through me, you wouldn't know it from the wound. Only a tiny scratch remained.

"Your body, in its transformative state, has this miraculous ability to heal itself. It may be an effect of the genetic coding I provided you."

I paced the floor. There he went again. Genetic mumbo jumbo talk. I was sick of it. "I'm really tired of getting shot. I might have some magic healing power, but one of these days, it may not work. I don't want to die. I'm just thirteen."

Cardan nodded. "You're right. We will choose our moments more carefully until you are older and more prepared for such battles."

I gritted my teeth. Questions needed to be answered. Too much didn't add up. Dreams of killing Ghost's men by the waterfront. Even the news coverage said I killed. Yet, I blacked out, so how could I have harmed anyone? Now this mysterious being in the park with my face. Something wasn't right.

My lips puckered. I tugged at my hair. "In the park, I wasn't alone."

"I know. I was there." He lit a cigarette and leaned against a table. His eyebrows twitched. "I saw the gang members, the police. You bravely handled a deadly situation and saved countless lives among those officers and, dare I say, the people in that neighborhood. They all owe you a debt of gratitude."

"That's not what I'm talking about!" I gripped the table with both hands. "Cardan, after I was shot, someone who looked exactly like me passed over me. I swear it was my face staring down at me."

Cardan blew smoke from his mouth. "That's just not true."

I pounded the table. "I'm telling you I saw myself standing over me in that park."

He frowned. "Ilan, I was there when you were shot. There was no one else in the park like you—just the gang members and the police. Perhaps you were seeing things, which wouldn't be a surprise considering your condition."

"But—"

He stopped me. "There is more you must know. I never saw you fall to the ground. When you were shot, you went… berserk."

"What?"

"You ran at the gang member who shot at you and blasted him at close range, killing him instantly. You then ran back into the park and attacked the other gang members, killing four more, before police shot at you. At that point, you ran off into the night. I couldn't find you. I searched for hours and when I could not find you, I took a chance that maybe, just maybe, you found your way home. And that's exactly what you did, sort of. I found you unconscious in a subway car, your shoulder already mostly healed."

He placed a hand on my wounded shoulder. "Ilan, you must face the fact that you killed again, and while that was not my intended outcome, those deaths will create fear in the hearts of those who would do evil."

I grabbed him by the shoulders. "No, it's not true! I fell when I was shot. I didn't hallucinate seeing someone else there. Maybe that stranger did those terrible things. It wasn't me. You have to believe me."

Cardan spit out the cigarette. "There is no other like you in this world. You are special. You have an ability no one else will ever have."

I released him and slumped into the cot. Not again! This couldn't be happening! Was I losing my mind?

Tears slid down my cheeks. "I'm not a killer."

He knelt beside me. "You are because you have to be. This isn't some movie. This is real and in the real world there are bad people who have absolutely no moral compass. They kill for fun. They kill because they can. Don't you understand? Evil must be stopped. They must know what it is to fear. If there is one out there willing to strike at them, then they will no longer have free reign. I created you, Ilan, to be the hero this world needs, and that hero cannot be soft."

"I don't want to be this hero." I buried my head into the pillow.

Cardan turned me over and held a circular mirror in front of me. My eyes burned red. Hair hung loosely around my face. I looked away. He gripped my chin and held the mirror up to my face again.

"This is the face of a hero," he proclaimed. "Get to know this face. Accept that this face is unique and special. This is you, Ilan. There is no other."

Chapter 23

The Anti-Hero

I poured over each word of the newspaper article for the tenth time. I could recite some paragraphs by heart. It chronicled the rise of a strange group of heroes, or vigilantes, and their increasing violence—even murder.

There have been appearances all over the burrows. It started with an elastic hero who pulled a child to safety from an underground pipeline near Jackson Heights. Then a slime creature saved zookeepers trapped when deadly animals escaped their enclosures at Queens Zoo. According to witnesses, a half man-half wolf stopped armed robbers at Queens National Bank. In each of those cases, no one was killed, though the wolf critically injured at least one gunman. Three nights ago, however, a bird man, as described by some, killed a group of men with mob ties while stopping an illegal shipment of guns near the waterfront in Brooklyn.

The most recent deadly appearance was last night in a Bronx park. Five gang members, including a reputed leader, were killed by yet another mysterious individual, this one described as a vigilante made of pure light, according to unnamed police sources.

The headline read: *Vigilante Heroes Hailed, Feared Across Burrows.*

One police lieutenant was quoted as saying, *"If this group of vigilantes thinks they're helping, they're not. They need to let police do their job before innocent people are hurt and, believe me, the longer this violence continues, the greater the chance for good people to be caught in the crosshairs."*

Police sources also said each one of the vigilantes was now wanted for questioning. Anyone involved could face murder charges.

I lowered the paper and shook my head. Is this what Cardan wanted—for his hero to be wanted for murder? What good was that? How could I be a hero if I was wanted by police? The newspaper, just like police and every citizen out there, had no idea their group of vigilantes was just a kid named Tripp… or Ilan.

I flung the paper on the ground.

"Don't damage that." Cardan placed a glass filled with orange juice and a plate of eggs and toast on the table in front of me. He bent down to pick up the paper. "I'm keeping a file of all your media coverage. This story is the best yet."

"You're crazy," My mouth watered at the sight of the food and the orange juice. I swallowed saliva.

A train rushed by. The table shook and some of the orange juice jumped from the glass. It dripped from the table before I spoke again.

My body quivered with adrenaline. "You read the article. I'm wanted for murder. The police think I'm dangerous. This isn't the kind of hero I want to be. Not some killer."

My heart thudded loudly. I tore at my hair. If I killed, there was no going back. I couldn't fix it. I crossed some kind of line. This is what Doc Torren warned me about. Why my dad tried to stop me.

Cardan dusted off the paper. "Is that all you get from this article? Did you not read the positive comments from people on the street who feel safer because you're out there making a difference… doing what the police can't or won't."

He cleared his throat and read, *"Say what you want about these vigilantes, but they're real heroes. It's time someone takes these gang members off the streets and make them pay for what they've done in our neighborhood."*

Cardan peered at me. "Did you not read that comment? Or what about this one? *'I hope these heroes are here for good. They're exactly what this city needs. I hope the police leave them alone and focus on the real criminals.'*"

He carefully placed the newspaper on the table. "Don't you see, Ilan? You've already given this city hope."

My temples throbbed. I rubbed my forehead. My thoughts swirled inside my brain. I didn't ask for this. I didn't want to be a symbol. I wanted to be left alone. To get back to my life. But that wasn't possible. I'd killed—even if I had no memory of it.

I knocked the newspaper to the ground. "All I know is because of you I'm a killer, and I don't even have any memory of killing anyone. And now I'm going crazy and seeing things, like myself standing over me. I've had enough. Why can't you just let me stop? I don't want to hurt anyone else."

Cardan pulled a syringe from his lab coat. "This will make you feel better and prepare you for your next mission."

I pushed away from the table and abruptly stood, knocking over my chair. "More of that enzyme?"

He nodded and stepped closer. "Yes, a slightly stronger dose. It will bring back your confidence and help with your transformation. Once I've injected you, this meal you see before you will be yours to enjoy."

"No!" I shrunk away. He wanted to drug me. Turn me into a mindless drone to do his bidding. "No more. I don't want it. You can't make me. Just leave me alone."

"Ilan, please, calm down." He approached a second time. "You know this helps. You felt it before."

I searched for something to defend myself with. I grabbed the pillow from my cot and waved it at him wildly. "If you were really my dad, you'd let me stop. What kind of a nut are you?"

Cardan stepped back. "Son, you're tired and scared. This enzyme will help. I'm not trying to hurt you. I want to protect you. Believe me."

"I don't. I don't believe anything. I don't know what to think anymore." I charged, striking him over and over again with the pillow. I caught him with one good shot across the face. He fell over a chair.

I had to eat. And morph. Steal his phone before he hurt my dad. I lunged at the table before Cardan could climb to his feet and grabbed a handful of eggs with one hand… the toast with the other.

"Ilan, let me give you the enzyme first." Cardan, his eyes bulging, reached for me.

"So you can control me? No more." I placed my hands to my mouth and chomped on the eggs and toast at the same time. I chewed loudly and then swallowed, dropping the remaining food. "Isn't this what you want, *Dad*?"

"Oh, Ilan, this struggle is so needless." He pulled out a revolver, the one he held when he killed Doc Torren. He aimed the barrel at my chest.

"What are you doing?" My body tensed. I backed away, my hands held in front of me as if they could somehow deflect a bullet. They couldn't.

"I'm so sorry, my son, but in such an agitated state, I do not know what will happen during the change. Step back into the control room." He waved me toward the tiny glass chamber he had first placed me in when experimenting with my transformation. "This is as much for your safety as my own."

"I'm not going in there." My hands shook uncontrollably. Was it because of the change or the rage building deep in my gut?

"I must insist." He cocked the gun. With his other hand, he reached into his pant pocket and lifted the phone.

"Give me your cell," I demanded. Heat licked at my skin. My lips curled up in a sneer.

"Please, Ilan, step into the chamber before you do something you will regret later when you realize the error of your ways.

Before you force me to take action to kill the imposter you love so much." He waved the phone in front of me.

My stomach rumbled. Limbs burned as if fire coursed through my veins. Head throbbed. The change neared. In that moment, a new realization struck me. "Just give me the phone. You won't kill him because without him you can't control me. And you won't shoot me. I'm your prized possession, remember? You made me this way. I'm your answer to the world's problems."

Cardan extended his gun hand until the barrel was a foot away. His finger pressed slightly against the trigger. "You're very wrong, Ilan. I don't need you. There is another."

"What?" The rumbling in my stomach grew louder. My chest tightened as if someone twisted a vise around my body. My legs wobbled.

Before I could take another step, a spasm shot through my body. My limbs shook violently. I fell against the table, bracing myself against the quake rattling my insides. *Br… breathe…, Tripp. Y… you… can do… this. You… ha... have to… change. Only way… to escape.*

The spasms stopped. I took a deep breath and slowly lifted from the table. Reaching my full height, I scanned my body.

I hadn't morphed into anything.

That can't be—

An explosion tore through my gut, igniting a firecracker under my skin. Scalding bile rose from my stomach up my throat. I screamed. My torso and joints stiffened. My hands curled into fists and froze. My legs refused to move.

Cardan backed away, gun still aimed at me. "You see, Ilan, how you suffer needlessly? You must allow me to administer the enzyme. It's not too late. I can still help ease your pain. Let me inject you with the enzyme."

He dropped the phone into his lab coat pocket and lifted the syringe. Lunging at my arm, he tried to plunge the needle through my flesh, but on contact with my skin, it smashed into pieces. The blue enzyme dripped uselessly to the ground.

Stone spread to my torso, neck and face, encasing my skin like a mummy enclosed within a tomb. I could no longer move my mouth, blink my eyes or wiggle my nose. I couldn't rotate my hips or bend my knees. My neck wouldn't twist.

My heart pounded. Each beat clattered like two rocks striking each other. I twisted left and right but my body wouldn't budge. I grunted, but the sound never left my throat.

A prisoner in my own body, I hyperventilated though I had no sensation of air sliding from my lungs. How was I even breathing?

Cardan's eyes opened wide. He kept the gun pointed at me.

I could only imagine the monster I'd become.

"Oh, my son, you must see yourself." Cardan slipped over to another part of his lab and quickly returned with the small mirror. "You are magnificent."

He held it to my face.

I was a freaking statue. I shrieked in silence. My body vibrated under the stone exterior.

The image staring back at me reminded me of ancient Greek statues at the museum. Only smaller. I remained my normal size. Chiseled stone replaced skin. Blood still pumped through my veins. I could see even though my eyes were empty white orbs. Air flowed in and out of my lungs, but the stone cocooned me.

If possible I would have cried.

Cardan put away the mirror and placed the gun into his pocket. "I know you're scared right now, but don't be. You're still in control. You're still you. You just need to figure out how to use this transformation, just like you learned to use every other transformation. Use your mind. Think and you'll master whatever power this change provided you."

I tried to listen but couldn't quiet my thoughts. I screamed again. Cardan couldn't hear me. Deep under the stone, my muscles twitched. I envisioned myself pounding my hard exterior with a sledgehammer, each blow more violent than the next, but nothing happened. I couldn't break free.

Cardan placed his hands on my face. I couldn't feel his touch.

"Son, you can do this. Listen to my words. Use your mind. Concentrate on the little things like breathing. Hear your heart. Feel the oxygen move in and out of your lungs."

I concentrated on each limb, trying to imagine flesh and bone underneath the shell.

A train zipped by overhead. A tiny piece of concrete dislodged from the ceiling. It crashed against my shoulder with a loud thud and bounced onto the floor.

Crack!

What was that? Did that come from my stone shell?

I tensed my muscles. Nothing at first. No movement at all. *Try, Tripp!* I wiggled my shoulder. It rotated! *Yes!* I jerked my right elbow. My arm bent. I rotated my writs. They responded with a slight twist. Then I wiggled my fingers. Like a statue coming to life, I flexed my legs.

Each movement came with a crunch, as if my arms and legs might break off, but they didn't. I swiveled my hips. Bent my knees. I took one tiny step. Then another.

"Yes, Ilan, you are stronger than you think." Cardan held his hands high.

Struggling to keep my balance, I staggered, like the Frankenstein monster in old movies, to one of the concrete walls of Cardan's underground lair. With a fist, I smashed through solid rock, puncturing a hole in the wall.

"Magnificent." Cardan smiled and rubbed his chin. "This is not the way I planned for your next transition to occur, but I think we can forget the glass room. If you are quite ready, it is time to reveal yourself once again to the city. Let us prepare for—"

Slowly rotating back toward him, I smashed my foot into the ground. The concrete beneath me fractured. How else could I protest? How could I make him understand? I didn't want to be seen like this. I didn't want to go up to the streets and be chased by police or shot at by bad guys.

I didn't want to hurt anyone. This game had to end.

"Ilan, we have been over this now far too many times." He reached for the gun handle. "Now pull yourself together and let's—"

I slammed my other foot into the ground.

He raised the gun but did not point it at me. "Son, please. Listen to your father. I know what's best."

No! I was done listening to him. Done listening to everyone. I no longer knew my true name. My true self. Was I Tripp or Ilan? The hell with it. I no longer cared. I just knew I wasn't following this jerk anymore. Still wobbly, I stumbled forward, my hands extended toward him. A loud thud accompanied each step. I couldn't speak but had to make him understand.

"Ilan, listen to me." Cardan once again aimed the weapon at me.

I lumbered toward him. *No, you listen to me. I'm not your Ilan. I'm not even Tripp. Maybe I'm no one, but you don't get to tell me what to do anymore.* There was something freeing in that thought. Like I could have a new beginning. And be whatever I wanted.

"Ilan." He retreated until he bumped up against the door to the glass chamber. "Ilan, stop!"

I took one more step, got within an arm's length of him, and he fired the gun.

The blast echoed like a tiny explosion. My stomach turned to ice. I gasped in silence. *No!* As the round launched from the barrel, I couldn't duck or get out of the way. I couldn't even close my eyes. Couldn't flinch. The bullet struck me. A spark of light bounced off my chest, but I never felt it. The round ricocheted off my stony outer layer.

The bullet cried out as it streaked away from me and found another target—Cardan.

His head snapped back; knees caved. Cardan fell onto his back and dropped the gun. His phone slipped from a pocket onto the concrete.

Blood oozed from his scalp.

Oh, no! What did I do? Was he dead? I couldn't even bend down to check.

Cardan! I shouted silently. *Cardan!*

He didn't budge.

Next to his body was the phone. I tried reaching for it but failed. I couldn't lower my arms to it. *Come on!* I strained but my limbs wouldn't bend that far. How was this possible? The means to call for help was within my reach. *Damn it! Try again!* I stepped toward the phone but lost my balance. I took a second step to balance myself, but... crack... my stone foot landed on the phone. *No! You stupid dumb ass! What have you done?*

What was I supposed to do now? I should have listened to Doc Torren. Never used my powers. I should have let him lock me away for good. I was a monster. I wish... I wish I was never born. Then none of this would be happening. No one would have died because of me. I should just stay down here in the dark and rot away.

I stood there crying. I was tired. Empty. Broken inside. *Yes, I should just disappear down here forever.*

Then another thought cut through the despair. My dad—the man who raised me—was out there somewhere, probably dying. My tears quieted. A spark ignited deep inside my chest. Whether he was my dad or not, I couldn't let that happen. I had to do at least one right thing in my life. Save him. But how? I just busted my one chance to reach him.

Maybe Lucas and Mrs. Ramirez could help. I have to find them.

I twisted my body with great effort to scan the lab. I had to get out of here.

With clunky strides, I trudged toward the hidden doorway. By now, I memorized its barely visible outline in the wall. I had no key, but I could use my strength to break through. *Wait, I'm naked. What the hell are people going to think of a naked statue walking the street?* I stopped by a shelf filled with clothes. A gray hooded jacket lay on top of folded white T-shirts and gray sweatpants. I tugged my stone arms into the jacket and pulled the hood over my head. Cardan's trench coat hung from a nearby hanger. I grabbed it and wrapped it around my shoulders. It stunk of cigarette smoke, but it would hopefully be enough of a disguise.

I continued toward the door, each step coming a bit easier. Maybe the change had already started to pass or my body was becoming use to this form.

Once at the doorway, I slid my fingers over the crevice that marked the door's outline.

From behind me came the squeak of Cardan's shoes. I froze. A hot breath blew across my stone neck. A soft voice whispered my name. *"Ilan".* Cardan lived. My body numbed inside my shell. The chance for escape passed.

Unable to swing around, I awkwardly turned, expecting to see him, but he hadn't moved. I could still see his legs crumbled on the floor where he'd fallen. Was I losing it? Hearing things? Could there be someone else in here with me? Watching me? Cardan said there was another, but who? No one else snuck up behind me. The vision of a creature with my face standing over me in the park invaded my thoughts.

I couldn't worry about that now. *Just get away, Tripp.*

I returned my attention to the wall. With no key, I slammed my fist into the wall. The concrete started to chip away, small chunks at first, but soon larger sections. I jabbed as hard as I could until an entire slab of concrete crashed to the ground, revealing a steel door underneath.

Damn, one more barrier to my freedom.

I drove my fists into this reinforced blockade over and over until a gap formed. My pulse raced. I would have smiled with relief if I could have. My escape was close.

"Ilan." The whispery voice came from behind.

I slowly turned, but no one was there. Cardan still hadn't budged. Was his ghost already haunting me? *Leave me alone!* I took a deep breath and waited to hear the apparition speak my name again. Nothing. *Come on, Tripp. Don't lose it.*

Turning back to my work, I forced my fingers into the opening and yanked with all the strength this strange transformation gave me.

The door moaned in protest but with one last wrench, the grinding steel separated from the wall enough for me to squeeze through.

I peered into the darkened, cold tunnel deep underneath the city. The time had come for me to surface for good.

Chapter 24

Stone Man Rises

I wandered from the darkness of the lower tunnels where the homeless huddled together in rags. Poor souls forgotten by the city hiding in this dank, foul-smelling underworld. I truly belonged here with them, but not yet. Not until my dad was safe.

It didn't even matter if he was really my dad. He raised me, so I guess I owed my life to him, even if he was a jerk. Once he was out of harm's way, I'd return here. Best to live in the shadows away from everyone else.

I reached the upper levels and treaded as lightly as I could onto the terminal past the crowds waiting for the trains. I concealed myself in Cardan's trench coat, my head covered by a hood. His cigarette stench surrounded me as if he held me in an embrace. He might be dead, but somehow I feared he'd never be truly gone from my thoughts. I'd forever be his prisoner in my mind.

Despite my best efforts, each step I took landed with a clump on the concrete. People stared, but I kept my head bowed and hands in the coat pockets.

When a train screeched to a halt, I mixed in with the crowd and clamored inside.

With no room to sit and legs that wouldn't bend, I stood and held onto an overhead railing. A mistake. The trench coat slid down my arm, revealing my stone wrist.

"Mommy, look." A little girl, maybe five, with ponytails, sitting near me pointed at my hand.

The young woman sitting beside her wrapped her arms around the girl. "That's not polite, sweetie."

I lumbered deeper into the train. See, I was a freak. The girl and her mother knew it. I lowered my head, making sure the hood hid my face.

The doors swished shut. A woman's voice declared through speakers that the train was headed toward midtown Manhattan.

Good, I could get lost in the hustle and bustle of Times Square.

The train lurched forward, quickly picking up speed as it raced toward its next destinations. I lifted my head just enough to peer at my fellow passengers. The young woman with her daughter. An elderly man with a cane sat in front of me. Men and women dressed in business suits and skirts. Touristy types in jeans and T-shirts that read, *I love NY*, carrying bags from local stores. Maybe twenty or so of us crammed into this cabin.

Some glanced at me but quickly looked away. I lowered my head again.

Were any of these people trailing me? Even if I'd escaped Cardan, those government agents could still be searching for me. They probably thought I was the one who killed Doc Torren and those others inside their facility. Whatever flesh remained under my stone outer layer prickled. My heart pulsated faster with each breath.

Were they all staring at me? I glanced again at the others on the train. No. Unless they shifted their eyes away from me at just the right moment.

I didn't like this. A bead of sweat dripped off my brow, down my chiseled face. How was that possible? Were my powers fading? Somebody brushed past my coat. A young man with a goatee wearing a New York Knicks jacket. He carried a basketball and a duffle bag. A shiver raced up my spine. I trembled. The woman with the child glanced at me from the other end of the train, and then she reached for her phone. Why? *I need off the train! I'm definitely being watched!*

I pushed those thoughts away. Told myself no one paid attention to me. It was just in my mind. *Keep it together, dude.* I had to figure things out. Find a way to reach my dad before it was too late.

After several stops, with New Yorkers jumping on and off the train and doing their best to shuffle around me, a voice over the intercom announced, "Nearing Manhattan Terminal. Next stop, 34th Street Terminal."

Manhattan was as good as place as any to get off the train. I'd mix in well with some of the crazies who walked the streets above. No one would notice a stone man among the street performers who lined the sidewalks. I needed to let this strange transformation fade away, and then think about my next step—getting home. Plus, I couldn't stand another second on the train. The feeling of being watched made me want to tear a whole through the train and run away. My pulse raced. I breathed in short shallow bursts.

The train slowed.

Just breathe normal, Tripp. Okay, let's get off this—

A blinding flash of light flooded through the train's windows.

What the…!

A roaring boom violently rocked the cabin. An unseen force smashed against me with a whump, jolting my neck and hurtling me backward. I slammed hard against something.

What's happening?

Glass shattered. Shards bounced off my stone skin. People screamed. The train screeched like a wounded animal. Steel tore apart. I was tossed about like a raggedy doll. My brain rattled. Did I hear my chest crack? Others landed on top of me, burying me, their cries deafening.

Then came silence and blackness.

***

Pleas, muted like wadded tissues stuffed in my eardrums, jarred me back to consciousness.

Suffocating smoke and the stench of burnt gas engulfed me. *What's… happening? Where… am… I?*

My ears rang. My head pounded, and thoughts raced at a dizzying pace. I couldn't budge. *What…? Wait a second. On a subway train. Something bad happened. Did the train flip? Oh my God!* It did!

I silenced my thoughts and blocked out the constant whine blaring in my ears. New sounds—distant and garbled, as if I were under water—filtered through. Coughing and crying.

"Help… me!" someone begged.

Dim lights flickered. A red glow bled through the choking black smoke hovering through the cabin.

I lay flat, my arms wedged underneath me. I had to get up. I tried lifting myself. The movement caused something to slide from my back and land next to me. I rotated my neck just enough to stare beyond my hood at what had been on top of me.

A woman.

She lay crumbled beside me, her eyes open but vacant. Broken glass wedged deep into her neck. Blood pooled around her, creeping closer to me. Her mouth was agape in what must have been a final moment of pure terror before death took her.

I screamed in silence. Grunting deep inside my throat, I struggled to lift my heavy stone body.

A second body rolled off me. An elderly man. A steel rod pierced his chest. He landed next to the dead woman. His limbs bent and twisted like a marionette puppet. Their blood mixed together, coating the bottom of the train.

I staggered to my feet, legs wobbly despite my stone form.

My lungs burned. I wheezed out each breath, searching for fresh air, but the cabin filled with smoke and dust.

What the hell happened? Did another train hit us? Was there an explosion? Was it a terrorist attack?

I sensed movement around me. Others were still alive. Their grunts and cries, their pleas for help all blended together into a confusing racket.

A reddish flare tinged the black smoke.

"Fire!" someone shouted.

"God, help us!" another cried.

"Save my child!" the woman with the girl blurted.

Run away, Tripp. Don't get involved. You don't owe these people anything. Where was the door? The smoky haze hid the exit. I didn't know which way to turn.

Those around me huddled on their knees, leaning against seats turned sideways. The train had flipped on its side. The door was beneath us. A steel beam crashed through the door above us, blocking that exit. We were trapped. I gasped. My heart crashed inside my chest. Panels over our heads creaked and moaned. A window above us shattered, showering us with glass. Chunks of concrete dropped through the broken windows, striking some on the head. New screams echoed around me.

"The train's caving!" a man in a torn business suit shouted. Scratch marks covered his forehead. "Jesus, we must be buried under a ton of rubble. "We're not going to make it."

"Mommy," the little girl cried.

Someone pounded against steel inside our cabin.

"The door back here is jammed." The man was too far away to see his face. "It won't open."

I gritted my teeth. *Come on, Tripp! Do something!* We had been nearing the terminal, hadn't we? A way out of this had to be close. *You're freaking made of stone. That has to be good for something."*

The reddish glow brightened. Flames pierced through cracks in the windows above us. People cried, pounding their fists against the cabin. They crawled over broken glass, fleeing to the back of the train, pleading for anyone to help between coughing fits.

Whatever you're going to do, do it now!

Making sure my face was still hidden underneath the hood, I clambered over broken benches and twisted bars until I stood at the train's ceiling. *Now, Tripp!* Balling my stone hands into fists, I pummeled the steel over and over.

"What's he doing?" a woman asked through coughing fits.

"I… I don't… know," a man wheezed with each breath.

The ceiling began to bend and break. The stone coating over my hands chipped away. Each blow sent shockwaves of pain deep into my muscles, but I dare not stop.

One last blow busted a hole through the train.

"Look, he's doing it!" someone declared.

"But how?" another cried.

The side of the train over our heads moaned louder. How much longer until the cabin completely caved in?

I gripped the twisted steel, tearing it away, widening the hole.

"Please, hurry!" a woman pleaded.

More stone chipped off my arms and shoulders. Would my powers last long enough to save us?

They had to.

One more tug. At last! My heart leaped. I pried away enough of the ceiling for everyone to exit the car one at a time. No! My hopes for a quick exit were dashed. A steel beam and slabs of concrete blocked our way. My stomach clenched. Chest tightened. My stone head drooped against the beam.

The fire crackled. Flames danced around us.

"Damn it!" I turned back to the people behind me. All on their knees, trying to stay beneath the black smoke filling the train.

"Mommy, it burns," the little girl squealed.

"Just hang on, baby," her mother whispered as if barely able to talk.

I couldn't let them die. I had to plow through. And fast. The steel overhead creaked louder and louder.

I rammed my shoulder against the beam blocking our escape. Once. Twice. Three times. *Come… on…, Tripp. Do… this!* A fissure crisscrossed the stone over my chest. Each blow hurt more than the last, like my bones were crushing beneath my tough exterior.

Again, I struck the beam. This time it broke in half, falling away from the train. Chunks of concrete crumbled.

Our path cleared.

I motioned to the others to pass through the opening.

"Thank God for you." The young mother, her face bloodied, smiled at me as she led her daughter outside the train.

Others patted my back as they exited.

"Hey, this guy's still alive, but he's trapped," a man with a raspy voice shouted from one end of the cabin. Young and muscular, he wrestled to lift a beam crushing the legs of an elderly man who lay motionless.

I crossed to them. Jeez, how much time before the train crumpled under the weight of debris? The panels overhead cracked. We were almost out of time.

I pointed for the young man to get out of the train. He shook his head.

"I'll stay and help." He gasped for a breath. "He's breathing. Alive. Got to get this off him."

Nodding, I grabbed the beam and lifted. The stone shielding my legs splintered. My body shook, but I hoisted the steel just enough.

The young man, his arms wrapped around the elderly man, tugged him from under the beam. Once they were far enough away, I dropped the steel. Flames overhead licked at my head, my shoulders, my arms. Pinpricks of heat stabbed through the cracks in my stone. I cringed. Much longer and I'd roast.

Lifting the unconscious man, I staggered after the younger one through the exit.

Rumbling thundered overhead. The cabin collapsed. Debris flooded the compartment.

We were safe, even though I landed hard on the ground and dropped the old man. I gasped for one clean lungful of air but breathed in smoke and ash.

"We're still trapped!" the mother with a young daughter cried. "The way to the terminal is blocked."

I peered through the murky haze, lit only by the yellow flames rising from the wreckage behind me.

The train's engine car was a heap of bent and twisted steel. Two men—I guessed the conductors—lay dead, arms and legs ripped from their bodies. Had the engine blown up? Why? And what about the cabins behind ours. Were more people trapped? Piles of debris and the growing fire blocked my view of the rest of the tunnel. And ahead of us, a barrier of concrete slabs, rebar and more fallen beams blocked our way to the terminal.

Our passage was blocked on both sides. What was I supposed to do? Try to get these people to safety? Go deeper into the tunnel, looking for others who were trapped or hurt? What would happen if there was another explosion? These people here with me now would die. I had to free them first. Then go look for others. My stone head felt so heavy, like I couldn't hold it up anymore. So tired. Weak.

No, get up, Tripp! Be the hero these people need! But I didn't want to be a hero. Maybe, I didn't have a choice. Maybe Cardan was right.

Cardan! Had he done this? Was this another test? No, even that bastard wasn't this cruel. Or was he? That didn't matter now.

Move!

I slowly stood. The fact that I could bend my limbs was yet one more sign my powers were failing, but I needed them just a bit longer.

Lumbering to the barrier, I grabbed large chunks of concrete and shoved them out of the way. Others joined me, forming a line to haul away what they could lift.

This was taking too long.

The stench of gas hung heavy in the tunnel and from somewhere came the sizzle of a broken power line.

Gripping a fallen beam, I hefted it over my head and slammed into the barrier. Crunch. Large sections of concrete gave way. *Again, Tripp!* I drove the steel into the blockade once more. Then a third time. And a fourth.

My muscles screamed. Sweat poured off my stone forehead. My arms shook. Legs wobbled. I wasn't going to last much longer.

One… more… time!

I smashed through.

Light streamed through the hole. The terminal lay just ahead.

Firefighters and police officers on the other side stopped their own efforts to reach us and stared in disbelief.

"You did it!" a woman declared.

"You're a hero." One of the men patted me on the back.

I limped back to the unconscious man. Two others had already lifted him. I pointed for them to head toward the light.

"What about you?" one of them asked.

I shook my head. I couldn't leave the tunnels yet. I had to see if others had been hurt. I couldn't abandon them.

A group of firefighters and officers streamed through the hole I created. They placed their arms around those having a hard time walking.

One firefighter approached me.

"Are you okay?" He shined his flashlight on me, and then he stopped. "What the—?"

An explosion tore through the tunnel. An orange ball of fire raced toward the terminal. Those just crossing through the barrier would be hurt. Killed maybe. I shoved the firefighter toward the barrier. Grabbing a slab of fallen concrete nearly as large as the tunnel itself, I lifted it in front of the charging blaze.

With me on the wrong side.

Goodbye, Dad.

Flames slammed into me. Surrounded by agonizing heat, I screamed out, but none could hear my silenced voice. My stone skin blistered and popped.

God, help me!

The fire's cry was deafening, the white-hot center, blinding. Then the inferno whooshed back into the shaft. Pitch black surrounded me. Images of my dad, then Lucas, Maria, even Mrs. Ramirez, flashed through my mind. Cardan's face, sneering, eclipsed them all.

Then nothing.

Chapter 25

Seeking Home

"Is he alive?"

"I don't know. He's a damn statue."

"Everyone, just grab and lift."

Voices stirred me awake, but my vision was blurred. Hands grasped my body. Men grunted as they lifted, but I didn't budge.

"We need more help," someone called.

More hands. More grunts. My body slowly rose. I was being carried, but from where? What happened?

More voices filled the void.

"Have an oxygen mask ready?"

"Chief, the full blast of the fire got him. There's no way he could have survived. No one could."

"I've seen the impossible tonight. We're not going to give up on him. Oxygen mask, now! Have an ambulance ready. Make sure St. Vincent's is prepped for an unusual patient."

No! Not the hospital. *Get up. Get up!*

"What are his vitals?" someone asked.

"Any pupil movement?"

"You're kidding, right? He's made of stone or rock or something. He's got no pupils."

My vision cleared. I could make out a swirl of activity around me. In the distance, red lights flashed.

More clarity came. A dozen firefighters hovered over me. I lay on a stretcher beside an ambulance.

"Thank God for him," a woman uttered. "He saved us."

I had to get away. I couldn't go to a hospital. They'd contact the men in dark suits, or worse, Cardan might find me… if he still lived.

I shot up in the gurney. A blanket covering my naked stone body slid away from my chest. My clothes must have burned to ashes. The firefighters pushing me let go and retreated an arm's length away.

Climbing from the stretcher, I stood on the street, a nude statue, cracked and blackened by fire. I would have blushed if I could. The stone covering my legs fractured. I wouldn't remain stone for long. What would be left of my flesh? I could be burned beyond recognition, but I no longer felt pain. I coughed with each breath, but my lungs still worked.

The scene around me became eerily quiet.

Firefighters, police, ambulance crews, the media—everyone stopped to stare at me. Then something even stranger followed. The police and firefighters saluted me. I wish they didn't. I didn't deserve it. People had died. I had no way of knowing how many. How many had been trapped in the train cars behind mine?

A woman in a white fire helmet with the words *Battalion Chief* emblazoned on the side stood next to me.

She removed her helmet. "I don't know who or what you are, but you saved lives tonight. That makes you a hero. But you were in an explosion, and we have no way to tell if you're hurt or not. We just want to get you to the hospital to make sure you're all right."

I shook my head.

Run, stupid. I grabbed the blanket, wrapped it around me, and lumbered past the chief and everyone else. Reporters followed me.

When they wouldn't stop trailing me, I slammed my foot against the pavement. A fissure formed in the concrete sidewalk. The photographers and cameramen retreated, but they wouldn't stop for long.

I had to evade them.

My only option—find another hole to crawl into.

***

I awoke to someone pounding against a door.

My eyelids flittered open and the haze of sleep quickly lifted. I lay on a hard, cold floor. A rat itched itself just a few feet from my face. I snapped to my feet and backed into a sink. The pounding continued.

"Hey, let someone else have a chance," an old scratchy voice complained. "You don't own this bathroom."

I rubbed my eyes. "Oh, yeah, I hid from the reporters in a bus station bathroom. Smelly choice."

Sleep must have overtaken me, but for how long?

"And where did I find these crappy clothes?" I wore a grease-stained T-shirt two sizes too big and a pair of damp jeans torn at the knees and shredded at the bottom. I had no shoes or socks.

I turned toward a cracked mirror. My face, my human face, stared back at me. The stone transformation had faded and my skin returned to normal. No signs of burns. Incredible! How was that possible? The stone saved me. My powers finally did some good for others, but not everyone. Some died. My eyes reddened, and tears came. I lowered my head to the sink. *Get a grip, dude.*

The pounding at the door stopped. "Screw you," the man on the other side of the door declared. "I'll be back and you best not be in there."

I splashed cold water across my face. Images of the saluting firefighters flashed through my mind. The faces of those trapped on the train lingered. I splashed more water in my face then peered into the mirror again. Thin, pale face. Eyes rimmed by black circles. A young version of Cardan. I shuddered. Was I really his son? Was I Tripp, the name I grew up with, or Ilan?

A last splatter of water and I reached for the bathroom door. What would I find on the other side? What if Cardan was there? I paused before turning the handle. An ache rose from deep within my gut. I thought I might throw up, but nothing came. Taking a deep breath, I pushed open the door.

An old man with a long gray beard shoved me out of the way. "About time." He limped into the bathroom and locked the door.

An unusual calm filled the station. A handful of people sat or slept on wooden benches. On a far wall, a round clock revealed the time—three o'clock. With only a few drifters in shabby, torn clothing wandering in and out the doors, I assumed that meant three in the morning. This was good. I could move more freely under cover of the early morning quiet and find my way home.

I missed my house. My bedroom. My dad. If I was to find him, I could start there. Even if it was risky. A sign on the wall read, 31 West 43rd Street Station. That put me several blocks from the cave-in. From here, I'd have to hop on a couple of different busses, but I'd eventually get back to Queens. That would have to wait until morning. The busses didn't run this early in the morning. I'd have to figure how to sneak aboard without money.

I sat on a wooden bench, but the little hairs on the back of my neck stood at attention. That feeling of being watched swept over me.

I whirled around, but no one was there. Mostly, a few vagrants tried to stay warm for the night. But I still had that creepy feeling of unseen eyes on me. Unable to shake the feeling, I ran out of the station.

Stillness had settled over this part of the city. A smoky haze partly masked the starry night sky. Gray smoke billowed over the skyscrapers. Must be the remnants from the explosions.

I distanced myself from the station.

Walking along the sidewalk past store fronts, some with blinking neon signs, a sharp ache in my stomach stopped me. Weakness spread through my body. I braced myself against a brick wall. My guts rumbled, and I wrapped my arms around my torso. Was I about to change? No, that wasn't possible. I had no food in me. I was starving.

"What the hell am I supposed to do? Try to find some food? But If I eat, I turn into a monster." I rubbed my fingers over the valves in my belly. "If only there was a N.E.R.D machine at the local 7-Eleven. I could really use some of Doc Torren's concoction right now."

I sighed. "Sorry, Doc. Sorry I let all of this happen."

I willed myself to ignore the hollow feeling in my insides. Food would have to come later. So how would I get home? I buried my head in my hands.

Just then, a taxi pulled up to the curb alongside me. Its driver, an older man with graying hair and thick hands, peaked through the passenger window. He stared at me and tilted his head.

"Need a lift, kid." He waved for me to enter his cab.

"I… I don't have any money," I told him.

He scratched his head and peered at his watch. "I was going to take a break soon anyhow. Let's say I just take one now. I'll give you a ride on the house."

I stepped away from the cab. Why would a taxi driver offer me a ride for free? Was he a black suit in disguise? A friend of Cardan's? A crazy old man looking to kidnap a kid on the streets?

"No thanks." I walked away.

The cab inched forward. "Look, kid, just looking to help… that's all. You don't have to be scared."

I stopped. "Yeah, why help me?"

The cab's breaks squeaked. The old man kept his hands on the steering wheel. "You look like someone who needs help. Let me tell you, tonight some hero saved a bunch of people from that subway. I guess I'm feeling a little inspired to do something to help others myself. Figured I'd start with you. Look kid, you want a ride or not?"

My heart ground to a halt when he mentioned the subway. Did he know I was the one? No. How could he? Was he lying? I couldn't trust anyone, but I needed to get home. I had no ride. No phone. No money.

"Okay, I'll take that ride." I climbed in the back seat.

He eyed me through the rearview mirror. "Where to?"

"Jackson Heights in Queens."

The cabbie turned to face me, one eyebrow raised. "That's quite a trip. Is that home? What's a young one like you doing so far away? And so late at night?"

I stared through the window at the mist hanging over the city. "Don't want to talk about it."

"Suit yourself, kid." He swung a U-turn from the curb. We drove in silence until my stomach rumbled loud enough for anyone to hear within a few feet of me.

"Hungry?" With one hand, he opened the glove compartment and pulled out what looked like half a sub sandwich wrapped in tinfoil.

I reached for it, but quickly recoiled. What was I thinking? "Uh, no thank you. Can't eat right now."

"Well, it's here if you want it." He dropped it onto the front passenger seat.

Knowing it was there made my stomach hurt even more. My body trembled. He was just trying to be nice, but this was torture. I bit my lip and squeezed my hands until my knuckles turned white.

At times, I caught him staring at me, but he quickly looked away. He never asked me any other questions other than for my specific stop in Jackson Heights. I directed him to a street a block shy of my house.

Based on the clock on his dashboard, it took forty-five minutes to make our way to Queens. We arrived just before four in the morning. My neighborhood was just like I remembered with a row of nice two-story homes and clean sidewalks. Streetlights cast the cement and parked cars in a soft orange glow. How long had I been away?

"Please stop here," I directed.

He pulled to the curb. "Are you sure this is where you want to be?"

I shrugged. "No."

"Are you going to be all right?"

I shook my head. "I don't know."

"Do you have a mom and dad or someone I can hand you off to? I don't feel right just leaving you here alone."

"Thanks, but you've done enough." I started to exit the cab but stopped. "What happened on the subway. Do they know what caused it?"

He frowned. "I don't know. I heard over the radio, though, something about suspecting a broken gas line. No terrorism or anything like that. Not that it matters to those who lost loved ones, right?

"Do they know how many died?" I didn't want to ask the question, but I had to know how many I failed. "I mean, that person who helped people. He only saved people in one train car. What about the others?"

The taxi driver tilted his head. "How did you know that?"

"Uh, that's what I thought I heard."

He scratched his chin. "I don't know how many died, but reports from the news are that most got out alive."

I took a deep breath. "Thank, God."

The driver offered a slight grin. "You know, this city's been through so much. A lot of bad crap. It could really use a break. Maybe what we need our more of those freaky vigilantes popping up or the hero on the train tonight."

"Maybe." I left the cab and slammed the door. My head swooned. I wasn't sure whether to be sick of the word—*hero*—or just accept the destiny Cardan had chosen for me. Maybe I could help others—but on my terms. No one else's.

"Wait, kid." He pulled out a wad of cash from his pocket. "I don't know how much is there, but I want you to take it."

"I can't."

"Yes, you can." He winked and extended the cash to me. I reluctantly took it. "Good luck to you."

He drove away, and I stood alone again. Dirty, smelly, tired. Without a clue what I would find at home.

With soft steps, I walked toward my house. The leaves hung silently without a breeze to sway them. I paused at each hedge or parked car I passed, sure Cardan would be hiding behind one. I snuck by each house, careful to avoid the beams cascading from the streetlights.

Still, I couldn't shake the feeling someone followed me. I peered over my shoulder. Shadows of trees lurked on both sides of the street. Off to the right, a bush rattled. I lunged behind a car. A cat jumped out and slunk across the street. I released a lungful of air, gazing at its sly stroll.

Wait. Did I see a puff of white smoke behind shrubs? No. I sighed. I was just seeing things that aren't there.

Slithering from parked car to parked car, I safely reached my house. But it no longer felt like home. It seemed more like old ruins, cold and lifeless. Coming home at night from Lucas' in the past, the front porch light would beckon me inside. More comforting light welcomed me from the front window. Not now. Shrouded in darkness, a heavy gloom oozed from the windows. Sure, my dad wasn't the most loving man, but I felt safe growing up in this house. Now, a chill spread between my shoulder blades.

I stood frozen on the sidewalk.

"You have to see what's inside," I told myself.

After glancing one last timeread2242242242242242242242242242242242242242242242224 224224242242242242242242242242242242242242242242224 224224242242242242242242242242242242242242242242224

2252252252252252252252252252252252252252252225225
2252252252252252252252252252252252252252252225225
2252252252252252252252252252252252252252252225225
225225 at the sleeping neighborhood, I took my first step toward the front door. My bare feet touched the icy stone walkway.

I hesitated before grasping the doorknob. Placing my ear against the door, I listened for movement. Silence greeted me. I reached for the doorknob but recoiled. The door would probably be locked anyway, and I didn't have a key.

I tried it anyway.

The latch clicked; the door opened. Strange to find it unlocked. I should have run away. That was a bad sign. No, I couldn't run. Not yet. I had to find something inside that could lead me to my dad. Something that would help me uncover the truth about my past.

I gently cracked the door and peeked inside.

What the…?

Everything had vanished. I threw the door open all the way and blinked away tears. The chairs, the couches, the tables, the pictures—all of it had been stripped away, like we had never lived here.

I charged past the living room into the kitchen. The refrigerator, microwave, the oven—all gone. Even N.E.R.D., the feeding machine I hated so much.

I slammed a fist on the counter and bolted toward the stairs.

"Dad," I called even though I knew he wouldn't answer.

My words echoed off bare walls. I tried to switch on some of the recessed lighting in the ceiling, but nothing happened, like the power had been cut off.

I climbed the stairs to the darkened rooms on the second floor. Every room—empty—just like downstairs. Drapes and shudders removed from windows. I lingered in my dad's room. A black-marker drawing of me and him should have been on the wall next to the bed. I had drawn it when just a toddler. Now, someone had erased it.

I flew back down to the living room and crumbled to the plush beige carpet. I ran my fingers through it and cried some more. How long had I been away? I needed answers.

"I have to get to Lucas!"

***

"This is a mistake," I mumbled. "I'm putting him in danger just by being here."

I crouched in the bushes circling Lucas' two-story house. His bedroom window was just above me. I shouldn't be here, but I needed to see him—needed to see someone I trusted. I needed a reminder I was still Tripp, not Ilan.

That feeling of pins and needles pricked. I glanced at the street. No one. I picked up a handful of rocks and launched the first one at my friend's window. It bounced off the glass with a loud pang.

I flinched and cursed under my breath. Ducking, I waited to see if anyone stirred. I half expected his dad to storm through the front door. A rather large man, he scared the crap out of me, especially since he never seemed to like me much. He thought his son should spend more time with *normal* teens, I guess. He was probably right. Lucas could be popular if he wanted to. He even knew how to ride motorcycles, way cooler than anything I did.

Lucas had no stomach for popularity. Still, why he chose to be friends with me, a kid with lots of problems, I never knew.

No one threw open the front door. Lucas' window remained closed. I hurled another rock and like the first it clanged off the glass. This time the drapes swished apart and the window slid open.

Lucas' face peeked through. I shuddered. Was it him? Really him? I wanted to shout up to him, but my voice cracked. Tears slid down my cheeks. What a pathetic loser to cry like this, but I couldn't help it.

When he finally woke up enough and spotted me below, his eyes bulged.

"Dude," he nearly shouted.

I nodded, still unable to speak. My legs trembled, barely able to support my thin frame. I had found my way back to my best friend. Finally! For the first time in a long while I felt—safe. I slumped to my knees.

"Dude, I'm coming." He disappeared back inside his room.

I turned back to the street. Three houses down, a cloud of white smoke snaked out from behind a tree. I shook my head and rubbed my eyes. It couldn't be. In the murky layer before daybreak, my mind made me see something not really there. *You're safe. Cardan can't get you now.* I wasn't sure I really believed that.

The lock to the front door unlatched with a click. Lucas threw open the door and tackled me to the ground.

"Dude, is it really you?" He sat on top of my stomach.

"Yeah it's me." I pushed him off, finally able to utter words.

"What's going on, Tripp? There's been some crazy stuff going on at your house." He grabbed my hands and lifted me to my feet.

I didn't answer. I fought back more tears.

"What is it?" He placed a hand on my shoulder.

"You called me Tripp, dude. It's been a while since anyone used my name."

"What are you talking about?" He ran a hand through his hair.

"Let's talk inside," I suggested.

We snuck up to this room, and he closed the door behind us, careful not to make a sound. I peeked through his window at the street. Still quiet, but I quivered anyway.

Lucas sat at his desk. "Okay, man, tell. All I know is two weeks ago you stopped coming to school, then your dad disappeared, and I found your house empty. I mean it's like you never lived there. One day you're here. The next day—poof, you vanish. What's the deal?"

"Wait, so I've been gone two weeks?" I slid to the floor.

"Yeah, more or less." He rocked in his chair.

Two weeks had passed—it felt like so much longer. I laid on my back, legs curled up close to my chest. It helped ease my aching stomach. "Are you okay, Lucas? Nothing has happened to you? Or Maria. Or Mrs. Ramirez."

"We're fine. Why?"

"Thank, God." My stomach rumbled louder than ever.

"Uh, what was that? Are you going to transform right now?" He scooted away. "You're not going to—you know—kill me or anything? That seems to be your thing lately. I mean are you losing it? Should I be scared?"

"To be honest, I don't know anymore, but right now I'm just super hungry. I can't eat, though. Can't risk it." I pulled my knees even closer to my belly.

Lucas held up a finger. "Wait here."

He rushed from his room but quickly returned with a thermos and something round wrapped in foil. Smiling wide, he handed both to me. "Dude, remember the last time you spent the night, when you brought that strange colorless shake and those green patties? Well, you left your thermos here with about half of the shake left, and you left behind one of the patties. I saved them, man. Don't know why, but I did. Don't know what their shelf life is, but what the hell. Eat up."

I stared at thermos and the foil. My stomach gurgled again. It was months ago when I spent the night but this strange goo never went bad. Still, I shook my head.

"No, I can't. Too dangerous." I pushed the thermos away.

Lucas glowered at me. "Even if you change, you're not going to hurt me. At least, I don't think you will. Now take it. You need it."

He was right. Like a wild beast, I snatched the patty from him, unwrapping it and devouring it. Green bits and saliva fell from my mouth. The tasteless patty, dry from age, scratched my throat, but that didn't matter. I washed it down with the slimy liquid inside the thermos. The shake oozed over my tongue down my esophagus.

When I finished, I stood and backed against a wall. I gazed from the empty thermos lying on the floor and then to my hands. They shook wildly. What had I done? I held my breath, waiting for the change to come.

Lucas's eyes grew large. "Are you okay?"

I breathed in rapid bursts. "I... uh... I don't know. Do I look any different? Am I sprouting horns or anything?"

"No change." He stood and approached. "Just your same ugly face."

I slowed my breathing. Maybe I was going to be okay. Doc Torren's food was supposed to keep me from transforming. This time it worked... so far.

"You're okay, Tripp." Lucas motioned me to sit. "Just take it easy and tell me the rest. I need to know what's going on."

I crumbled to the floor. My eyes watered. "Man, things are messed up bad. I don't even know who I am anymore, and my dad—he's locked up somewhere and I don't know where to find him. I just—"

Lucas shook his head. "Wait, slow down. Tripp, what's going on? Where have you been?"

"I was kidnapped—I think."

Lucas joined me on the floor. "What are you talking about? I don't get what any of this is about, but I do know ever since you went missing, some very strange things have been going down in the NYC. Freakish creatures have been showing up everywhere, and I figured they were you."

"That's right. It's all me."

He frowned. "But man, you've been killing as many people as you've been saving. Some call these things heroes and—"

"Don't say that word," I blurted much too loud. "This hero thing is bull. Everyone just needs to back off. There's no superheroes, man. Especially not me."

"Whoa, whoa, dude, take it easy." Lucas held his finger to his lips to quiet me. "I get it. You're sick of it, but didn't you save some people from a subway tonight?"

"How do you know about that?" My body tensed.

He smiled. "Facebook, man. Video of a naked statue running down the street after pulling a bunch of people from a collapsed tunnel."

"Damn it, I don't want to talk about that." My voice was still too high.

"Okay, just keep quiet." He glanced toward the door. No one came. He turned back to me. "Look, you didn't let me finish before. I was saying, some call you—well, those things you become—a hero, others a vigilante out for blood. You know I love your powers, but since when did you become a killer?"

"Since Cardan came into my life." I rubbed my eyes. I just wanted to sleep but couldn't. Not now.

"Who?" Lucas slid closer.

"He calls himself Cardan. Says he's my father." I took a deep breath. "I have to start from the beginning, so you understand."

I wove the story from that first night I met Cardan at the park after my transformation to my final confrontation when the bullet he fired bounced off me and struck him.

Lucas' mouth hung wide open after I finished the story. "Do you think he's dead?"

"I don't know. But if he's not, you and Maria and Mrs. Ramirez are in danger. He said he'd hurt you if I didn't obey him."

"Just let him come after me." Lucas crossed his arms. "I'll take him out."

"This is serious, Lucas." I looked up at him.

He raised an eyebrow. "I'm nothing but serious. This dude needs to be taught a lesson. Hopefully, he's already getting his ass kicked in hell. But hold on, you said you were kept in some kind of military base?"

"Yeah."

"That explains why some Army types were hanging around for a day or two. There were also a bunch of choppers flying over this area for forty-eight hours straight I'd say, and men in dark suits and black SUVs driving around the school and our neighborhood. I hid in the bushes and watched as a few military jeeps packed with armed soldiers circled the streets around your home. Man, this is some crazy stuff."

I sat up and punched his arm. "Thanks for stating the obvious. What happened to the soldiers and those in the black suits?"

He shrugged. "I don't know. Like your dad, they just disappeared."

I laid my head on the floor. "Lucas, what am I going to do? I have to find my dad before he runs out of time. I don't know if he's losing air or starving. I can't let him die."

He reached onto his desk, grabbed his phone and threw it to me. "Try calling him."

I hastily punched in my dad's cell phone. My heart raced. I held my breath. The phone rang once, twice, three times. "Come on!" After the fourth ring, a computer voice came on the line and stated the number was no longer valid. "What?" I tried again but got the same response. My heart sank. "Damn it." I lowered the phone.

Lucas placed a hand on my shoulder. "Don't give up. We'll think of something."

"Like what?" I threw up my arms.

"I don't know. Maybe Mrs. Ramirez could help. We'll sneak you into school tomorrow, and you can talk to her. For now, crash here."

"Your parents would love that."

"Who cares?"

I started to rise, but my head spun as if I'd just gotten off a spinning cups ride. I fell onto his bed. Then tried to stand again. "No, I've already put you in danger. I should go."

Lucas raised an eyebrow. "You're not going anywhere. You need to sleep, man. We'll figure stuff out in the morning."

I gave him a hard look. "Okay, but Lucas, I want you to know something. I can't remember killing anyone. I don't want to hurt anyone anymore. I never wanted any of this. You have to believe me."

Lucas sat beside me in the bed. "I do, dude. I do."

Chapter 26

Back To School

Students streamed through the front gate onto the grounds of Poopter Junior High. I checked the watch Lucas gave me. Seven fifty. In ten minutes, the morning bell would ring. They would rush to their classes.

I frowned as the students mingled inside the gate. My life might be screwed up, but not theirs. They remained normal teens. I lowered my head into my hands. *Never thought I would miss school.* Two weeks ago, I might have belonged there. No more. I was a fugitive.

A block from the front gate, a crowd of students passed my hiding place behind a parked car. Blending in with them, I might go unnoticed.

After the last student passed, I joined the group and slowly wove my way to the center. Lucas had lent me a pair of jeans and a brown T-shirt emblazoned with a surfer emblem. The hood of my sweatshirt concealed my head, and the book-laden backpack I toted made me fit right in.

Lucas offered to walk with me, but I couldn't put him in danger. He reluctantly agreed to let me sneak onto campus alone. I didn't want to place him in any more danger than I already had. But, he loaned me his cell phone. Said he would borrow—or more to the point—sneak away with his mom's phone, so we could stay in communication.

I patted the bottom of the backpack and felt the outlines of a folder. That's where I hid the phone. Safer there than on my body. You know, just in case I transformed or something, I didn't want the phone to be smashed.

At the front gate, a security officer—security-dude Max, as Lucas called him—stood stone faced. Every morning, he ushered in students and rounded up stragglers. Hopefully my plan to mix in with the other students would work. Max might be under orders to hand me more over to anyone who might be hunting me.

I couldn't take that chance.

Walking beside a girl who chatted with a boy, comparing photos of some singer on their phones, I pretended to join their conversation. I giggled when they did. Nodded in agreement. And moved my lips as if talking.

A few feet from the gate, I slowed and held my breath.

Max towered over everyone. He was a big guy with a round face and large gut atop thick legs the size of tree trunks. The jacket of his brown security uniform barely reached around his belly. His raven-black eyes shifted from student to student. He never smiled, not even at the students who greeted him.

I peeked at him from under my hood, and he immediately focused on me like Superman zeroing in with his X-ray vision. A cold sweat swept across my forehead. My heart pumped three times faster. *Oh no!* He knew. He was going to stop me!

I started to retreat. A familiar person darted past me. My best friend slammed into Max as if he hadn't seen the massive security guard. Despite Max's size, he stumbled backward and nearly fell.

"I'm sorry, sir." The concern in Lucas' voice sounded convincing.

"You know the rules. No running onto campus," Max responded, his voice deep and raspy.

"Sorry, sir, really sorry." Lucas needlessly brushed off dust from Max's uniform even though Max never fell. "So clumsy of me."

I rushed through the gate. Once far enough away, I turned toward Lucas. He winked at me, and I nodded.

Taking a deep breath, I slithered past students gathered in the quad. Out of the corner of my eye, I spotted Maria talking to a group of girls. I started toward her but stopped. My heart beat fast. I wanted to talk to her. To tell her I... liked her. But that wasn't possible now, so I skulked away to the bathroom. Would I ever get to see her again? Maybe someday ask her out to a movie or something? *Get real, Tripp.*

As the morning bell sounded, I checked each of the stalls to make sure I was alone before entering. I would hide here until the lunch hour when Mrs. Ramirez might make her way from the counseling office to the trailer where we usually ate. If she didn't go there, I'd have to find some other way to make contact with her, but right now that was my best shot.

I needed to speak with her. She believed in me. Told me my powers were a gift, not a disease.

Locking the door, I sat on the toilet and prepared for a long wait.

***

My watch alarm startled me back to consciousness. I still sat on the toilet, my legs tucked against my chest. My head rested against the stall. Drool slid down my mouth and dried, gluing my chin to the side of the stall. When I lifted my face away, my skin sounded liked a suction cup.

I cursed myself for falling asleep. I could have been discovered, but a lack of sleep overcame me. Fearing I might doze off, I had set the alarm for five minutes before the lunch break.

Rubbing away the remnants of sleep, I listened for movement in the bathroom. Hearing none, I slowly unlatched the lock and cracked the door. I was alone. I crept toward the exit and peeked outside. A few school staff walked by, but quiet filled the largely empty campus. Students remained in their classrooms. That would change in a couple of minutes when the lunch bell blared.

After one more glance in both directions, I dashed across the field and ducked behind the trailer. No one followed me.

A minute later the lunch bell rang, classroom doors flew open and students rushed toward the cafeteria. The campus came to life as hundreds of students laughed and talked. I wished I could be like them. Was I ever? Not really. I was stuck in this stupid trailer at lunch every day with Mrs. Ramirez.

Two minutes passed, but Mrs. Ramirez hadn't arrived. Damn! She wasn't coming. Why should she? The only reason she ate her lunches here was to watch over me. Now she was free of the hassle and could eat anywhere.

I waited another few minutes. "Come on, Mrs. Ramirez, I need you here."

I ran my fingers through my hair and sighed. Too much time had passed. My head dropped to my chest. What now? I had to get off the school grounds. What a dumb idea to come in the first place. I turned toward the back gate, a nearly impenetrable fence of black metal bars meant to keep students in and everyone else out. Maybe I could climb it, but could I do it without being seen?

"Tripp, is that you?"

I froze at the familiar voice.

"Tripp?"

I turned to face Mrs. Ramirez and struggled to fight back tears. Another friendly face; another person I could trust. She smiled at me, just like she always did—the kind of smile that made me believe things would be all right.

"Uh, yeah… it's me," I mumbled.

"I can't believe it." She wrapped her arms around me. "When you disappeared, I feared the worse. I went to your house when your telephone number no longer worked and found it abandoned. I am so happy to see you."

"I'm, uh, happy to see you, too." I pushed away from her embrace. "Can we talk inside?"

"Of course, come on." She ushered me into the darkened trailer, and we sat at a table. "Now, tell me everything. I am so sorry for whatever has happened. I never should have suggested you use your powers."

I blinked away a tear. "That doesn't matter now."

"But—"

"Mrs. Ramirez, what happened isn't your fault."

"Well, yes it is… Ilan."

I stood. "What did you just call me?"

My jaw dropped. The blood rushed from my head. Dizziness overcame me, and I grabbed the table to keep from falling. How did she know? Something was wrong. Very wrong.

"Aren't you Ilan?"

I stumbled away from the table. "Mrs. Ramirez, I don't under—"

"You will." She sneered at me and then threw open the door. Daylight flooded the trailer, blinding me. "I think he's ready for you."

The shadows of two figures slid inside. A familiar stench filled the trailer. Cigarette smoke! My breath froze deep in my lungs. My pulse pounded in my ears. I retreated to the back wall, my hands in front of me to fend off the dark figures. Was this a nightmare? Was I still inside the bathroom stall fast asleep? No, this was real.

"Who are you?" I squinted for a better look, but I didn't need to see. *He'd* come for me. Somehow, Cardan lived.

"Ilan, don't you recognize your father?" Cardan's voice bounced off the walls.

Mrs. Ramirez closed the door and locked it. The click-clack of the bolt stole my short-lived freedom. My knees wobbled. Limbs shook like jelly. I gasped, forcing my lungs to move air. I was *his* prisoner again. Darkness, like deep under the subway, returned to the trailer. *Wait, I can't give up! My dad's out there!*

Cardan stood by the door, paler than I remembered. A bloody bandage wrapped around his forehead.

He wasn't alone. Someone shorter than him, roughly my size and build, held him. This mystery person's face was shrouded by a hood.

My weakened legs failed me. I dropped to the floor. *Please, I can't be his prisoner again. God, help me!*

Cardan hobbled toward me, aided by the stranger. He stopped to take a deep breath, then shuffled the rest of the way, dragging his feet with each step until he hovered over me like a ghost. A twisted grin revealed his yellow teeth. His eyes blinked rapidly. Drops of blood stained his tattered trench coat. Wet with sweat, his greasy hair matted against his forehead.

My gaze shifted to the newcomer. His head bowed, I couldn't see his face underneath the hood. I didn't want to. Something about him chilled my insides. I wanted to run from him even more than Cardan.

I scrambled away from both of them, crawling backwards until my back struck the bookshelf. "What... what...?"

"What am I doing here?" He knelt on shaky legs and massaged the bloody bandage. "You are my son, and I am your father. We have a connection. I had to return to you."

I shook my head. How was this possible? He survived the bullet and got to Mrs. Ramirez. Made her betray me. I had to get away, but there was no escape.

"But the bullet hit you in the head." I stuttered my words. "I saw you lying there. Blood was everywhere."

"And you thought I was dead, so you left me. I understand. You didn't know what else to do." He smiled. His damp hair hugged his forehead. "My son, the bullet merely grazed me. For a time, the pain was so bad I wished I was dead, but I couldn't leave this world—not when there is still so much for us to accomplish."

He extended a quivering hand to my face, but I turned away.

"I understand your shock right now, but together we can rebuild what we started." He tried to stand but lost his balance. The hooded stranger grabbed Cardan's arm and helped him to stand.

"Ilan, we must put our disagreement into the past and move forward." He patted his helper on the shoulder. Who was this other freak?

I stared into the hood. Just a hint of brown willowy hair curled out from underneath.

"Who is this?" I climbed to my feet.

"That answer will be revealed in due time," Cardan answered.

I turned my attention to Mrs. Ramirez. "What have you done?"

"Secured my future and my daughter's." She stepped closer to Cardan. "This good man—your real father—came to see me not long after I was assigned to watch over you. I am sorry, Ilan, but his offer of payment for convincing you to use your powers was something I couldn't turn my back on."

My heart ached. Hands formed into fists. "You never cared? You were just serving him and using me? All those talks we had. I confided in you. I thought you were my friend."

She shrugged. "Like I said, I'm sorry, but everything I told you was true. You should use your power, so I never really lied to you, did I?"

My body trembled. Mind raced. Head pounded. "Is anyone else in on this? The principal? Is that why he let us eat out here away from everyone else?"

"No, it was easy to keep him in the dark. See for yourself." Cardan crossed to the supply closet aided by his hooded caretaker, then slid open the door. The principal and Max, the security guard, lay crumbled on the floor on top of each other.

Oh my God! I searched the trailer, desperate for a pair of scissors or a sharp pencil. Anything to strike at Cardan. "Did you—?"

"They live." He closed the closet door. "They are good people, but I needed them out of the way for this little meeting. When we are safely away from here, they will awake unhurt."

"Why?" A sharpened pencil lay on a counter to my right. I inched toward it.

Cardan grimaced as he touched his head again. "Son, this has all been for your own good."

I glanced again at Mrs. Ramirez. "That day when you convinced me to help the boy—Maria's brother—trapped in the drainpipe, you didn't care about the boy or me, did you? You wanted the money?"

Cardan answered for her. "Actually, the boy falling into the drain was no accident. I made that happen. I had to, so you could break out of your shell. I needed to bring out the hero in you."

"I don't believe it." I grasped the pencil.

"It is the truth." His eyes focused on my hand.

"What about that first night when I transformed in the 7-Eleven and stopped that crook?"

"I paid him handsomely to rob that store, and I promised to ensure he never saw a day in jail after you stopped him, which I knew you would." He clasped his fingers under his chin. "And do not fear. The scum will do his time."

"No!" He played me from the start. Turning me into something I wasn't. Something I never wanted to be. A monster! Damn him! I had to make him pay for what he'd done. My body trembling, I pointed the pencil at Cardan.

Stepping in front of Cardan, *no face* raised his fists. The dude behind the hood slightly lifted his head. His face remained hidden, but his intentions were clear. Protect Cardan. But why?

Cardan gripped his bodyguard's arm and tugged him back. "There's more, my son. That little incident in the zoo was my doing as well. I had Theresa, or should I say Mrs. Ramirez as you affectionately call her, lie to you about her daughter being there."

"And the bank?" Blood surged to my head. My checks burned red hot. He was responsible for everything. Why didn't I see it?

"I watched you and that imposter of a father long enough to know what days he went to the bank. So yes, I set that up, too. Had those fools put a gun to his head because I knew you would save him."

"What about the subway cave-in." My fingers tightened around the pencil. "Innocent people died. I couldn't save them. You were behind that, too?"

Cardan glowered at me. "I would never take an action that would knowingly result in the deaths of good citizens. Unless, of course, I knew you could save them. You were not ready for such a test. No, that was not me. It was an unfortunate accident—the fault of no one—and you performed admirably, my son."

"Shut up." I held the pencil like a dagger. "I don't need your praise. I don't even believe you. You were playing me all along."

He shook his head. "No, I was helping you discover your true self. That's all. This world needs a hero. That's why I created you—to save the world."

"You turned me into a killer." I threw myself at him, thrusting the pencil at his chest. I wanted to drive the tip into his heart.

No face tackled me to the floor like a professional wrestler. I slammed hard against the tile and lost my grip on the pencil. This unknown scum pinned me. A fist hovered over me, ready to crash down if I struggled.

Cardan held up his hands. "Please, there is no need for such violence, especially among brothers."

What!

My attacker stood. With both hands, he slowly removed the hood.

I nearly spewed.

He had my face. The same brown hair. Same brown eyes. Same thin, pale face. I stared at my double, covering my mouth as dry heaves overtook me.

"Ilan, allow me to introduce you to your twin brother, Nicholas." The smile on Cardan's face was sickening. Like a madman witnessing his freakish creation come to life. Only he'd created two of us.

It couldn't be real. My stomach convulsed.

Something penetrated my arm, and an icy sensation flowed through my veins. My body numbed, my head drooped, my vision grayed.

The last thing I saw was *Nicholas* reaching for me.

Chapter 27

Reunited

Wake up, brother. The words sounded faint, distant, but there on the edge of my thoughts. A haze surrounded me, and my mind spun. Then, like the unexpected flash of a camera in a pitch-black room, it all came back in a blinding frenzy. Mrs. Ramirez's treachery. Cardan's return from the dead. A stranger who looked just like me.

Cardan's voice echoed in my head. *Ilan, allow me to introduce you to your twin brother, Nicholas.*

My eyes shot open. My mind spun out of control. Cardan lived! Damn it! The freaking bastard drugged me. Dragged me back to his lab and locked me inside the impenetrable glass box. Made me a caged animal again. I lay on the cold floor, my knees scrunched to my chest. High above hung the pipes and exposed steel rods lining the ceiling of his underground lair.

Hot tears formed. He'd stolen my freedom again—maybe this time forever. Now some twin added to the madness.

My head ached; hands felt clammy. My stomach gurgled. Bile rose up my throat. I was going to be sick, but I squeezed my mouth shut and swallowed the hot phlegm. Now was not the time to spew. I stood on trembling legs.

The twin stood just outside my glass prison.

"Father, he is awake." Nicholas, as Cardan called him, spoke softly, kind of like me, only with a slight British accent.

"Oh, thank goodness." Cardan, wearing his white lab coat, rushed forward. A bandage still covered his head. "Ilan, it took you longer than I expected to awaken. I was worried, but it is good to see you are finally back with your family."

My family?

I studied Nicholas. It couldn't be real. This had to be a trick Cardan played—had to be. I had no twin brother. No brother at all.

My face boiled as blood rushed to my head. "What is this, Cardan? What have you done?"

Nicholas studied me just as closely. He placed his hands against the glass and curled his upper lip in a sneer.

I fought to keep my balance on wobbly legs and staggered toward him. Every curve of his cheeks, his chin, even the pointy shape of his earlobes resembled my features. His eyebrows were just as thick. His brown hair long and tangled. His eyes deep set as mine. We shared the same skinny body, judging by his spaghetti-thin arms, though the baggy sweatshirt hid his true size.

I glanced at my own clothing. Cardan dressed me like Nicholas. No one would be able to tell us apart—except for one small difference. This twin wore a golden triangular locket around his neck.

"Do you like it, brother?" His English accent seemed to mock me. He didn't wait for me to answer; instead he opened the locket and revealed a faded picture of a woman with long brown hair and brown eyes, just like mine. She smiled as she looked toward some distant point. "She is our mother."

I stepped away from the glass. "Enough of this crap. Who are you?"

He looked puzzled by the question. "Father has already told you. We are brothers. Isn't it obvious?"

"Stop saying you're my brother." I gritted my teeth.

"But it's true." He grinned and placed his hand on the glass.

My attention shifted back to Cardan. "Answer me, you bastard. What have you done? Who's this person? How'd you make him look like me?"

Cardan pulled up a chair and sat close to the chamber. He lit a cigarette, puffed on it once, then a second time.

"Cardan—"

"Ilan," he interrupted, "as I told you, this is Nicholas. Yes, he is your twin brother, but really he is so much more than that. Both of you should sit as this will be hard for you to understand. What I am about to tell you will have a profound effect… I hope in a positive way."

"Father?" Nicholas raised an eyebrow.

"Nicholas, do as I say." Cardan peered over his shoulder. "Theresa, please bring a chair to Nicholas."

Mrs. Ramirez strolled up to us from a far corner of the lab with a chair and placed it next to Nicholas. She barely glanced at me as she stepped behind Cardan and placed her hands on his shoulders.

Traitor! You'll pay, lady. My knuckles turned white as my hands balled and trembled.

I slammed my fists against the glass. "Let me out of here. Tell me where my dad is!"

"Ilan, you are much too agitated. You are upsetting your brother." Cardan didn't look at me. His gaze focused on my twin. He motioned for him to sit.

Nicholas refused. "Father, what do you mean we are so much more than twins?"

"Nicholas, do not make me ask you to sit again." Cardan snapped his finger.

Like a dog, my twin did as directed.

"Thank you." Cardan crossed his legs and puffed on the cigarette. Smoke rose around him. "Nicholas, Ilan, to say you are brothers does not do either of you justice. It suggests the normal process by which siblings are born into this world, and the kind of siblings you are goes beyond that very basic human process."

"Speak English." I pushed against the glass.

"Yes, father, I don't understand." Nicholas' foot tapped against the floor.

Cardan lowered his cigarette. "Nicholas, my son, I took you from your mother's womb when you were still in an embryonic state, so that I could better manipulate your genetic code. In a sense, you grew in an artificial womb I prepared just for you. That's why you are better than Ilan in all ways."

My *twin* jumped to his feet. His chair fell backwards and crashed against the floor. His stare flitted from Cardan, to me and back to Cardan. "Father, what are you saying?"

Cardan wrapped his arms around Nicholas. "You are my son, Nicholas, as much as Ilan, but you were not bore naturally. And, in fact, I had to freeze you while still in a fetal stage until I could perfect my science. You are the perfection. Ilan, who was bore by your mother, was my failed experiment."

A numbing tingle spread through my body. What? I really had a brother, and I was the failure? This had to be more lies. All of this had to be a lie. But how else could you explain this stranger with my face?

Nicholas grasped the pendant in his hand and stared at the picture—the one he called our mother. "I don't understand. Is she not my mother then?"

"She is very much your mother just as I am your father." Cardan eyed the pendant. "You were just raised artificially for your own good and the good of science."

I mashed my face up to the glass wall. This boy seemed genuinely upset. Then again, he might be a great actor. "Hey, Nicholas… Nick… don't listen to anything he says. All he does is lie, man. Look, I don't know what's going on here, but don't buy into it. We're probably not even really brothers. He's playing us, man."

I wasn't sure what to believe, but if this twin dude was angry, maybe I could get him on my side. Maybe he'd free me.

Nicholas slammed his fist against the glass. "Don't you dare call him a liar. He's a great man."

"Nick, bro—"

"Ilan, that's enough," Cardan barked. "You continue to be a disappointment to me."

"Do you think I care?" I spit. My saliva slowly slid down the glass. "You've lied to me and now it's clear you've lied to this poor fool."

"Shut up." Nicholas pounded the glass again. He had tears in his eyes. What pissed him off so much? Because he knew I was right? Because he was coming over to my side—that everything Cardan told him about his mother was crap? I had to keep pushing him. But I wasn't sure what I believed anymore. A stabbing pain shot through my skull. My brain pulsated.

"Both of you stop and listen." Cardan pushed Nicholas away from the glass. "Ilan, everything I told you is true. Before you were born, I manipulated your genetic code, so you would be better than the average human. You would be superhuman—a new breed to serve the greater good and protect the weak. I did it to both of you. But I made a mistake with you, Ilan. I thought I could restructure your genetic material while you remained in your mother's womb. But it was a dangerous approach. As a scientist, I had to ensure the success of my experiment, so I removed Nicholas from his mother and treated him under more controlled conditions inside a tube. I still wasn't sure which one of you would prosper. I hoped you both would, but I decided if I lost one child, I'd still have the other."

"You crazy bastard. How could you do that? How could the woman you say is my mother just let you do that?" I pointed toward the pendant.

He shook his head. "I did not give her the choice. I kept her sedated throughout the pregnancy so that I could perform the necessary procedures. Afterward, it took time, but she came to forgive me and realized what I had done was for the good of humanity. You were born a perfect child, but I soon realized the error of my bio-engineering. While you were consuming your mother's milk, you started to transform into something… monstrous. And every time we fed you, the transformation was different. I couldn't control it."

"And what about me, father?" Nicholas asked.

"I froze you long before your birth, so that if I failed to engineer Ilan correctly, I could right my mistakes with you. Though you are twins, you were born a year after Ilan."

"You're full of it." I turned my back to him. It couldn't be true. My reflection, misshaped and bent in the scratched glass, stared back at me. He did this to me… somehow. Yet, I knew he was spinning lies. How could I tell what was real? What was bogus? "If it's true, why would you experiment on your own unborn sons? Why?"

"Because I didn't want anyone else in the world to face the kind of life I had." Cardan threw down his cigarette and stomped on it. He immediately lit another. "My parents, my sister, my little brother were killed in our London home by murderers who broke in to steal what little money we had. I vowed to make sure no one would suffer such pain, and I decided science was the way to achieve such a goal. Ilan, even though I failed with you, I could have helped you control your transformations if my colleagues hadn't reported me… if the government hadn't taken you away from me."

"But why didn't they take me, Father?" Nicholas picked up his chair and sat again. He rocked with his head bowed like someone praying.

Cardan smiled at him. "You were already frozen in your embryonic form. When I feared Ilan might be taken from me, I hid you away. And after I escaped the prison, they threw me into, I returned to you and continued my work while still searching for Ilan."

I scoffed. "It's not true. None of it."

"Why do you continue to doubt the proof you see?" Cardan approached the glass. "You have a twin, and he is better than you in every way. It took some time, but I determined the flaw in the genetic code that makes it impossible for Ilan to control his transformation. I fixed that in Nicholas."

"I don't get it." I pushed away from the glass.

"Nicholas can eat whatever he wants, and it will not immediately trigger a transformation. He controls when he transforms and after years of research, we know specifically what foods cause what transformation. He is perfect—the new breed of human I set out to create, but failed, with you."

Cardan's words stung.

Nicholas spoke the thoughts swirling through my mind. "So why have you sought out this pathetic version of me, Father? What value is he to you, to us? We don't need him. Let's return home, like we were never here. I will be the hero you want me to be. I will prove myself to you every day. Please, Father!"

"Because, with all his imperfections, he is my son—my first-born—and I had hoped I could help him." Anger tinged his voice. He kicked away his chair. "When I finally discovered where they had taken you, I had to find you, Ilan. I still believe I can help you control your abilities."

"*Dad*, since you got it right with Nick here, why don't you just fix me?"

"Because it is too late to change your genetic coding," he took another puff on his cigarette.

"Well, isn't that just great." I threw up my arms.

"Ilan, I can still help you. I have tried, but you fight me. The world needs a hero unafraid to do what needs to be done to remove the filth and scum of this planet. Not someone who is weak-minded and afraid to act."

"You mean... kill," I responded.

"When necessary, yes."

I paced in my little glass prison. "Wait a second, I get it now. All this time, I didn't kill those people. It was Nick, wasn't it? He changed into whatever monster I became and did as you ordered. He killed for you."

"Yes." Cardan dropped ashes from his cigarette.

Thank God! Whatever my fate would be—even if I was to be locked away forever—at least I knew I wasn't a killer. I was still… me. Tripp! Not Ilan. It was as if a heavy bag lifted off my shoulders. I could stand tall. Breathe a little easier. No matter what, Cardan didn't change me.

I scratched my head. "You know, when you freed me from whatever hole Doc Torren had locked me in, I saw some green slimy thing moving into a vent. Was that Nick, too? Did he help free me? Did he help you kill those people, too?"

Cardan didn't answer. He only grinned, which was answer enough.

A chuckle escaped my lips. Not sure why? Maybe relief. Maybe because I started to believe this crazy nightmare was real. I had a brother named Nicholas who'd been following my every move this whole time.

My laugh ended, and then I threw myself at the glass. "So what happens now, Pop? What are you going to do with me and my brother?"

He again placed an arm around Nicholas's shoulder. "Ilan, I brought you here one last time in hopes of convincing you to truly be my son again so we might begin a journey together as a family to save this world from the evil that infests it. Alas, I have failed to make you understand. I hear it in your voice. Nevertheless, I ask once again, will you be my son? Will you allow me to help you, so our united family can bring an end to evil?"

I ran my fingers through my hair. My gaze wandered to the doorway out of his lab, the door I ripped open. All I needed was one last chance to escape. If I could get him to free me, I'd escape this freak show and find a way to stop him. "Yes, I will do whatever you want."

Cardan glared at me. He offered a grim smile. "My son, I love you so much, but I see through your lies. You contemplate an escape even now."

I shook my head. "How could I escape? You have my killer twin here to stop me. Besides, the man who raised me was a fake. The government wants to imprison me. I know that now. Just give me a chance."

Tears dripped down Cardan's cheeks. "This pains me, but I do not believe your words. I see deceit, not love, in your eyes. You have left me no choice. I must end your life. From this point on, I have only one son."

I struck the glass with a fist. "What are you saying?"

"When they ripped you from my arms all those years ago, and even though you still live, in a way you died then. I have come to realize you are dead to me now." He lowered his head. "So you must die now just as a piece of me died when you were taken from me."

What did he just say? I couldn't have heard him right. "Let me out of here!" I screamed. My chest tightened. A hollow sensation spread from the pit of my stomach to my limbs, stealing my courage. He was going to kill me? *God, no!* "I'll be your son. I won't try to escape."

Mrs. Ramirez whirled away from me. Nicholas's eyes bulged.

"Tripp, isn't that the name you prefer?" Cardan crossed his arms. "Well, Tripp, this little glass box is rigged with tubing that enables poisonous gas to seep into the chamber. I promise you it will not be a painful death."

"No, Cardan! You don't have to do this." I thrashed my arms and legs against the glass. "Please, Father—"

"Forgive me if I do not watch your death. Theresa will be here to record your passing. I take my leave so that my true son, Nicholas, and I can carry out one more mission to make your city a safer place for its citizens. I have discovered the compound that is home to *Ghost* and his family. You remember him, don't you? The crime boss responsible for bringing illegal weapons into the city and putting them into the hands of children. The sacrifice of his life and the lives of his family will announce to the world that a new breed of hero has arisen to put an end to such filth. It saddens me to kill his sweet little girls, but you can't rid the streets of evil by showing mercy. Good-bye, Tripp."

"No! Don't do this!" I slammed myself against the glass door, but it didn't budge. "Nick, don't let him do this. We're brothers. Don't let him kill me like this. Don't let him kill those girls. Mrs. Ramirez... help me!"

Cardan turned on his heels and strolled to two air tanks. Tubing wound from them to either side of my prison where they connected to holes in the glass.

"You planned to kill me all along, didn't you?" I struck the glass one more time.

"No, I wanted you to join me, but you wouldn't. I can't leave loose ends that might stand in the way of my efforts for all of mankind." Cardan turned gauges on the tanks and gas hissed as it raced toward me. A green mist poured through the holes.

I threw off my sweatshirt to cover one vent. "How can you call your son a loose end? You're crazy, man. I knew it all along." *Oh my God! I don't want to die!*

I shifted my gaze to Nicholas. "Is this the man you want to serve? One day he'll do the same to you."

Nicholas tugged on Cardan's lab coat. "Father, is this really necessary? I mean—"

"Hush, Nicholas. Come, we must leave." Cardan walked toward the doorway of his labyrinth.

The gas poured in faster. It smelled of rotten eggs. I coughed and gasped. My heart thudded louder and louder. I crashed my hands against the glass. "Nick..."

"Sorry, brother." He followed Cardan.

My vision blurring, I watched them slip from the lab. Mrs. Ramirez, tears in her eyes, ran to a far corner and stared at the wall.

I coughed and slipped to the floor. This was how I would die. What about my dad? I never had a chance to see him. To tell him I was sorry for everything. Was he safe? Was he slowly dying somewhere because of me? I would never know. This was no way to die. I pounded against the glass some more, but I couldn't escape.

I tried to hold my breath but wheezed and coughed some more. "Please, someone, anyone… help me."

Chapter 28

Just Breathe

Poisonous gas seeped into my mouth, burning my insides. Sprawled on the floor, I clawed at my throat. My chest convulsed. I spit up white hot foam. It sizzled as it dripped from my lips. *God, I'm dying! Dad… please… help.* My body spasmed, arms and legs shaking uncontrollably. I rolled onto my back. *Can't… breathe!* Salty liquid slid from nose into my mouth. My own blood! *So… much… pain. Just… let… it… end!*

"Hang on!"

A familiar voice cut through my agony. But it quickly fizzled. Fogged with gas, my mind played tricks.

"Tripp, I'm here."

The poisonous gas blanketing the chamber muffled the voice. No one was there. Gray shapes flashed before me.

Then a black mask hiding a face.

My fingers touched the glass as I mouthed.

"Tripp, I'm going to get you out of there."

Whoever was there said something else, but I could no longer hear his words. I couldn't even hear the deadly gas anymore. My world went silent.

A ghostly floating vision struck the door with something. Then again. A third and fourth time.

Was any of this real?

Darkness overcame me.

***

"Chew, man! You have to chew. If you don't, you'll die."

The words penetrated the emptiness that enveloped my mind.

"Eat... damn it!" The words floated to me as if on a soft breeze.

I bit down on something soft, something sweet. Juice flowed down my throat. I chewed faster. I didn't recognize the flavor at first. Then it came to me—an orange.

The citrus ignited an explosion in my stomach. Flames, real or imagined, rose through my body and forced open my eyes.

"Eat more. It's working." Hands forced more food into my mouth. Whoever was feeding me grasped my chin and forced my teeth to move. Pieces of banana moistened in my mouth and slipped down my throat, adding fuel to the fire deep in my belly.

I think I screamed. My body trembled.

"Come on, man, transform. Stay with me."

I rolled over as my bones cracked and muscles bulged. Bones ripped through my back. My face twisted and contorted. I screamed again—a wail that no longer sounded human.

Somewhere beyond my view a woman whimpered. *Mrs. Ramirez?*

When the pain eased, I stood on heavy legs. I could see. Breathe the musty air of the tunnels. I was alive. The pain gone.

But what had I become? Blue muscles and brown fur covered my shoulders, arms and thighs. My hands, long and thick, only had two fingers and a thumb, each with long razor-like nails. I peered over my shoulder. Demon wings extended from my back.

Mrs. Ramirez covered her eyes and ran to a corner of the labyrinth.

A stranger in a dark leather jacket, jeans, and black motorcycle helmet stood an arm's length away from me. A crowbar lay at his feet. He slowly removed the helmet, and my heart did a somersault. Lucas!

"What? How? You saved me." I fought the urge to wrap my massive blue arms around him.

"I wasn't going to abandon my best friend." Lucas held his helmet to his chest.

"I don't know what the heck to say, but thanks."

"We're buds. That's what buds do."

My eyes watered, but I sniffed back tears. "What am I?" My words came out high pitched like a hyena's laugh.

Lucas shrugged. "You look like some kind of gargoyle, but whatever man, you're alive. That's what matters."

"I need to see what my face looks like." I stepped toward Lucas. He retreated.

I lowered my head. "Sorry, I didn't mean to scare you."

"I'm not scared, man… really." He reached into his backpack and pulled out a cell phone. His mom's with her heart-shaped cover. Flipping it around, he took a photo of me. "Here, look."

A monster glared back at me. Yep, I resembled a gargoyle. Blue skin and a patchy black beard covered my face, and pointy cheek bones extended out so far that my glowing yellow eyes buried within my skull. Two rams' horns rose from either side of my head and my ears—large, thick and bony—ended in jagged points. Like a saber-toothed tiger, fangs protruded from my mouth.

I handed him back the phone. "Jeez, now I'm a demon?"

"You're alive," Lucas reminded me. "That's what matters."

"How'd you get here. How'd you do this?" My gaze flitted back and forth from Lucas to the glass prison where I almost died. The keypad locking mechanism was smashed to bits.

"It's all here." He lifted the backpack he'd given to me from the floor beside a table. He grabbed his phone from inside. "Looks like they didn't search the backpack. That's how I found you. I'll tell you more, but first we have to deal with Mrs. Ramirez."

Lucas dropped the backpack and hefted the crowbar, pointing the tip at her.

She held her cell phone.

"Yo, lady, don't you dare make a call." Lucas held the crowbar over his head and took long strides toward her.

She dropped the phone. "Please, don't hurt me. I'm sorry."

"Sorry doesn't cover it. Tripp trusted you." Lucas was close now, just an arm's length away from Mrs. Ramirez. Close enough to strike her if he wanted.

"Lucas, I'll handle this." I tucked my wings in tight against my back and stomped toward her with clunky legs and feet the size of a grizzly bear's paws.

Mrs. Ramirez backed against a wall. She held up her arms up as if to fend me off. "No, Tripp, please don't hurt me. I didn't mean you any harm."

I shoved a table out of my way. It flipped over and crashed against a cabinet. "Don't tell me you didn't mean any harm. How long, Mrs. Ramirez... how long were you working for him?"

"Tripp—"

"How long!"

"Since the school year started. I don't know, maybe four months ago."

Tears spilled down her cheeks.

I took another step closer. "How did he get to you?"

She sobbed. "H... he spoke to me at a co... coffee shop ne... near school. W.. we went out a fe... few times. Then he re... revealed the truth t... to me. As... asked for help. He... pai... paid me a lot. Offered me more. T... to get yo... you to use yo... your powers. He really cared for you."

"And you believed him?" I bared my fangs. Rage boiled my insides. My wings fluttered open until they surrounded her. The beast in my wanted to tear her arms off for what she'd done. No, that's not me. I wasn't a killer.

She fell to the ground. "Please, I'm so sorry."

"Tell me the rest." I knelt. My massive hands formed into fists. I wouldn't hurt her, but I could scare the crap out of her. "How much money did he offer you?"

"A quarter of a million." She lowered her head into her hands. "He said he had the money in a European bank in my name. He was going to take me to Europe to begin a new life."

I smashed my fists into the floor. The tile splintered. "How could you do this to me?"

"I'm so sor—"

"Don't. Just don't." The kid in me wanted to cry. The gargoyle in me still wanted to rip away her flesh. No, I was not a monster. No matter what Cardan tried to make me. "Where's my dad?"

"I don't know, Tripp… really."

"She's lying, Tripp." Lucas, helmet back on, held the crowbar with both hands.

I leaned in close. "Tell me the truth."

"I'm not lying. He never told me anything about your dad, except that he was a government agent or something, not your real father." She clasped her hands together as if praying. "I'm telling you the truth, Tripp."

I sneered and rose to my feet. A lead pipe, one that had probably fallen from the ceiling, was exactly what I wanted. I grabbed it and returned to Mrs. Ramirez.

"What are you going to do to me?" Her eyes were wide with fear.

"Nothing. I'll let you go, but not quite yet." With super strength, I wrapped the pipe around her as easily as bending a plastic straw. The pipe's weight would keep her anchored to the wall. She might eventually be able to stand, but it would take her a while.

Lucas grabbed my arm. "What do you mean, let her go? She's going to get out of here and tell that evil dude you're alive."

"I'm done with her. For all I know, Cardan expected me to escape and then kill her. I'll never do things his way." I crushed the phone into jagged pieces. "Besides, it doesn't matter what she tells him. I will face him and Nicholas long before she's able to contact them anyway. I'll make them tell where my dad is. Let her escape. She'll move slowly with that heavy pipe wrapped around her."

I walked away from Mrs. Ramirez, stopping once by a table covered with yellow notepads. The same notepads he used to compile information about me during his tests. Like an explosion, visions erupted in my mind of Cardan forcing me to eat and transform. It hurt every time. He never cared. He never really wanted to help. I wanted to tear the pads to pieces, but maybe there would be something about where he'd imprisoned my dad.

"Lucas, look. Maybe there's a clue to my dad." I opened one of the pads. Nothing inside but page after page about me and my transformations. The writing of a madman. Nothing about my dad. I opened another. Still nothing about my dad.

Lucas rifled through a handful of them. His eyes large, he held one open to me. "Dude, there's an address here, but the name *Ghost* is written next to it."

I glared at it. "That's the crime boss. Cardan and Nick are going after him and his family. Said he's going to kill them all. Even the children." I took a deep breath. How could I let him kill children? "Lucas grab all these pads. Let's take them."

He did as I directed, slipping them into his backpack. Then we crossed through the doorway out of Cardan's lair and never looked back.

Inside the darkened tunnel, I scanned for Cardan or Nicholas but they had vanished. Quiet surrounded us.

I turned my attention back to Lucas. Even with shoulders the size of cannonballs that caused me to hunch over, I towered over him.

"So how'd you find me?" I marched through the tunnel, heading for the upper levels. Lucas hurried beside me.

"I gave you my phone, right? My parents, who have never completely trusted me, have one of those phone tracking apps to keep tabs on me. When I snatched my mom's phone, I trailed you." He patted his jeans pockets where he placed both phones.

"They carried you out like you were drunk or something when everyone else was in class. They made it look like you were walking, but your feet dragged along the ground. I knew something was wrong."

"Thanks for coming after me. How'd you get here so fast?" I cringed at my ear-piercingly high voice.

"I ran home, got my motorbike, and I tracked you all the way here."

We climbed a shaft to the subway terminal, but Lucas stopped.

He tightened his grip on the crowbar. His knuckles turned white. "Man, I heard all that about you having a brother. That Nick seems like a real ass. And I heard when he said he was going to kill you. I didn't know what to do. If I should charge in, swinging for their heads, or what? If they hadn't left, I guess I wouldn't have had a choice. I'm sorry I waited so long, dude. You could have died. I shouldn't have waited. But I was scared. I was a—"

"A hero." I placed a heavy hand on his shoulder. "My hero. You saved my life. If you came in any sooner, they would have killed you. You never should have come."

"I had to."

We stood in silence, for the moment, and then I chuckled. "You're going to be in a lot of trouble."

"Totally worth it."

We started our climb again, reaching the upper tunnels. Soon we would reach the terminal. I hoped it would be shutdown after that subway cave-in near Manhattan. That way no one would see me. No one would scream

"Whose crowbar?" I asked.

"My dad's." He slipped it into his backpack. "Good thing I brought it. Otherwise, I never would have gotten that stupid cell open. I jammed it into that control box on the door over and over, and finally something popped. You were coughing up yellow stuff and couldn't breathe. I was afraid you were a goner."

"And you just happened to have some food?"

"Like I said, I figured things would go bad, so I brought a bunch of supplies in case you needed, you know, to change. And it worked. Your change brought you back to life."

"I guess."

"Don't guess, man, it's true. I always told you this change you go through is not a curse."

"I just don't know what to think. All I know is I'll never be free of this. I'll always be this freak."

We reached the terminal. It was abandoned. I motioned for Lucas to stop. "I have to go after Cardan and Nick. They're going to the home of a crime boss named Ghost to kill him and his family. I can't let them."

Lucas looked surprised. "What about your dad?"

I shrugged. "I'll find him. I will, but I can't let Cardan and Nick kill those kids. Maybe I can even convince Nick to switch sides. I don't know if he's really my brother or not, but Cardan has twisted his mind."

"You don't owe that crime boss or his family anything." Lucas shook his head. "You certainly don't owe that crazy twin of yours anything. He left you for dead."

The beast in me exploded. Fire burst from my mouth. Flames soared over Lucas' head. He ducked just in time.

"What the hell?" Lucas patted down his body as if checking to see if he'd caught fire.

I retreated. "Sorry, man. I didn't mean to. Didn't know I could do that, but I'm just so damn sick of Cardan. I can't let him win. I have to stop him. Can't let him hurt anyone else. Especially kids. And Nick—I don't know. If he's my brother, he deserves a chance to turn. If he won't, then I'll….

I let that thought trail off. "What was the address with Ghost's name beside it on the pad?"

"Yeah. It's 2295 West Hills Lane, Catskill, New York," he announced. "I know where that is!"

"How?"

"My dad works for the Transit Authority. Maps are his life, and not just of NYC. Made me memorize his maps, too. Like I needed to know to keep me safe. Maybe he was right, after all."

I clapped my massive hands together. "Tell me how to get there?"

Lucas started for the tunnel exit. "I'll guide you there. Come on."

I grabbed his arm. "No! This I do alone. You've done enough. I can do this part on my own. Go home. Your parents are probably already tracking with you with your dad's phone."

He smiled broadly. That's right, so we better hurry. We don't have time to argue right now."

"Lucas, please. Just tell me how to get there or give me your phone. I'll find it on GPS."

Lifting his phone from his pocket, he showed it to me. "Can't. My phone's out of juice. It's dead. Happened while we were in the tunnels."

"Then give me your mom's phone."

"No can do." Lucas again started for the exit. "You're stuck with me till the end. I'm not letting you out of my sight."

I growled at him, then relented. "You do everything I say, and if things get bad, you hide."

"Whatever you say, buddy." He reached the steps leading out of the terminal. "I guess we can take my motorbike."

"Don't think I'll fit." I raised my wings. "Let's fly instead."

I followed him up the steps. An image of my dad frowning at me drifted across my thoughts. *Hang on, dad, just a little longer. I'm coming for you. I promise.*

Chapter 29

Ghost's Castle

The Catskill Mountains were about an hour and a half drive from NYC. By air, thirty minutes tops.

Night had already fallen by the time Lucas and I left the tunnels. People screamed when we emerged onto the street. A little girl cried and hugged her mother. A man shielded a woman in his arms. A police officer drew his weapon.

I ignored them all and grabbed Lucas, spread my wings and raced toward the peaks of the city's skyscrapers.

An orange moon hung low in the eastern horizon. A cool breeze washed against my face. The stink of car fumes and urban life gave way to the pine scent of the mountains. My senses in this form worked on overload. Like telescopes, my eyes zeroed in on sights a mile away, registering the shock on the faces of the people who stared and pointed at me. My nose picked up a mash of odors from the sizzling meat at a hotdog stand to the sweetness of a running spring in the mountains.

"Dude, not sure I like this kind of closeness," Lucas shouted through the wind ruffling his hair. His arms wrapped around my neck. "I really would have preferred to take my bike."

"This is faster."

"Yeah, well, you better not drop me."

"You're like a feather in my arms."

"Still, this is the first and last time we fly together." He tightened his grip.

"I agree."

"Do you have a plan?"

"No."

"What are you going to do?"

"Just try to stop Cardan. Save those kids. Then smash his bones until he tells me where my dad is. If this leads me to my dad… well, I'll tell him I'm sorry for being a lousy son and ruining his life." I thrust my wings back and we cleaved a faster path through the air.

We passed wintertime resorts and lakefront cottages.

"There." Lucas pointed to a secluded road snaking underneath large pine trees. Offshoots from the road led to mansion-like homes surrounded by trees and brush.

The road ended at one superstructure larger than all the rest—more castle than mansion. Towers, kind of like turrets, rose above the tree line. Lights from hundreds of narrow windows pierced the stronghold's gloomy solitude. Walls around the property made it seem like a fortress.

"That has to be it. This had to be Ghost's home" Lucas shouted. "If I were a crime boss, that's where I'd be."

I bit my lip. Lucas was right. It was time to face Cardan one last time. Force him to tell me where my dad was. If I had to break every bone in his body, he'd tell me."

I circled once, using my super vision to scan for trouble. No sign of Cardan or Nicholas, but something else caught my attention. Two bodies were near brush by a front gate. Four others lay scattered on the grounds just inside the compound walls. Two more were crumpled on the steps leading to the front door. Blood pooled around the bodies.

The front door—really a two-door entryway—hung uselessly off its hinges. Someone had blasted their way into the home.

Blood rushed from my head. My face felt numb. I shivered. Cardan and Nicholas had already arrived and brought death.

"Do you see what I see?" I asked.

"Yeah, gruesome stuff," Lucas answered.

I landed on the road leading to the front gates.

"What are we doing here?" Lucas removed the crowbar from his backpack.

"Hide in the brush. If I'm not back in a half hour get out of here."

I spread my wings to take flight.

"Wait a second." He grabbed my wrist. "I came here for a fight, not to sit on the sidelines. I can help."

I shook my head. "I know you can, but you've risked too much already. I can't let you get hurt in there."

"Tripp, I'm a big boy." He swung the crowbar at the compound.

"I'm sorry." I ripped my wrist free. "Just please do what I'm telling you. If you were hurt I couldn't live with myself."

I flapped my wings once and leaped over the gates into Ghost's compound.

Lucas ran up to the gate. "Tripp, get back here. This isn't cool." He kept his voice to a whisper but made his frustration clear.

I glanced back once, gestured for him to head into the brush and then swung back toward the front doors. I hoped he would understand and forgive me, but I wasn't sure I was going to walk away from this battle. If I fell, I wouldn't be able to protect him. Better he stay as far away as possible. His dad was right about me. I was a bad influence. I never should have gone to Lucas's home, but if I hadn't, I'd be dead already.

I hopped across the grounds, passing two of the bodies, both large men. Military-style rifles lay by them. One man's eyes were wide in terror. Blood dripped from his mouth. His neck had been slashed so deep his head nearly separated from his body. What kind of creature had Nicholas become?

My wings fluttered, and my body trembled. "There's no going back. Keep moving."

I sprinted toward the entrance. Claw marks had been scratched into the wooden doorframe. More blood!

Peering into the house, two more bodies lay just beyond the entryway. Their blood spilled across a stone floor along a cavernous hallway. A chandelier hung over head, its lights doused. Moonbeams cast the only glow.

I crept into the mansion. A chill surrounded me. Paintings of people covered the walls. Maybe the history of Ghost's crime family. The largest painting was of an elderly couple dressed like they were from the early 1900s—the man had a thick mustache and wore a stiff suit; the woman wore her hair up and was dressed in a formal gown. Other paintings showed couples and their children in more modern clothing.

I continued deeper into the castle. My thick, heavy feet clopped on the icy stone tile.

The hallway emptied into a living room as spacious as a fancy hotel's lobby. Two separate fireplaces marked opposite ends of the room, but no blaze burned in either one. Leather couches and chairs filled the center of the space and marble tables lined each wall.

A staircase curved up to the second story. Light from some unseen point upstairs licked at two more bodies, one at the base of the stairs and another about halfway up the staircase.

I lumbered over to the stairs, peering over my shoulder more than once.

At the base, I knelt at the body. Blood poured from a slash wound at his neck. I leaned closer and his eyes shot open. *What the...?* I tried to scramble away, but he grabbed my hand. He gasped, tried to speak and then fell silent. One more breath escaped his mouth, and he died.

The crack of a gunshot from the floor above shattered the silence. I flinched. My body tensed. Wings spread.

A child's scream followed.

I raced up the stairs. At the top smashed tables and broken lamps, some still lighted despite lying in pieces on a carpeted floor, littered another hallway.

A child cried from somewhere nearby. A door hung off its hinges at the end of the hall. I dashed toward it but toppled to the floor when I tripped over one more body.

Someone spoke. I recognized Cardan's voice. I slid along the wall to the doorway where I dropped to my knees and peeked inside.

A little girl's pink lamp atop a dresser shed pale light through the room.

Four people knelt on their knees, facing away from me. Two looked like young girls, beside them a woman and a man. Blood dripped from a wound on his shoulder blade. His body wobbled. He struggled to keep his head up.

Cardan held an automatic rifle in his hands and paced back and forth.

Where was Nicholas? He had to be nearby. What kind of beast had he become to cause so much death?

Cardan stopped to light a cigarette. He took a long puff and then blew out the smoke. Cigarette between his lips, he pointed the gun's barrel at his captives. The girls whimpered. The woman leaned close to both, embracing them.

"You've cast your evil over New Yorkers long enough, Ghost." Cardan's voice sounded icy. "It's time for your reign to end and for the people to once again know what it means to feel safe."

"Look, I don't know… who you are, but… I'm just… a businessman. Not… some crime boss… called Ghost." The man took long breaths between his words. His head bobbed.

Cardan grabbed him by the hair and jerked up his head. "How dare you lie rather than confess your sins and face your death like a man. Your lies condemn your wife and children to a painful death, and you will watch them suffer before your own end."

"The girls… no!" the woman cried. "Please, no."

"Leave my family… out of this," the man pleaded. "They've done… nothing."

"Oh dear, I'm afraid that was not a confession." Cardan released his grip on the man's hair. He glided from the man's wife to the two little girls. "You have left me little choice."

The woman pulled the girls close. "Stay away from them."

Cardan stopped behind the smaller of the two girls.

"Daddy," she sobbed.

"Don't hurt my daughter," the man begged.

"You have brought this on yourself, old chap." Cardan glanced toward the ceiling. "It is time, Nicholas."

Nicholas came into view. I bit my upper lip to keep from gasping. A man-sized spider with eight spindly legs and arms crawled along the ceiling. A spider's head replaced his human one. Eight yellow eyes blinked down at the victims. He opened his mouth wide and hissed, like a snake. A thick layer of prickly insect hair covered his body. His jaw split apart, revealing razor sharp teeth. Green saliva oozed from black lips.

He dropped from the ceiling and landed next to Cardan.

Both girls screamed. The man's wife squeezed the girls, but Cardan pulled her away.

"Ghost, say goodbye to one of your girls." Cardan showed no mercy. "Nicholas, let it be done."

The girls screamed.

"Please!" the woman yelled.

Nicholas reached for one of the girls.

"Okay, you're right," the wounded man shouted. "I am Ghost. Is that what you want to hear? It's true. And I don't just run New York City. I control the whole state. Right now an army of state troopers and police are racing here. You're not going to survive this night. Now, let my family go and we'll talk like businessmen. You can leave here with as much cash as you want, and you and this thing will see the morning. Harm my family and you're dead."

Cardan laughed. "Very brave of you to finally speak up for your family, and your words are spoken with such confidence, too. But I am not here for your money. I am here for the good of mankind. I appreciate your confession, but you and your wife and your offspring must pay for the pain and suffering you brought on your fellow man. Your deaths will be a message to all like you—that the time of evil has passed."

He puffed on his cigarette. "Nicholas, if you will."

Nicholas raised a leg as sharp as a spear over the youngest child.

My heart thumped painfully. *Move!*

I pounced on him. We tumbled to the floor and rolled several times. Our momentum separated us, and I stood first. "Stop, Nick! Don't do this!"

Stunned, Nicholas slowly gathered all eight of his legs under his body and stood with some effort. Eight eyes blinked several times. He shook his spider head and green spit sizzled through a plush throw rug.

The girls wailed. Their mother shielded them with her body.

My muscles tensed. Eyes burned. Drool dripped from my fangs. A fire raged in my gut. The spider beast was an enemy. *Destroy your enemy. Show no mercy.* Those words echoed through my mind. I couldn't think. I raised my fists to pummel Nicholas. *Do it! Kill him!* I took one step then stopped. The monster controlled my thoughts. I couldn't let that happen.

I lowered my claws and took a deep breath. "Nick, if you can understand me, this isn't the way. You've killed enough tonight. Don't hurt these kids."

Cardan applauded, the rifle tucked underneath his arm. "Ilan, you are stronger than I gave you credit. All the better that you should witness the acts of a true hero. Nicholas, my son, do not let your brother stop you from your righteous task. Nothing has changed."

"Don't listen to him, Nick," I pleaded. "If you're really my brother, you can't do this. It's not who we are."

"Evil must be stopped." Nick's words slithered from his lips.

"Killing kids isn't the way." I extended my hand toward him. "Come on, Nick, listen to me, not him."

Nicholas shifted his view from me to Cardan.

"Do your duty, my son," Cardan ordered.

"Yes, Father." Nick's body started to twist and contort. His extra arms and legs slipped back into his body. His remaining arms and legs pulsated and popped as muscles bulged through skin. His spider-like face became human then stretched and morphed. Cheek bones extended out; eyes pushed back into his skull. Wings ripped through his back and extended behind him.

When the transformation completed, I stared at a mirror image of myself. He had become a gargoyle, just like me. The only difference—around his neck he wore the locket with the picture of his... our... mother.

I stood confused. How could he instantly change without eating anything? How could he become whatever he wanted? Did I have that power?

Nicholas roared and spewed fire from his mouth toward the ceiling. He then tackled me like a football player around the waist. My back smashed against the floor, my wings tucked underneath me. He knelt over me, grinning with yellow fangs.

"I've listened to you enough, brother." He raised a set of dagger-length fingernails to strike me.

I spit flames into his face, and, as he turned away, wrapped my legs around his head and threw him to the floor. He rolled once but quickly shot to his feet. I stood as well. *Kill him. No. I can't do that.*

The girls' shrieks bounced off the walls. Ghost and his wife dragged them to a far wall.

Cardan lifted the rifle and aimed it at me.

Nicholas arched his back and blew a fiery ball at me. I ducked. The blaze singed my head and struck the wall behind me. The flames instantly ignited curtains. Fire spread through the room, rising up the walls and onto the ceiling.

The monster in me fought for control. *Kill him now.* I shook the voice away.

Nicholas must have noticed my distraction. He slashed at me, ripping two lines through my chest. I yelped like an injured dog. I felt each nail rip through my flesh, tearing skin away. Thick, warm blood oozed from the wounds. I touched the torn skin. Crimson liquid flowed over my claw.

Enraged, I wildly slashed my nails at Nicholas. He avoided each strike then grabbed my wrists and flung me across the room. I struck the far wall with a thud. More flames flew from his mouth toward me. I dove out of the way. The blazing spit crashed into the wall.

The flames crackled and danced. Choking black smoke spread along the ceiling.

"Mommy," one girl shouted.

"You are weak, brother, because you show mercy." Nicholas crossed to me.

Dazed, I hunched over, wheezing through shallow breaths. He grabbed me by the neck with both claws and lifted me off the floor. I pounded on his arms, but Nicholas was stronger.

"End this, Nicholas," Cardan commanded.

Nicholas squeezed tighter, his grip like a vice. Choking, I grasped his wrists, but couldn't break his clasped claws. He smashed me against the floor as if I was nothing more than a stuffed toy.

His claws tightened.

No, you can't lose this easily. The voice inside my head stirred me to life. I stood one leg at a time. My own claws tightened into fists, and I brought them crashing down on Nicholas's arms over and over again. His grip loosened, and I smashed him across the face. He crumbled to the floor.

Flames leaped from wall to wall. Ghost, his wife and children coughed, but they couldn't escape. Cardan, rifle in hand, blocked the doorway.

"Maybe it's best we all die here in this fire," he uttered. "Maybe that is appropriate."

"No." I picked up a table, engulfed in flames, and hurled it. Cardan tried to get out of the way, but a wooden leg struck him. He dropped the weapon and fell to his knees.

I pointed to Ghost and his family. "Get out."

They slipped from the room out of sight.

My attention was turned away from Nicholas too long. A razor-sharp nail slashed across my waist, like a hot blade ripping my flesh. I screamed and swung toward him. Blood dripped from his claws. He grinned with satisfaction. Warm thick fluid dripped from my shredded skin. I backed away from him, gritting my teeth against the stabbing pain.

"Nick, stop this—"

He launched at me, driving a foot into my right thigh with the force of a sledgehammer. Hard enough to snap bones, but my hardened muscles withstood the blow. I still struggled to remain on my feet. "Nick, listen to me!"

His claws joined into fists. He brought them down as if to crush my skull. Damnit, I wouldn't be beat that easily.

The beast in me took over. I roared back at him, sidestepping his blow with the speed of a wild animal in a life and death battle. Instinct fueled each movement. *Take the fight outdoors. Face him in the skies.* Burying my claws into his shoulders, squeezing through muscles and tendons, I pushed him toward the window. He howled, raking his nails across my chest. I felt each cut, but I couldn't stop.

"You wanted this fight, Nick. Well, let's do this." I tightened my hold on his shoulders and threw us both through the glass.

Chapter 30

Must Fight On

Nicholas and I dropped two stories, are wings entangled. Nothing to slow are plunge. I landed with a thud on my right arm against a stone walkway. Air rushed from my lungs. My wrist bone snapped, cutting through my tough blue skin. The crack echoed in my ears. Fiery pain radiated up my arm. Rolling onto my side, I grasped the break with my good claw and squeezed the bone back into place. A bellow exploded from deep in my throat. I screamed like a rageful beast.

Out of the corner of my eye, I spotted Nicholas. He slowly rose, shaking his head like a wild dog. He landed in the soft grass and showed no sign of injury.

Gasping for a breath, I climbed to my feet, lifting myself with my one good arm, but was too slow. Like a rampaging rhino, Nicholas barreled toward me, head bowed as if to impale me on his ram's horns.

I couldn't escape. I gritted my teeth, shoulder bent toward him. Better he impale my arm than my chest.

A gunshot cracked like thunder.

Nicholas skidded to a halt just a few feet away.

"Stop!" Lucas stepped from the shadows. He held a handgun pointed skyward. Smoke rose from the barrel. "Nobody move."

"Lucas, you shouldn't be here?" I stood, my broken wrist, hanging limp.

He turned the gun on me. "Quiet, one of you is not my friend. I just need to figure out which one."

"Lucas, shoot him." Nicholas' voice perfectly matched mine. He pointed at me. "He's Nicholas."

Lucas scoffed and aimed the gun at Nicholas. "Dude, you just solved my problem. The real Tripp wouldn't want me to shoot his brother—or anyone for that matter."

An explosion ripped through the mansion, shattering wood and glass. A fireball burst through the second-story windows, lighting up the compound as if day had cut through the night. The mansion moaned and creaked in protest. The grounds shook. I nearly lost my balance. Jagged pieces of timber and glass tore into the grass all around me. Slivers pelted my back and legs but bounced off my thick skin.

Lucas flinched, ducking to avoid the projectile debris.

Another figure emerged from the murky cover of night behind him. Cardan!

"Lucas, look out!" My warning came too late.

Cardan struck him over the head with the butt of his rifle. Lucas dropped to the grass and didn't move.

"No!" I lunged at Cardan.

Nicholas' claws tore into my arm from behind, ripping me from mid-air, forcing me to my knees. I shrieked. His claws were like steel rebar digging deeper and deeper through every muscle fiber in my arm.

"You will not harm, Father." He squeezed tighter, slicing down to my bone.

I roared in agony. *Oh my God! He's trying rip off my arm! Do something!*

A rush of fear and hate erupted from deep in my gut. My muscles hardened, bursting through my skin. "No!" I leaped to my feet and twisted around, smashing my elbow into his stomach. His ribs crunched. I then raked a wing across his face, slicing through his cheek. Nicholas' blood splattered across my chest.

He let out a scream, falling to his knees.

I thrust out my wings and took flight, racing into the sky high above the compound. I peered downward. Nicholas recovered and leaped after me.

"You can't escape, brother." Gaining speed, he was nearly upon me.

"I have no plans to. Come and get me." I spread my wings wider and climbed farther into the night.

Nicholas was a killer. He'd already proven that. Now I was his prey. But the monster I'd become could kill, too, and I burned with hate.

I flew higher and fast, then rolled to the right and hovered. *I'm waiting, brother.* Nicholas soared past, fluttered his wings to brake, and swung back toward me.

"This ends now." He thrust his wings back and attacked.

Yes, it does end now. I wanted to give in to the voice in my head and let the creature take control. If I gave into the hate seething deep in my chest, I would tear Nicholas in two, even with a bad arm. I desired blood and his would do just fine.

He slammed into me, and I held back a cry as my broken wrist crushed against my body. We tumbled over and over across the sky, tearing at each other. Each slash of his claws drove me deeper into rage. *Kill him!* a voice in my head screamed. *Kill him now!*

He smashed my cheek with a bone-jarring punch. I slashed at his mid-section as if to cut out his insides. Nicholas roared and stabbed at my neck, but I dodged and plunged my nails into his chest. Just a little deeper, and I'd rip out his heart. The beast in me rejoiced at that thought. *Do it!*

Spitting fire into the night, Nicholas broke away from me and flew higher, but I would not be denied my kill. My nose wrinkled with the stench of his fear. I caught his foot and dragged him toward me. He thrashed about like a caged animal, but I had him. Jumping onto his back, legs wrapped around his waist, I chomped down on one of his wings, ripping through his flesh with my fangs. His blood was sweet. With my one good claw, I slashed at the wing. My nails sliced it like sharp knives cutting through meat.

He bellowed in agony.

Hurts, doesn't it, brother?" One final swipe severed the wing. Nicholas roared. His blood coated my claw. I released my hold. With only one wing, he fell hard and fast. He landed with a thud on his side.

I floated down to him and knelt beside him. *Time to die, brother.* I lifted my hand over his head and extended my nails to their fullest length.

"That's right, Ilan, my son, kill without hesitation." Cardan's eyes were wild. "This is what I wanted all along. Kill your brother and you will take the first steps toward becoming the hero this world needs."

He's right. You're a beast. Kill. Nick is nothing but my prey. How exhilarating it would be to see his warm blood drip over my claws as his life slowly ended. He deserved death. *Do it! Now!* I crashed my nails down toward Nicholas' neck but recoiled. What was I doing? I glared at my claws, then Nicholas. *I'm not a killer. Not a monster. A hero doesn't kill. Take control.* The voice was mine—my human self. My body shook. I took a deep breath and willed myself to lift away my claws.

"Sorry, Nick." I spoke just loud enough for him to hear.

He stared up at me, confusion in his eyes.

I shifted my attention to Cardan. "I'm not going to kill my brother... or anyone. That's not why I have these powers."

Cardan aimed the barrel of his gun at me. He slowly stepped forward, and I retreated. When he reached Nicholas, he lowered himself while keeping me in his sights. Like a concerned father, he examined the wounds, then stood.

With some effort, Nicholas climbed to his feet, but his legs trembled, body hunched. A whimper slid from his lips. His breathing was raspy and wet. A mix of blood and foamy mucus gathered around his mouth. More blood seeped from his chest. He held his flesh together over his heart with his claws.

What had I done? How could I have allowed myself to inflict such pain? I'd allowed Cardan to turn me into a beast, but never again.

Cardan patted Nicholas' arm then turned his attention to me. "You are wrong, Ilan. I gave you these powers to make a difference. Removing those who are evil from this world, rather than allowing a corrupt justice system to let them walk free, is the right path."

I ignored him. "Nick, a second ago *our father* told me to kill you. How can you stand by him?"

Nicholas didn't answer.

"Silence." Cardan's forefinger tightened against the gun's trigger. "Ilan, I found you too late to make our family whole again. Some wrongs of the past cannot be fixed, no matter how much I desire it."

Behind him, the fire raged. Flames bled through each window and danced above the roof. The inferno cast a red glow over the compound. The crimson color spread across Cardan's face. He looked crazier than ever.

"I guess you're right, *Dad*."

My mind raced. Cardan was going to shoot me. How could I stop him? Off to the side Lucas stirred. Beyond him, Ghost lay in the grass. His wife struggled to drag him away. No sign of their children. They must be hiding. If I didn't stop Cardan, he would kill them and Lucas, too.

My bulging arms started to shrink. Nails slid back as my claws started to reform into hands. More blood dripped from my wounds. My body ached. Powers were fading. I just wanted to lay in the grass and sleep.

No, I had to fight on for everyone, including Nicholas. Maybe I could still save him. My hands formed into fists. I tensed what was left of my muscles and I spread my wings. My only escape…

skyward. Maybe I could fly fast enough to avoid being shot. Let him waste his rounds. Circle back. Stop him. I just prayed Nicholas was too hurt to fight.

"No, Ilan, you will not escape this," Cardan declared. "The time has come for you to leave this world. Find comfort in knowing you will join your mother in the afterlife. Goodbye, my son."

He squeezed the trigger. I leaped into the air, but a round cut through my side. I screamed and dropped to the ground. My head slumped against my chest. I waited for more gunfire to tear though my body, but it never came.

Only the blaze roared.

"What are you waiting for?" I clutched my side.

"He cannot respond, brother." Nicholas' voice was weak and labored. He held the rifle. Cardan lay at his feet, eyes closed.

My head dropped into the grass, and I stared up toward a smoke-filled sky. Had Nicholas just saved me? My eyes wanted to close. Sleep would be so sweet. So tired.

I blinked and in that instant Nicholas stood over me. He tossed the gun away and extended a claw to me. What was he doing? I tried to slide away, but he shook his head.

"Take my hand, brother," he urged. His claw transformed back into a hand.

I lay still.

"Please, Ilan."

I cautiously grasped his hand. He lifted me to my feet and held my arms until I was steady.

"I don't understand." I stared into his yellow eyes.

"You showed… me mercy." He took long breaths between each word. "You could… have killed me… you didn't."

"I'm not a killer." I reached out to him, but he backed away.

"I decided you deserved the same mercy you showed to me." He bowed.

"You know, it would have been cool if you decided that a few moments before he shot me." I tried a slight smile.

Nicholas offered no response.

"Did you kill him?" I pointed at Cardan, who still lay motionless.

Nicholas looked at the man he called father. "No, he will have a headache when he awakens."

"Dude, he'll be pissed at you."

"I don't know this word, but if you mean, angry, yes," Nicholas responded. "It is time for Father and me to have a talk, anyway."

"Nick, we're brothers, man. Stay with me. Don't go with him. He's just going to twist your mind to his screwball way of thinking. He's already made you kill tonight, but that's on him more than you."

"He is not a bad man," Nick challenged. "In many ways, he's right about this world."

"Nick, it would have been wrong to kill those kids."

"Maybe."

"Nick—"

"Ilan, I let you live because you let me live. It is time for me to take Father away from here. Please do not try to stop me and do not attempt to follow me. I may not show mercy if we meet again."

"Where will you go?"

"Home."

"Where's home?"

"It doesn't matter. We will no longer exist to you."

He closed his eyes and took a deep breath. His body creaked and popped. His wounds sealed themselves as if he had never been hurt. The wing I cut in half regenerated. His legs no longer wobbled, and he stood straight and strong.

"Wait, how did you—?"

"Remember, Ilan, do not come looking for us. Let us continue our mission without you. Let Cardan learn to love me as his only son." Nicholas stomped away. When he reached Cardan, he picked him up and cradled him in both arms.

He glanced at me one more time. "Ilan, you will want to return to the tunnels to our father's laboratory. There is a door hidden in the floor. I am sure you will be interested in what you will find on the other side of that door."

I raised an eyebrow. "What do you mean?"

Nicholas spread his wings and took flight with Cardan tucked against his chest. In moments, they disappeared from view. My brother was gone, but somehow I knew our paths would cross again. Cardan would not forget me, and I wouldn't forget them either.

"One way or another, I'm going to save you, brother," I said loud enough for my own ears.

In the distance came the blare of sirens racing toward the fire.

Lucas and I had to escape. I started toward him but froze after the first step. The round lodged in my side was like fire penetrating my flesh. Taking a deep breath, I sunk my own nails through my flesh, probing for the bullet. I quickly found it. Fortunately, the round was not very deep thanks to my tough hide. Suppressing a cry, I tugged it free. The human part of me gagged at the site of my own blood dripping off the hot metal. The beast was stronger than that. I didn't have time to be sick.

I dropped the round and lumbered to Lucas, who moaned and rubbed the side of his head.

"What happened?" he asked

"How do you feel?" I painfully bent toward him.

"Not good, dude."

"You saved me again. Thanks."

"Uh, anytime."

Despite my wounds, I still had enough gargoyle strength flowing through my veins to help him to his feet. My muscles ached, but I wrapped my arms around his waist, and we stumbled over to Ghost and his wife. Their girls now joined them. The two cried and hid behind their mother. Ghost tried to lift himself but fell back.

His wife aimed a gun at us. Ghost placed a hand over hers to lower the weapon.

I got my first good look at his face. For a crime boss, he looked young with jet black hair tinged by just a bit of gray. Blood soaked his goatee. His right eye was swollen shut. Cheeks were cut.

"I don't know who or what you are under that Halloween costume, but you saved my family." His voice barely rose above a whisper. He cringed and coughed. "Thank you for what you did here tonight. I want to repay you. Tell me how?"

Lucas responded first. "A million bucks."

I rolled my glowing eyes and sighed. "I don't want anything from you. I came here tonight to save your family, not you. If you're the one known as Ghost, we may see each other again, and you won't like it."

"I understand," he answered. "You may not like it either."

Without another word, with what remaining power I had left, I grabbed Lucas and flew into the night—toward the subway tunnels.

Chapter 31

The Discovery

I flew hard and fast toward NYC, straining to stay aloft, but my powers faded. My wings were retracting, slithering back into my flesh. The muscles in my cannon-sized arms drooped like balloons deflating. My body screamed from the weight of holding Lucas. The Manhattan lights illuminated the night in the distance, but, jeez, after all I'd been through, I wasn't going to make it back.

We jerked up and down. I nearly dropped Lucas. In panic, I squeezed him against my chest.

Glaring up at me, he tightened his grip around my neck. "Hey, dude, don't let go!"

I grunted, trying to gain altitude. "I'm losing my powers. I can't keep us up."

"Then land. We'll hitch a ride into the city."

"You don't get it. I'm losing my wings. We're headed for a crash landing."

"What… do you realize how high up we are? Do something, Tripp. Don't want to smash into the ground."

"Duh." I flapped my shrinking wings harder to slow our descent.

"Can you get us over there?" He pointed to a body of water up ahead. "That's got to be the Hudson River. A wet landing is better than a splatter landing."

"I'll try." A grunt escaped my lips. I thrashed my wings and arched my back into a dive toward the river. From this height, I couldn't tell the difference between the night sky and the murky water. What if I missed the river and struck land? I focused on a barge in the middle of the water and prayed my eyes weren't fooling me.

"We're not going to make it," I cried.

"Shut up. You can do it."

"No, I can't!"

About thirty feet up, my wings vanished all together. We plummeted toward the Hudson. Our screams broke the silence of the night. Flipping over and over, I lost my hold on Lucas. *No! No! No!* I lost sight of him. My view shifted at dizzying pace from the dark water rushing at me, to the starry sky and back to the water. The river was like a black wall curving across the shadowy land. We'd both be crushed.

"Lucas... Luc!"

I struck the Hudson head first. The freezing water smacked me in the face, jarring my neck. A haze of unconsciousness engulfed me. *Stay... awake!* I sank fast. The murky water boxed in my vision. I thrashed and kicked but had no idea which direction led back to the surface. I screamed, but water rushed down my throat. I couldn't breathe. My head became heavy. Numbness spread through my limbs. I couldn't die like this. And what about Lucas? I couldn't let him die. *Fight for it, Tripp! Swim, damnit!* I kicked hard and extended my hands above my head.

From above, a hand grabbed hold of my shoulder and tugged. I shook away the haze, then grasped the hand. My heart danced. Whoever had me was like a lifeline. I kicked my legs even harder.

Finally, I breached the surface, coughing water.

Lucas glared back at me. He wrapped an arm around my shoulders to keep me from sinking back into the dark waters.

"You saved me again." I placed my human hand on his arm. I was human. No longer a monster.

"You really do owe me, huh? He joked. "How you doing?"

"Not sure." I bobbed in the gently rolling water.

"Bad timing, but I guess it's good to see normal Tripp again." He pushed hair out of his eyes.

I did a quick self-examination. Not only was I human, but all my wounds disappeared. Even my broken wrist healed. "I guess I'm fine. Good to be me again, but I'm freezing." Mist drifted from my nose and mouth.

"All right then." Lucas' teeth chattered. "Let's get to land and figure out our way to the city."

***

We stood on the Upper East Side in the early morning hours. One more block and we'd reach the subway entrance. Deep beneath the city Cardan's lab and a hidden door awaited us.

We were so close now to the answers I needed. It seemed like it took forever to get here, but only an hour passed since we crashed into the Hudson. My transformation left me naked, but I found an old jacket and oversized torn jeans mixed among the brush along the riverbank. Soaked and cold, we trudged to a nearby roadway.

We walked along the roadside, watching for a passing car. What else could we do but hitch? Lucas had a cell, but the river damaged it. We didn't walk far before a kind old man in a Ford pickup stopped to see if we were all right. Lucas made up a story that we ran away from home but were mugged and abandoned. Don't know if the old man believed the story, but he offered us a ride to NYC anyway.

Now here we stood.

I turned to my best friend. "Lucas, you've done enough." I placed a hand on his shoulder. "If you still have your dirt bike somewhere around here, just take it and go home. Your parents must be crazy worried. Your dad's already going to kill you. Just go."

'Look, I'm in this all the way," Lucas protested. "You're right. I'm already dead. So what's the difference? Can't call him now."

He lifted his mom's cell to show me. A blank screen proved his point. The river had killed the phone.

"Let's finish this." Lucas grinned and started toward the subway.

Shaking my head, I chased after him. We leaped over the turnstile and dashed through the terminal. Jumping onto the tracks, we snuck through the tunnel until we reached the steel door to the abandoned passages far below.

I stopped. "Are you sure you want to come?"

"You know it."

We made our way into the lower catacombs. The air, cold and musty, made me shiver. The hairs on the back of my neck stood tall. I felt Cardan's presence all around me, like a trailing shadow I could never escape.

We stepped around a familiar bend and reached the doorway into the lab.

Lucas nodded and together we stepped inside. The lab was quiet; pale lights still cut through the darkness. Mrs. Ramirez was gone. Kind of a surprise since she had a pipe wrapped around her, but I didn't care. She no longer mattered to me.

"Nick said there was a door hidden in the floor." I tiptoed through the lab. Cardan might be far from here, but images of him flashed through my mind. I saw him everywhere I looked.

Lucas noticed. "You okay?"

"Yeah, this is just a bad place, you know."

We searched the concrete floor for anything that resembled a door, or crevices to reveal the presence of a door but found nothing.

We met in the center of the labyrinth.

"Damn, there's nothing here that looks like a door." I punched the air.

"There has to be something." Lucas dropped to the floor. "Wait a second, have you ever paid attention to this rug?"

I lowered to my knees. A dingy square rug, enough to cover a small bedroom floor, stretched out beneath us. The gray rug nearly matched the concrete. Dirt, mud and who knows what else stained it.

We stared at each other and then crawled to one side of the rug.

"Roll," Lucas ordered.

We rolled the rug into a tube and slid it out of the way. I intertwined my fingers and placed them against my mouth. Lucas grabbed my arm. His eyes bulged.

"You see it?" he asked.

"Yep."

In the center, a slab of concrete had been cut out and shaped into something like a door that could be lifted away on hinges.

We grabbed one end and pulled as hard as we could. At first the door didn't budge. We tugged harder. The door creaked and gave way.

"We've got it," Lucas grunted. "Don't stop now."

We yanked once more and the door swung open as far as the hinges would allow. A second door, this one steel with an attached handle, lay beneath the concrete.

Lucas and I glanced at each other without saying a word.

We both gripped the handle and tugged. Though heavy, with some effort we lifted the steel door.

"Oh my..." Lucas' words trailed off.

I gasped and slumped to my knees. Beneath the steel door was a hidden chamber about the size of a closet. Candy wrappers and empty bags of chips littered the floor. Jugs of liquid—maybe water—were stacked in one corner.

The stench of urine rose from the chamber.

A small lamp attached to one wall provided meager lighting. The hiss of air came from a hole next to the lamp, but the air was thick and barely breathable.

"Do you see him?" Lucas pointed at the wall opposite the lamp.

I leaned forward, my mouth agape. My body shook. Hands formed into fists. Oh my God. It was him. Finally. My dad lay slumped against the wall, his head tilted toward me. Though barely open, his eyes focused on me. A slight smile cracked his lips. He mouthed my name in silence.

"Dad!" I jumped into the chamber and grabbed his hand. His skin was warm. "God, please be okay."

"I'm… alive." my dad mumbled. He tried to lift his hand to my face but couldn't.

"Dad, I'm so sorry for this" I touched his face. My heart pounded. Tears streamed down my cheeks. I couldn't hold them back. He had been so close all this time. I should have known. I should have been able to help him. How could I have let Cardan do this?

"Tripp… you… okay?" Dad whispered, blinking his eyes.

I gripped his hand. "I'm better now. Dad, this is all my fault. I'm sorry I let this happen to you. But I stopped him. That man who did this to you… I beat him."

"Tripp, you're a real hero," Dad uttered. "None of this was your fault. Don't ever think that."

I wiped my eyes. "We're going to get you out of here." I turned toward Lucas, still at the top of the chamber. "Go get help."

"No." My father found the strength to grab me with trembling arms. He pulled me into his chest. "Oh, my son. I thought I'd never see you again. Never be able to tell you…"

His words trailed off into tears. We stayed in an embrace for a long time. I didn't want to pull away. I didn't want to let him go. But I had to.

"Dad, we have to get you help."

"Tripp," Lucas called. "Dude, I just checked my mom's phone. It's a miracle. It's back to life. I'll call an ambulance."

"No… ambulance," my dad said. "Lucas, throw down… your phone… to me."

Lucas did as my dad asked.

"Tripp." Dad's eyes fluttered. His head slowly drooped to his chest.

"Dad!"

His head shot up. He blinked his eyelids. "I'm still with you. Just weak. Look, this will be hard for you to understand, but I'm going to contact… the CIA. I'm one of them. They'll send help. But, they'll also take you, Tripp, For your own sake…, you shouldn't be here… when they come."

My thoughts raced. My dad was really working for the government. What did that mean? Had Cardan been right about everything? Was this man an impostor? I took a deep breath. Right now that didn't matter. He was still my dad. The man who raised me, even if he was a jerk most of the time. For now, he needed me.

I held his shoulder. "I'm not going to leave you, not like this."

"Son, the government… knows about you." He coughed some more. "They'll imprison you… like before."

"I know. That's okay. I'm ready."

My dad sighed then dialed a number. He tried dialing over and over. "Damn, no… reception."

I snatched the phone. "I'll climb above and make that call. Lucas, is there a line or something you can lower to get me out of here?"

"I'll check." He disappeared and soon returned. "I think this will work." He had two sheets tied together and lowered them down to me. "Hold on. I'll pull you up."

A moment later I stood next to him with the phone in my hand.

"Is your dad okay?" he asked.

"I think so."

"What can I do to help?"

"Lucas, dude, I'm about to place a call to the government, but you can't be here when they arrive. If you are, it'll be bad for you."

"Tripp—"

"Lucas, you're the best friend a guy could ask for."

He grabbed my hand. "I don't know about that twin of yours, but we're brothers. I'll always have your back."

"Same here. By the way, I'll make sure the black suit dudes don't get your mom's phone."

Lucas grinned then started to turn, but stopped. "Will I see you again?"

"I hope."

"You better be at school next week." He wiped red eyes and walked from the labyrinth.

I watched him leave, fighting back my own tears. The truth was, I knew I'd never see him again. He was better off without me. I was nothing but trouble. But I'd miss his stupid sense of humor. I'd always remember how he was there for me when I needed him the most. Somehow, if Lucas ever needed me, I'd find him. I'd save him, just like he did for me.

"Goodbye, Lucas." I turned my attention to the phone and pressed redial. It rang twice, then someone with an official voice answered.

"My name is Tripp Taylor," I said into the receiver. "You've been looking for me. Well, I'm here in a tunnel under the subway. I'm sure you can track this phone to me. I'm with my dad. I think he's one of your agents. He's been hurt and needs medical attention. Please hurry. When you get here, you can do whatever you decide is best with me. I won't put up a fight."

Chapter 32

In Custody

"Wake up, my son. There is work to be done."

My eyes fluttered open; a haze drifted away. I was back in the glass prison inside Cardan's labyrinth. He stood at the door in his white lab coat, his clipboard in one hand and a lighted cigarette in the other. How did I get back here? It couldn't be. Nicholas took him and flew away. I was supposed to be safe now.

"You have been asleep much too long." Cardan smiled kindly. "It is good to have you back. Your family has missed you."

He motioned to a series of massive transparent tubes behind him.

"Look at how your brothers are growing." He turned from me and strolled to one of the tubes, patting the glass like a father caressing his child on the back. "They will need you to teach them, Ilan."

I gazed closely at the tubes. A glowing green liquid filled each tube. Floating inside the liquid were creatures that looked like me. Clones in different stages of development. Some looked my age. Others years younger, some just babies. A few were bent and twisted, their faces misshaped and contorted. They shook inside the tubes, writhing in pain.

"What have you done?" I gasped. "Cardan, no."

I pounded the glass.

All the clones awoke and started chanting, "Ilan, return to us. You belong to us. Ilan, we need you. Why do you stay away? Ilan… Ilan… Ilan."

I closed my eyes and covered my ears. "No!"

A blaring alarm sounded, startling me awake.

My eyes shot open. I lay in bed back in my room. Well, not really my room. The one set aside for me inside whatever military installation I'd been taken to after the CIA rescued my dad and took me into custody.

I blinked away the remnants of that nightmare and silenced the alarm clock next to my bed. Every time I fell asleep, the same images returned. The doctors here said to expect dreams like that. They diagnosed me as having something like post-traumatic stress disorder. The effect of being someone's captive. How long would this last? After two weeks in here… two weeks of restless nights… I was starting to lose it. I just wanted Cardan out of my head.

Beads of sweat covered my forehead. I wiped strands of damp hair from my eyes. My thoughts turned to my dad—the man who raised me. At least he was safe. He was somewhere in this facility, or so I was told. I guess it was true since he came to see me once a day.

I lived in a white windowless room with a bed, a television, iPod with all my favorite songs, and a laptop with restricted Internet use. Oh yeah, and a stupid alarm clock that would wake me up for a morning round of tests. Recessed lighting in the ceiling activated in the morning around six a.m. and turned off at night around ten. I had no control over the lighting. A few times a day staff in lab coats led me down a long hallway to a recreation area with a pool where I could exercise, swim a little and watch the latest movies on a theater-quality big screen.

Everyone treated me well, especially the new doctor assigned to my case. A younger man than Doc Torren, Doc Barrington called himself a genetic specialist and said he would devote himself full time to help fix the segments of my DNA that brought the transformations whenever I ate.

He never called my transformation a disorder. In fact, Doc Barrington referred to my powers as *cool*.

I liked him.

My dad—not really sure I could call him that anymore—told me I wouldn't be held here permanently. It would just be a matter of time before those in charge released me to live a *normal* life.

Honestly, I didn't care. My setup was good. Sure, I was a prisoner and they'd never really let me go, but that's life.

I grabbed my iPod and headphones and turned them on. As I listened to music, I thought back to the conversation we had about Cardan and how I came to be his son.

***

Four days after we arrived, my dad visited me for the first time. He wore hospital-like bed clothing and robes. He walked slowly, still weak from his time in captivity.

We sat at the small round dining table in my room.

I was quiet at first even though thousands of questions spun through my mind.

Dad broke the silence. "How are you, Tripp?"

"I'm doing better, I think." I tapped my fingers on the table. "You?"

"Getting stronger every day," Dad answered. He reached for my hand but pulled back. "Tripp, none of this was your doing. None of this. We should have told you the truth from the start to prepare you for the day you might face him."

"You mean Cardan?"

He nodded. "Yes."

"Is he my real father?"

Dad cleared his throat. His eyes grew large and red. "Yes…, I'm sorry I never told you before. But, Tripp, to me, you're my son, and I couldn't be prouder of you. For a time, I forgot how proud. I let my own crap—my own pain—get the best of me and I forgot to be the man you needed me to be. I'm more sorry for that."

I shook my head. "So Cardan was telling the truth."

"Not about everything, Tripp." My dad rubbed his forehead. "I read the report by the team that interviewed you here. If what you told them about Cardan is true then much of what he shared with you was tainted with lies."

"I don't understand."

Dad leaned forward. "You reported that Cardan told you he was a genetic scientist who manipulated your DNA while you were in your mother's womb. Cardan said you were taken from him and his wife when you were a baby by the British government and that his wife died while in their custody."

I blinked, remembering Cardan's every word about the death of his wife, the woman he said was my real mother. "That's right."

My dad's hands formed fists. "Tripp, as far as we know, his science background is true, and he is responsible for your... condition. But the British government never kidnapped you, and your mother didn't die in their custody."

"What?" I rose from the table.

"Tripp, please listen. "Your mother—your real mother—died in childbirth because of what Cardan did to you and to her."

"How do you know this?" I asked.

Dad took a long breath. "You had a grandfather—your mother's father—who was a scientist employed by the British Royal Navy. He saw Cardan for the monster he was. Your grandfather was the one who took you away from Cardan to keep you safe. Your grandfather had ties to the United States and figured it best to bring you here rather than try to hide you in England. Your grandfather had a friend, a fellow scientist, in the Secret Service."

"Doc Torren," I reasoned.

"Yes. Your grandfather left you with Doc Torren and under the protection of our government to keep you hidden from Cardan. Believe it or not, Tripp, a Secret Service team was assigned to your case with Doctor Torren as the lead."

I leaned back in my chair. "And you?"

He rubbed his hands together. "I am an agent, too. By now you obviously figured that out. Tripp, I was a good field agent. So was my wife. We had a child together. A little boy." His voice cracked. "On a vacation, while I was driving, we were struck by a truck." His eyes reddened. "My wife and son were killed. I was left with this permanent injury. I'd never be a field agent again. I was stuck behind a desk."

"Dad—"

"Let me finish. Doctor Torren was a friend. When he was given authority over you, he asked me if I would be your guardian. Take on the role of your father. Do you understand? We would shield you from the truth. Your life would be a lie, but you'd be safe and have some semblance of a normal life. We didn't fear you. Just wanted to help. Well, we might have feared you a bit."

I wiped a tear from my eye. "Why did you agree? I always thought you hated me."

He shook his head. "No, Tripp. Never. I agreed to the assignment. Torren thought it would be good for me. Help me heal. Maybe I thought so, too. But I was wrong. I never forgave myself, and I shouldn't have put you in the middle of my crap. I was angry. And I never lost that anger. And I took it out on you. I'm sorry."

"So you made me believe my mother, your wife, died because of my birth." I gripped the end of the table. "You made me think it was my fault."

Dad nodded. "I'm so sorry. I can't ask you to forgive me for any of this. What I did was inexcusable."

My heart pounded. I wasn't sure if I wanted to slug him or throw my arms around him. Instead, I asked, "What about my grandfather?"

"When he brought you to this country, he was already dying." Dad leaned back. "I don't remember what illness he had, but he succumbed to it shortly after we met him. He died knowing you were safe and cared for."

I lowered my head. Sad for a grandfather I'd never known. Sad for two mothers I never had a chance to know. One real. One not. But both connected to me.

I stood from the table. "What do you know about this twin of mine? Is he really my brother or was it a disguise, or what?"

Dad shrugged. "I read about that in the report. I don't know what to say to it. I suppose it's possible you have a brother. Our counterparts in England and other parts of Europe are following this, so we may discover the truth."

"Do you know how Cardan found me?" I paced in front of him.

"I don't, Tripp." He stood and limped toward me. "But I have a theory. If you do have a twin, maybe he has some kind of mind link with you. I know it's crazy, but we can't rule anything out. Have you tried peering into his thoughts?"

I raised an eyebrow. "Uh, no." Maybe it was time I tried, especially if I wanted to find him and save him from Cardan. I didn't say that to my dad. I folded my arms over my chest. "So what happens now? Do we go our separate ways? Do I stop calling you dad?"

He smiled slightly. "If you want, I'd like to try again—no more lies. I've petitioned to have you rejoin me. I hope you want to stay with me, but I understand if you don't. It is up to those in much higher positions than us to decide what happens. But if you want it, I'll fight for you. Then, we'll figure out the future together. And what to do with those powers of yours. I will leave that up to you."

I gazed at my dad. This man who lied to me my whole life. Who had been cold and angry when I needed someone to just tell me everything would be okay. Those thoughts gripped me like a vice with anger. My face tightened. My teeth clenched. *Just breathe, Tripp.* Other thoughts filled my mind. He'd kept a roof over my head. Cared for me when he could have abandoned me. None of it could have been easy for him. Losing his wife and child. Maybe he deserved another chance. Maybe we belonged together.

My face softened. Lips parted in a smile. "I... I guess... I'd like to stay with you, if that's all right."

He grabbed me and tugged me into his arms. "It is more than all right. I promise you things will be better."

I held him tight. I no longer cared if Cardan was my true father. This is the man I chose to be my dad.

I just hoped we'd have the chance to be together.

***

I paced my room inside the compound. I remained in custody a week after the conversation with my dad. Still no word on what would happen to me. Whether I'd be released, so I could be with him or remain a prisoner. My dad came to see me every day, and frustration etched deeper and deeper into his face, but he forced a smile and told me we'd be able to leave this facility soon.

I knew he was lying. Just trying to hide me from the truth. They'd never release me. I was too dangerous. They'd never let us be together. I even decided to tell my dad the next time he came that he should stop visiting me. I don't know if I would have the courage to tell him that. The thought of it was like a weight against my shoulders. Without him, I had no one, but he should get on with his life.

I also decided that I'd have to figure out a way to escape on my own. How else could I get to my brother, Nicholas?

I had to get out of here to help my twin. Who knows what Cardan had him doing? Killing more people Cardan thought were evil? My brother deserved better. There has to be good in him. I just know it. He deserves a chance to live his life free of that tyrant, but from here I couldn't help him.

Sure, we didn't really know each other, but he's still family. And he knows how to control his powers. Maybe he could teach me to do the same. We could help each other, then. Really be brothers.

I tried several times to use my mind to build some kind of hyperlink between us, like my dad suggested, but couldn't sense him or hear his thoughts. It just made my head hurt, but each failure just made me try harder.

Studying each wall of this prison cell, no clear escape route was visible. No vent. No windows. Just a door that slid open but remained locked from the outside.

If only I could get my hands on some real food instead of the liquid diet they forced on me. Even a scrap of food would turn me into something that might let me break out of here. I stomped my foot against the floor. *Stay calm, Tripp. Someday, you'll figure out a way out of here.*

"One day, Nick, bro, I'll figure out a way to reach you."

Chapter 33

The Breakout

I lay in my bed in the darkness, staring up at the ceiling. The medicine-like odor of the air pumped into my room surrounded me, tickling my nose. I turned to the digital clock on my nightstand. Four in the morning. In another two hours, the lights would turn on and a new day would begin.

It was Tuesday, at least I think it was. My third week in captivity. But I was losing track of time as one day faded into the next, and the routine of my life dulled my senses.

Wake up at six. A pretty nurse named Jessica brings me my morning breakfast, a dose of N.E.R.D. juice. After that, Doc Barrington visits me for a checkup and to remind they are doing everything they can to control my powers. An hour after his visit, a security detail leads me from my room to a gymnasium for a workout—a little basketball, a swim in an indoor pool, weights—whatever I want. Then, lunch—more N.E.R.D juice. Later, a little schooling with a young curly-haired agent named Mike. Finally, a visit from my dad around dinner. At night, some television and then bed. Each day the same.

I asked for a laptop or iPad, but they told me that was not possible right now for my own safety.

I'd grown numb to the routine, except each time they led me to the gym I contemplated an escape. Somehow, without my powers, I never found the courage to try.

"Coward!" I gripped my sheets until my knuckles turned white. "So I'm just going to give up? Is that it? You have to—"

The door to my room swished open. I froze. That wasn't supposed to happen. At least not until the lights hummed to life. My room remained dark. I slowly twisted my neck to peer at the door.

No one stood there.

"What the hell?" A cold sweat spread across my forehead. My pulse quickened. Stomach tied up in knots. No, had Cardan come back for me? I sat up, trying to keep my limbs from trembling. I wouldn't go with him. Not again. I'd rather die than be his slave.

I slowly stood, gazing through the dim room at the shadowy layer covering the open doorway. "Cardan, I'm not going to join you." The words flowed meekly from my mouth. How could I fight him without my abilities?

"It's not Cardan." My dad's voice cut through the darkness.

He limped inside, his cane in one hand, a revolver in the other. He wore the same dark suits as the agents who first abducted me. I wiped sweat from my brow. Short gasps of air rushed from my mouth. My chest heaved. Something was wrong? But what?

Crossing to me, he slid the gun into his jacket and placed a hand on my shoulder. "We have to go." He had a wide grin on his face, but his eyes darted back and forth from me to the door. "We don't have much time."

"What is it?" I shoved his hand away and retreated a few steps. "Is it Cardan. Is he coming for me?"

My whole body shook at that thought. My stomach gurgled as if I'd be sick. How much did I fear that crazy dude? What had the bastard done to my mind? My eyes watered at the thought of once again becoming his prisoner.

"It's not Cardan, Tripp." He lifted the gun from his jacket. "It's just time for us to get out of here."

I shook my head. "I don't under—"

"Tripp, now!" he barked. "There'll be time to explain if we make it."

I grabbed my tennis shoes, clutching them to my chest. He didn't even give me time to get out of my pajamas and into some clothes. He ushered me out of the room with one arm around my shoulder. His gun extended out in front of him, but for what? Who was the enemy we were escaping? We hustled down the hallway, one I had traveled through many times to the gym. All the lights were dimmed. Video cameras monitored our movement.

"Dad, the cameras…. They'll see us." I pointed at one camera directly overhead.

He nudged me farther down the hallway. "We've got them on a loop, which we'll give us five minutes to make our move. Right now, they think you're still asleep in your room."

"But what are we doing? These are your people?"

He glared at me. "I told you, I'll explain later."

We stopped at an elevator. I'd been in it only once when they delivered me to my room. Since then, this hallway had been off limits to me. So many times I'd fantasized about sneaking from the gym to this elevator and riding it to freedom, but I'd never tried.

Damn me for being afraid, but now my dad had come for me. I just didn't know why. My head spun. He was CIA, and now he was treating his own agency as the enemy. Why? This didn't make sense.

Could I trust my dad? He'd lied to me my whole life. Was he just as crazy as Cardan? Who the hell could I trust? Maybe no one. But right now, what choice did I have but to follow him.

He pounded on the elevator button. "Come on, hurry."

"You're scaring me." I fumbled over my words.

"Don't be. It's simple. I'm breaking both of us out of here, so we can begin a new life. That's all. And we're going to make it.

We have a lot of support for what we're doing." He winked at me.

"What does that mean?" I asked.

He didn't respond.

His face became rigid. He aimed his gun at the elevator doors. "Get behind me just in case."

Just in case what? I tightened the grip on my shoes. Held my breath.

The elevator swished open. No one rushed at us. It was empty. I released a breath of air lodged in my throat. I followed my dad inside. Stale air greeted us. A window ceiling above revealed how ragged I looked with my uncombed hair stuck to my damp forehead and pajamas hanging off my thin body.

A digital display on the control panel read B-4. The "B" had to stand for basement, which meant they kept me four levels below ground. I hadn't really paid attention the last time I rode on the elevator. I was too freaked out then. I was scared now, too, almost to the point of hyperventilating, but my mind focused on the display. I was so much of a threat the government had to hide me four levels below ground. Holy crap. They were never going to let me out. That's why dad had come for me.

The elevator slowly ascended the shaft. I wanted to scream. This was taking far too long. They'd know we'd escaped, and they'd stop us. Lock me up again. I didn't want to go back down to that room. I wanted to see daylight. Wanted to breathe real air again.

The elevator finally stopped, and the doors opened. No one greeted us. Thank God! Dad limped through the doors, aiming the gun to the right and left. He kept his finger on the trigger, the weapon cocked and ready to fire.

"Hey, watch that thing." I recognized the voice before I saw the person who spoke the words. Doc Barrington. I peeked through the doorway. He stood just beyond the elevator, his hands out in front of him, urging my dad not to shoot.

Dad took a deep breath and lowered the weapon. "Good to see you."

Doc Barrington nodded. Dressed in his white lab coat, a blue tie visible underneath, he stepped closer to my dad. The young doctor, short but muscular, with the thinnest of beards—like dirt across his tanned face and chin—smiled at both me and Dad.

"It's all set," the doctor whispered. "All the gates are unlocked. Get to the docks. The ship leaves tonight at 8 o'clock.

What was he talking about? The docks? This was getting freakier by the minute. I needed answers. Why had this doctor I barely knew conspired with my dad to free me? He knew what would happen to me if I ate real food, yet he was willing to let me go. What the hell did he know? Was the government going to kill me or something?

Doc Barrington nodded to my dad then looked at me. "Tripp, I wish you all the best, kid."

"What's going on here?" My eyes darted to him, my dad and the two agents. "Tell me something, please."

"Just go… now," Doc ordered.

A black Mercedes, with a heavy tint, screeched to a stop in front of us. A driver, also in a black suit, climbed out. My dad slid into the driver's seat and Doc Barrington motioned me over to the passenger side.

"Tripp, hurry, we're almost out of time." Dad threw on a pair of sunglasses.

"Someone please tell me what's going on," I cried.

"When we're free of the facility," my dad answered.

With a nod to the doctor and agents, he revved the engine and sped away. I glanced back at the doctor. He didn't owe me a thing, and yet he helped me escape. I guess he risked a lot for me. How would I ever be able to repay him for this?

The Mercedes wound its way up the parking garage until it reached ground level. A gate at the garage entrance had already been opened, so we flew by without slowing down.

We emerged into the sunlight, blinding even with the tinted windows. Shielding my eyes, I twisted around in my seat to see my prison one more time. A towering glass complex shaped like a pyramid rose high over pine trees nestled against a mountainside. I shifted my gaze forward. A two-story solid steel fence blocked our escape.

Dad raced toward the barrier. If it was supposed to open so we could pass, it hadn't.

He wasn't slowing the car.

"We're going to crash," I shouted.

"It's okay, Tripp," Dad reassured me.

"What are you talking about?" I leaned forward. "It's still closed."

When we were almost upon it, a doorway in the steel barrier cracked and started to swing open but too slow. We would slam into it for sure.

"Stop!" I closed my eyes.

The collision never came.

"You can open your eyes now." Dad chuckled. "We made it."

I looked toward the facility. The fence we passed through was slowly closing. I rested back in my seat and took a deep breath. "Please tell me what's happening."

Dad gazed through the rearview mirror. "The decision came down that you were to remain in custody for the foreseeable future. They were not going to let me care for you. They were going to treat you like a lab rat, and I just couldn't let that happen. Doctor Barrington and a lot of the other agents agreed. They helped me plan your escape and made it possible for me to get you out of there unnoticed."

My dad and the others rescued me. Unbelievable! I owed them all so much, but what did this all mean? Were we going to be on the run for the rest of our lives?

"We're upstate right now, so we have a long drive to the city. You might as well relax," my dad suggested.

"Relax? They're going to hunt for us." I stared out the window. Rolling mountains surrounded us on either side. We drove on a lonely two-lane highway with no vehicles around us. "They're never going to leave us alone. You shouldn't have done this. Now you're stuck in this with me. You should drop me off and drive far away from me."

My dad squeezed the steering wheel. "Don't worry, son. I have a place in Alaska—a nice home I've kept quiet. I've booked you passage on a cargo freighter leaving for Alaska tonight from the port. You'll make your way to the house. There I have another N.E.R.D. machine with plenty of fluids for you. I've even stocked the refrigerator, so you can eat when you feel like it. It's quiet enough there so when you transform no one will notice. There's a bank account with a fictitious name that I'll provide a password for, so you will have plenty of money. I have a few ends to tie up here, and when I do, we'll be free. When I can, I'll join you. I'm not going to leave you. Ever."

Dad spoke like an agent planning a detailed mission. This was all too much to take in. "What are you going to do?"

"Just trust me."

"I can't let you do this." I raked my hands through my hair.

"It's already done." Dad reached back and patted my leg. "I've made my choice. Now I plan to make my superiors understand. I think in the end, they'll realize this is for the best and leave us be."

"But how?"

"Not your concern."

We drove the rest of the way in silence and reached NYC by four o' clock. We stopped at a Manhattan hotel just a block from the port. My dad had already reserved a room. When we entered, he pulled a bulky backpack from the closet, and he showed me the insides.

"This should be enough to get you settled in Alaska." He slumped onto the bed, covering his eyes with his arm.

He had packed a portable version of N.E.R.D with enough liquid to last at least a week. He'd also placed a packet inside with five thousand dollars in one hundred dollar bills. Clothes, enough to last days, took up much of the pack.

But I craved real food. My stomach gurgled. I hadn't had a feeding yet, and right now a steak sounded better than a N.E.R.D shake. I kept my mouth shut. I wasn't about to complain after all my dad had been through. I knew he still wanted me to hide my powers. He was right. But that didn't curb my hunger.

I ignored the empty feeling in my gut. "So how am I supposed to know where to go once in Alaska?"

Dad rose up on his elbows and pulled a piece of paper from his pant pocket. "I've written everything down."

He handed me the paper. Written in black ink were directions on what to do when the cargo ship docked in Alaska and how to get to the house.

Dad reached into his other pocket. I also have this for you. He removed a cell phone and placed it in my hands. It was one of those old-fashioned flip phones. "Only use it to contact me. No one else. Not even your friend, Lucas. And only use it in an emergency."

I dropped the phone on the bed and chuckled. "Are you kidding me? My whole life is an emergency."

Chapter 34

Fateful Choices

We hid in the room until seven at night. I had a feeding with the portable N.E.R.D. machine. Not very satisfying, but I was no longer hungry. My dad didn't bother to eat. He kept checking his watch and peering through our fourth-story window at the docks. When he didn't think I was watching him, his face became rigid. When we made eye contact, he softened and smiled to reassure me everything was all right.

I didn't believe it.

"What are you looking for?" I asked when he gazed through the window for what could have been the hundredth time. "Are we being followed?"

He flashed a grin. "We're not being followed, Tripp. I promise you. I'm just keeping an eye on our path. Guess I'm being overly cautious. Can't help it. It's the agent in me. But we're fine. Things are going to work out. You'll see. I've got it all worked out."

I tried to remain calm, but my heart raced. Fear clawed at my insides. Despite what my dad said about striking an arrangement, so we could be free, one thought in my head eclipsed all others. *We'll be fugitives always looking over our shoulders.*

When darkness settled over the city, and the clock struck seven, Dad patted me on the shoulder. "Time to go. Your ship awaits."

He handed me my backpack filled with supplies and money and started for the door. I grabbed his arm.

"Dad, just come with me. Forget about striking some deal. Let's get on that ship together. Come with me to Alaska." I gripped his arm tighter. My chin quivered. Jeez, after all I'd been through, I was still a scared kid.

He embraced me. "Tripp, it has to be this way, but you'll be okay. And I will join you. We're both going to be fine."

I lingered in the warmth of his arms. My chest ached. I could hardly breathe. This was the last time I was going to see him. Didn't matter what he said. I knew the truth. He might want to get back to me, but the black suits would stop him.

We separated, but he held onto my shoulders. In that moment, my dad looked younger. He was still gray, but his wrinkles vanished, like the stone of his cold, hard exterior chipped away revealing the man he used to be. "I know I don't deserve it, son, but have a little faith in me."

I nodded and forced myself to take a breath. "I'm ready. Let's go."

We made our way from the hotel onto the docks. Dad wore jeans, a Polo shirt and brown leather jacket. I dressed in a thick blue jacket, gray T-shirt and Jeans. No one paid any attention to us.

Workers on the docks in orange jumpsuits and white hard hats remained busy even after dark, unloading cargo. The revving of tractor engines, the whine of hydraulic lifts and the crash of the rolling ocean against anchored ships echoed around me. The dizzying mix of sounds added to my unease.

My gaze shifted from one worker to the next. My shoulders felt heavy, maybe because of the backpack, maybe because I felt their eyes on me, weighing me down.

Still, no one stopped us.

I walked beside my dad. The handle of his revolver peeked out from the pocket of his jacket.

Lifting my face into a soft breeze, I closed my eyes. The salty sea air was soothing but did little to ease the sense that any minute, we'd be jumped. My mind screamed at me to turn and run, but I stayed by my dad's side.

We walked along one dock until it made a ninety-degree turn. At the far end of this wharf was a cargo vessel. The ship was massive, stretching maybe the length of a football field, and the deck towered high above. It stunk like old seaweed and was covered in rust and sea barnacles.

"This is your ship." Dad patted me on the shoulder.

I nudged his hand away. "Looks freaking scary."

Dad laughed. "After everything, don't tell me you're scared of a little sailboat."

"Sailboat?"

He nudged me forward. "Just come on. I have someone for you to meet."

We shuffled toward the ship, my dad peering back just once. He kept one hand on the revolver's handle.

We neared a walkway that led into the vessel and at the base stood a gray-haired man dressed in a dingy white captain's uniform. He had a scruffy beard that covered most of his face. I think he was smiling, but it was hard to see his lips underneath his graying whiskers.

He nodded to my dad. "Everything is ready."

Dad released the revolver and shook the man's hand. "Good. Tripp, this is Captain Leon. He's an old friend from way back. He's going to watch over you during your journey. I promise I'll meet you in Alaska. I won't fail you ever again. I love you. Tripp."

He hugged me, and I returned the embrace. I couldn't remember the last time he told me he loved me. Maybe never. "I love you, too." I think I meant it.

"Leon, give me a minute with my son." Dad pulled me aside and leaned in close. "Tripp, I know you're scared, but I trust Leon with my life. He got me through some scrapes when we were both younger men. You'll be okay."

I swallowed my fear. "Okay, I'll do this."

He leaned even closer so that I felt the hotness of his breath. "Tripp, it's important that you not try to use your powers for now.

I'm not telling you to never use them. We're going to figure this out together once we reach Alaska, but for your own safety, be careful for now. Promise me, Tripp."

"I promise." Even though I uttered the words, I wasn't sure it was a promise I could keep. My head pounded. This was all happening so fast. My entire life was changing. Could I ever live a normal life again? Maybe I wasn't supposed to. I had done some good with my powers. Saved people. How could I just turn that off now?

Dad ended the embrace, and we returned to Captain Leon. "I have to go, but we'll be together soon. Have faith, Tripp."

"I will."

He grasped my shoulder one more time, then limped into the night, stopping only once to flash one more smile. He then turned and continued on his way. I watched him until he was out of view. A pain filled my chest and my stomach rumbled, not because I was hungry. I didn't know how to feel.

"Well, my boy, it looks like you're my charge for the next week." Captain Leon spoke in a friendly voice. "Shall we climb aboard?" He started up the walkway toward the ship's entrance.

I started to follow.

Just then fire trucks raced by the port. I followed the flashing red lights charging up the street just beyond the port. They headed toward an orange glow rising among the distant skyscrapers. A fire! That meant people could be in danger. *Damnit!*

I glanced back at the cargo ship and Captain Leon, then back toward the orange glow. More sirens roared past the port.

Images flashed through my mind of the boy I saved from the pipe, the people I rescued in the zoo, and the night of the subway cave-in. I'd made a difference, and not because of Cardan. Because of me. I still didn't want to be a hero. Not in the way movies portrayed them, anyway, but maybe I could go on helping people. Do what I thought was right. Not because destiny demanded it, but because I wanted to.

But I just promised my dad I wouldn't use my powers. He has a plan. I should follow it, right? If I go to that fire, maybe all the bad stuff would happen all over again. How could I be this stupid?

"Are you coming aboard?" Captain Leon motioned me to join him.

I pounded my fist into my open palm. What the hell! I was never going to be *normal* anyway. "Let's hero up one more time."

The pain in my chest disappeared. The rumbling in my stomach eased. I turned back to him and smiled. "Sorry, Captain. I just can't right now."

I took off running in the direction of the blaze, stopping only once to grab a half-eaten pizza resting on the top of a trash can.

Darren Simon has been a writer for much of his life. His career has included working as a journalist in Los Angeles, Israel and Southern California along the Mexican and Arizona borders. He presently works in government affairs on California water issues, teaches college English for the California Community College system, and does free-lance writing for regional magazines.

His work as an author focuses on middle grade and young adult readers to inspire them to read the way he was inspired, first by comic books and then the science fiction and fantasy novels that were so important to his youth. He resides in California's Desert Southwest with his wife and sons.

***